THE RANSOMED MADONNA

Botticelli's *Madonna and Infant* is on loan from the Vatican, insured for two million dollars. It arrives in New York safely and is well guarded. But a small group of thieves have worked out the perfect heist to ransom the famous painting. Posing as a relative of the museum's namesake with his secretary, they manage to finagle their way back in after closing. Unfortunately, a young pregnant woman passes out in front of their getaway car, and assisted by a beat cop, gives birth in the back seat. When the thieves return, they now have a mother and child to deal with. Unfortunately, Nick Dekota is financing the heist, and he wants to dispose of them both, and quickly. In no time, the heist goes from bad to worse.

THE HOUSE ON K STREET

First Mrs. Margulies receives obscene phone calls. Then her apartment is vandalized. And finally, her pet mynah bird is shot dead. It's all too much for her, and she makes plans to take a much-deserved vacation, sub-leasing her rooms to a nice, young man who has been seeing one of the girls upstairs. What Mrs. Margulies doesn't know is that the nice, young man is a member of the Sons of Columbia, a right-wing group that has plans to use the apartment to pull off the perfect assassination. With Mrs. Margulies gone, they now have access to the basement, where a bomb will be assembled that once it is exploded, will change the world.

LIONEL WHITE BIBLIOGRAPHY (1905-1985)

Fiction
Seven Hungry Men (1952; revised as *Run, Killer, Run!,* 1959)
The Snatchers (1953)
To Find a Killer (1954; reprinted as *Before I Die,* 1964)
Clean Break (1955; reprinted as *The Killing,* 1956)
Flight Into Terror (1955)
Love Trap (1955; reprinted in UK as *Right for Murder,* 1957)
The Big Caper (1955)
Operation—Murder (1956)
The House Next Door (1956; first published in *Cosmopolitan,* Aug 1956)
Hostage for a Hood (1957)
Death Takes the Bus (1957)
Invitation to Violence (1958)
Too Young to Die (1958)
Coffin for a Hood (1958)
Rafferty (1959)
Run, Killer, Run! (1959; re-write of *Seven Hungry Men,* 1952)
The Merriweather File (1959)
Lament for a Virgin (1960)
Marilyn K. (1960)
Steal Big (1960)
The Time of Terror (1960)
A Death at Sea (1961)
A Grave Undertaking (1961)
Obsession (1962) [screenplay published as *Pierrot le Fou: A Film,* 1969]
The Money Trap (1963)
The Ransomed Madonna (1964)
The House on K Street (1965)

A Party to Murder (1966)
The Mind Poisoners (1966; as Nick Carter, written with Valerie Moolman)
The Crimshaw Memorandum (1967)
The Night of the Rape (1967; reprinted as *Death of a City,* 1970)
Hijack (1969)
A Rich and Dangerous Game (1974)
Mexico Run (1974)
Jailbreak (1976; reprinted as *The Walled Yard,* 1978)

As L. W. Blanco
Spykill (1966)

Short Stories
Purely Personal (*Bluebook,* May 1953)
"Sorry—Your Party Doesn't Answer" (*Bluebook,* July 1954)
The Picture Window Murder (*Cosmopolitan,* Aug 1956; condensed version of *The House Next Door*)
To Kill a Wife (*Murder,* Sept 1956)
Invitation to Violence (*Alfred Hitchcock's Mystery Magazine,* May 1957; condensed version of novel)
Death of a City (*Argosy,* Jan 1971; condensed version of novel)

THE RANSOMED MADONNA
THE HOUSE ON K STREET

Lionel White

Introduction by Bill Kelly

Stark House Press • Eureka California

THE RANSOMED MADONNA / THE HOUSE ON K STREET

Published by Stark House Press
1315 H Street
Eureka, CA 95501, USA
griffinskye3@sbcglobal.net
www.starkhousepress.com

THE RANSOMED MADONNA
Originally published by E. P. Dutton & Co, Inc., New York, and
copyright © 1964 by Lionel White.

THE HOUSE ON K STREET
Originally published by E. P. Dutton & Co, Inc., New York, and
copyright © 1965 by Lionel White.

"Expect the Unexpected: Two Lionel White Crime Novels" copyright ©
2024 by Bill Kelly

ISBN: 979-8-88601-102-9

Book design by Mark Shepard, shepgraphics.com
Proofreading by Bill Kelly
Cover art by James Heimer, jamesheimer.com.

First Stark House Press Edition: September 2024

Expect the Unexpected:
Two Lionel White Crime Novels

by Bill Kelly

Lionel White (1905-1985) wrote nearly two score novels between 1952 and 1978. Nearly twenty of these were published in hardcover, mostly for Dutton, the remainder being paperback originals, eleven of which were published by Gold Medal. White also published one novel as L. W. Blanco, riffing on his own name for the pseudonym. White also made occasional appearances in magazines with condensed versions of his novels and with a few short fiction novelette and novella length works. He was, however, primarily a novelist, today regarded as the crime writer who basically created the template for the heist/caper novel.

Stark House Press has previously published twenty of White's novels in ten "two-fer" editions. All books offer fine introductions to White's life and work and are excellent resources for those seeking additional information about this mid-twentieth century crime fiction pioneer.

Several of White's novels were adapted for the movies and television, most notably Stanley Kubrick's *The Killing* from the quintessential heist novel *Clean Break* and Jean Luc-Godard's chase thriller *Pierrot le fou* from the novel *Obsession*.

As a former crime reporter White was of course able to draw on his experiences with crime and criminals for plot and characterization, but White's artistry lies in his ability to start with some basic ingredients common to most crime situations and produce works that are unique from each other. In other words, his works are not formulaic and even within the heist subgenre for which he is most famous, no novel can be considered a clone of another. White was a writer who ensured originality in each new work because he himself, based on the few extant interviews with the author, had no tolerance for redundancy in story or character. So the issue of producing a work unlike those preceding it, beyond the basic necessities of qualifying the work as a "crime novel", was a challenge that may have been less of an issue for White than it has been for many other writers. And apparently whatever pushback he may have gotten from editors/publishers (if any) did not inhibit his ability to create "originals".

Of the two novels in this volume, *The Ransomed Madonna* and *The House on K Street*, the former's title obviously indicates a heist novel, while *The House on K Street*, although containing some elements in common with a criminal caper yarn, can most accurately be characterized as a political thriller and more specifically a Cold War political thriller.

The main issue for the reader who has read several White novels may be: "Gee, another White heist novel, why bother?" The answer to the question lies in answering three other questions: Will the plot be much different from one (or more) plots found in previous White novels? Will the characters driving the events in this story seem familiar? Is there a moral or ethical issue in play whose resolution determines the outcome of the story? For the two novels in this volume at least, those already familiar with White's work will not be disappointed: both books feature plots unique to White's other work; his characterizations in each work portray both major and minor cast members who are well-drawn (seem like actual human beings and not mouthpieces for the author) and each book features an ethical issue that gives the story a spine that is not mere proselyting or philosophy, but has a major influence on the resolution of the story.

The Ransomed Madonna (1964) is a Sandro Botticelli painting entitled *Madonna and Infant* on loan from the Vatican to a museum in New York. Obviously, stakes are high as any theft or damage of such a valuable work will have official international repercussions at the highest levels. So when the painting is stolen in order to extort a ransom from the company that has insured it, law enforcement, corporate entities and government officials are in full scramble mode. At stake are the reputations and careers of the museum staff and various government officials, so the one-million-dollar price tag demanded by the heist gang becomes a secondary detail, taking a back seat to job loss and ruined careers. The painting itself is highly valued as a work of art by the museum of course, as well as by Clifford Johns, an insurance investigator, but also an artist himself, who has been assigned to guard the painting while it resides at the museum. As usual in a White heist story, the plan devised by the crooks is a good one and White performs his typical meticulously detailed step-by-step unveiling of the robbery and the ransom collection as the plot develops. A difference between this book and other White heist novels is that the tone of the book, in the beginning at least, is serio-comic, both for story and characterizations. A key figure, ironically, in ensuring that the heist goes smoothly is one Patrolman Dullin, whose actions enable the crooks to make a smooth getaway and include delivering a baby in the back seat of the getaway limousine, all the while oblivious that a robbery is in progress. When being debriefed after the robbery, Dullin is asked:

> "Tell us why you think he [a member of the robbery crew] might not have been an American."
> Dullin gulped. "He—well, he didn't like baseball."

Justice is off to a rough start but any thought that the story will resemble a Donald Westlake Dortmunder escapade is soon dashed as the woman and newborn baby (a human analogue to the *Madonna and Infant* painting) become hostages whose lives are at stake, as the mother of course can identify the crooks, shifting the tenor of the situation from one with comic elements to one of utmost gravity.

So officialdom meets to ponder the problem and does what officialdom do: point fingers, make threats and find a scapegoat, so if things go well they can assume (at the worst share) credit and if things go bad they have someone to focus the attendant grief on. The chosen pawn is Clifford Johns, judged the best candidate to act as a go-between in negotiations with the "Botticelli Gang" as he is an employee of the insurance company and is motivated to solve the crime committed on his watch. As the biggest tragedy in this situation for those in charge would be the firestorm of retribution that would fall on their heads if the painting is lost, preventing public knowledge of the theft is their initial primary concern. The ransom money and the fate of the kidnapped mother and baby are lesser concerns. The meeting of "concerned parties" has an underlying satiric tone, but once the process of ransoming the artwork and (hopefully) rescuing the hostages begins, White returns to his straight crime caper mode of telling the story.

There is no one more motivated to recover the painting than Johns, for both professional and esthetic reasons, but from the beginning he wrestles with the question of relative importance: what is his primary objective—recover the painting at all costs (including the hostages)—or sacrifice the painting if he must, to ensure the safety of mother and child? Losing a masterpiece artwork would be considered a tragedy (reasons varying) by most of the people involved in this case. Therefore recovering the painting—at any cost—is pressed upon him continuously as the primary objective. So Johns is pitted against his superiors and his own conscience as each step in the ransom/recovery process develops:

> Again Cliff began to sense a feeling of guilt and also a feeling of shame. He was as bad as the others. The girl was in trouble, probably in danger of being murdered, and all anyone had been thinking about was the safe return of a piece of painted canvas.

Typically in White heist novels fate and character flaws play a role in undoing what is usually an ingenious plan. In *The Ransomed Madonna*, the execution of the robbery and ransom collecting plan, explored in typically fascinating detail by White, is no exception. The accident of the mother staggering into the getaway vehicle and giving birth is a twist of fate that the crooks are, at least initially, more than equal to. However, as the story progresses we find that their main conflict from the situation is between those who want to ensure the safety of the mother and child and those who want to eliminate the mother as a witness. Will this be their undoing? Heck no! White has another deadly sin in mind to contribute to the unraveling. As always in a White novel, plot twists are dictated by character and not clever author sleight-of-hand with the characters dancing to string pulls.

Cliff Johns is always in there pitching, but the ending relies on events neither he nor the crooks can exert complete control over as relationships and conflicting values render the ending completely unpredictable but nevertheless logical on its own terms.

White also avoids the typical mystery conclusion reveal choices as the loose ends are tied up by characters new to the story. A heist novel, yes, but with the heist subservient to the moral/ethical battles waged by participants on both sides.

The House on K Street (1965) is a story "ripped right out the headlines" as the old chestnut goes. Cold War tensions, after abating somewhat in the late 1950s, begin once again to peg out the fear meter during the Cuban Missile Crisis (1961) and the John F. Kennedy assassination (1963). Russian leader Nikita Khrushchev had visited the United States in 1959, following a visit earlier in the year to Russia by Richard Nixon. Optimists hoped that both visits would help ease the tension between the world's two superpowers locked in deadly opposition since the conclusion of World War II. In 1956, the Russian leader had uttered the immortal threat, "We will bury you!", so it was hoped the communist firebrand had mellowed, at least a little. Khrushchev's visit had US law enforcement forces worried sick and his visit to Disneyland was canceled due to security concerns. Other than that, the visit was mainly positive for both sides with the threat of nuclear war seeming less a possibility as the 1950s made way for the 1960s, due to various proposed plans and agreements designed to bring both sides closer to common ground.

A biproduct of the JFK assassination was a whole array of conspiracy theories regarding possible assassin Oswald string-pullers, and accomplices, individuals for whom the assassination might only be the first step in the overthrow of the US government. Naturally, many books and movies were produced whose subject was either the assassination or possible events that portrayed the next step toward nuclear war between the US and Russia. The fascination, analysis, ax grinding and exploitation of this seminal event in US history continues to this day.

The House on K Street appeared early in the initial post-assassination cycle of books that used the assassination as a touchstone. A Russian premier is scheduled to visit the United States, starting in Washington, DC and an elaboration assassination attempt is being planned. To White's credit, his novel is a straight thriller and although the perpetrators are members of a far rightwing group called The Sons of Columbia, White eschews any soapbox harangues for straight storytelling. As it is 1965 and Americans can hardly be more fearful of nuclear war at this time, there is no need to gild the lily and White doesn't. Instead we have a seemingly foolproof and complex assassination plot with law enforcement totally in the dark for most of the novel.

The novel begins with an assassination: of Joe, a mynah bird, but Joe is a mere stepping stone. The bird belongs to Carolyn Margulies, owner of a building on K Street in Washington, DC. The "assassination" is another in a series of efforts to harass Margulies to the point that she abandons her home. This occurs and those plotting the assassination of the Russian leader have completed the first step in their plan. Margulies only occupies the ground floor of the building so the conspirators must find a way to neutralize the other tenants, which include a magazine editor and two young women sharing an apartment. The perpetrators of the conspiracy are a varied lot: a political dilettante who bankrolls the operation; his front man and organizer; a zealot for the cause; a professional assassin just doing a piece of work per usual and two lower-level Sons of Columbia members who do the grunt work of tunneling underground from the house on K Street to facilitate the planting of a bomb on the route the Russian premier is to take from the airport to his hotel.

The organizer of the plot is Francis Blantz, dedicated to the cause but not above embezzling the dilettante's money, an expediter who troubleshoots conflicts within the gang. The Really Scary Fanatic in the mix is Jerry Townsend, whose successful manipulation of the residents of the house on K Street is vital to the success of the operation:

> It wasn't that Townsend was too stupid or dull to realize that the crime might be traced to him; in fact it was almost sure to be. No, Townsend, the dedicated fanatic, was firmly convinced that in the long run he would be considered a hero. He fully realized that he might also be a martyr, but he was prepared to take that risk.

The only professional criminal in the group is a man known only as Marko, who regards the others in the group with disdain but approaches his bombmaking task and its consequences with emotional detachment. At one point Blantz, clearly in denial regarding the full consequences of their actions, confronts Marko, because he is concerned that one of the gang may be lost in the explosion:

> Blantz stared at him with mild horror. "You are a cold-blooded bastard," he said.
> Marko again shrugged. "Cold-blooded? How about yourself? You are paying me so much money to kill a certain person. ...

I am no different than any other public executioner. No different than the man at your Sing Sing who throws the switch, or perhaps the soldier who lifts the rifle. Not the judge. Only the paid executioner.

"Ah, but you. You pay me to kill one man, but you know very well that in order to do so I must probably kill another dozen. Two dozen, perhaps fifty. Perhaps even a hundred. You know this, you understand this, but it does not faze you? So what are you worrying about one more for? Why does one additional one make the slightest difference? Is it because it will be one of your own perhaps?"

Blantz shook his head helplessly. "You wouldn't understand," he said, "No—no it's not because it will be one of our own. God knows there are plenty of them we can spare. It's only …"

"You amateurs are all alike," Marko said. "All alike. You are constantly killing, either because of stupidity, or greed, or avarice, or neglect. You think nothing at all of it.

"But I am a professional. I kill only for one reason. Because I am paid to do so. If I refused the job, someone else would take it. The victim would not be saved."

Townsend occupies the apartment of the now departed Margulies and proceeds to seduce Joan Harrington, one of the two upper floor boarders in order to gain an ally in detecting and neutralizing any suspicions that may arise in the minds of the remaining two boarders as the tunnel is being dug. Paul Dabney, the magazine editor, is smitten with Mary Eden, so sees little else, but Mary herself, already suspicious of Townsend, will play a role in undermining the plot. Jan Majeska, a police detective, originally involved in the investigation of the shot through Margulies window that took out Joe the mynah bird will eventually tumble to what is going on, but as is typical in a White devised criminal operation, the conspirators' plan proceeds with complex ingenuity and skill unimpeded by law enforcement.

The ethical issues underlying the plot and its consequences are obvious, but White never lectures and once again allows the story to unfold, all plot points driven by character strengths and weaknesses. He introduces a generally hopeful public view as counterpoint to the sense of paranoia and hysteria driving the Sons of Columbia:

No one, of course, was childish enough to assume that an

official state visit, a motorcade down Pennsylvania Avenue, a meeting on the White House lawn between the heads of two great governments, and the usual social hubbub which surrounded such events would really solve any basic problems. But there was a general feeling that the entire thing was a step in the right direction.

Prodded by Mary, the sole boarder not to be hoodwinked by Townsend, Detective Majeska is finally able to rally law enforcement at all levels to combat the impending plot. White combines cliffhanger style pacing evocative of old-time movie serials with a documentary like unfolding of the final scenes to produce page turner suspense leading up to the conclusion.

As in *The Ransomed Madonna*, White adopts a technique appropriate to a conspiracy situation involving the government for the "summing up." The reader of course knows what has happened but we see a red herring story fed to the public regarding the events that have transpired, providing a deft realistic touch to the proceedings, subtly reminding the reader that the reasons for an event as reported by the media may have little resemblance to what has actually happened.

This latest two-fer addition to Stark House Press's Lionel White collection has added two lesser-known works that showcase White's abilities both in the crime caper subgenre novel that he is famous for and his less explored realm of political thriller. Both novels feature ingeniously conceived crimes that seem destined for success but as in most White novels, the successful initial execution and eventual ultimate failure of these enterprises turns on the characters of those executing the crimes and those opposing them.

—May 2024
Mesa, AZ

Bill Kelly has proofread many Stark House releases since 2017 and recently has contributed introductions to several volumes, including *The Deadly Pay-Off* by William H. Duhart and *Hollow Triumph* by Murray Forbes, as well as having edited short story collections by Helen Nielsen, Nedra Tyre and Lorenz Heller. Kelly received a B.A. in English from Columbia University and was a technical writer and illustrator for several corporations. His first exposure to crime fiction was the works of Raymond Chandler, Penguin UK editions, purchased in Singapore.

THE RANSOMED MADONNA
Lionel White

This book is for
William P. Lewis
A Most Knowledgeable Fellow

CHAPTER ONE

1.

Being Monday, a traditionally "slow day" for news, the story, carried by the major wire services, made most of the important morning newspapers throughout the country. In New York, Boston, Philadelphia, Washington, and a number of other cities which take a certain pride in assuming a knowledgeable attitude toward culture, city editors displayed it on the first page. Some even used a two- or three-column picture to accompany the story. *The New York Times*, indeed, blew the picture up to four columns, feeling that anything less would hardly do justice to the subject.

The *Times* and the *Herald Tribune* in New York and the *Enquirer* in Philadelphia went even further. They were not content to print merely the wire-service report verbatim, but devoted considerable space on inside pages to the background of the subject matter.

It was felt, and rightly, that this secondary treatment would be of considerable interest to a wide group of teachers, schoolchildren, members of women's clubs and those general readers who had a sincere interest in art, history, and culture. The city editor of the most widely read Boston paper, keenly conscious of his Catholic audience, saw certain added values and played the story accordingly. On the other hand, the *Christian Science Monitor* gave it equal display, feeling the religious significance of the material was of sufficient import to cross denominational lines.

Despite the shrewd reasoning of the various editors involved in estimating the type of reader who might be enchanted by the article, it is doubtful that any of them would have suspected that Nicholas Dekota would find it acutely absorbing.

They all knew Nick Dekota, of course.

The fact is Nick—whose concern with the news of the day was limited to the sports pages—would not have been interested at all had it not been for Jack Reason. The city editors had never even heard of Jack Reason, but if they had, it is highly unlikely they would have numbered him among their audience.

As a general rule, horse players on the verge of insolvency have very little curiosity concerning art and even less for world-famous religious paintings.

As a matter of truth, had anyone asked Jack Reason six months before to identify Sandro Botticelli, Jack would very likely have replied that he was probably a barber up on Columbus Avenue. As for Botticelli's world-renowned *Madonna and Infant*, one of the Vatican's most precious treasures and now for the first time to be placed on exhibition in New York's exclusive Glickenstein Museum—well, Jack Reason couldn't have cared less.

Six months ago.

Nick Dekota's closest approach to art was an elaborately framed original Varga nude which he had purchased to grace the oak-paneled billiard room of his Fort Lee, New Jersey, mansion.

At precisely ten-thirty, on Friday morning of the first week in April, Nick Dekota was sprawled out in a leather chair in this same billiard room, beneath and to the left of the aforementioned Varga. His personal barber was completing Nick's morning shave, and Judy Monica was diligently manicuring the square fingernails of his already flawlessly manicured left hand.

Nick was looking at the front page of *The New York Times*. For a moment his eyes went to the reproduction of the *Madonna and Infant*, and then at once turned back to the headline of the accompanying news story. It was the headline which really interested him. It contained all the news that he really needed. It read:

MUSEUM INSURES
VATICAN PAINTING
FOR TWO MILLION

Nick waited until the barber had finished patting his face with powder and was collecting his instruments. He retrieved his hand from Judy's grasp and hunched forward in his chair.

"That's enough," he said. "Take off, Pete."

When Pete had closed the door behind him, he spoke again.

"Get ahold of that clown Reason, Judy," he said. "He's staying at a flea bag on upper Broadway. The Winslow. Tell him I've decided to go along. Have him here by eight tonight."

Judy Monica started to reach for the telephone on the table at her side.

"Not on the phone, stupid," Nick said. "Tell Morry to bring the Caddie around and have him drive you over. Park a couple of blocks away and telephone. Tell him to meet you in a bar someplace. You think I want the whole world knowing my business?"

Judy stood up and pushed a lock of platinum blonde hair from her forehead.

"Sure, Nick," she said.

"And while you're at it, do some shopping. Get some clothes."

"I've got plenty of clothes already, Nick," Judy said.

"Not the right kind of clothes. Go to Klein's, or Ohrbach's or someplace like that. Get some ginghams or whatever an ordinary housewife wears. Plain stuff."

"Klein's? Gingham? Have you flipped? What in the world would I—?"

"You're going to be a suburban housewife for the next few weeks," Nick said. "So you gotta dress like one. And get rid of that platinum mop on top of your head. Dye it brown."

Judy took a step back and stared at him. "A housewife?" she said. "I am? What are we doing? Giving up this place?"

"Not me, dope," Nick said. "Reason. Jack Reason. You're going to be his wife—for a month or so. I'll explain to you when you get back."

Judy shook her head. "It will take a little explaining," she said.

Nick leaned forward and gave her an affectionate pat on the fanny.

"Not really his wife, you dummy," he said. "You just have to pretend. While he's handling the deal. I want someone with him all the time. I want to be sure my interests are protected. So you are going to be his wife."

"Well, you better explain to *him*, then," Judy said. "And about the clothes …"

"Use your judgment," Nick said. "You're smart. You know what I want. So get going now. And be careful. I don't want anyone to make a connection between me and Reason. Now or ever. So tell Morry to play it cool when he brings him over tonight."

"Maybe you should tell me—"

"Later. I want you to get over to New York and make the contact as soon as possible. Just tell him I've decided to go along. And to be here tonight."

Nick dropped the paper on the floor as she left the room and his eyes went to the Varga nude on the wall.

"Two million," he muttered, a certain awe in his voice. "No broad in the world is worth that, let alone a picture of one."

2.

Charleton Manners, chairman of the Glickenstein Foundation, raised ice-blue eyes from the mahogany table on which he had spread the newspapers. He moved with deliberation, first taking the black horn-rimmed glasses from his patrician nose and then delicately flicking the ash from his cigarette. He looked over at Miles Dangleader, his gaze lingering for a moment of disapproval on the brown Van Dyke beard.

When he spoke he made no effort to keep the dislike he felt out of his voice. Manners' Board of Directors had overruled him on the selection of Dr. Dangleader as the new curator; it was too late now to do anything about it. The man had a two-year contract, signed, sealed, and delivered. But Manners had taken an immediate dislike to Dangleader, in spite of his excellent background and reputation. And certainly this matter of the *Madonna and Infant* was proving Manners correct.

"Extremely bad taste," he said. His slender finger pointed to the newspapers in front of him. "Blatant sensationalism. This sort of publicity may be fine for a Hollywood production, but it certainly has no place here. The Glickenstein Museum, Dr. Dangleader, is an institution which has always been proud of its reputation for integrity. Frankly, I shudder to think what the late August Glickenstein might think if he were to see these stories in the morning press."

Dangleader, a short, heavyset man with slightly thyroid eyes, a muddy complexion, and a tendency to sloppiness in his dress, dropped the ash from his cigar down the front of his corduroy jacket and smiled. Perhaps because it was his nature, or perhaps because he felt secure with that two-year contract firmly in his possession, he spoke casually, almost flippantly. Neither Charleton Manners' exalted position in the world of business and art, nor his exaggerated dignity, particularly impressed him.

"This sort of nationwide publicity is the finest thing that could happen," he said. "Why, it is beyond value; will probably bring thousands of people in for the exhibition. It will put the Glickenstein Museum on the map."

"The Glickenstein Museum has always been on the map, Dr. Dangleader," Manners said coldly. "And certainly, Botticelli is hardly in need of a cheap publicity stunt. I might add that when this is brought to the attention of the Vatican, I wouldn't be at all surprised if they should change their minds...."

"But the Vatican itself insisted we insure the painting," Dr. Dangleader remarked. "It was only on that condition they agreed to loan us the Virgin."

Manners winced at the casual way in which Dr. Dangleader referred to the world-renowned oil.

"Insuring the painting, Botticelli's *Madonna and Infant*"—he emphasized the full title—"is one thing. Giving the fact to the press is something else. We are not exactly running a peep show here, Doctor. We are not anxious to attract crowds of mere curiosity seekers. I fully appreciate your desire to bring fine paintings to the museum and put them on exhibition, but this sort of shocking and sensational story is hardly—"

Dr. Dangleader raised a pudgy hand and Mr. Manners ceased speaking, offended by the abruptness of the interruption.

"May I remind you, sir," the doctor said, his furry voice suddenly quite as chilly as that of the man facing him, "that the principal reason I was given my job was to increase the depressingly low attendance at the museum. I was instructed to do everything in my power to stock as many fine paintings as our budget will allow or as we can obtain on loan. Certainly you will not quarrel with the fact that obtaining the Virgin"—Manners again shuddered—"was no mean feat. It is the first time in history the painting has ever left the confines of the Vatican. There isn't a museum in the world which wouldn't have given its eye teeth—"

"Dear Dr. Dangleader," Manners interrupted, "I do wish, if you must refer to the painting, you would give it its proper title. The title of the oil is *Madonna and Infant*. A title which—"

"Which Sandro himself wouldn't have recognized," Dr. Dangleader said. "He called it simply *Virgin and Infant*."

"Sandro?"

"Sandro Botticelli."

Mr. Manners swallowed and brushed a morning *News* aside and extracted the fourth page of the *Herald Tribune* from the pile in front of him. Putting on his glasses, he began to read.

"Alessandro di Mariano dei Filipepi was born in Florence in 1447. Unable to learn to read or write, he was apprenticed by his father to a goldsmith named Botticelli in his early years and it was from him that he took his name. Later he was transferred from the school of the goldsmith to that of Fra Filippo Lippi, a Carmelite brother, then at the height of his practice and reputation as a painter. It was under the master that the youth obtained his proficiency.

"A rich and fanciful colorist, Botticelli soon became famous for his religious paintings, often using gold to enrich lights on hair, tissue, and foliage, a truly exquisite effect.

"Perhaps the most superb example of his work is the *Madonna and Infant*, believed to have been painted by Botticelli before he fell under the political influence of that evil genius, the Dominican Savonarola. During the period when, together with Domenico Chirlandio, upon his return from Rome ..."

Manners suddenly tossed the newspaper aside.

"Now that," he said, "is the sort of newspaper story which we not only approve, but which ..."

Dr. Dangleader bobbed his head. "Of course," he said. "I approve as well. But my dear Mr. Manners, you must realize that that particular story would never have been given such prominence in the newspaper if the editors had not been made conscious of the news value of an insurance company taking out a two-million-dollar policy! I might also add ..."

Before he had a chance to add anything, the telephone on the table rang, and he hesitated and picked up the receiver.

He listened a moment and then said, "Send him right in." Turning to Manners, he smiled. "The art detective—from the insurance company."

Manners tossed up his hands. "Detective," he said. "Good God, what next?"

"Well, perhaps not really a detective as such," Dr. Dangleader explained. "A fellow named Johns. Clifford Johns. Something of an artist himself. He is actually an art expert employed by the Continental Assurance Company. My understanding is that he will check on the Botticelli when it is delivered and will be assigned to watch it while it is in this country."

"You mean he's a sort of guard in case someone might try to steal—?"

"Hardly that. The painting is far too famous to attract thieves. There could be no possible market for an oil as well-known as this one. But there have been cases of vandalism, of willful destruction...."

He ceased speaking as the door opened and his secretary said, "Mr. Clifford Johns, gentlemen."

3.

Mary Donahue quickly pushed the bankbook under the pillow of the daybed as the knock sounded on the door. She hadn't really had to look in the book to know exactly how she stood. She knew the figures by heart.

A week ago there had been three hundred and eighty dollars. She had drawn thirty on Thursday: seventeen to pay the week's room rent, four for the prescription she'd had filled at the drugstore a couple of blocks over at the corner of Broadway and Sixty-ninth Street, and eight for groceries, which included her quota of cigarettes.

At least she had cut down on the cigarettes—not exactly taking the doctor's advice and quitting altogether until the baby was born, but anyway getting down to half a pack a day.

She looked up as the door opened and smiled wanly. Minnie Finkle held the clipping from the newspaper along with a pot of tea. She had a face like a newly sharpened hatchet, and her narrow, dark eyes took on a shrewd expression as they passed over the bare room before coming to rest on the small figure lying on the daybed.

"Hum-m-m," she said. She put the teapot on the counter of the kitchen sink behind the opened draw-curtain of the kitchenette. "I thought so—no breakfast as usual."

Mary Donahue forced a weak smile. "I'm still having morning sickness," she said. "Less than a month to go, and it's still with me. I thought by now ..."

Her eyes were on the older woman as she spoke, and she noticed the newspaper clipping in her hand. When she saw that there were no letters, she was unable to conceal her disappointment.

Minnie Finkle knew exactly what was going through the girl's mind.

"No letter, honey," she said. "Now you listen to me. Forget him. I know men. God knows I've been married to two of 'em and one was worse than the other. I've raised three children of my own, and I made every cent to support them. You're better off. At least you won't have to be taking care of some useless, drunken bum the way I did."

"He isn't a drunken bum," Mary said. "It's just that he's a musician and like all artists he has no sense of responsibility. He probably doesn't even know that he's going to be a father. If Jerry—"

"Jerry, Schmerry!" The landlady's voice was rich with disgust.

"You're lucky he doesn't know," she said. "You're lucky you aren't married to the bum. I know those jazz musicians. I've had 'em here in the house, and there wasn't a one of them worth a plugged nickel. They give you a line of sweet talk, take what they want, and then they're gone. Now you be glad that he is. I know, you aren't feeling so good right now, but once you have the baby why you'll get back to modeling again and then there will be just you and the baby, the two of you, and you'll make out fine. Now, while you're drinking this tea, I'll go down and make some toast and eggs."

"I'll try the tea. You were good to bring it," Mary said. "But I'm not up to anything solid just yet. Anyway, I have plenty of groceries and I ..."

Mrs. Finkle wasn't listening. She finished pouring the tea and then opened the icebox to see if there really was some food. Satisfied, she turned back to the girl on the bed.

"You shouldn't be worrying yourself at a time like this," she said. "It's lucky you have me to look after you, sitting around all day mooning about that no-good bum."

"Jerry isn't a bum," Mary repeated stubbornly. "It's just that he's young and irresponsible."

"Irresponsible—I'll say!" Mrs. Finkle said. "If he shows his face around here, I'll soon tell him—"

"I'm afraid you won't have the chance," Mary said wistfully. "He's probably out in Chicago or San Francisco or somewhere by now and—"

"And good riddance," Mrs. Finkle said. She moved over to the bed and sat next to the girl, handing her the cup. She spread the news clipping where Mary could see it.

"Thought it might sort of inspire you," she said.

It was the four-column reproduction of the *Madonna and Infant* which had been published in the morning paper.

"Look at that expression on her face," Mrs. Finkle said. "Beautiful. Real beautiful. It's the way you're going to feel when you wake up in the hospital and see your baby for the first time. You won't be thinking of no musician or anything else. Just that beautiful, lovely baby you have and how much he's going to mean to you. I clipped it out of the paper this morning to show it to you. And you know something else?"

Mary looked up from the painting with a trace of a smile. "What?"

"It's going to be right around the corner!"

"What's going to be right around the corner?"

"That painting. That's what. At the Glickenstein Museum on Central Park West. Less than two blocks away. That's what. It's in the newspaper. The Vatican has loaned it to us, or at least to the museum, and it will be there for anyone to see. Why, when you get out of the hospital you can go over there and look at it for nothing. At two million dollars, yet."

"What's two million dollars?"

"That's what it's worth. The paper said so. That's what they insured it for. I should have brought the whole paper up, I guess. But I wanted you to see the picture anyway because I thought it might cheer you up. Some famous Italian fella, Botti something-or-other, painted it hundreds of years ago. Can you imagine—two million dollars and anyone can go right in and look at it. Myself, I don't see how an old picture can be worth that much and it probably isn't. It's just some sort of story to make people think so, so that they'll go and look at it, but anyway, it's going to be right here, or at least a block or so away and you can see it." She continued without stopping for a breath, "You going to see the doctor today?"

Mary shook her head. "No," she said. "I don't have any money to waste on doctors. It's going to be a little while before I can get back to work, and I want to save every cent...."

"Now, child," Mrs. Finkle said, "I've told you not to worry about money. As long as I'm running this place, you ain't going to have to worry about a roof over your head. I know that you're a good girl, and when you get back to work again you'll—"

"I wasn't such a good girl when I got this way," Mary said and smiled weakly.

"We all got our moments of weakness," Minnie Finkle said. "My God, Sam Finkle and I weren't married until after the second one came and we only did it then so he could go on relief. Anyway, I know a decent girl when I see one. I've had enough of the other kind in this house, I can tell you."

She promptly did tell Mary, going into elaborate details concerning no less than six young ladies who had been her tenants at one time or another.

When at last she was ready to leave, she again pointed at the picture which was still spread out on the couch next to Mary.

"*Madonna and Infant,*" she said. "Being Jewish, I never have quite understood how a virgin could have a child, but that doesn't matter. Just look at that picture. A beautiful face. Real angelic. And that darling baby! Like you are going to have, young lady, if you take care of yourself. I gotta go now, but I'm going to be back right after I get my shopping done. And morning sickness or no morning sickness, I'm going to make us some lunch. Some nice boiled chicken. You'll be able to keep that down. And I want you to think about going to the doctor. I know you're healthy and all, but you see the doctor anyway. You should be getting prepared." Her eyes took in Mary's swollen stomach. "You want to know just about when it's due so you'll be ready," she added.

"I'll know," Mary said. "I'll know. And I'll just call a cab and go to the hospital and—"

"You should have some family with you," Minnie Finkle said. "I wish you'd just let me know who—"

"I've told you, Mrs. Finkle," Mary said. "There is no family. At least none that I would want to know...."

"Someone should know. If you would only give me the name of your doctor and the hospital you are going to."

"I just want to see this through alone. And I appreciate all you are doing," Mary said stubbornly, "but I got into this by myself, and I must see it through—"

"Such foolishness," Mrs. Finkle exclaimed. "You got nothing to be ashamed of. Husband or no husband, you got nothing to be ashamed of."

"I'm not ashamed," Mary said.

"Don't be. As I said, I had three kids. Two bastards and one legitimate. The legitimate one's in state prison and the other two— well, one's a fine lawyer and the other's a very high-class bookmaker."

4.

Jack Reason put the telephone receiver down and wiped his forehead, which was completely dry, but which he felt should have been dripping perspiration. It was the call he had been waiting for, hoping for, but fearing would never come. He had been gambling that it would come, and he knew that if it ever did, he'd be in.

Shaking his head, he sighed. It had been a long shot, but it had paid off. Just those few little words. She hadn't even identified herself, but somehow he knew—knew that the message must come from Nick.

She had said, "It's about Mr. D. Meet me at the tavern at Seventy-second and Amsterdam in fifteen minutes. I'll be sitting alone at a booth in the back. Drinking a martini. Platinum hair and a mink stole. Come alone."

He walked across the room and stood in front of the mirror above the dresser and looked at himself in the glass. His thin mouth smiled as he patted his dark, well-combed hair and then straightened his striped necktie. He drew back his lips and admired his even white teeth, before he leaned down and scraped the few bills and the change into his side coat pocket. He didn't have to count it. Sixty-two dollars and eighty cents.

He'd been planning to call the bookie and lay fifty on the second at Aqueduct. It was a long shot and a desperate chance, but he was going to have to take it. The hotel rent was due; there were all those small but annoying bills. He just had to hit.

Again he smiled. He wouldn't have to bother now. A much longer shot was about to pay off.

For a moment his eyes went to the newspaper lying open under the mirror. He leaned forward and with one hand caressed the picture on the front page.

"You paid off, baby. I just knew you would," he said, under his breath.

He pulled on his jacket and took the soft felt hat from the chair. He didn't want to keep Mr. D.'s friend waiting.

She was not too tall, slender, a blonde—which he understood not because of the platinum hair, but because of the light blue eyes and fine-grained white skin of her face. She wore a little too much make-up; it made her look older than her twenty-four or five years. Her clothes were expensive but somehow not just quite right. From a distance he would have said, "Dumb blonde." But she wasn't dumb by a long shot and this he knew at once. It was an old habit, making quick appraisals of people, and he was rarely wrong.

The martini, untouched, was sitting on the table in front of her. Except for two men who stood at the end of the bar, up near the front, she was the only customer in the place.

He dropped his hat on the seat and moved in opposite her. She merely looked at him and nodded.

He lifted his hand and beckoned the waiter. "Sherry," he ordered. He waited until the waiter turned toward the bar and said, "Never take anything stronger."

"Ulcers?" she asked.

He shook his head. "Caution," he said.

"And your name is?"

"Jack Reason," he said. "Were you expecting someone else?"

"Only wanted to be sure," she said. "Guys—strangers—have picked me up before this, you know."

"I would have guessed," he said. "And you are ..."

"It doesn't much matter who I am," she said. "What I have to say will only take a—"

She stopped speaking as the waiter returned with the drink. They waited then, quietly appraising each other until he had returned to the bar, where he stood reading a scratch sheet.

"Mr. D. wants to see you. This evening. Eight o'clock. You'll be picked up. Be at Broadway and a Hundred-and-second Street, northeast corner, at seven-thirty exactly. A car will stop by. Be alone and don't talk with anyone between now and then. And you are not to let anyone know about it."

"Your Mr. D. is pretty cautious himself," Jack said.

"Very cautious, Mr. Reason."

He smiled, thinking she really is quite smart. But of course she would have to be. Anyone in Nick Dekota's confidence could be trusted to be smart.

Looking over at his slender, long-jawed, youthful face, Judy Monica was also doing a little thinking.

So this, she thought, is the man who is going to be my husband for the next few weeks. Well, at least he isn't too bad. He looks all right, even if he is a bit on the thin side and has that cagey look about him. But he's probably about as entertaining as a racing form, from what Nick has told me.

All these professional gamblers are alike. If it isn't a horse race, a crap game, or a baseball pool, it doesn't exist. Sort of too bad in a way. He's young, at least compared to Nick. And he's certainly a lot better looking than Nick could ever hope to be. In fact, if it wasn't for that sharp, gambler's look ...

She shook her head and frowned. This was no way to start thinking about the man she knew she was going to have to start playing house with for the next few weeks or so. It was strictly a business deal, and it was going to remain on that basis. It would have to be that way if she wanted to remain healthy. Nick Dekota wasn't in love with her; he treated her pretty much the same way he treated one of his favorite police dogs. But she was Nick's property, and Nick was pretty selfish about the things he owned.

"Is there anything else?" he began, but she smiled and shook her head.

"Just that Mr. D. says he'll go along. Isn't that enough?"

"Plenty," he said. "So we can skip it and go on to more important things. Like for instance, would you like to have lunch? And what would you be doing with the rest of the day? And—"

"And you are getting way ahead of yourself," she finished for him. "It's too early for lunch and the rest of the day I'm going to be doing a little shopping. You see, I must get ready to play house."

He looked at her quizzically. "Play house? Someone I know, maybe?" he asked.

"Oh, very likely," she said, standing up. "I'm afraid I'll have to be going now."

He shrugged, a little disappointed. "Well, I'll be seeing you, I guess," he said, hesitantly.

"Yes, I should imagine you will," she said. "Be on time tonight. Mr. D. doesn't like—"

"I'll be on time," he said.

He waited until she was gone and then reached for his glass and sipped the sherry. He noticed that she had not touched the martini. She's even more cautious than I am, he thought. He hoped he'd be seeing her again. That makeup had been pretty bad, but the face behind it ...

CHAPTER TWO

1.

Clifford Johns met his fiancée in the lobby of the 21 Club at a quarter to two. Patricia Bentley had been waiting since one-thirty, and she was annoyed. Patricia was not used to waiting for anyone, and she felt she certainly shouldn't have to for the young man she had agreed to marry. It wasn't merely that she was meticulously punctual herself. She just couldn't tolerate carelessness about little things. It was one of those habits of Cliff's which she hated and which she was determined to correct once they were man and wife— this casual, easygoing, dreamy way he had of ignoring the conventions.

He blew in from the street, his handsome tanned face all smiles when he spotted her sitting in the deep leather chair. She noticed at once that his hair needed grooming, that he was wearing a colored sports shirt, and that his tweed coat could stand a pressing. Tall, broad-shouldered, and lean-waisted, there was no doubt but what he was good-looking. But why couldn't he have seen to it that his shoes were shined? And the dark shadow of beard on the square jaw certainly testified that he had shaved the night before rather than that morning.

Her family was right. There was no doubt about it. She was crazy even to think of marrying him. No family, no background, and a pretty questionable future. But that was all beside the point: he did have an irresistible quality. She would simply have to make him over. She was sure that the raw material was there. Of course, he would never amount to anything as a businessman, but he certainly was charming—after all, he had made her fall in love with him— and she supposed he had talent in his own field. In any case, she certainly had all the money either of them would ever need. But he would have to start learning that he was not to treat her as he treated his other women. She was not a girl to be kept waiting.

Patricia looked down at her platinum wristwatch. "You are late," she said. "I've been here—"

"Darling," he said, leaning down to take her hands and pull her to her feet. "Darling, it was unavoidable. I got tied up at the Glickenstein and—"

"It is embarrassing for me to sit here like some little shopgirl waiting while you—"

"No one would ever mistake you for some little shopgirl, Pat," Cliff said, propelling her by the elbow toward the dining room. "I made it as soon as I could. Sorry to be late, but business, you know...."

"Business? That silly job of yours. I can't understand why you don't just stick to your painting. Why you want—?"

"Why I want to make a living?" he finished for her. "It's simple, darling. I like to eat. Painting pretty pictures is all fine and good, but it doesn't exactly earn me a living."

"And I suppose that playing at being some sort of detective is a solution?" Patricia said, making an effort not to let the annoyance show in her voice. "If you must work, Daddy has told you a dozen times that he will bring you into the brokerage business. For someone as smart as you are—"

"Smart enough to get Daddy's favorite daughter," Cliff said, laughing. "Anyway, I am not some sort of detective, as I have explained a dozen limes. I am an investigator. I work for an insurance company and I am an art expert and investigator. I'm doing something I like and know how to do. It doesn't pay a lot of money, as you well know, but at least I'm in a field which interests me. Now let's not argue and spoil our appetites. I'm hungry as a wolf."

The waiter led them to the table and he pulled out her chair. Cliff ordered Scotch sours while they looked at the menu. He waited until they had the drink before breaking the news.

"About tomorrow," he said at last. "I'm afraid I have bad news. I won't be able to go out to the Hamptons with you after all. Something has come up, and I'm going to have to work."

Patricia put her drink down and looked up at him. Her eyes were suddenly cold and her chin quivered when she spoke. "Clifford Johns!" she said. "You simply can't. The family's expecting us and all of my plans have been made. You promised and you will simply have to come. I can't just go out there again and tell them that you—"

"Afraid you'll have to, honey," he said. "It's like I told you. Something has come up. Important. Really important."

"More important that I am, Cliff?" Patricia said.

"Nothing is more important than you are, Pat," Cliff said. "You know that. But this is different. The S.S. *Vulcania* docks at ten in the morning, and I have to be down at the pier to meet her."

"What's so important?"

"The picture, darling. I've explained it all to you. The picture gets in and I—"

"That silly picture! Cliff, it's just out of the question. I'm quite sure—"

"It isn't a silly picture, Pat. Botticelli never painted a silly picture in his life. In any case, I have no option in the matter. The company has ordered me...."

"And just why is it so necessary?"

"Don't you read the papers, honey?" Cliff asked. "Continental has insured the painting for two million dollars. So I must—"

"I would assume that they will have the proper armed truck and what-not," Patricia said, sarcastically. "I can't see why it is necessary that you be on hand. And it is important that we don't let the family down again. They are expecting us."

"And they'll just have to be disappointed, Pat," Cliff said. "You see,

I have to be with that picture from the minute it leaves the ship's safe until it is hung in the gallery. And even then it is going to be my job to keep a constant eye on it. I'm afraid that for the next two or three weeks, at least, my time isn't going to be my own."

For several moments she stared at him. She was boiling inside, but she made an effort to control herself. She knew him well enough to realize that he wouldn't change his mind. He never did.

"Oh, Cliff," she said. "It all seems so ridiculous. Your excuse for living the way you do, being the way you are, is that you are an artist, that you want to paint. And here you are, acting just like any other dull little clerk. If you insist on doing what you want to do, why don't you just paint great pictures yourself, instead of standing around like a Pinkerton and babysitting someone else's art work?"

He smiled at her indulgently. "I've explained it to you a thousand times, honey," he said. "I'm just not good enough."

"You are. You're very good. You do beautiful portraits. Why even Daddy said the one you did of me—"

"Your Daddy knows less about art than I know about the price of IBM," Cliff said. "Sure, I can do a nice little likeness. I can even do the kind that fond parents like to hang above their mantlepieces. But that isn't what I want. I want to do something really great, something—"

"Then why don't you? Why don't you just sit down—"

Cliff sighed and reached for his fresh drink. "Listen," he said. "Listen, will you? *I* know I have the talent. I even know what and how I want to paint. And some day …"

"Someday? What day? What is it you're waiting for?"

He shrugged and tossed out his hands in a futile gesture. "Maybe the right model," he said. "I know exactly what—"

"If you know exactly what, then you should be able to go ahead and do it. The model shouldn't hold you up if you can see in your mind's eye just what it is you want to do."

"Listen, Pat," Cliff said, leaning forward and looking at her seriously. "Listen and try mand understand. I can describe the Mona Lisa to you. I can tell you everything there is to know about the color of her complexion, the size of her eyes, the way the nose fits the face. I know it by heart. I know the picture I want to paint by heart, also. The girl, the way she is built, everything. Except the expression. And that is something you have to see in order to understand and interpret. Can't you see what I mean? I need a certain girl—not just any girl. It isn't the design or the draftsmanship or the color or anything else. It's an expression I'm looking for. And when I find it …"

"Order another drink," Patricia said.

"Every great artist had one really great model," Cliff said. "At least every great artist who did figures and heads. If you can find one in a lifetime, you're lucky. And someday …"

"And someday you will come to your senses," Patricia said. "I just hope it won't be too late. I'm getting a little bit tired of being stood up. Tired of trying to explain to my family, and myself as well, just why …"

"Now, Pat," Cliff said. "You know—"

"I know that when some damned painting is more important to you than I am—"

"Botticelli's Madonna is not some damned painting," Cliff said, coldly.

"I think that I'm a lot more important than any picture, no matter who painted it or how much it's worth." She pushed back her chair and stood up. "I don't believe I care about lunch," she said, "and in any case, we've wasted so much time that I must go if I'm to keep my appointment at the hairdressers'. As far as tomorrow is concerned, you'll just have to have your office make other plans. I shall be expecting you to pick me up at noon, exactly as we have arranged."

"But the Madonna," Cliff began. The words died on his lips as Patricia swept out of the room. He looked after her helplessly for a moment, and then noticing the people at the next table staring at him, he shrugged and slowly sat down. He realized that he had been talking at the top of his voice. He saw that his neighbors were still watching him curiously.

He turned to them and smiled sweetly. "Madonna must come first," he said. "Madonna must be served."

The woman at the next table giggled, and her escort turned away, his jaw at an indignant angle.

2.

Morry Shine was wearing a chauffeur's uniform as he wheeled the Cadillac out of the curved drive of the Fort Lee mansion just after midnight. Jack Reason sat beside him on the front seat.

"When we get into Manhattan, you can drive down Broadway and drop me at a Hundred-and-tenth," Jack said.

"I'm dropping you at Columbus Circle," Morry said. "That's where Mr. D. said to drop you."

Jack cocked one eye to look over at his companion. "Oh? You always do just what Mr. D. says to do?"

"Everybody does what Mr. D. says," Morry said.

Reason was silent for several minutes. "And suppose that I just want to get out before—"

"You get out when I let you out, Buster," Morry said. "Understand?"

"I understand."

"Good," Morry said. "We'll get along better that way." He sighed and after a minute said, "Say, you was with the boss a long time. Got some business with him maybe?"

Again Jack looked over at him, this time covertly. Instinctively, his hand went to his breast pocket where the wallet rested—the wallet holding the ten bills. The ten, one-thousand-dollar bills.

"Now you don't think Mr. D. would be wanting me to discuss his business affairs with his chauffeur, do you?" he asked.

"I ain't just a chauffeur," Morry said in a surly voice. "But I guess you're right. It ain't none of my affair what you and the boss got going."

"I didn't think it was," Reason said. "No, I hardly thought it was."

"Don't matter none, what you think," Morry said. "I know all about it anyway. I'm going to be along. Going to be with you when you get the place."

"Oh?" Jack took a long breath. "I guess you *are* more than a chauffeur," he said at last. "Who said you are going to be along, as you put it?"

"Mr. D. said so," Morry said. "You see, I'm going to be out at the place with you, to sort of watch after the boss's interests."

"You are, eh," Jack said. "That's interesting. Mr. D. said that a young lady was going to be out there with me—to, as you say, watch after his interests."

"That's right," Morry said. "Judy. Judy Monica. And that's what I mean. She's the boss's interest, in a way of speaking, and that's why I'm going to be along. To watch after Mr. D.'s interests."

Jack waited several minutes. He remembered Nick had said that he would be sending along someone to act the part of a gardener and a handyman around the place. It must be the man beside him.

"You seem to know all about it without my telling you," Jack said.

"Perhaps you can tell me...."

"I can tell you nothing," Morry said. "I already told you too much. Anything Mr. D. wants you to know, he'll tell you himself. If he don't, Judy will. And that's all I got to say. I'm dropping you at Columbus Circle."

"You can drop me at Columbus Circle and you can drop dead yourself, as far as I'm concerned," Jack said.

"We'll get along fine," Morry said. "But *you* can't drop dead. You got important things to do."

"That's right, I have," Jack said. "Yes, we'll get along fine—just so long as you mind your own business and don't interfere with mine."

"I ain't interfering with nobody," Morry said. "I am just going to be there to watch—"

"To watch the boss's interests," Jack finished for him. "Right."

3.

It was after one in the morning, and the old man was tired. He sat propped on pillows in the big leather chair, the card table drawn up across his knees. He was wearing a silk dressing gown over his regular clothes; he hadn't removed the striped bow tie or taken off his expensive, narrow shoes, in spite of the fact that his corns were hurting again.

The cards lay spread out on the table in front of him, and his slender, almost transparent hands moved like tiny bird's claws as he turned up one after the other. He'd been playing solitaire since eleven o'clock, and he had still to win his first game. It would have been very easy if he'd wanted to peek or cheat just the slightest bit, but he made it a practice never to cheat when he was playing with himself.

A cup of lukewarm beef tea sat at one side of the table, and his old-fashioned gold watch lay in a corner. He strained his eyes and looked over at it, shaking his head. He wished Jack would arrive.

He dealt three cards from the top of the deck, turned them over, and carefully put them on the stack in front of himself. The king of spades showed. This was the second time through without a play, and he knew that he'd lost the game again.

He swore a particularly foul oath in a voice with an amazingly cultured accent and threw the cards into a jumble with his left hand. As he started to get up, the bell rang.

Mark Liebman waited for the second ring before he pushed the button which released the lock on the downstairs front door of the apartment house. He was back in his chair waiting when the soft knock came on the door. He called out to come in.

"About time," he said, neither turning nor raising his eyes as Jack Reason entered the room and tossed his hat on the couch.

"Sorry to be late," Jack said, "but it took a little while. He wanted to know everything and I had to go over it all again. In detail."

"And?"

"And okay. I got it." He reached into his pocket and took out the wallet, laying it on the scattered cards. "Ten," he said. "Ten thousand. I tried for fifteen, but ten was all he'd go for. Later, if we need it …"

"Ten should do it," the old man said. His face was without expression as he looked down at the wallet. He didn't touch it.

"What else?"

"A half," Jack said. "I tried, Mark. Tried every way I could, but he insisted on an even split. There was nothing I could do about it."

Mark Liebman turned and looked up at the other man. "You should have told him to go to hell," he said.

"I did," Jack said. "And he was perfectly willing to go, but he wasn't budging about the split. It was either that way or not at all."

"And what does he do for his split?" Mark asked, sarcastically. "Put out a lousy ten grand and—"

Jack spoke quickly, interrupting him. "Well, he'll ante in more if we need it, but we got to show we need it. Other things, too. He agreed to supply the lawyers and the bail bond boys if we need them."

"We can't afford to need them. I told you that, Jack. I'm an old man now, and I've done all the time I can do."

"I know. I know, Mark," Jack said. "We are going to pull this off. Don't worry one little bit about that. But it didn't hurt to figure the mouthpieces and the bail just in case. After all, the worst that can happen would be a couple of years or so."

"A couple of years or so is fine for you, son," Liebman said bitterly. "But not for me. I told you. I'm too damned old. I've done too much time. One more jolt, even a couple of years, and I've had it."

"There won't be any screwup," Jack Reason said. "You know that, Mark. This is one that can't miss."

"I still don't like the split," he said sourly. "Even so, I'm surprised he went for it. He must have thought it was gilt-edged."

"It is gilt-edged," Jack said. "Nick could see it right away. My God, just think about it. A snatch—and the worst they can do is get you on a larceny rap. Not only that, but the only witness who could talk afterward can't talk at all. Instead of maybe a bump off to protect ourselves, the worst that could happen would be they'd get us for willful destruction of property. It's perfect."

"Nothing's ever perfect," Liebman said. "The last rap I did was a jewel switch which was also supposed to be perfect—but I spent three years, two hundred and fifty-six days with nothing to do but find the flaw in it."

"There's going to be no flaw in this one," Reason said. "Anyway, the hell with all that. The thing is we got the nut money. He went for it, even if he did insist on a fifty-fifty deal."

"Well, I'm still surprised," Liebman said. "What was the convincer anyway? I didn't think Nick Dekota would put out ten grand in cash to get his own mother out of purgatory."

"The convincer was the story in the papers this morning—the two-million-dollar insurance policy they took out on the picture. Up until then, he just couldn't get it through his head that any picture was worth that kind of dough. Didn't believe for a second that a damned old piece of canvas …"

"Well, he believes it now or he wouldn't have come up with the front money," Mark Liebman said. "The point is, will he play it our way? Will he let us handle it? Did he have any suggestions or want to move in on the caper itself?"

"Anything but," Reason said. "He hardly had a word to say. Just wanted the plan, was all. Except one thing. Instead of just you and me and Neddie out at the house, he's sending along his girl. She's supposed to be my wife when we take the place. Mr. D. said it would look better if I was married instead of just moving in with my old man and chauffeur."

"A girl? What girl?"

"Nick's own girl. But you won't have to worry about her. She's all right or she wouldn't be Nick's girl, you can bet on that."

"I don't like women in on these things."

"She isn't going to be in on it, Mark. Just going to be out at the house so things will look legit. I think maybe Nick is right about that part of it."

Liebman drew in his thin shoulders and shook his head. "Dames!" he said. "Anything else?"

"One more. There will be one of his boys out at the place. Right now, he's Nick's chauffeur, but he's coming along as a gardener."

"What the hell do we want him for?"

"We don't," Jack said. "But it was one thing that Nick insisted on. He wants to have someone there, in case anything happens."

"What does he mean, anything happens? What does he expect to happen? That we'll take the dough and just move on and cut him out?"

"I wouldn't be surprised," Jack said. "After all, Nick Dekota is nobody's fool. I can see why he might want his own end protected. Of course, he didn't put it quite that way. He just felt that an extra man might just possibly come in handy. As he puts it, you never know when you might need muscle."

"We got Neddie for muscle," Mark Liebman said. "If I thought we would have to be using muscle, I wouldn't be in on this myself. You know very well I have never—"

"I know—I know, Mark," Jack said quickly. "But don't worry. There isn't going to be any violence, nothing rough at all. This thing is going smooth as silk. Mr. D. is merely protecting—"

"His interests," Liebman said, sarcastically. "Doesn't the damned fool know we wouldn't dare double-cross him? Hell, he's the only person in this world, outside of ourselves, who will ever know what's happened. We couldn't cross him if we wanted to. He should know that. We don't need this muscle man of his. The girl's bad enough, but at least she adds up. But a muscle man—"

He stopped speaking suddenly and looked up at Jack Reason sharply. "What does this woman of his look like?" he asked.

"A real doll," Jack said.

The old man shook his head again.

"It's adding up," he said. "I guess I understand why the muscle is being brought in. By God, boy, you better make damned sure he isn't going to be needed. I knew I didn't like the idea of a girl along with us. And now ..."

"Oh, don't worry about it, Mark. Don't think I would be crazy enough to let some dame screw up anything this good. And I wouldn't go for a girl of Nick Dekota's, no matter what. You should know me better than that. You can trust me, Mark."

"If I didn't trust you, I wouldn't be with you," Liebman said. "It's because I do trust you—"

"And because there's nothing wrong with a couple of hundred thousand dollars for your own cut," Jack Reason said.

"Nothing at all wrong with it," Liebman said. "So what's next?"

"Neddie," Jack said. "I want us to be settled within the next week. We have to move fast. There's no extra time. I'll be in touch with Neddie tomorrow. We'll arrange for the cars, and then go on out and see the place on Long Island. You want to go up with us?"

"Won't be necessary," Liebman said. "You know what you're looking for."

"I know. I can handle that part without any help. But once I make it on the cars, you should be the one to—"

"I'll be here whenever you need me," Liebman said. "You're sure Neddie is all right?"

"I'm sure, Mark. He isn't bright. I've told you that. But he's loyal and he keeps his mouth shut. I've known him since I was a kid. He's been a good friend. No record and a clean background. Has a chauffeur's license and he's driven a cab, too. Just the man for the job. You don't have to worry one bit about Neddie. I'd trust him with my life."

"I hope you won't have to," Mark Liebman said, dourly. "Well, you better be getting along now. I want to get to bed and get some sleep. At my age ..."

"At your age and at your weight I'd match you against a pair of wildcats," Jack said and laughed. He patted the old man on the shoulder. "We're in, Mark, in," he said.

"Sure," Liebman said. "I just hope we stay that way. This is out of my line you know, boy."

"It's out of mine too, Mark," Jack said. "That's one reason we should be good at it. With your front, my brains, and Neddie's brawn—"

"And a hell of a lot of luck—"

"We don't need luck," Jack said. "This one is perfect."

"Get out and let me get to bed," Liebman said. "Call me tomorrow night."

"You'll be here?"

"I'm always here."

4.

At the bottom of the last page, Mary Donahue wrote, "With all of my love," and signed her name. She took the envelope from the drawer of the small desk and carefully addressed it: Mr. and Mrs. H. D. Donahue, RFD #4, Spring Valley, Kansas. And then, not bothering to enclose the letter, she stood up and went to the two-burner stove.

She turned the heat off under the pot that held the boiled chicken.

She wasn't in the least hungry, but she was going to have dinner anyway. The doctor had told her she must eat regularly. She would follow his directions even if the mere thought of food almost gagged her.

A few minutes later, sitting at the table with her dinner still untouched in front of her, a very strange thing happened. She was thinking of Jerry again, but now, for the first time, the thought didn't bring that tight pain to her heart, didn't choke her up so much that she was barely able to breathe.

She knew all his vital statistics. Jerry McHenry, thirty-two years old, five-foot-ten, a hundred and fifty-five pounds. Pianist, jazz musician. Brown eyes, curly black hair beginning to recede from a narrow forehead, a slightly turned-up nose, and a rather weak chin. A high color, caused by too much drinking.

But that was all. She just couldn't see him, could no longer conjure up his actual appearance. For the first time in all of these months of thinking of him, she suddenly no longer missed him. She didn't feel love, compassion, or even hate for him … he was just Jerry McHenry—a man she used to know. Someone who'd been nice enough to her in his way.

The father of her unborn baby.

She picked up the knife and fork and cut off a piece of the boiled chicken, and when she put it in her mouth, it tasted good. It tasted like food used to taste when she'd enjoyed eating.

She slowly smiled. And then she laughed. It was marvelous knowing that she was able to laugh again. She felt as though she had just recovered from a long siege of illness.

"Jerry McHenry," she said. And laughed again.

She'd never liked the name Jerry anyway. So she would name the baby Harold—Hal—after her dad. Hal Donahue, not Hal McHenry.

Thinking of her father, she remembered the letter. The letter with all of the lies she had found so hard to write. She reached for it, inclined for the moment to not send it at all. She started to read it, inwardly knowing she couldn't tear it up. Much as she hated to lie, she knew that she must protect those old people out in Kansas. Someday they would have to know, but not yet.

Carefully she reread the letter.

Dear Mother and Dad:

I am sorry to have been so long in answering your last letter, but so many things have been happening and I've been so busy that I just never seem to get around to the things I really want to do.

I'm still modeling and have been doing quite well. I expect to have my picture on the cover of an important fashion magazine sometime next month, and when it comes out I'll send you a copy.

Now I have some news. Sometime within the next thirty days I'm going on a trip. I've taken a job with a steamship line and am going to work as a hostess on a cruise ship which will be sailing in the Caribbean for six weeks. It doesn't pay a great deal, but I'm sure I'll like the work and the people are very nice. I'll be doing a little singing, and that's what I've wanted all along. Of course it isn't exactly a Broadway musical or anything, but it's a start.

Actually it is to be more of a vacation than a real job. Of course it will mean that I'll be away from New York for more than a month, but this shouldn't interfere with my work when I come back again. I will, of course, keep my room here. The only bad feature is that I won't be able to write very often, since the boat doesn't touch port for the first couple of weeks. So, if you don't hear from me for a while, don't worry. I understand letters from the tiny islands that the cruise ship touches sometimes take forever to get back to the States.

I've been feeling quite well, but have put on a little weight, which I hope to lose before I return. After I get back, I'm hoping that I'll have enough money saved up to be able to come home for a visit. In any case, I'll surely be home for Christmas this year.

I hope Daddy is going ahead with his plans to sell the farm. It is time he started taking it easy.

With all my love,
Mary

She folded the two sheets of paper carefully, inserted them in the envelope, and sealed it. She only hoped that when they really knew what had happened during that time she was supposed to be on a

Caribbean cruise, they would forgive her for her deception. There was no doubt in her mind that she would tell them, but it was better that they knew nothing until after she'd had the baby. It was bad enough she had to hurt them. She didn't want them worrying now. Besides, once they saw their grandchild and fell in love with the baby as she was sure they would, it would take some of the edge off of their shock.

She would mail the letter in the morning. There was no hurry—no hurry about anything now. She had a full month, as near as she could guess, before anything important happened. And then it was going to be the very most important thing in her life.

That night Mary Donahue fell asleep within minutes after she pulled the sheet up under her chin. She fell asleep with a small smile on her face. She was happy again for the first time since that day when she had received Jerry's letter telling her …

But she didn't even want to think of Jerry anymore.

CHAPTER THREE

1.

Dr. Miles Dangleader took his feet off the polished top of his desk, flicked the ashes from his cigar to the floor, and leaned forward to look at the face of the leather traveling clock.

"Three-thirty," he said. "Three-thirty, Friday afternoon, April twenty-fourth. Another half an hour to go and it's all over. The greatest two weeks the Glickenstein Museum has ever had, if I say so myself."

Cliff Johns put his half empty glass on the desk and grinned. "You certainly can say so," he said. "I wouldn't have believed anything in this world could have gotten this many people in to see good art."

"To see one particular piece of good art," Dr. Dangleader corrected. He took the pint bottle from his top desk drawer, filled his own glass halfway full, and looked at the other man. "Say when."

"When," Cliff said, as the other poured.

"If we could do this every week, why I'd—"

"It would be too much of a good thing," Cliff said. "Frankly, when you close up at four today, I won't be sorry. These last fourteen days have been a hell of a strain. I could use a little rest."

"You won't be getting much, I'm afraid," the curator said. "Aren't you going to Washington with the picture?"

"Flying down Monday morning," Cliff Johns said. "As you know, the picture will be picked up tomorrow by the Brinks people and they are responsible until it's hung in the National Museum. I take over again then for a week. Stay with it until she's back on the Italian liner, heading home. Well, it's been a great experience babysitting something worth two million dollars."

"Worth a lot more than that actually," Miles said. "I dare say the Vatican wouldn't part with it at any price. Amazed in fact that we were able to arrange the loan."

"Probably a gesture to cement good international relations," Cliff said. "And of course you're right about its worth. There is only one such Botticelli *Madonna and Infant*, the same as there is only one *Last Supper*, one—"

"I'm just glad to have had the opportunity to have seen it in my lifetime," Miles said. "A reproduction gives nothing resembling the thrill of the original. I guess a lot of people must feel the same way. Even Manners was amazed at the turnout we got. I think he's coming around a little to my way of thinking. Publicity, for a good cause, never hurts."

Cliff nodded and sipped his drink. "The old boy been around lately?" he asked.

Miles nodded. "Out in the gallery right now." he said. "Giving a private showing in the North Wing. You know we closed the room to the public at three today. Mr. Manners showed up at three-ten with a Very Important Person."

"Yes?"

"Yes. Baron Manfried Glickenstein. A cousin of the late August himself, no less. In town from Munich."

"Baron Glickenstein? I thought they were all dead."

"Hardly," Dr. Dangleader said. "The Glickensteins are like the Rothschilds. Europe is full of them. The Glickensteins were originally a mercantile family, and I understand that this particular branch— that is the German offshoot—made their fortune in jewels. Diamonds in South Africa, rubies, emeralds."

"Manners is probably putting the bite on the old boy for an endowment," Cliff said. "Odd that he should have shown up just at this time. Did you meet him?"

"Charleton brought him in and introduced him when they arrived. Guess they'd had lunch together or something. Weird old duck. Tiny and beautifully dressed. Spoke with a thick accent. So old that his personal man, a tall, thin, sort of unbelievable fellow in striped pants, if you please, had to hold him by one arm when they came in. But he's still sharp as they come. Asked a hundred questions about the Botticelli and then, just as I was about to feel a little sorry that he had never seen it, he explained that the last time he'd viewed the picture was when he was a dinner guest of the late Pope John in Rome. Quite a character."

"He sounds like one. I'll bet Manners is really laying it on thick."

"Always does when he has a rich art patron in tow. Funny thing about him. He treats art patrons as though they were God Almighty, and yet he can't stand artists."

"He wouldn't be able to stand me then," Cliff said.

"That's right, you paint, don't you?" Miles said. "I used to dabble a little myself."

"Why did you give it up?"

"Oh, I was never any good and knew that I would never be. But I liked paintings and I had a leaning toward museum work, so I went in for this end of the thing. But tell me, how come you aren't painting now?"

"I do a little now and then," Cliff said. "But I like to eat, too. So I decided that I'd take a couple of years off and work for a living. Try and save some money and then, when I get a small stake, I'm going to take a shack up on the Cape or out on the Monterey Peninsula and really give it a whirl again."

"I know what you mean," Dangleader said. "Always wanted to do the same sort of thing, although I knew I would never amount to a damn. Would have tried, anyway, if I hadn't gotten married and had a child. The only solution is to find a rich wife, I guess."

"I found one, but it didn't seem like a very good idea," Cliff said, a little bitterly. "I gave her up, fortunately before the marriage. Actually, she gave me up, I guess you can say, as it was she who broke the engagement."

"Objected to the art bit?"

"No, oddly enough, it wasn't that. The fact is, she wanted me to quit this job and devote my entire time to painting. Had confidence in me, which didn't mean a thing, as she wouldn't know a Modigliani from Whistler's Mother."

"Sounds like an ideal wife," Miles said. "Rich and stupid."

"Oh, she wasn't stupid. As a matter of fact, that was probably the trouble. She was one of those strong-minded girls. It would have had to be her show—all the way."

"Know what you mean," Miles said. He finished his drink and started to reach for the drawer again.

"Not for me," Cliff said. He stood up and stretched. "Been pleasant, but I think I better push off." He looked at his watch. "Almost four. I have an early date."

"You going to stop by and check the North Wing before you go?" Miles asked.

Cliff shook his head. "No need," he said. "I saw the picture right after the guard closed the door at three. Been no one in there since except your Baron Glickenstein and Charleton Manners."

"There won't be anyone else, either," Miles said. "Old Farquharson, the guard assigned to the gallery, has had strict orders to open the door for no one at all. Of course, with Charleton Manners, it's different."

"Of course. Well, I'll be seeing you."

"Probably be down in Washington one day while the painting's still there," Dr. Dangleader said. "I'm anxious to see how it looks in another setting."

"I'll buy the drinks when you come," Cliff said.

A moment later, passing the North Wing, he observed Farquharson standing at the door which was opened a crack. He nodded to the old man and said, "They still inside?"

"Yes, sir," Farquharson said. "Expect they'll be through any moment now, sir."

"Well, be sure and lock up tight after they leave," Cliff said. "We wouldn't want anything to happen now with just a few more hours to go."

"You can be sure nothing will, sir," the guard said. "That door gets locked, and I'm not leaving this spot until I'm relieved at ten. You may rest assured of that. Nothing short of an atomic bomb can hurt that picture, sir, now that the crowds have gone."

Cliff wished him a good night and strolled through the main lobby and out of the double front doors. He nodded at the uniformed watchman standing outside and went to a cab sitting at the curb. The cab was not in the usual taxi stand directly in front of the steps leading to the museum. That space was occupied by a long black Rolls-Royce town car with a colored chauffeur sitting erect in the front seat, oblivious to the sign which said: "Reserved for Taxicabs."

Baron Glickenstein does right well by himself, Cliff thought as he climbed into the cab and gave the driver a downtown address.

2.

Mark Liebman, leaning heavily on a gold-headed walking stick and accompanied by Jack Reason, who supported him by his elbow, hesitated as he left the North Wing of the Glickenstein Museum. It was exactly five past four. The old man was dressed in a black broadcloth suit, cut in the old-fashioned continental style. He wore a starched winged collar and a maroon foulard, Oxford gray trousers above patent leather shoes; the effect was topped off by a fresh gardenia in his buttonhole. His hands trembled just slightly, and with his pale complexion, heavily lined face, and pure white hair he looked ten or twelve years older than his actual seventy-three years. His voice quavered slightly as he turned to Charleton Manners.

"Deeply grateful," he said. "It has been a pleasure, Herr Manners."

Manners nodded, pleased. "Your cousin has given us a truly magnificent museum, Baron." He noticed Farquharson as the guard was about to turn the key in the lock of the massive door. "It might interest you, sir, to know that Farquharson here was the first employee, hired by the late August Glickenstein himself, almost forty years ago." He turned to the guard. "Farquharson," he said, "this is the Baron Manfried Glickenstein, of Munich. A cousin of the late Mr. August."

The guard bowed, spoke in a slightly awed voice. "How do you do, sir," he said. "I knew Mr. August well, sir, that I did. A great man. A truly great man. His death came as a terrible blow to all of us."

"Thank you, thank you very much." Liebman returned the bow. Jack Reason, standing at his side, also made a short bow and then turned, again taking the old man's arm. The three of them went to the lobby and passed outside where Mark Liebman hesitated, obviously to catch his breath. He stopped midway through the door, so that the guard was forced to stand there holding it open.

"May we drop you somewhere, Herr Manners?" Liebman asked.

Charleton Manners shook his head. "Very kind of you, Baron Glickenstein," he said. "Most kind. But I am old-fashioned and still like to get my stroll in each day. I live just across the park on Fifth Avenue and I always enjoy the walk."

He held out his hand and the old man put his cane under one arm in order to take it. "It has been most good of you to let us view the painting," he said. "Most good, Herr Manners."

Manners smiled, shaking his head. "Not at all, Baron," he said. "The pleasure has been all ours. I am quite sure your cousin would have been deeply gratified if he could have known that you would pay us a visit."

Liebman nodded. He still made no move, and the guard continued to hold the door as he listened to the exchange.

"Ve leave for Europe tomorrow, so I must bid you now goodbye, Herr Manners," he said. "Again, it is most good of you. And when you visit Germany, you must be my guest."

"I certainly shall, Baron," Manners said. "I certainly shall." He turned and nodded to Jack Reason. "A good journey," he said.

Reason bowed and the old man started to walk again. Neddie had got out of the Rolls, and he now climbed the steps and supported Liebman by his right arm as the three slowly made their way to the street.

Manners stood watching them as the chauffeur and the old man's secretary loaded him into the back of the Rolls-Royce. He turned to the uniformed guard who was closing the door, preparing to lock it.

"Fantastic old fellow," he said. "The Baron Glickenstein. A cousin of the late Mr. August."

"Indeed, sir?"

"Indeed. By the way, has everyone left?"

"Dr. Dangleader was the last, sir," the guard said. "He left about five minutes ago. We're closed for the night now unless you want to go back inside."

"No, no, I'll be on my way, too," Manners said. "Good night."

"Good night, sir."

3.

Jack Reason leaned back into the deep upholstery of the limousine and let out a long breath.

"Thank God," he said, "that's over. You think everything went all right, Mark?"

Mark Liebman nodded sourly. His voice was strong when he talked and there was no trace of the German accent.

"Of course everything is all right," he said. "He went for it, hook, line, and sinker. And it was a break about that guard. That guy

Farquharson. We couldn't have had it happen better."

"You were splendid, Mark," Jack said, with obvious admiration. "I'll be damned if I didn't have to keep pinching myself to remember that you weren't actually Baron Glickenstein. The old Baron himself couldn't have done a better job."

"You made a pretty good secretary yourself," Mark said grudgingly. "Glad you watched it and kept your mouth shut."

Jack nodded and raised his wrist. "Ten minutes," he said. "Plenty long enough." He picked up the speaking tube at his side and spoke into it. "Okay, Neddie," he said. "Let's get back. And if there's a cab in that parking space, get out and give the driver a couple of bucks to move it. Explain about the old man finding it hard to walk. You know."

"I know," Neddie said.

He swung at the next corner and again headed back uptown.

As the Rolls slowed down and approached the museum, Neddie saw there was a cab parked in the space where he had previously been, but that it had pulled up so that there was a spot behind it. A uniformed patrolman leaned against the door of the cab and was talking to the driver through the opened window.

Neddie gauged his distance and figured he would have just enough room to crowd in behind the taxi. The policeman stopped talking to the cab driver and watched curiously as Neddie climbed down from the front seat and opened the door of the town car. Jack stepped out of the opposite door, rounded the car, and helped Liebman out. Again he held him by the arm, as the two slowly walked up the few steps leading to the main door of the Glickenstein Museum.

Jack Reason pressed the bell button at the side of the door and, looking through the glass, saw the uniformed guard getting up from a chair just inside the lobby. He heard an engine start and turned. A passenger had gotten into the cab, and it was pulling away from the curb.

The policeman had walked over to the Rolls and was saying something to Neddie.

4.

After thirty years with the New York Police Department, Sergeant Francis O'Brien had retired on a liberal pension. His record during those thirty years was clean, if not spectacular. Though he was neither particularly bright nor the possessor of any unusual imagination, he had been reliable and trustworthy, and so his superiors gave him excellent references. Although the pension was adequate to support him for the rest of his life, he had still wanted something to keep him busy, and so he had at once gone to an employment agency. The agency had sent him to the Glickenstein Museum.

After having pounded the Manhattan pavements for more than a quarter of a century, he found the museum job a sinecure. Nine to five, five days a week. He was stationed at the front door, and his employers didn't mind if he occasionally took a break and sat down for a rest. Of course, these last two weeks had been a little different.

The museum people had offered to bring in an additional man, but he had volunteered for the extra duty, and the extra pay. He still worked his nine-to-five shift, but since the Botticelli had been on exhibition, he had continued working until ten in the evening, at which time a special man hired from a protective agency came on to relieve him.

The hours were long, but it really wasn't too bad, as once the doors were closed at four, he could just sit on the chair inside the main lobby. The only thing was that he found it pretty hard to keep awake, and he had to go over to the box and ring every other hour. Fortunately, Farquharson, the other guard, was also on during the early evening hours, and he punched the clock at the entrance of the North Wing.

On this, the last night of his extra duty, ex-Sergeant O'Brien recognized them at once. It was the old man whom Mr. Manners had called Baron Glickenstein, and his skinny companion. He couldn't for the world imagine what had brought them back.

Under normal conditions, he would never have unlocked and opened the door. He would merely have shrugged his shoulders, shaken his head, and pointed to the sign marked "Closed" which hung on a chain from the bar across the plate glass of the door.

But this was not a normal occasion and these men were no mere sightseers who had arrived too late for the regular visiting hours.

O'Brien looked past them, as they stood waiting. His eyes took in the Rolls-Royce, noticed Patrolman Larry Dullin, whom he knew very well, standing at its side and talking with the chauffeur perched behind the wheel. Class, real class.

He began turning the heavy night latch, while he muttered to himself, "That Dullin! Any excuse to shoot the breeze and keep from pounding the beat. He'll pound that boy's ear as long as he's parked there and then likely enough he'll be coming and ringing the bell and wanting a cup of coffee with me."

He finished releasing the latch and opened the door a crack, cocking his head in inquiry as he looked out at the two men who stood in front of him.

"Baron Glickenstein forgot his briefcase when we left a few minutes ago," Jack Reason said. "He believes he left it either in Mr. Manners' office or in one of the galleries. If you recall, we were with Mr. Manners and …"

O'Brien nodded quickly. "Yes indeed, sir," he said. "You left just as I was closing up for the night. I remember quite well."

"The Baron had some very important papers in the briefcase, and since he is leaving for Europe in the morning, it is essential that we get the briefcase now."

O'Brien nodded, sympathetically. "I'll be glad to look for it," he said.

"In the office or one of the galleries," Jack repeated. "The Baron will be glad to identify the contents and …"

"Just step inside, please," O'Brien said. "Perhaps you had better come with me, so that I get the right one. Of course this is against the rules—no one is supposed to enter once we're closed for the day—but I'm sure that Mr. Manners would have no objection."

"Kind of you," Liebman said in a thin voice. "Most kind. Won't take but a minute or so of your time. Doctor, would you—?" He turned to Jack who ostentatiously reached into his breast pocket for his wallet.

"That won't be at all necessary," O'Brien said. "I'm only too glad to be of service. That I am. Now, if you will give me just a moment, I want to relock the door. Have to be very careful, you know. We have a very valuable painting on the floor."

He again snapped on the night latch and then turned and led the way down the long hallway toward the rear of the building. Farquharson was sitting on a chair just outside of the locked entrance to the North Wing as they passed. He looked up curiously.

"The gentleman left a briefcase in Mr. Manners' office," O'Brien explained. "We'll be only a minute."

Farquharson nodded.

Heavy drapes had been drawn over the windows of the office. O'Brien snapped on the light switch at the side of the door and stepped into the room. He was moving toward the large flat-topped desk when he heard the door close behind him. Instinctively he started to turn.

The hard rubber blackjack caught him just behind the right ear and Jack Reason dropped it on the carpet and grabbed him under the armpits as he began to fall.

It took them less than a minute to force the gag into his mouth and cover it with a wide strip of adhesive tape. They used short lengths of braided nylon cord to tie his wrists behind his back and secure his ankles. They then rolled him on his stomach and pulled his legs up and bent them, tying them tight to the cords which bound his hands.

Neither man spoke until they were finished.

"He's going to be pretty uncomfortable, but it won't be for too long," Liebman said. "When no one hits that time clock at six, the Holmes people will be all over this place in a matter of minutes. You didn't hit him too hard, did you, Jack?"

Reason shook his head. "Help me get him behind the desk," he said.

Leaving him on the floor so that his body was out of sight of the door, Jack went back and picked up the blackjack.

"Your turn next," he said, handing it to Liebman.

He closed the office door gently behind him, as Liebman pressed against the wall just inside of the room next to it.

Farquharson looked up in surprise as Jack quickly approached him. He started to his feet.

"It's Baron Glickenstein!" Jack said, the words coming out in a rush. "He's had a heart attack. In the office. We need help."

He turned, not waiting for the other to speak and started back toward Mr. Manners' office.

Farquharson started to say something, but then realizing that the other man was not hearing him, quickly followed. They arrived at the office simultaneously and Jack reached for the doorknob and twisted it. He stepped aside and Farquharson strode past him into the room.

It wasn't a hard blow and it was badly aimed, but he was an old man so it was enough to stun him. Jack Reason had the tape across Farquharson's lips as he moaned and began to struggle. It took a little longer to bind his hands and feet.

They turned off the lights after taking the keys from the guard's pocket and closing the door behind them.

The only light in the North Wing, in which there were no outside windows, came from the narrow fluorescent bulb hanging over the Botticelli.

Reason had to stretch to get the frame off the wall, and he was very careful. He turned the light off before he took the picture down, and Liebman held a pencil flash for him as Jack lay the picture on its back on the floor.

The painting and its original frame had been enclosed in a custom-made glass-faced box to protect it while it was away from the Vatican, and it took Jack several minutes to remove the painting from the box.

He used a razor blade holder to cut carefully around the borders of the canvas. The ancient paint cracked in tiny slivers as the blade found its way through. The canvas had been backed up by a piece of heavy board and stuck to it with some sort of mastic, and Jack had to use a putty knife very carefully to free it. The operation took more than twenty minutes.

Liebman stood by patiently as the other worked. When Reason was finished, Liebman played the flash on his wristwatch.

"A quarter to five," he said. "Right on the dot."

Reason stood up and quickly removed his jacket. He took the folded-up cellophane he'd brought with him and spread it open and laid it over the painting, covering both back and front. He used Scotch tape to secure it. He lifted the canvas carefully and handed it to the other man.

Liebman bent it very cautiously and when he heard a slight crack, stopped at once. Holding it straight, he laid it against Reason's back. He used clips to attach the top of it to the tape which extended a few inches below Reason's collar, and then Jack held out his arms as Liebman very carefully helped him put his jacket back on.

Jack could feel the edges of the canvas where it curved under his armpits. But it was completely concealed by the garment.

He started for the door, walking cautiously and holding himself as erect as possible.

Liebman was turning the night latch to open the front door when he heard the startled gasp at his side. He looked up quickly.

"What in hell is going on?"

His eyes followed his companion's and he looked through the glass door down into the street.

More than a dozen people were standing around the Rolls-Royce. Among them was Neddie, in his chauffeur's uniform. Several of the onlookers had their faces pressed to the rear windows of the limousine. But not Neddie. He was staring directly at them, and there was a shocked, almost horrified expression on his broad face. His huge hands hung helplessly at his sides.

5.

Mary Donahue had the first pains around noontime. They didn't particularly alarm her. She'd been feeling a little queasy all morning, and since her breakfast hadn't stayed down, she'd decided to skip lunch. She supposed that the pain came because her stomach was empty.

It vaguely occurred to her to call her doctor around one-thirty, when the pain began to be a little more severe, but she shrugged and dismissed the thought. It was just too silly. After all, the baby wasn't expected for at least another week. Of course, she couldn't be too sure about the exact time, but that's what she had figured and that's what the doctor had told her.

Getting off the bed, she heated some water and made some bouillon, and this time it did stay down. But the pain didn't go away.

She'd read about women going into labor and having their babies hours, even days, later. And sometimes, they had their babies quite a bit ahead of time. Mrs. Finkle would probably know all about it; she'd had children of her own.

Mary decided to go downstairs and talk with the older woman. It wouldn't hurt to ask her advice. Anyway, she had to talk with somebody—anybody.

But there was no answer when she knocked at her landlady's door, and so she went back upstairs. She got out her sewing basket and decided to work on the tiny garment she was knitting.

Keeping busy would get her mind off of it.

By three-thirty she really began to worry. The pains were worse than ever, and they were coming at regular and frequent intervals.

She took a couple of aspirins in water and once more went downstairs. Mrs. Finkle was still out.

Returning to her apartment, she found the baby book. She'd read the chapter a dozen times, but she wanted reassurance.

At four o'clock she telephoned her doctor but only managed to get an answering service. The answering service said that if she'd leave her number, the doctor would call her back as soon as he reported in.

At four-thirty the pains became almost unbearable and very frequent. She realized that she wasn't going to be able to wait. She thought of telephoning the hospital and asking them to send an ambulance, but decided she couldn't stand waiting for it to come. She'd probably get there quicker by cab.

She stood up and almost doubled over in agony. Then the pain went away for a moment, and she found her jacket and her bag. She took only a second to scribble a note which she left on the table by the daybed.

> Mrs. Finkle:
>> Have gone to hospital. I'm afraid it's come.
>>> Mary

The pain hit her again on the way down the stairs, and for a moment she didn't think she was going to make it.

There was no cab in sight and so she determined to walk to the corner. After all, she assured herself, she was a strong, healthy girl and she wasn't going to panic. She'd get to the hospital in time.

But when she reached Central Park West, there was still no taxi. Several passed but their flags were down. She suddenly realized that this late on a Friday afternoon, it would be difficult to find an empty one. But there was a cab stand in the next block in front of the Glickenstein Museum. She'd often walked there before for one.

She would just have to try to get that far.

As she reached the corner of West Sixty-eighth, she stopped and bent over and groaned. Something had happened—something sharp and agonizing and terrible inside her. She felt a wave of faintness and leaned against a building; a man and woman passed her and stared. She thought vaguely that they probably thought she was drunk.

She straightened up. There were only a few more steps to go and she would be in front of the museum where there was bound to be a taxi.

She could feel the tears on her cheeks, and she found it hard to see. But she would simply have to keep on.

Yes, she had certainly misjudged her time. Misjudged it badly. Someone should have told her....

She staggered and almost fell and a small scream escaped her lips. She took another step and again it came. This time she sank down slowly. She just couldn't stand for another minute.

Then she felt an arm under her own, and she looked up quickly through her tears.

"Oh God," she said. "Oh God!"

She was aware that whoever he was he was picking her up, one hand under her back and one under her bent knees. She started to cry out, but the sound never came. She had already fainted as the door opened and she was placed on the wide back seat of the car.

6.

Patrolman Dullin leaned against the front door of the Rolls and looked at the big black man with an amused expression.

"Rented car, eh?" he said. "Probably another one of these ten-thousand-dollar-a-year millionaires."

"No, sir," Neddie said. "He's the real thing. A foreigner. Royalty like. A baron. But how'd you know this was a rental heap?"

"License tag," Officer Dullin said, a little smugly. "The license tag is the tipoff. You work for the company?"

"No, sir. I was hired special for this job. By the Baron Glickenstein himself."

"You don't say," Dullin said. "Well, it must be a soft touch pushing one of these buggies around. Not like standing on your feet on a hot pavement all day. Is this guy the Glickenstein the museum was named after?"

"Can't say," Neddie answered. He took a handkerchief from his pocket and began to polish the already shining rear-vision mirror. He wanted to end the conversation, wanted to get rid of the cop before they returned.

"How about turning that radio on and getting the game?" Dullin suggested. "I'd like to know how the—"

"Radio's busted. Don't work at all," Neddie said, a little too quickly.

"You mean to tell me," Dullin said, "that a heap like this—why it must be costing your boss a good hundred bucks a day—has a radio that don't work? I tell you, it's a cryin' shame—"

"The boss don't like radios," Neddie said. "If you want that ballgame, you can most likely get it at the bar up on the next corner."

"Sure," Dullin said. "A hundred dollars a day for a car and a man has to go to some lousy bar to get a ballgame. Why you'd think—"

He stopped talking and instinctively stepped back, away from the car.

Patrolman Dullin had been on the force for more than eighteen years and had never advanced past his present rank. He was frankly lazy and without ambition. He had a number of rather bad habits, none of which had helped him along in his job. He liked to talk, he liked to drink, and he hated physical exercise. He was quite content to continue on for the rest of his twenty years and then retire on his pension.

But he wasn't a bad cop. He'd made the usual number of arrests, handed out the usual number of tickets, and kept trouble from developing on his beat when he saw it coming. He had an instinct for trouble. Of course he'd never done anything especially spectacular, but then he hadn't been called upon to. As a matter of fact, aside from the times at the pistol range, he'd never even fired his service revolver.

He had, on two occasions, broken up pretty bad barroom brawls. Once he'd broken down the door of a gas-filled room and given artificial respiration, which had saved a woman's life. And twice he'd delivered babies in an emergency.

He had seen her out of the corner of his eye as he stood there shooting the breeze with the fancied-up chauffeur. Just another girl, coming down the street toward him. Hadn't paid much attention except to notice that she was very very pregnant. And then, while he was still standing there talking, he'd subconsciously realized that there had been something wrong. It was almost like second sight, that odd instinct of his.

That's when he'd stepped suddenly back and swung around.

He was just in time to catch her as she fell.

It was lucky he'd had those two previous experiences. He didn't need any doctor to tell him what was happening and what he must do. He yelled to Neddie to open the door of the Rolls as he lifted the girl in his arms.

That first time he'd had a chance to call the ambulance, which of course had not arrived. He'd been damned nervous and after a bit had gone ahead and tried to remember what he'd learned in the police academy. It had taken him a good half hour and the woman had been a small Puerto Rican girl who'd had a tough time of it. He'd sweated it out, and by the time the ambulance did arrive, with an interne, it was all over.

Both mother and child had lived.

The second time had been even tougher, but again he'd managed, and again both mother and infant survived.

This time he knew that there would be no chance even to put in a call for an ambulance. No time to do anything at all except what he must do at once.

She was small, like the Puerto Rican had been, but it was an easy birth. Over almost before he had a chance to start. The sack broke of its own accord, and he used his pocket knife to cut the cord. The whole thing didn't take more than seven or eight minutes at the most.

The mother had quickly regained consciousness, and she knew what was happening. Yet she didn't make a whimper. It amazed him the way it was these little ones who had the stamina.

He was careful as he backed out of the car to see that she was lying comfortably on the seat, her newborn son in her arms.

Turning to the crowd around the car, he cursed and yelled for them to clear off. It was then that for the first time he noticed the frail old man with the flower in his buttonhole, standing at the side of the car and glaring at him. He remembered him as the one who had gotten out of the Rolls and entered the museum. It was the one the chauffeur had told him was royalty or something.

Dullin looked at the old gentleman and smiled. "You've just had a new baby in the back of the car, sir," he said. "An emergency. You'll have to get them to the hospital."

Jack Reason quickly stepped up. "An ambulance, maybe?" he asked. "Or can't we get a cab?"

Dullin shook his head. "Go up to Woman's Hospital on East One-Hundred-and-Fifth Street," he said. "I'll go inside and phone 'em to expect you. One of you better get in back with her."

"But—"

"You do as I say now," Patrolman Dullin ordered. "She's fine and the wee one is fine, but you should take 'em in to the hospital. There's nothin' to worry about. I'd go along with you, but I'd better go inside and telephone so that they'll be expecting you."

Without another word he turned and started for the front steps of the Glickenstein Museum.

Liebman stared at his retreating back. "Now what—?" he began.

"Get in the car. In the back. Quick," Reason ordered.

He opened the door and the old man crawled in the back, pulling down one of the jump seats.

Jack got quickly in front.

"Get going, Neddie." His voice was low and urgent. Neddie already had the engine running, and he threw the gears into mesh.

"Where's that hospital?" he asked.

"We're not going to any hospital," Jack said tersely. "By the time we got there, every cop in this town would be looking for this car. Looking for us. That museum door was left open and that cop is going to find those two guards within the next couple of minutes."

"Then what—where?"

"Follow the original plan," Jack said.

"But the girl—the baby ..."

"They'll just have to come along with us."

"Oh Lord!"

CHAPTER FOUR

1.

"In about five minutes," Deputy Chief Inspector Morris Gotterman said, "you, Dullin, and I are walking into the Commissioner's office. In that office there will be a number of Very Important Persons, along with the Commissioner himself, who is also very important. There will be a man from the FBI, a high official of the CIA, a representative of the State Department, who flew in from Washington last night. The head of the Glickenstein Museum will be present, as well as representatives of the insurance company which carried the policy on the painting. And all these important people are going to make you repeat everything you have told me. And they will ask questions—a lot more questions than you have had to answer so far. You better have your story straight."

"Yes, sir. I—"

"Don't interrupt, Dullin."

The Deputy Inspector frowned and scratched his nose with a lean tobacco-stained finger. "Just listen. You will have to repeat your story. And a damned unsatisfactory story it is, I might add. Thank God, Dullin, I was a patrolman myself at one time, so at least I can understand up to a point. But don't expect the others to. You as much as admit that you virtually helped the thieves into their getaway car. You failed to see the painting which they must have been carrying. You didn't get the license number, and you have only a meager description of the gang. You placed a young girl and her newborn infant in the getaway car, but you didn't so much as get her name or her address.

"Instead of climbing into that car and seeing that the woman and child were safely delivered at the hospital, you strolled into the museum to make a phone call. When you discovered the two private guards who had been attacked, you did think to call an ambulance. But you failed to understand there had been a major robbery; you overlooked the ransom note which was left behind; and apparently you were unable to make a connection between the thieves and the attack on the guards. As a result, valuable minutes were wasted and the criminals made a clean break while you were standing in front of the museum waiting for the ambulance to arrive."

The Deputy Chief Inspector drew a long sigh. "In fact, Dullin," he said, "you performed nobly as an obstetrician, but as an officer of the law you acted like a horse's ass."

Patrolman Dullin nodded his head sagely, in complete agreement.

"I have but one piece of advice to give you," his superior officer said. "Listen very carefully. I don't expect the full implications of this thing to sink into that simple brain of yours, but try and follow as best you can. There is only one way in which you can further contribute as an unconscious accomplice in this matter. You can fail to keep your lip buttoned.

"I want you to try and understand exactly what has happened. A painting, a world-famous painting worth at least two million dollars in cash, and actually beyond price so far as its real value is concerned, has been stolen. That painting belongs to the Vatican in Rome."

Again the Deputy Inspector hesitated and scratched the other side of his long nose. "Are you a Catholic, Dullin?" he asked.

Patrolman Dullin nodded brightly.

"In that case, perhaps you will understand. To repeat, that painting belonged to the Vatican and was on loan to the Glickenstein Museum. But it was really on loan to the government and the people of the United States. As trustees, you and I, and every other citizen of this country, are responsible for its safety. We have failed and the picture has been stolen. Should this fact become public knowledge, there is no telling what the international political and diplomatic repercussions might be. The very prestige of our country is at stake. The thing has assumed proportions far beyond a mere case of breaking and entering and larceny. Why, if word of this were to seep out …"

The Deputy Inspector ceased speaking, obviously struck dumb for the moment by the staggering implications of the possibilities.

"And don't forget, sir," Dullin suddenly said, "the girl. The girl and the wee boy who were kidnapped."

Deputy Inspector Gotterman glared. "Forget, you fool?" he roared. "How *can* I forget? That is the very thing I am about to mention. Not only have you been involved in an international incident and a major art robbery, you have been the witless agent to a kidnapping. Why do you think that FBI man is waiting inside to take us over the coals? If one word of that missing woman and her newly born child should get out, the whole thing will be in the fire."

The buzzer at the Deputy Inspector's elbow came to life and he quickly stood up.

"This is it," he said. "Come on now and just remember what I have been trying to say. A straight story and the truth, exactly as it happened and as you remember it."

2.

The Police Commissioner got slowly to his feet, holding the piece of paper as though it were a snake. He reached for his reading glasses and took a deep breath.

"The picture will be returned upon receipt of one million dollars," he read. "Negotiations will be conducted only with a representative of the insurance company. Should the authorities or the public in general be made aware that the painting is missing and is being held for ransom, the painting itself will at once be destroyed.

"If you wish to see the picture safely returned, be assured that the only way in which this can be accomplished is by keeping the theft private and by making no effort to avoid payment of the money. The responsibility is all yours. Contact will be established Tuesday afternoon."

The Commissioner slowly dropped the paper to the desk. "Signed 'The Botticelli Gang,'" he said.

Dr. Miles Dangleader, sitting next to Charleton Manners, shifted in his seat and said, "I hardly think …"

The Commissioner turned and stared at him coldly. "I agree," he said bitterly. "You hardly do. I will remind you that the New York

City police offered to post guards at the museum, but you people turned down the suggestion, preferring to arrange for your own protection. Please do not interrupt."

It was obvious that the Commissioner was in no mood for small talk.

"Gentlemen," he said, addressing the audience as a group, "we are all more or less familiar with what has happened. Under ordinary circumstances this would be merely a police matter, and as such would fall solely under the authority of the New York City Police Department. However, such is no longer the case. I would like at this time to let you hear a word from Mr. Harwood Davies Granell, of the U.S. State Department, who has flown in from Washington to attend this meeting." He bowed to a slender, gray-haired man at his left and resumed his seat.

Mr. Granell smiled thinly and spoke without getting up.

"As you will readily understand," he said, "this matter has been brought to the attention of a Very Important Person in the capital. Because of all the ramifications, it was felt that only the highest authority could outline a pattern of behavior."

He paused long enough to let the significance of his information sink in before continuing.

"You may have been surprised to read in this morning's newspapers that the painting is on its way to Washington in an armored car. That story was deliberately planted. It was felt, rightly or not, that the matter is far too delicate to trust to the integrity of the press. I might also add that security on this matter is so tight that no report of the theft has been made even to Interpol, again for fear of a leak. I tell you this only to make it clear how essential it is that knowledge of the theft be kept quiet until every effort has been exhausted to repossess the painting.

"It is not the policy of the federal government to cooperate with criminals, any more than it is the policy of your local police department. On the other hand, in this particular incident, we have no choice at all in the matter. We are convinced that the writer of that ransom note meant exactly what he said. In short, should the gang of criminals responsible have the slightest suspicion that we are not acting in good faith, they would at once destroy the painting. I believe you can understand what this would mean."

The State Department man hesitated and took a silk handkerchief from his breast pocket and wiped his forehead. "If any news of this gets out, even if the painting is returned intact and undamaged, the United States will become a laughing stock in the free world and a subject of utter ridicule to our enemies. The very prestige and reputation of the country as a whole is at stake. Herein lies the heart of the problem."

Granell stopped abruptly. He took a slender cigar from an aluminum case and clipped the end before he lit it and settled back in his chair.

The Commissioner again arose. "We have another representative of the federal government present," he said, "and I suggest he speak for a moment. Richard Riley of the FBI."

Riley was a youngish man with a dark crew cut, wearing a blue sports shirt under a tweed coat. He smoked a pipe and his square, strong hands rested nervously on the table in front of him, one playing with a silver pencil and the other tapping the blotter. He didn't look up when he spoke.

"Our interest," he said, in a gentle voice, "is not really so much in the painting itself as it is in the woman and child who were spirited away in the thieves' car." He looked up then and smiled slightly. "Oh, of course we *are* concerned about the Botticelli. Should it prove to have been transported across a state line we will be very much interested. But at the moment, from the evidence we have available, it would appear that a young woman and her newborn infant have been kidnapped. And kidnapping is very definitely in our province. Even though no official complaint has been filed, and there is no missing persons report, the fact remains that the woman was in the car when it left, and that she has not turned up at any hospital or other institution since. And so, we are working on the theory that the gang is holding her and her child as hostages. If such is the case, the matter will sooner or later come under our jurisdiction.

"This unknown woman would prove an excellent witness against the members of the gang should they ever be arrested, and so it is more than possible that her life, as well as the life of her child, is in jeopardy. As a result, any publicity which this case might receive would only increase that risk. As in all cases of kidnapping, our first responsibility is the safe return of the victim, and only then the apprehension and conviction of the criminals involved. The entire resources and the full cooperation of our organization have been offered to both local police and other federal agencies, but at this time, we are leaving the overall handling of the case to those other agencies, at their request."

Riley was followed by another federal man, an Earl W. Willoughby, connected with the CIA.

"Speaking for my own organization as well as for the office of the Attorney General," Willoughby said, "I can only reiterate what my colleague in the State Department has said. The painting must be returned safely at all costs and at any price. Knowledge of the theft and the ransom demands must be a matter of utmost security. Until the Botticelli is safely back in the Vatican, any public awareness of what has taken place would be most damaging to the United States. Even then, it will be a matter of the most delicate nature to determine our policy. Apprehension of the criminals, their punishment, the payment of a million dollars are all mere details and very unimportant ones by comparison. The return of the picture, and that alone, is the paramount issue involved."

Julius Balch, executive vice president of Continental Assurance, sitting in a stiff-backed oak chair off to one side, quickly looked up. He moved forward in his seat, his chin outthrust, and spoke quickly.

"The matter of a million dollars, or to be more exact, two million dollars, for which my firm has insured the painting, is not a mere detail," he said. "We took out this policy in good faith. I will remind you gentlemen that the Continental Assurance Company is a publicly owned corporation and that stock in it is held not only by Americans but by the nationals of a number of foreign countries, including Italy. They would hardly take kindly to the idea of losing so vast a sum. I have been instructed by my superiors to tell you gentlemen that we are prepared to pay the demanded ransom, but only so as to ensure the safe return of the painting and thus avoid paying out an even greater sum in case it is irretrievably lost or destroyed."

"And I would remind the gentlemen from the insurance company that had they seen to it that proper precautions were taken to safeguard ..." the State Department official cut in, getting quickly to his feet.

He in turn was interrupted by the Commissioner, who also rose and spoke in a loud and authoritative voice.

"Gentlemen—gentlemen," he said. "I implore you. This line of argument will get us nowhere. I feel sure that we are all aware of the gravity of the situation. We are anxious to protect the insurance company as well as being concerned with the return of the painting and the safety of the missing woman and her child. But if we are to solve this case satisfactorily, we must all work together. That is the very reason for this meeting."

He sighed, looked around at the others, and his eye came to rest on Patrolman Clarence Dullin, standing stiffly at attention next to Deputy Chief Inspector Morris Gotterman.

The Commissioner frowned and his nose wrinkled like that of a man suddenly encountering a foul odor.

"We must get to the business which brought us together," he said. "I have made a point of having present at this meeting not only the police official who has so far been in direct charge of the case, but three persons who had the dubious distinction of actually seeing the members of the gang at the time the robbery took place. I would like you first to hear Deputy Inspector Gotterman, assigned to special details out of Centre Street, who has been on the case almost from the moment the robbery was discovered."

3.

Following some five minutes during which he outlined the bare facts of the robbery, or at least those bare facts of which the authorities had a sure knowledge, Deputy Inspector Gotterman proceeded to explain what steps the police already had taken and what steps they intended to take.

"Every effort has been taken and will be taken to avoid alarming the criminals and frightening them off before they are given the opportunity to negotiate. We are working on the assumption that we are dealing with an extremely clever gang and that it is quite possible that they may have sources of checking our own activities.

"Certain things I feel free to tell this audience at this time; other things are a matter of top security. As to our progress to date, we have found the getaway car, a rented Rolls-Royce. The usual thorough scientific examinations have been made; the usual checks with the company which rented the car. They have led us nowhere.

"The two guards who were attacked at the Glickenstein Museum have spent endless hours going over mugshots down at headquarters. Patrolman Dullin"—he looked over at his companion with a glance of false friendliness which was all too apparent—"Patrolman Dullin, who observed at least three members of the gang as they made their escape, has also gone over hundreds of mugshots. Again without results.

"The usual underworld sources—stoolies and so forth—have been carefully questioned, while we made sure we didn't tip our hands of course. Also without success.

"We have picked up and grilled a good many persons whose dossiers indicated that they would possibly have been involved in this sort of an affair. But again we have not struck any pay dirt. At the moment, we have exhausted most of the obvious possibilities. It may well be that until the first contact is actually made by the mob itself, we will be powerless to make our own first real move."

He hesitated, looked over at the Commissioner as though seeking help, but, receiving no encouragement, continued.

"Realizing," he said, "that we may possibly have overlooked some obvious conclusion, I have, at the Commissioner's suggestion, seen to it that Patrolman Dullin, as well as the two museum guards involved, are present at this meeting. These men are here to answer any questions you gentlemen might choose to ask. But before you question them, let me assure you that once they leave this room, they will be kept under the tightest possible security until this case is solved. At their own request, they will be held in protective custody, and so you gentlemen may rest assured there will be no leak of the story through them."

Again he hesitated, obviously catching his breath. He was fully aware that the fragments of information he had to offer were far from adequate and reflected no great credit upon the department.

"The man who posed as Baron Glickenstein was a phony. We have been in cable contact with the actual baron, who, of course, has not been informed of the robbery. The person who acted as the false baron's secretary is very probably a well-known international crook, but so far we have been unable to pinpoint his identity. Neither Mr. Manners nor Dr. Dangleader has been able to offer any special leads, since the criminals made their appearance seem so plausible.

"That brings us to the chauffeur of the getaway car. It would appear that he is an American Negro. Patrolman Dullin spent some time talking with this man while the robbery was taking place. The patrolman is here with me, ready to answer questions."

The Deputy Inspector took a step back, at the same time taking Dullin by the arm and pushing him forward.

Riley, the FBI man, was the first to speak up. "Just why," he asked, "do you figure the chauffeur is an American?" he asked.

Dullin shuffled his feet for a moment and blushed. "Well," he said at last, "to tell you the truth, I'm not all sure he is an American."

The Commissioner stared at him, quickly raising his eyes, but before he could speak, Riley shot his second question. His voice was no longer soft and unassuming.

"No?" he said. "No? And what makes you reach that conclusion, officer?"

"Well …" Dullin felt the Deputy Inspector's bony fingers tighten on his arm, and he knew he was about to say the wrong thing. He began to stutter, but Riley was impatient.

"Speak up, officer," he said. "Speak up. Tell us why you think he might not have been an American."

Dullin gulped. "He—well, he didn't like baseball," he said at last.

"He told you he didn't like baseball?"

Dullin nodded. "Said his radio didn't work, but I knew better," he said at last. "I knew that in a rented car like a Rolls, the radio was bound to work. So when I asked him to turn on the game he … he …"

Dullin, suddenly realizing that not only was the Deputy Inspector about to create a lasting bruise on his arm, but that the Commissioner himself was throwing daggers at him, again hesitated.

"So he told you the radio didn't work and you concluded that he didn't like baseball. Hum-mm. But he was a Negro, is that right?"

Patrolman Dullin nodded.

"And his accent?"

"Accent?"

"Yes—the way he spoke. Did he have a Southern—?"

"Oh, I see what you mean. Sure. Like Harlem, only more so. Just like one of those Georgia—"

"I think we can safely assume that the chauffeur was an American Negro," Riley said, "in spite of the fact that the officer feels it is un-American not to like baseball. After all, perhaps he did like baseball, but having a job to perform, considered it wasn't a part of his duties to be listening to a game while working."

The look Deputy Inspector Gotterman gave Patrolman Dullin should have turned him to stone on the spot. Dullin, however, feeling that he was being understood at last, merely nodded brightly.

"I knew that that radio *had* to work, in an expensive rented limousine like that," he said.

"Any more questions?" the Commissioner quickly interrupted. Instead of glaring at Dullin, he was now looking murderously at his Deputy Inspector. Why had the Inspector been stupid enough to suggest that the patrolman attend the meeting and answer questions?

"I would like to know a little more about the officer's impression of the girl who gave birth to the child in the back of the car," Mr. Manners said. "Do you believe, officer, that this could have been a possible plant to divert attention? Perhaps a prearranged ..."

This time the Deputy Inspector gave Officer Dullin no chance to reply.

"Only God could have prearranged that," he said quickly. "The department feels that Patrolman Dullin acted completely correctly in taking care of the girl and seeing to the delivery. Certainly it was the most natural thing in the world for him to have placed her in the rear of the nearest vehicle. I believe we can be quite confident that the incident came as a complete surprise to the criminals and that the birth of the child was as much of an inconvenience to them, at that particular moment, as it must have been to the mother herself."

Riley again spoke up. "And this girl said nothing at all during the time she was having this child?" he asked, looking sharply at Dullin.

"She didn't even whimper. Now usually when I make a delivery, there's a lot a screamin' and ..."

"You've answered the question, officer," the Commissioner said. "Now if you gentlemen have no more questions ..."

"I would be curious to know why the officer failed to take the license number of the Rolls," Riley said. "It would appear—"

"The matter is being taken up at a departmental hearing," the Commissioner quickly answered. "Dullin, I believe you may leave now?

"We have the two private guards," he began again. "I think you have all had the opportunity of going over their testimony, but if anyone here wishes to ask ..."

His voice trailed off.

4.

At the conclusion of the meeting, it was agreed that all interested parties would refrain from any activities, at least until such a time as actual contact between the so-called "Botticelli Gang" and the authorities had been established. It was further agreed that the Commissioner's office would act as a sort of central clearance agency, not only so far as all governmental activity was concerned, but also in regard to what releases would be made to the press so as to offset any suspicion that there might be something amiss.

In view of the ransom note's demand that the thieves deal only with a representative of the insurance company, it was further agreed that Clifford Johns should serve as the direct intermediary, but only with the understanding that he keep in constant touch with police authorities.

It was felt that the less the Glickenstein Museum had to do with the case from this point on, the better for all concerned. The museum itself had been only too happy to foist the job off on Johns. They knew that Johns was thoroughly qualified to establish the true identity of the painting, should negotiations for its return be successfully concluded. And as a representative of the firm which would be supplying the ransom money, Johns would be in a strategic position to make certain demands.

It was Julius Balch, the insurance company executive, who had pointed out Johns' rather unique qualifications to act as the go-between in any negotiations with the ransom gang.

"Our man," he had said, "has a background which I believe will be of great value under these circumstances. His function with our firm has been that of an investigator, and before he came with us he had a rather wide range of experience in the United States Armed Services. He was a major serving with Intelligence in Korea, where he distinguished himself. He has, of course, the further advantage of being an expert on paintings as well as an artist himself."

He smiled indulgently at Johns, who stood by rather embarrassed. Balch had personally hired Johns at Continental because Balch's wife had been a friend of the young man's family and had admired several of his pictures. Balch considered that it had shown a certain degree of character when Johns had been willing to give up something as trivial as painting to take a position with his firm.

The Police Commissioner hated to have a rank amateur in the so-called driver's seat, but, because of the necessity for complete secrecy, he was powerless to do anything else.

Riley, the FBI man, disliked the idea of a private party interfering in an official case, but he too realized the pressures and understood that the time was not ripe for his department to move in. Nevertheless, he made a mental note to have Johns' record checked a lot more carefully.

Very much a part of all of these considerations in the choice of Johns was a human factor, for if the picture were destroyed or lost, the others knew Johns would make as good a scapegoat as anyone.

And should the negotiations for the return of the picture prove successful, there was no question of his stealing the credit from them, as no one in the outside world would ever hear of it. His company would merely make the payoff for a crime which would never be known to have taken place.

It was agreed as the meeting broke up that Johns would be given a free hand but that he would maintain a constant liaison with officials, should he be fortunate enough to establish contact with the mob. In the meantime, they must play it by ear. At the moment, the emphasis would be on secrecy.

Balch and Manners left the Commissioner's office together, followed by Dr. Dangleader and Johns. The men from Washington stayed on for a few minutes longer, but as there was very little to say which had not already been said, they too soon departed. Inspector Gotterman was anxious to be on his way, but the Commissioner indicated he would like to have a few private words with him after the room was cleared.

Dr. Dangleader, sitting with Clifford Johns in a restaurant a couple of blocks from Centre Street a half hour later, made his point with a wry smile.

"Personally," he said, "I would hate like hell to think that anything could happen to the painting. It would be an irreparable loss to the art world. On the other hand, I am far from distraught at the thought that the State Department might be embarrassed. That particular branch of the government has embarrassed us often enough with its boners in the past."

"The image of this country as a nation of integrity means a little more to me than it apparently does to you," Cliff said a trifle coldly. "But, as you say, the safety of the picture itself is the prime consideration. But you didn't even mention the other consideration."

"Yes?"

"Certainly. The girl. The girl and her child."

Miles looked at his companion with a certain amusement. "Let me ask you to consider something," he said. "On the one hand we have an irreplaceable masterpiece in this portrayal of the Madonna and Infant. On the other hand, we have a real live girl and her infant. Suppose—just suppose—one mother and child should have to be sacrificed in order to save the other. Now which would you take? Are you prepared to lose to humanity forever the work of a genius in order to save the life of an unknown waif and what might very possibly be her bastard offspring? Does a single human life mean so much to you that you can overlook your integrity as an artist and as a connoisseur?

"Or, on the other hand, are you able to overlook the value of two human souls in order to save for all humanity a truly great painting?"

Cliff stared at his companion. "What a hell of a question!" he said at last. "Are you kidding?"

"Not at all. I am propounding a very simple problem. Of course I understand that it is all a matter of hypothesis, that the thing probably would never happen. But what would you actually do if it did and the decision was solely yours?"

"You must be a little sick," Johns said.

Miles laughed. "You're evading the question," he said. "All right, I gather that you'd let the painting go and save the girl. Of course, you know as well as I do that hundreds, yes thousands of real artists have sacrificed their health, their families, even their very lives, in order to give the world something which was great or at least which they thought was great. Why, then, shouldn't one simple little girl who very likely has nothing at all to offer humanity sacrifice herself to preserve that which is surely established as great?"

"I still think you are—"

"Sick? Not at all. Just logical. Let's say then, that you wouldn't sacrifice this unknown girl and her child for the Botticelli. Now would you sacrifice her for ten Botticellis? For ten Botticellis and perhaps a handful of Michelangelos? Don't shake your head. You have to have a price somewhere. If not ten Botticellis and a handful of Michelangelos, let's throw in all the great works in the Louvre. If you still hesitate, we can toss in—"

"Miles, you really are sick," Cliff said. "Finish your coffee and let's get out of here." He looked at his watch. "I want to get back to the museum in plenty of time. If that gang lives up to the ransom note, we should be hearing from them in another couple of hours."

Dangleader grinned and nodded. "We should, and I hope we do," he said. "I think we can count on a rather cryptic message, however. You can be sure the police have already tapped that phone, and you can also be sure the gang will have figured as much. However, we might as well be on our way."

Standing up, Cliff reached for the check. He smiled at the other man.

"About the girl and her child," he said, "I might have to think for a second or two. But if it was a case of turning you in for the picture, old boy, you can be sure I wouldn't hesitate a minute. Curators are easily replaced—Botticellis are not. Perhaps that girl, or her child, might someday do a picture even greater than the *Madonna and Infant.* You, according to your own testimony, are damned sure not to."

"For a guy who spent a couple of years playing cops and robbers in the Army, you're one hell of an idealist, Major," Miles said, his voice edged with good-humored sarcasm.

CHAPTER FIVE

1.

County Patrolman David Parker pulled the prowl car over to the edge of the shady, tree-lined road, jerked on his emergency brake, and crawled out of the front seat. He walked to the side of the station wagon parked directly in front of him and, leaning on the door next to the driver, pushed his cap back on his forehead and spoke in a slow drawl.

Lou Storey, who carried the mail on route #4 out of Glen Head, was an old friend with whom the patrolman liked to pass the time of day. Parker's beat covered one of the last fine old residential sections of the Long Island North Shore and nothing very much ever happened there. Lou, who had been delivering the mail for more years than he cared to remember, had a reputation as a gossip, and he was generally good for a spicy story or two concerning the goings-on of the wealthy people who still hung onto the great old estates.

"What's new, Lou?" Parker asked.

Lou Storey shrugged. "New? Nothing's new, Dave," he said. "The old ones are all dying off, and the young ones move away."

Parker nodded. "Well," he said, "that's progress I guess. Won't be long before these places are broken up and the developers move in. I see the old Asher place is being occupied again."

Lou Storey nodded. "Yep," he said. "New tenants. Thought they'd tear down the place after those people from the UN gave it up, but it looks like the family changed their minds. It was sure a great place in its day. Forty rooms, stables, tennis courts, indoor swimming pool. Used to have fifteen in help inside and five full-time gardeners. A real white elephant. They'll never sell it, that's for sure. Not with help the way it is today."

"I'm surprised they were able to rent it," Parker said. "Have you—?"

Lou shook his head. "Nope," he said. "Haven't even hardly seen 'em and they've been in a couple of weeks now. Why, you know—"

Patrolman Parker smiled. "Come on now, Lou," he said, "stop kidding. You probably know more about them than their own lawyer does by this time. Don't tell me you've reformed and stopped steaming open the mail!"

"I don't think that's very funny, Dave," Storey said, reproachfully. "Anyway, that reminds me of something. I knew there was some reason I thought it was a sort of odd outfit that took the Asher place. Do you know, since they've been here they haven't received one piece of mail? Not one single letter. Not even a bill. And they don't have a box over at the post office. I checked and—"

"I'll bet you did, Lou," Parker said. "But that is strange. Haven't been around to the back door, looking for a handout or a little hot news or—?"

Lou shook his head. "Gate's been kept locked," he said. "I did talk to a gardener, though," he added. "Damned unpleasant sort of fellow he was, too."

"If he's like any of the other gardeners around here, he probably knows more—"

"Didn't know nothing," Lou said. "He's a big ape—looks like a prize fighter. Said he was hired through an agency in New York and claims he doesn't know a damned thing about the people. Did tell me their name. Beddingham or something like that. There's an old man, and he's supposed to be dying. His daughter and son-in-law moved in to take care of him, I understand. There's a colored man who doubles as chauffeur and butler, but so far as I know they don't even have any inside help aside from him. Quiet people. You never see them. Understand they rented the place furnished for a year. The gardener didn't seem to want to talk about them. In fact, he was downright unfriendly."

Lou Storey pushed a stack of mail to the side and turned his ignition key. "Well, I got to be moseying along," he said. "Got enough to worry me without bothering about some nut who is crazy enough to take on the old Asher place. But it is a damned funny thing, their not getting mail."

Parker nodded and moved away from the car. "Yeah," he said.

"Maybe I'll just stop by and say hello. After all, they're on my beat and I—"

"You're just as damned nosy as I am, Dave," Lou Storey said and laughed. He pulled off as Patrolman Parker went back to his prowl car.

Five minutes later the police officer was standing in front of the high wrought-iron gates at the beginning of the long blue-stoned driveway leading up to the old Asher mansion. The gates were closed and a small freshly painted sign hung on the chain which held them together. The sign read: *Private—Keep out.*

For several moments the patrolman scratched his head casually. Then, observing that the chain had no lock, he snapped open its latch and pushed apart the gates. Moving up the driveway bisecting the expansive lawns at the front of the mansion, he noticed a heavy-set man in a sweat shirt and dungarees off to one side. As he watched, the man brought a large estate grass cutter to a stop and climbed down from the seat.

Then, at a half trot, the man headed for the wide porch which fronted the rambling white mansion. The officer received the very definite impression that the gardener was moving fast in order to block him before he would have a chance to ring the doorbell.

2.

She lay on the chaise longue, flat on her back, her loose russet hair spread over the pillow, and her eyes wide open and staring at the ceiling. She was wrapped in a silk dressing robe, too large for her small frame, and someone had tossed a light quilt over her legs and feet. The shades of the room had been drawn, but there was enough light so that she could see quite clearly.

She had breastfed the baby, and then the girl had come and taken the infant and put it in the portable crib a few feet from the chaise.

It was daytime, probably somewhere around noon, but Mary Donahue was not sure what day it was. She didn't know the day and she didn't know where she was or how she had happened to come to this house and this room. They had fed her, several times, and she was not in pain any longer. She had slept—slept and awakened and then gone off to sleep again. It must have been a few days.

She turned her head slightly so that she could see the girl who sat in the corner of the room, watching television. The sound of the program didn't annoy her, nor did the presence of the girl.

For a brief moment she was tempted to call out. But she quickly discarded the idea. She had already learned that it was pointless to ask questions. She had tried and each time she had been told to be quiet and rest.

It had been the same with all of them.

Of course, she was happy to realize that the baby was all right. A fine, healthy little boy—and from the few times she had really had a chance to see him, one who took after her family and not his father.

But she was stronger now, feeling almost normal again. And she was no longer satisfied just to lie there and be taken care of. She wanted to know.

She closed her eyes then for a moment, trying to think back. To remember.

She recalled leaving the house where she lived. She knew that she had started looking for a cab when those pains suddenly became so terrifying. She had started toward Central Park West and she remembered turning the corner near the museum where she'd hoped to get the cab.

Then it had happened. She knew that she must have fainted. About later, she couldn't be sure, but there had seemed to be a uniformed policeman and a group of people crowding around.

And then she must have blacked out again. She remembered coming to in the back of a speeding car. A deeply upholstered car. It certainly had been no taxicab. The little old man was sitting on a seat near her, holding her baby.

She probably had been only semiconscious, but it seemed to her they had stopped and changed to another car. She was sure it was another car.

The second car had been like the first, a large, luxurious limousine, but she remembered that this one had gray, opaque curtains which pulled down over the side and back windows.

They had driven for a long time.

When at last the car had stopped, she expected that someone would come with a stretcher, or at least a wheelchair, to take her inside.

But there had been no stretcher, no wheelchair. A huge colored man with a soothing voice had lifted her bodily from the back seat and carried her through the doors of the house. She remembered that she had cried out for her baby and that the colored man, who'd been wearing some sort of uniform, had muttered to her not to worry, that they were bringing the baby in, and she would have him with her as soon as she was in bed.

There had been a long blank period then, and the next thing she recalled was awakening between white sheets, the child lying in the hollow of her arms and nursing avidly.

That was when she first saw the girl, who had been standing at the side of the bed, staring down at her.

The colored man was again in the room, but this time he was no longer in uniform. It was he who had taken care of her, had bathed her and combed her hair. It was he who had told her she had a boy child and that the child was well and healthy and there was nothing to worry about.

"Six of my own," she'd remembered him saying, "and not a real doctor for a one of 'em and all turned out to be strong as oxen. None of 'em as big as this fella here when they was born."

He had gentle hands and a gentle manner, and he must have had a lot of experience around sick people as well as newborn babies.

But he, like the girl later on, had not answered any of her questions.

During the next day or so—she just didn't know whether it was two or three days—she had seen the others several times. The old, white-haired, tiny little man who must have been the one who'd been in the back of the car. The tall, thin, silent one who never said anything. And one other, a great hulking animal of a man who had poked his head into the room to stare at her and had merely grunted and looked as though she were some sort of unwelcome intruder.

The sound of a bell came through the open door of the room and interrupted her thoughts.

It was the first time she had heard the bell since she had been in the house. It startled her.

It must have startled all of them.

The girl across the room leaped to her feet and reached for the television set. But instead of turning it down, she turned the volume up.

The tall, thin man, who couldn't have been more than a few feet from the door of the room, suddenly appeared, and as he entered the room, he slammed the door behind him.

He wasted no time at all.

In a second he was at the side of the chaise. He leaned over her, staring into her startled eyes. His own eyes were no longer indifferent, no longer bored.

"One sound—one little peep out of you," he said in a low husky voice barely audible over the sound of the television, "and I'll—I'll …"

His hand went out and circled her throat, and he raised his other arm, the fingers of his hand forming into a tight fist.

He hesitated then for a moment as Mary's eyes went wide in shock. He motioned toward the girl, who quickly crossed the room to stand at his side.

They all heard the second ring of the doorbell. "Watch her," he snapped.

He turned back, looking down again at Mary. "If you want to see that baby again, you will be quiet. Absolutely quiet."

His hand released her throat, and he turned quickly toward the door as the bell again sounded.

3.

Jack Reason turned from the window as the patrol car circled down the driveway and disappeared through the front gates. Looking over at Morry Shine, he shook his head.

"You played it stupid," he said, "coming up to the house like that. You're supposed to be a gardener, not a bodyguard."

Morry shrugged, his face sulky. "I don't like it," he said. "What the hell is a cop doing coming around and asking those questions? I tell you, there's something wrong. He musta suspected somethin'."

Liebman took the cigarette from his mouth and spoke. "I was listening," he said. "That cop suspected nothing. The trouble with guys like you, you think all cops are alike. You don't understand these local clowns. This place is on his beat and it was only natural that he should stop by. Jack is right: you played it dumb. All he wanted to do was introduce himself, find out who we were."

"I still don't like it," Morry said. "I don't like nothing about the way things have been going. First we get saddled with that broad inside and her brat. Now we got cops. Mr. D. isn't going to like this one bit."

"It doesn't matter what Mr. D. likes," Jack said. "I'm running this caper, not Mr. D. You take your orders from me and don't forget it."

"I take my orders from the boss and no one else," Morry said. "Yeah?"

Jack moved across the room, speaking over his shoulder. "I'm leaving for town in a few minutes to make the contact. While I'm there, I'll be in touch with your boss. We'll damned soon find out who you take the orders from. In the meantime, you better get back outside. The idea is you are out there to keep anyone from nosing around. Anyone means neighbors or kids or someone who might just happen to wander by. It doesn't mean cops who are just doing their duty. You want to ask for trouble, all you have to do is act the way you did. As though there's something going on we're trying to conceal. While I'm gone, just listen to Mark and do what he tells you and make sure you don't pull any more dumb plays."

"The dumb play was picking up the girl," Morry said. "When the boss finds out about her and the kid—"

"What the hell would you have had us do?" Mark Liebman asked. "Just toss her out along the road someplace?"

Morry nodded. "Sure," he said. "Sure—that's exactly what I would a done. You guys act like a bunch a amateurs. Now you got yourself a nice live witness. I don't care so much about you two, but there's me and there's Judy. Nick ain't going to like it one bit when he finds out that his girl—"

"Worry about yourself," Reason said. "Let Mr. D—"

"I am worrying about myself," Morry said. "I worry plenty. That dame has seen me and can identify me. They make a kidnapping thing outta this, and I could hit the chair. Just wait until Mr. D. hears about that broad. He'll know what to do all right."

"I'll wait," Reason said. "In the meantime, stay away from her. The less she sees of you, the less chance of her being able to identify you later on—just in case."

He started for the door, looking at his watch. "Time I got going," he said. "Neddie will take me to the train and then come on back. Anybody need anything from the stores?"

"Neddie can bring me a bottle of cognac," Liebman said.

Jack Reason nodded. "Right. And maybe you better go in and give that dame some kind of a story. I probably scared hell out of her. Try and calm her down. There's no reason she should know anything unless she has to. I don't want her flipping her lid."

Following Reason out of the room, Liebman waited until they were out of ear shot before speaking.

"When you see Nick," he said, "maybe you better mention something about a little more dough. This picking up the girl changes a few things. There'll be extra expenses."

"I'll ask for it," Jack said, "but getting it is something else. Once Nick makes a deal—"

"I know," the old man said. "He won't change. Or else he'll want a bigger cut. That he isn't going to get. But try for the extra money anyway."

4.

At exactly two-thirty on Tuesday afternoon the telephone on Miles Dangleader's desk rang, and Clifford Johns leaned forward in his chair.

"Maybe this …" he began as his companion reached for the receiver.

Miles shrugged his shoulders. "Maybe."

He took the receiver from the hook. It was the girl in the outer office.

"Continental Assurance Company, Dr. Dangleader," she said. "They—"

"I'll put Mr. Johns on," Miles said. "Just one sec—"

The girl interrupted him. "They asked for you, Dr. Dangleader."

Miles raised his eyebrows. "Put them on," he said. Holding his hand over the mouthpiece, he looked at Cliff. "Your office," he said. "They want to talk to me."

"Dr. Dangleader?"

"Yes."

"Do you have one of our people with you, Doctor?"

Miles looked surprised. "Why yes," he said. "Your Mr. Johns is here. Would you like to—?"

"If you please."

Miles took the receiver from his ear and turned to his companion. "For you," he said, a baffled look on his face. "Apparently your office is a little confused."

Cliff took the instrument. "Johns here," he said.

"Listen carefully, Mr. Johns." It was a soft voice. "I will say this only once. You are to leave the museum immediately. You are to be alone. Understand? Alone and no one is to tail you. You will be watched. Get the nearest cab. Go to the subway entrance at Ninety-sixth and Broadway. Take the downtown train, transfer at Times Square to the shuttle, and get off at Grand Central. Go to the lobby of the Roosevelt Hotel. At three o'clock, when a Mr. Charles Hardy is paged, answer."

Cliff opened his mouth to speak, but as he did the sharp click of a receiver being replaced struck his ear.

"This is it, Miles," he said, quickly getting to his feet. "I'll be in touch."

The cab stand outside of the museum was empty and Johns quickly turned and started north on Central Park West. Within three minutes he had hailed a taxi and was on his way uptown. He couldn't help looking behind and wondering if he were being followed, as the taxi wound its way through the early afternoon traffic. Later, as he rode downtown on the Seventh Avenue Express, he again found himself watching the faces of the other passengers.

He changed trains at Times Square as he had been instructed to do and checked his wristwatch. A few minutes later, walking into the lobby of the Roosevelt, he again checked and saw that he had less than two minutes to spare.

Mr. Charles Hardy was being paged as he walked toward the desk.

Cliff turned and crossed to the head bellhop's desk. He gave the fictitious name and was handed a sealed envelope.

"A Western Union messenger just left this for you, Mr. Hardy," the clerk said.

Cliff turned away and slit open the envelope.

The message, printed on a piece of plain note paper, read:

"You have four minutes exactly. Go to east concourse, main floor, Grand Central Station. There is bank of telephones to left of newsstand next to Newsreel Theater. One phone booth will have Out of Order sign. Remove sign and enter booth. Put this note in your pocket, speak to no one. Start now."

Quickly, he crumpled the note and stuffed it into his jacket pocket. He turned and headed for the stairs leading to the passage to Grand Central Station.

It was the third booth down, and he quickly looked around as he reached for the Out of Order sign, hung by a cord outside the closed door. A woman, about to enter the next booth, looked at him curiously. But he had no time to react. The phone was ringing as he closed the door.

He lifted the receiver.

"Mr. Johns?" It was the same soft, slightly muffled voice he had heard earlier.

"This is Mr. Johns."

"You are empowered to act for Continental?"

"I am."

"Your company is prepared to meet our terms?"

"They are."

"Have you or the museum reported this matter to the authorities?"

For a brief second, Cliff hesitated. The question came as a surprise. As he fumbled for an answer, the voice, suddenly sharp, interrupted his thoughts.

"You hesitate, Mr. Johns? You have been warned. If you want a deal, you must completely disassociate yourself from the police. Warn the museum and warn your company. We are prepared to break off negotiations at once and with no risk. Think it over. If you want to do business it must be our way."

Cliff spoke hurriedly.

"We want to do business. But we also want to be sure nothing happens to the painting. It was dangerous to remove it from its protective case. It must be kept away from dampness and the canvas must not be bent. It should not be exposed to any extremes in temperature. Any damage would seriously detract from its value. You must take every precaution. Yes, we do want to do business, so just tell me—"

"Keep the police out of the picture, Mr. Johns. You have six days to get rid of them. A letter will be mailed to H. M. Harrington, General Delivery, Newark, New Jersey. Collect it personally. After three o'clock. It will be up to you to see that you are not followed. It will be your only chance. Don't muff it. We already have an offer from a private collector, and unless you play it our way, all deals are off. It will be up to you. Give me your full name and address."

"Clifford Johns, the Beaux Arts, East Forty-third Street, New York."

As he finished speaking, the line went dead.

5.

Before leaving the telephone booth, Jack Reason carefully wiped the surface of the black, hard rubber receiver with his handkerchief and then, twisting a piece of the material around his index finger, poked it into the hole which read "Operator" and circled the dial. A moment later he crossed the drugstore aisle and left the building. There was a cab at the curb and he climbed into it.

"Nearest express subway stop," he directed the driver, at the same time checking his watch.

Nick Dekota had said six o'clock. He'd have plenty of time. He was hungry, not having eaten since breakfast, but he decided to go out to

Coney Island immediately and get some seafood when he got there. He could kill an hour or so that way and still be at the baths in time for his appointment.

The subway ride took longer than he'd expected and he had time to eat only a dozen steamed clams at a seafood bar before he moved on and turned in at the Bayside Baths. He climbed the four steps leading to the entrance and saw the sign on the door: "Closed for Repairs."

His hand was reaching for the bell at the side of the curtained glass door when the door suddenly swung open. Morry Shine stood facing him.

"What the hell are you doing …?" Jack began, surprise and anger blending in his expression as he instinctively stepped back.

Morry shook his head, half nodding at a white jacketed attendant over at the desk in the lobby.

"Inside, buddy," he said.

As Jack stepped past him, the attendant got up and, looking first at Morry, who nodded, signaled Reason.

"This way," he said. Morry relocked the outside door.

The attendant waited outside the door of the dressing room until Jack came out with the towel wrapped around his waist. There were no words exchanged as the two men went into the steam room.

Nick was sitting on the marble slab, stark naked, perspiration running in streams from his pudgy face and body. He waited until the door was closed and they were alone before he spoke.

"Well, you sure screwed it up," he said.

"Morry was outside," Jack said. "What's he doing here?"

"He's here because I told him to be here."

"You mean he called you from out on the Island and you—?"

"Right. He called. And it's a damned good thing he did. Why the hell didn't you let me know about the girl and her kid? You and that old man must be crazy. Of all the messed up—"

"Morry shouldn't have called, shouldn't have left," Jack said, his voice furious. "I could have told you—"

"But you didn't tell me. Nobody told me. And Morry has his instructions. Anything goes wrong—"

"Nothing has gone wrong."

"Good God! You got a woman and her kid out there with you. You're probably facing a kidnap rap, and you tell me nothing has gone wrong!"

"I would have told you about the girl and the child," Jack said. "You yourself said not to make contact until now. Everything is coming along all right and—"

"Everything is not coming along all right," Nick said bitterly. "Morry did just what he should have done—got in touch with me the second something happened. And any time you snatch a mother and her newborn brat—something has happened."

"Listen, Nick, we got the painting," Jack said. "That's the important thing. Contact has been made and we got the picture."

"Yeah, and I got the picture, too. Morry has given it to me loud and clear. Maybe you and that old man don't see it, but, brother, I see it. If you hadn't snatched that broad and her baby, it is just possible the cops could have been kept out of it. Only just possible. But not now, my friend. Not any longer. Morry gave me the whole story. A cop delivering the kid in the back seat of the car! I never heard of such a thing in my life. And then the cop going into the art gallery to call the hospital. You know damn well he found those guards. You know damn well he reported it. You can bet your last buck that the police know all about the picture by this time and that you got that girl and her kid. The insurance people may swing enough weight to keep the robbery quiet, and may even have enough pull to keep the law away until they get the painting back, but now with a real kidnapping added, no one is going to—"

"I tell you it isn't a kidnapping," Jack said. "We didn't snatch the girl and her kid. The cop himself put them in the car."

"Oh sure. And I suppose she is hanging around with you now because she's taken a fancy to you or something? What are you doing, planning to cut her in on the caper or something? What about her husband and her family? What the hell you think they are going to do once that dame fails to show up in a hospital? You think some broad and her newborn kid can just disappear without anyone giving a damn?"

"I tell you, Nick, there's nothing to worry about. Sure it was a tough break, but what could we do? Anyway, what real difference does it make? We get the dough, you get your cut. That's the end of it. The girl hasn't seen you, doesn't know you exist. Neddie and Mark and I are the ones that are running the extra risk."

"Nuts." Nick threw up his fat hands in disgust. "The girl has seen Morry and she's seen and talked to Judy. And *they* know I exist. Damn it, I told you that I wasn't to be tied in this in any way at all.

You understood that. And now—"

"What could we have done?" Jack asked. "We didn't ask for the girl. Could we help it?"

"You didn't have to take her out to the hideout," Nick said. "You could have dumped her."

"If we'd have stopped at a hospital—"

"Who's saying anything about a hospital? You could have tossed her out of the car someplace. Dumped her along the side of the road."

"With a newborn baby? What the hell do you think we are anyway? Murderers?"

Nick raised his eyebrows and turned slowly to his companion.

"What are you doing, kidding yourself?" he asked. "Let me straighten you out, boy. Snatching that picture is one thing. The girl and her kid is something else. Who the hell would give a million bucks to get back a woman and her kid? I'm asking?"

Jack stood up, shaking the sweat out of his eyes. "Just what do you want us to do about it?" he asked. "We didn't ask for her, but we got her. So what? Do you want out?"

Nick lifted his head and stared at him. "You got my investment money to give back? You got my money and the cut I should get for getting this much involved?" He didn't wait to have his question answered. "No, Buster, I don't want out. But I want to get rid of that dame."

"It's too late now, Nick," Jack said. "We dump her now and she has descriptions of all of us and—"

"I'm not suggesting you call a cab and send her on her way," Nick said. He looked at Jack significantly.

Reason paled and shook his head. "We haven't bargained for murder, Nick," he said.

"Well you better figure what you have bargained for then. All I know is I made a deal to put up so much dough and to get a certain cut of a certain profit. Without risk. Already, I don't like the risk."

"We don't like the risk either," Jack said. "Anyway, we'll just have to cope with that problem when it comes up. The point is, because of the girl and her kid, things have changed. It is taking a little more money than we figured at first. It will complicate the negotiations maybe and it could take extra time. Also, solving the problem could run us a lot of extra expense—before we get the payoff. Liebman and I think you should let us have some more—"

Nick snorted. "Not a damned cent," he said. "I got enough in this already. We made a deal and we stick to that deal. I didn't bargain for the girl. She's your problem. Of course, if you want to change the conditions, want to give me another ten per cent of the take, I could let you have a few extra grand."

Reason shook his head.

"No thanks," he said. "We'll let it ride the way it is. Considering the risks we're taking, our end is pretty thin in any case. In the meantime, I've made contact with the insurance company and I am—"

Nick raised a hand. "Don't tell me about it," he said. "I don't want to know any details. None at all. Maybe you get away with this and maybe you don't, but don't tell me anything. Just see to it I get my cut when the money comes in. In the meantime, you better be getting out of here. I don't even like this business of meeting with you, not the way things are going at this stage of the game. From now on, I'll make my contacts through Judy or Morry."

"Morry should never have left—"

"He's already on his way back. And, by the way, that reminds me." He hesitated, looking up sharply.

"Reminds you?"

"Yeah, reminds me. I understand you and Judy have got real cozy. Sitting around playing gin rummy and—"

"Forget it, Nick," Jack said quickly. "It was your idea that the girl come along and make like a wife. Right now I got other things on my mind."

"Sure—just remember all she was to do was pretend to make like a wife. Keep that word 'pretend' in mind. Morry tells me you two make a real nice couple when you turn that jukebox on and dance and—"

"Morry's a damned troublemaker," Reason said. "You can be damn sure I'm not going to mess this deal up by fooling around."

"Morry is stupid, but he don't miss much," Nick said. "Anyway, get out of here now. And think about that woman and her kid."

"Don't worry about her," Jack said. "It's our neck—Neddie's and the old man's and mine."

"Sure—and Morry's neck and Judy's neck. And those two are my people. It comes right back to me. Remember that—right back to me."

CHAPTER SIX

1.

Deputy Chief Inspector Morris Gotterman was annoyed. Looking the FBI man straight in the eye, he didn't attempt to conceal his feelings.

"I thought we had an understanding," he said coldly. "It was my impression that you people were going to stay out of this. It was also my understanding that we had agreed to give Johns a free hand, at least until such a time as he has had a chance to regain possession of the picture. The federal people—your own people—are going to be damned upset if anyone throws a monkey wrench into things at this stage of the game."

Richard Riley shrugged. "You're jumping to conclusions, Inspector," he said. "We are staying out of it."

"You've been having Johns tailed—you just told me so."

"We aren't any longer," Riley said. "I merely explained that we followed him Tuesday when he left the museum. We were very careful. The operator is sure neither Johns nor anyone else observed him. We know that he took a cab, got out at Ninety-sixth Street, and went into the subway. We followed him to the Roosevelt, where he received a message at the desk. A check showed that the message had been delivered by a Western Union boy and we traced the boy, or rather old man, who delivered it. Turned out it had been mailed in to the Western Union office, and they no longer had the original envelope. The sender had enclosed a couple of dollars. Anyway that ended that. Our man followed Johns to Grand Central where he received a telephone call in a booth to which he apparently had been directed. Our man made no attempt to have the call traced—there wouldn't have been time—and he was unable to get close enough to try and listen in on Johns.

"Johns left the booth and returned to his apartment. We kept a close check on him for the next twelve hours. The following morning he got in touch with us and reported that he had been in contact with the gang who had the picture. He told us that they were suspicious, and he felt that there was a strong possibility they might discontinue all negotiations. He asked us to reaffirm our agreement to give him a free hand. Well, in view of the fact he came to us voluntarily and also because he promised that he would keep us informed of any moves he made as soon as it was safe to do so, we at once pulled off our operators.

"An hour ago Johns telephoned in and said that he would be calling us again within two or three days and again made a very strong request that we do not have him followed, or in any way interfere with him. I again reassured him. Aside from that, we have been in touch with executives at Continental Assurance, and they have promised that before any ransom sums are turned over for the picture they will give us an opportunity to list the serial numbers of the bills."

Riley stopped speaking and lighted a cigarette. "The thing which is disturbing us right now," he continued after a moment, "is the girl. Apparently you people have received no missing persons report; she hasn't turned up in any New York hospital, or in fact in any other private or public institution in this state or nearby states. Frankly, we are not too surprised that she hasn't turned up. But we are damned mystified that no one—no one at all—has reported her missing. Theft of the picture is serious enough, but a kidnapping and possible double murder is something again. We are prepared to play along on the first thing, but I can tell you this. The minute we receive a definite report that that woman is missing, we are going to stop pulling our punches and we're going to work."

Inspector Gotterman tightened his jaw and spoke through gritted teeth. "What the hell do you think we're going to do?" he said. "Do you think we like it this way? Like to just sit on our hands when we know a crime has been committed? No, we don't like it, but there is nothing we can do now. I can tell you one thing, however. We think we've made some progress. We figured that the girl must have come from somewhere in the immediate neighborhood. That she was obviously on her way for help when the baby came. Well, we made a very discreet investigation and we believe we know who she is."

Riley looked up quickly. "You know who she is?"

"We believe so. We've discovered that a certain young woman living in a small furnished apartment, actually a rooming house, not far from the museum, was in the last stages of pregnancy. She was unmarried and lived alone. According to the woman who rented her the apartment, the girl has disappeared. So far we have been unable to trace her family or even to turn up any friends. Of course we have had to work very carefully in order to keep it quiet. It isn't too surprising that she has not been put on the missing persons' list. Because she was unmarried, she was probably keeping pretty much to herself and was apparently planning to have the child in secrecy. The landlady, who was friendly with the girl, is worried and upset. But we have given her part of the story, without, of course, mentioning the picture, and we are sure that she will keep things quiet. We warned her if she talked it would endanger the girl.

"It is, of course, possible that it isn't the right girl. Our girl may just have disappeared to have her child without letting anyone know about it. But, I think it would be too much of a coincidence. In any case we haven't been completely inactive, at least so far as the woman and the infant are concerned."

Riley bit his lip. He nodded and stood up. "So what are you doing about it?"

"Nothing—at the moment. There is nothing we can do. Oh, we made the usual check on hospitals, as I have said, and that sort of thing. But until every chance of getting the painting back has been exhausted, we are powerless. Any publicity on the girl might throw the gang into a panic and not only jeopardize the return of the painting, but put the woman and her child in even greater danger."

Riley was annoyed that he had not been taken into the Inspector's confidence about the police activities and his voice showed it when he spoke.

"I shall expect you to turn over any information you have the minute we are officially brought into the matter," he said coldly as he prepared to leave. "I only hope it won't be too late."

2.

If Patricia Bentley had not formally broken off her engagement with Clifford Johns and returned his ring, along with a cold little note suggesting he might do better to "go find yourself a girl who is willing to believe what you have to offer is more important than I think it is," he probably would never have met Minnie Finkle.

The letter, in a scented violet envelope, was waiting for Johns when he returned to his apartment that Tuesday afternoon after he had made his contact with the "Botticelli Gang." During the following twenty-four hours, he gave it considerable thought. At first he felt nothing but a sense of guilt and a certain degree of depression. These feelings, however, changed gradually as he thought more and more about the matter, until at last he was amazed to realize that what he was feeling was more like indignation combined with a peculiar sense of relief.

Patricia of course was right about one thing: what he had to offer was pretty unimportant. At least to her. Cliff began to wonder if "what he had to offer" could be important to any girl. What about the girl who had given birth to the child in the back of the getaway car? Someone was certainly going to have to be important to her.

Patricia thought that she had a problem because he had merely broken a date or two with her. But here was a girl who really had a problem.

It certainly was strange that no one had reported her missing. The very fact that she had almost given birth to her baby right there on the street almost proved that no one had been thinking much about her at any time. She had obviously been living alone, as she had had no husband rushing her to a hospital.

Cliff began to wonder what sort of girl she was, what she looked like, how she had lived. It must be terrible to face an ordeal like that and find yourself alone and helpless and …

Yes, here truly was a girl to whom almost anyone would have been important. Her husband, her family, all of them must have let her down. And now the police and the authorities and society in general were letting her down even more. She had not gotten into that car because she had wanted to. So far as anyone could tell, the gang who had stolen the picture were still holding her—or had killed her and hidden her body somewhere. And who cared? Apparently no one.

Again Cliff began to sense a feeling of guilt and also a feeling of shame. He was as bad as the others. The girl was in trouble, probably in danger of being murdered, and all anyone had been thinking about was the safe return of a piece of painted canvas.

Somebody should do something. Someone should at least find out who she was, where she had come from, what had happened to her. Maybe there was no husband, no family. Not even a close friend. It can happen in New York. It happens all the time.

And it was at just about this stage of his thinking that Clifford Johns decided that it really wouldn't hurt if, during these next few days while he was forced to sit and await his next contact with the kidnappers of the Botticelli, he made a discreet effort to find out something about her himself. He would be extremely careful and do nothing which might jeopardize his position as a go-between. But certainly it couldn't hurt to find out who she was. It might even help.

It was a lot easier said than done. The extreme caution under which he was forced to move made any investigation difficult. All he had to go on was Patrolman Dullin's physical description of the girl. Unfortunately, the officer had failed to note whether or not she was wearing an engagement or wedding ring. There was the fact she had been where she was at the time the incident took place—and little or nothing else except the negative factors. No missing report, no unfilled maternity ward reservation, no frantic husband or family seeking information.

A couple of logical deductions might be reached.

It was very likely the girl was unmarried. She had been carrying no luggage, so she was probably a New Yorker. She had been walking, so it was more than possible she lived in the immediate neighborhood. She had probably been living alone, rather than with her family, and it was unlikely that she could have had a roommate.

Obviously, realizing her condition, she had been seeking a taxicab. Dullin had said she had seemed to be heading for the cab stand next to where the getaway car had been parked.

Cliff took out a large-scale map of Manhattan and carefully circled an area of some four blocks in radius, using the Glickenstein Museum as the focal point.

All apartment and rooming houses are supposedly licensed by the New York Housing Authority, and so that was his first stop. He was somewhat taken back when he discovered that the area he had circled was just about one hundred percent apartments and furnished rooms. He tried the apartment houses first, concentrating on the janitors and caretakers. It took him until late Friday, working both afternoons and evenings, to cover them all. He reached as many as he could by telephone; the others he visited personally. By the time he was at the end of his list, he was exactly where he had started, except for the knowledge that sexual activity on the middle West Side of Manhattan was a lot more prevalent than he had dreamed possible.

He had learned the identity and location of nine young women in one state or other of late pregnancy, as well as the fact that six newborn infants had arrived in the district within the last ten days. And all were present and accounted for.

On Saturday at eleven-thirty he began with the rooming houses and smaller apartments, and on Saturday afternoon at exactly four o'clock he rang the doorbell over the name of Mrs. Minnie Finkle on West Sixty-ninth Street.

3.

Minnie Finkle strained her neck so that she could see the slightly frayed card which the young man was holding out to her. She made no effort to take it and, being nearsighted and too vain to wear glasses, was quite unable to read the printing.

"Who did you say you are with?" she asked.

"Continental Assurance," Cliff said. "As I say, we are making a highly selective spot survey and I—"

"That name sounds familiar," Minnie said. "I've seen it somewhere lately."

"We're one of the largest and most important firms in the field," Cliff said, smiling. "Now if I can just ask a few questions?"

"What sort of questions?" Minnie didn't budge from her position in the doorway.

"Well, we are doing a rundown on the type of person who is the typical rooming house tenant in each section of the city. If you can just spare a moment or so, I would like to know how many people you rent to, their sex, age, general background...."

Mrs. Finkle threw up her hands. "Me, you don't need," she said. "I got just two tenants. One is a Mr. Cohen; he's in his sixties and he's retired. But he's not here now—he's visiting his daughter in Miami Beach. Then I have a young woman and she's—well, she isn't here either. She's away visiting relatives. You wouldn't be interested in either of them, and, anyway, I don't think they want any insurance."

She moved back, starting to close the door.

"But I'm not selling insurance," Cliff said quickly. "And actually, our survey covers only females, so I wouldn't be interested in Mr. Cohen. But if you can spare me just a minute, or perhaps tell me when your other tenant is expected back, so that I might make an appointment with her ..."

"I don't know when she'll be back," Minnie said, a little too quickly. "Anyhow, I'm busy and I—"

He caught the odd note of evasiveness in her voice, the peculiar look, almost of fear, which crossed her face. He realized that in another second the door would be shut in his face. He'd have to try a shot in the dark.

"Is she going to bring the baby back with her when she returns?" he asked.

Minnie looked up at him, her face suddenly hard. "What did you say?"

"I asked if she was going to bring the new baby back with her?"

For a moment she stared at him. Then she stepped to one side, opening the door wider.

"Maybe you had better come in," she said. "We can talk better inside."

She was remembering what the police officer had told her, what he'd instructed her to do. She felt an odd sense of fear, and for a moment she hesitated, but then the officer's warning came back to her.

"And remember, if you don't do exactly as I have asked, particularly about calling me at once, something tragic may very well happen."

Cliff could almost sense her fear as she moved to one side and gestured toward the couch.

"Sit down," she said, "sit down, Mr.—"

"Johns," Cliff said.

"Mr. Johns. Now what was that you said about a baby?"

Mrs. Finkle didn't sit down herself, but stood by the side of the door, almost as though she were waiting to turn and run through it.

"I wanted to know if this young lady who rooms here is going to bring her new baby home when she returns," Cliff repeated. "That's why she isn't here now, isn't it, Mrs. Finkle? Because she was going to have a baby?"

Mrs. Finkle hesitated a moment and then slowly nodded. "Yes— yes, that's why." She moved again, crossing the room. "I left some soup boiling in the kitchen," she said, "and if you'll excuse me a second, I'll just go in and turn off the stove. I'll be right back."

Before Johns could speak, she slipped through the door at the end of the room and closed it quickly behind her.

Passing into the small kitchen, she closed the door and listened with her ear next to it for a moment before she reached for the wall telephone. Her finger found the hole which read Operator and she swung the dial.

It was while she was saying, "I want the police, operator. This is an emergency," that the door opened.

Cliff Johns stood there watching her.

"You," she stammered, "you ..." The receiver fell from her fingers and she stepped back, her hand to her opened mouth.

"Don't you dare touch me," she cried. "Don't you dare."

"Pick up the phone," Cliff said, forcing a smile. "Pick up the phone, Mrs. Finkle. Ask to be connected with Deputy Chief Inspector Gotterman. Understand? Deputy Inspector Gotterman."

For a brief moment she stared at him, and then, almost as though she were mesmerized, did as he instructed.

It took several minutes to reach the Inspector, and then, once he was on the line, it took a few more before Mrs. Finkle was able to make him understand. When at last he did, the telephone almost exploded in her ear.

"Who did you say is there with you?" he roared.

"He says his name is Mr. Johns. From an insurance company and he was asking about—"

"Put him on!"

Cliff took the receiver from her shaking hand and put it to his ear. A second later he jerked it away as it again exploded into sound.

"What the hell are you doing there? Just what do you think—?"

"Now, now, Inspector," Cliff said quickly. "Please. Just talk with Mrs. Finkle here and tell her it's all right to answer a few questions. I—"

"I'll tell her nothing of the sort!" the Inspector screamed into the mouthpiece. "How did you get there anyway? Do you realize what you're doing? Do you know that you're interfering with police work? How dare you break your word and—?"

"You apparently have been breaking your word, too, Inspector," Cliff said. "Anyway, there is no point in having a discussion about it over the phone. Just talk to Mrs. Finkle and tell her—"

"I'll send a patrol car over and have you picked up, that's what I'll do," the Inspector roared. "I'll have you arrested and I'll have that woman put into protective custody. I'll—"

"No, Inspector," Johns said. "You'll do nothing of the sort. Unless you tell Mrs. Finkle to answer my questions, I may be forced to ask a lot of things which you would much rather I didn't ask. So play it my way. Our interests are the same, and I—"

"You stay right where you are until I can get there," Inspector Gotterman said. "Understand. Stay right there. And don't let that woman leave."

"I'll stay if you tell her to answer my questions," Cliff said. "Now talk to her."

He took the receiver from his ear and held it out to Minnie Finkle.

Mrs. Finkle replaced the receiver and turned to Johns.

"He said to wait until he gets here," she said. "Now just what is it you want to know about Mary Donahue, young man? I've already explained everything to the police and—"

"I want to know all about her," Cliff said. "Who she is, where she comes from, her age, her ..."

"Mary's a good girl," Mrs. Finkle said. "A fine girl, and I'm worried sick about her. She should call me, let me know."

"How about her husband, Mrs. Finkle? Her family. Why hasn't someone—?"

"I don't know anything about her family," Mrs. Finkle said. "Mary never talked about them, but I know they are from somewhere out in the Midwest. She didn't want them to know about the baby and—" She suddenly stopped, putting her hand across her mouth.

"Because she wasn't married?"

Mrs. Finkle's lips formed a tight, thin line. "And it's a lucky thing she wasn't," she said, defensively. "Mary isn't the first to be taken in by some smooth-talking bum. But I know her, and I can tell you she's a fine, decent girl, and if something's happened to her, I'll never forgive myself. She was a hard worker—she modeled you know—and she always paid her rent on time. A nicer little person you wouldn't want."

"Could I see her room?" Cliff asked.

Mrs. Finkle shook her head. "The police have put a lock on it," she said. "They didn't want—"

"Would you have a picture of her, Mrs. Finkle?"

"And why would you want a picture?"

"Well, when a person is missing it sometimes helps ..." Mrs. Finkle stood up. "Wait here," she said.

When she came back a couple of minutes later, she was holding two photographs. She handed them to Cliff without speaking.

The first was a studio portrait, and Cliff studied the rather small, slightly pointed face with the very large serious eyes under the wide clear brow. She was young—she couldn't have been more than eighteen or nineteen when the picture was taken. Hers was a sensitive face with something very innocent, very pure about it. The small chin was firm and sure. She had rather high cheekbones, a finely chiseled nose, and he guessed her shoulder-length hair must be some shade of red.

He realized he was looking at the portrait with the eyes of an artist. Nice as her features were, there wasn't one that he couldn't technically fault. But they seemed to fit each other perfectly, and the total effect was stunning. Mary Donahue was a really beautiful girl.

"She is very lovely," he muttered as he turned to the second photograph.

He was unable to resist the sudden low whistle.

She was in a bathing suit, and the picture had apparently been taken when she was modeling.

This time she was laughing for the photographer. But it wasn't her expression which brought the whistle to his lips.

Mary Donahue had the most perfect body that he'd ever seen. A small girl, almost tiny, she couldn't have weighed more than a hundred and six or eight pounds. But what there was of her was all woman, and as Cliff's eyes took in the beautifully rounded curves …

"All right, you've seen her, Mister," Mrs. Finkle said, reaching out and taking the photographs from his hand. "Now just what is it you have come here to find out? Why—?"

The sound of the pounding on the door interrupted her question. Quickly laying the pictures on the kitchen table, she turned to the door.

"That must be the police," she said. "Wait here."

Fifteen minutes later, Cliff and Minnie Finkle were escorted into the unmarked police sedan which stood at the curb in front of the West Sixty-ninth Street house. Cliff had in the breast coat pocket of his jacket the two photographs of Mary Donahue. He also had an overwhelming desire to find and to get to know the most enchanting girl he had ever seen photographed.

4.

Returning from the kitchen, Judy slumped into the chair across the table from Jack Reason and picked up her discarded gin hand, riffling through the cards.

"That," she said, "is the cutest-looking damned baby I ever saw in my life."

Jack raised his eyebrows. "You can say that again," he said. "She's some dish. A really good-looking chick."

Judy sighed and picked a card from the desk. "Don't be stupid," she said. "I'm not talking about the girl. I'm talking about her kid. You guys are all alike—see a pair of good-looking legs and set of puffed-up ..."

Jack laughed. "Nuts," he replied. "You think men fall all over backwards just because a broad is well stacked. How about you dames? Any guy with a solid bankroll and you fall head over heels."

"Sure—with the bankroll. Not with the guy."

"You certainly act as though you thought Nick Dekota—"

Judy looked up sharply. "Keep Nick out of it," she said. "There's a lot of things you don't understand about me and Nick."

"I understand that you jump when he cracks the whip," Jack said. "You take your orders—"

"You take your orders, too," Judy said. "When Nick speaks, everybody—"

"You're wrong, sister," Jack said. "I take no orders from Nick. Nick or anyone else. Nick put up the front money. Banked the job. But that's all. He gets his cut, but aside from his investment and his split, he isn't in the picture. I'm in charge."

"Well how about the old man? How about Liebman?"

"Liebman is my partner. I've told you that. We don't order each other around. I listen to him because he's smart. But I take no orders. From him or Nick."

Judy put her hand down slowly and dropped the cards. She looked into Jack's face and her eyes were suddenly soft.

"Listen, Jack," she said. "I like you. Don't ask me why. Maybe I just have a weakness for gamblers, and crooks and creeps or something. Anyway, you aren't a bad guy. But I want to warn you about something. Don't sell Nick short. And don't tangle with him. He's bad. Bad and dangerous. Next to him a cobra is as kind and trustworthy and loving as a mother bluebird."

"I understand about Nick," Reason said. "I just don't understand the hold he seems to have on a girl like you. People don't own other people, or haven't you heard? You've told me you hate to go to bed with him, that you don't even like him; and yet ..."

"Cut it," Judy said. "Lay off. And keep your voice down. If Morry hears you say something like that and it gets back to Nick, God only knows what he might do. I got enough troubles as it is."

"We all got troubles. But once this thing is over and I have a decent stake ..."

Judy shuffled her unplayed hand into the deck and stood up. "When *does* it get over?" she asked, her voice suddenly tired. "Tell me—when does it get over?"

"Why, when we get the dough for the painting," Jack said.

Judy shook her head. "No," she said. "No, it won't be over then. You see, you're forgetting something. You're forgetting about the girl in the other room. The girl and her baby."

"I'm not forgetting about them," Jack said, his voice sulky. "I've told you, me and the old man and Neddie are willing to take our chances. Once we get the money, we'll take the gamble and we'll let her go."

Judy laughed, without humor. "Sure—you'll let them go. But what about Nick? Can you honestly stand there and tell me you think Nick—Nick and Morry Shine—are going to let them go? Do you really think that? Are you that stupid?"

Jack rounded the table and took Judy by the shoulders, staring into her face, his own face suddenly stiff and white.

"Listen," he said, "we've made a deal, haven't we? I've told you that neither the girl nor the kid—"

"Who gives a damn about the girl?" Judy said, a trace of jealousy in her voice. "I don't want that baby hurt. Even animals don't kill kids."

"I've told you I made a deal," Jack said, squeezing her shoulders. "I'll see to it that neither the girl nor the baby are hurt in any way—and you, well it will be you and me when we make the break."

"And the old man? And Neddie?"

"Like I told you. I won't have to argue with them. Neddie wouldn't stand for it anyway, nor would old Liebman. These boys aren't killers—aren't cold-blooded murderers. My God, that's why we settled on taking a picture rather than snatching a person. We aren't taking a chance on the chair."

"You could get the chair anyway, since you grabbed that broad," Judy said.

"We could. But we still aren't killers," Jack said.

"Well, don't let Nick—or Morry—know. At least for a while," Judy said, her voice skeptical. "If either of them thought you'd chicken out, when it comes right down to it ..." She shrugged. "Hell, that girl is living on borrowed time."

"She's safe for the time being, at least," Reason said. "I've talked it over with Nick, and he agreed that it's smart using her as the front when we get together with the guy from the insurance company. And she's safe. She has to do what we want her to do. As long as we have the kid, she'll behave. Now give me a kiss and ..."

Judy struggled out of his grasp. "Not here you idiot," she said. "Morry—"

"The hell with Morry," Jack said. He reached for her and put his arms around her shoulders, pulling her slender body close.

He was kissing her hard on the mouth, his eyes closed, when the door softly opened.

Mark Liebman spoke in a hard, bitter, old man's voice. "Get her out of here," he said.

Waiting until the door closed behind the girl, Liebman slowly pulled the chair she'd been sitting in away from the table and dropped into it.

"You're a bigger fool than I thought," he said at last.

"My business, Pop," Jack Reason said.

"Our business. Isn't this thing going bad enough without your taking additional risks? Get Nick Dekota jealous and only God knows what could happen."

"Aw, no one knows...."

"I know. If I can walk in on you, so could Morry Shine. What you do is your own business only until it interferes. And believe me, messing around with that stick of dynamite could certainly interfere. I don't like it. I don't like this waiting, this stalling around."

"Sure." Jack took the other chair, his voice changing and sounding sympathetic and friendly. "I understand, Mark. I don't like it myself. But we had to stall. Had to have time to figure things out. If it hadn't been for the girl and her brat ..."

The old man shook his head. "So what have you figured out?"

"Well, I got this much figured. We're taking about ten extra days to collect the dough because we are going to need a lot more time to plan a getaway now that we do have the girl, whether we want her or not. And I've been thinking about something else. It is just possible that that girl isn't going to be half as dangerous as you might think. To begin with, we know damned well that neither the museum nor the government is going to want to come out and publicly admit that the picture was snatched even if they get it back safely. And the insurance company can't do one hell of a lot, if the government of the United States isn't in back of them. In the second place, we've found out a lot about the girl—that she wasn't married and that her family has no idea she was pregnant and that she doesn't want them to know about it. Gives us a sort of hold over her. Another thing, the way I am working it out, when we make her meet the insurance company representative and act as though she's now working with us, well, she's going to be pretty much implicated. Don't forget, she has to play ball on that. She isn't going to do anything to hurt the kid.

"Now, once we got the dough, and they get the picture back, I think we might just hand her a piece of money and let her go. To protect herself, she'll keep her mouth shut. At least long enough so we can get clear."

Old Liebman shook his head sadly. "You're dreaming," he said. "Maybe the girl could be convinced to keep her mouth shut, although I'm not so sure after talking with her. She didn't strike me as the kind who would worry too much what anyone would think, but she did strike me as the kind who would hesitate a long while before doing anything she might consider crooked."

"Hell," Jack said, "she had an illegitimate kid, didn't she?"

"Don't be a fool," Liebman said. "A lot of people do stupid things when they're in love. Why just look at you—when I walked in here—"

"Skip it, Mark," Jack said. "I'm just telling you that there's a good chance."

"There's no chance at all that Nick Dekota is going to buy it," Liebman said. "You know that. No, Nick isn't the boy to take chances. He's going to want her to disappear—for good. He's put his money in this, financed it, and he's just as connected as we are. And Nick doesn't take chances."

Jack looked up, his eyes half closed. "So what are you suggesting?"

"Nothing. I don't know what to suggest. Except that you better start thinking about it. Stop messing around with Nick's girl and start thinking."

"I am thinking, Pop," Jack said. "Anyway, we got a little time. Nick won't do anything about the girl for a while yet. I've convinced him that she can be the one who talks with the insurance company guy so that he'll never have to see any of us in person. At least that's something, and it makes it safer in a way for Nick himself."

"And it makes it just that much more certain that he'll insist on bumping her off," Liebman said.

"Look," Jack said, getting up, "I'm telling you what I just finished telling Judy. I'll work something out."

"You tell that woman too much," Liebman said sourly. He also stood up, leaning heavily on the table. "Well, you'd better get ready if you're going in tonight."

"I got plenty of time," Reason said.

"Sure—sure." The old man took out a handkerchief and spat into it. "Bring me back another bottle of cognac," he said. "I got a sour stomach. When I worry, I get a sour stomach. And when I get a sour stomach I start to think. And I don't want to think."

CHAPTER SEVEN

1.

Cliff Johns waited until he had left the lobby of the Newark Post Office before opening the envelope. Inside were two squares of cardboard, held together by Scotch tape. On one side was neatly printed the message:

"Take cab at once to Hotel Newark. When you reach hotel, use bank of elevators on right side of main lobby. Go to room 1401. Here is key."

He was the only passenger when the door of the self-service elevator opened at the fourteenth floor, and the corridor was deserted as he moved across the hallway to look at the room numbers. Fourteen hundred and one was to the left, the last doorway down before the corridor made an abrupt turn.

Cliff didn't hesitate. He inserted the key, twisted it, and heard the soft click of the lock. He opened the door and entered a large, single room. To his right a closet door stood slightly ajar; a second door next to it was half opened into what appeared to be a bathroom. There was a closed door next to this.

The bed was made up and there were no signs of occupancy except for a medium-sized suitcase lying on its side on the stand at the foot of the bed. The venetian blinds of the large window at the end of the room were closed, but there was a shaded light on over the small writing desk against one wall.

Carefully closing the room door behind himself, he snapped on the night latch and was moving across the room when the telephone rang. The sudden sound startled him, and for a moment he hesitated. Then the ring came a second time.

He reached for the phone.

It was the voice he had heard previously.

"Mr. Harrington?"

He hesitated a moment, the name coming as a surprise. And then he remembered the letter he had picked up at the General Delivery window less than half an hour ago.

"This is Mr. Harrington," he said.

"Open the suitcase."

The line went dead and Cliff took the receiver from his ear, looking at it oddly for a moment, before replacing it.

He opened the unlocked suitcase. Inside were several garments and a printed note.

The note read:

"Remove your coat, shirt, and trousers, and change clothes. Wear the dark glasses and the hat. The room key in the pocket of the new trousers opens the door next to the bathroom door of your room. Leave your clothes in this room. Use key to next room and go through it into corridor around corner from yours. Walk straight down the corridor and take elevator at the end. Go downstairs and leave hotel. Take cab to Newark airport. The square key, also in the trousers' pocket, will open locker number 517 in the airport. Be sure to lock door between connecting rooms in hotel before you depart."

Changing into the clothes he found in the bag, which, to his amazement, seemed almost a perfect fit, Cliff thought, they're cautious—very cautious. They're running as little risk of my being followed as possible.

He looked into the full-length mirror on the back of the bathroom floor and was surprised at the difference in his appearance. It was a garish outfit and certainly not the sort of thing he would ever have chosen. But anyone seeing him passing through the lobby would not, at first glance, have taken him for the same man who had entered room 1401 a few minutes ago.

It was shortly after six when he reached the airport, and it took him several minutes to find the locker. When he inserted the key and opened it, there was nothing inside but another envelope. Again the instructions were printed and the message was terse. It directed him to purchase a seat on the helicopter shuttle to La Guardia Airport, leaving at six-thirty-five. When he arrived at La Guardia, he was to leave the airport at once, on foot, through the main entrance, walk over the bridge which crossed Northern Boulevard, and go two blocks. He was to turn left at the second intersection and walk slowly north. Nothing else.

Cliff put the note in his pocket, glanced at his watch, and then went to the window where he could arrange for his seat ticket. He had less than five minutes to spare.

It was dark when Cliff Johns reached the intersection. He had been walking for more than fifteen minutes now and was wondering if the whole thing was merely a wild-goose chase. Cars lined the curb but the street itself was deserted, and as he reached the intersection and hesitated before crossing, the voice reached him.

It came from the opened window of a large black limousine which was parked a few feet from where he stood. "Get in the back, Mr. Johns."

A soft low voice, neither masculine nor feminine. It could have been the voice of an old man or an old woman: it had a querulous quality.

He hesitated a moment, his eyes going to the car. He saw that there was a uniformed chauffeur in the front seat, but the man's head was turned away.

The back door of the car opened and Johns moved toward it. As he crouched to enter the car, he was aware of the figure huddled at one side of the seat and then, a second later, someone pushed him from behind and he felt the blindfold going across his eyes. No words were spoken.

They made no effort to bind his hands or feet, but he was aware that there was one of them on each side of him as the car moved away. No one spoke, but he could feel the hands as the blindfold was made secure. Someone took the cigarette from between his fingers, and he was conscious of the car's window being raised as the draft died.

The car's radio came alive, obliterating street noises to the point where he was unable to guess whether they had turned onto a parkway, were riding through city traffic, or were traveling the back streets of the suburbs.

He made an attempt to estimate the time in transit, but when the car finally came to a stop, he couldn't tell whether they had been riding one hour or two.

No one spoke as they guided him, one on each side. There were steps and he knew he passed across a porch and through a door. Thick carpets made no sound at all. And then he was in a room and forcefully seated in an upholstered chair. A moment later he heard a door close softly.

Once more that thin, querulous voice spoke.

"Are you competent to identify the picture, Mr. Johns?"

"I am," Cliff said.

"Then, in a moment, you will be given the opportunity to see it. You have been brought here so that you may know you are dealing with the right people, that we have the picture, and that it has not been damaged. After you see the picture, you will be given your instructions. You are to ask no questions. You understand?"

"I understand."

There was a soft rustle and he was aware of someone stepping near him. He again heard the door open and close, and there was a click of a light switch. He started to move his head, and as he did a voice spoke from several feet away—a soft voice, the voice of a girl, and it had an odd, almost frightened quality, as though she were afraid to raise it above a whisper.

"I will take off the blindfold."

2.

Looking at the old man as he sat huddled in the oversized chair, Mary Donahue thought, I must be dreaming. These words, these hard, cold, bitter words cannot be coming from that fragile, delicate being. These impossible, insane sentences cannot be coming from those fine, sensitive lips, that cultured mouth.

But it was no dream, no nightmare, and there was no way in which she could make it one. Every terrible thing he was saying was the truth. Every threat.

Again she looked at the old man, and then decided it must be a trick of some sort. He wasn't like the others. There was nothing sinister or evil about him. Except his words, except what he was saying.

"You can't be serious," she said suddenly. "Are you just trying to frighten me? Is this some sort of silly game?"

"Yes," he said, "I am trying to frighten you. That is why I'm telling you the truth. And it is no game. You see, I want you frightened. Very, very frightened. Because unless you are frightened, you won't believe me and you won't do what I tell you you have to do. Your only chance, your baby's only chance, is if you are frightened."

Mary shook her head, as though to clear it. "And you mean," she asked, "you mean they would actually hurt my baby? Hurt me?"

"They will kill you."

"But why, why me? What have I done? Why should anyone want—?"

"You were at the wrong place at the wrong time. I have already explained that. And you are not to ask questions." The harsh, bitter voice softened then for a moment, and he looked up with almost an expression of pity.

"The less you know, the less you understand, the safer you will be," he said. "Perhaps not all of us want to hurt you. But there is nothing anyone can do about it unless you follow orders and do exactly as you are told to do. At least, for the time being, nothing will happen to you or your child, unless you disobey. Can you understand that?"

Mary nodded dumbly. "I—I guess so," she said.

"Then listen," the old man said. "Listen carefully. This man will be here within a few hours and you must have it down perfectly. You must make no slips. If the baby means anything to you—you will make no mistakes."

"I will make no mistakes," Mary said, dully. "But please, dear Lord, please …"

"Shut up and listen to me," the old man repeated.

3.

It took a moment or so for his eyes to adjust to the bright light of the room. It was a fair-sized, rectangular room, with walls painted an off shade of white. There were two windows at the far end, facing him, and the heavy drapes had been drawn. A large, old-fashioned chandelier was the source of light, and he shook his head a couple of times and rubbed his hands over his eyes.

It was then that he first noticed the easel standing some ten feet directly in front of him. The canvas was stretched on a frame which had been placed on the easel, and the full light from above shone on it.

Instinctively, Cliff started from the heavy upholstered chair in which he had been seated.

The voice spoke from behind him.

"You may get up and look at it but do not touch it."

For the fraction of a second he hesitated, half tempted to turn. But then he quickly rose to his feet and moved forward, his eyes riveted on the painting.

He knew, even as he approached it, that he was again looking at Botticelli's masterpiece. This was no copy or imitation.

Standing in front of the picture, he was overcome by a sense of relief. The painting had not been damaged or injured. That had been his greatest worry.

Yes, it was as magnificent as ever … superb in every detail. Those unbelievably brilliant colors. The exquisite design, the expression, the …

A million dollars? It was worth anything they cared to demand. Anything.

"If you are satisfied," the soft voice began, and Cliff, shaken from his mood of contemplation, swung around. For the moment, he had forgotten he was not alone in the room.

Mary Donahue had stepped back after removing the blindfold from his eyes, and now she was sitting on the couch at the opposite end of the room. She was following the orders she had been given.

A blue ribbon, borrowed from Judy, held the dark russet hair back from her clear forehead. She wore a short pleated skirt and blouse. Her legs, tucked half under her, were bare. Next to her, in the portable crib, was the child. Looking from one to the other, Cliff gasped and his eyes widened.

There was no mistaking her: it was the girl whose photographs he had seen on West Sixty-ninth Street.

Quickly he looked around the room to see whether they were alone.

Then he moved toward her, but Mary at once held up her hand and spoke.

"Stay where you are," she said.

He sensed it at once, her fear. And he knew that it wasn't he who inspired that fear.

"You are satisfied it is the picture?"

It was a question but the words came out in a whisper, without inflection, almost without meaning. It was as though a robot was speaking.

"I am."

"Do you have the money ready?"

"The money is ready."

"Where is the money?"

He hesitated a fraction of a minute. His firm had agreed to pay the ransom, but so far as he knew, nothing had yet been done about gathering the physical cash.

"Why," he said, "why, it is available when I need it. I can get it at any time."

"How long will it take to obtain the money?"

Again he hesitated, but only for a moment. "Any time after ten o'clock tomorrow morning," Cliff said.

"This is what you are to do," Mary said. "When you are released from here, you will return to your apartment. Tomorrow morning you will go to your office. You will arrange to have the money given to you in the form of cashier's checks. Twenty checks of fifty thousand dollars each. You must have the proper sort of identification so that these checks can be exchanged in any large bank in the country without question. At the time such an exchange is made, should any question arise, someone must be available at your main office who will be able to identify you over the telephone so that you may get the cash immediately."

Cliff stared at her and, as she hesitated, spoke. "But suppose," he began, "suppose ..."

"You are to listen and not ask questions," Mary said.

He nodded and moved over and sat down in the chair. He was baffled by her manner of speaking. She didn't quite seem to understand the very instructions she was giving him.

"When you have the checks," she said, "you are to leave your apartment and make absolutely sure that you are not being followed. You are being watched by our people, so that any attempt to tail you will be discovered at once. When you are positive you have evaded any followers, you will check into a small New York hotel of your own selection. Under a false name. You understand so far?"

Cliff nodded. "I understand."

"Next Wednesday you will run an ad in the used automobile section of *The New York Times*. It will read: '1919 Wills-St. Claire Roadster, mint condition, reasonably priced.' And then give the room number and the telephone number of the hotel in which you are staying."

She stopped speaking, and it was almost as though someone had lifted a phonograph needle and the record had come to an end.

Cliff stared at her face. He saw that her chin was quivering, and her eyes had unintentionally gone to the door. She looked like a small schoolgirl who had repeated a hard-learned lesson and was now apprehensively seeking approval.

"And that is all?" he asked at last.

Mary nodded. "That is all. You understand?"

He nodded his head slowly and his eyes half closed. He spoke barely above a whisper. "I understand," he said. And then he added, "But do you understand—Mary Donahue?"

She jumped as though she had been struck, and instinctively her hand went toward the crib which held the child. Again her eyes went to the door and this time there was no doubt about the fear in them.

Quickly he spoke, raising his voice. "I want to look at the picture again," he said. "May I look at it again?"

Mary opened her mouth but didn't speak.

He heard the rustle of sound outside the door and went on talking, again in a loud voice.

"The instructions are clear," he said. "I just want to assure myself that the painting has not been damaged."

He moved across the room, and again there was the sound beyond the door. But the two remained alone, and he turned and spent moments staring at the Botticelli. He heard the muffled sob behind him, but he didn't turn around.

"You must sit down again," she said at last.

Cliff turned and looked at her. He forced a tight smile, realizing that she needed courage and trying to give it to her, though he didn't know how to do so.

It was while she was tying the blindfold across his eyes that the whisper reached his ear. A thin, desperate sound, barely audible.

"Help me," she said. "Please God, help me!"

His hand went up and touched hers. He dared do no more. He was sure that everything that was said in that room was being overheard—was almost sure that they were being watched from some hidden vantage point.

But he wanted to reassure her, wanted her to understand that someone at least knew about her and cared what happened to her.

He held her hand only long enough to exact a brief pressure.

Forty-five minutes later the long black limousine pulled over to the side of the deserted street in Woodside, Long Island, and Cliff Johns, with the blindfold still on his face, stepped to the curb.

It took him another twenty minutes before he could find a public telephone booth and call for a taxi.

4.

Julius Balch, executive vice president of Continental Assurance Company, leaned across the desk and handed the long manila envelope to Cliff Johns.

"I hope you understand, Clifford," he said, "the tremendous responsibility which you are assuming. That envelope contains a million dollars in negotiable checks. When you walk out of this door, you are going to be on your own. Everything is going to depend upon you. There can be no mistakes. No failures."

"I'm sorry, Mr. Balch," Cliff said, "but that isn't quite so. I represent but one side in the negotiations. With the type of people we are dealing with, almost anything can happen."

"If you have any doubts, Clifford …"

Cliff shook his head. "I am hopeful," he said, "but that is all. So far as I can see, we have no option. We are risking one million to avoid a sure loss of two million. I can only assure you that I will carry through my end of it."

The older man looked doubtful and spoke in a worried voice. "I wonder," he said. "Perhaps we are doing the wrong thing. Perhaps it would have been best to have insisted that the government, the FBI, or the police handle it."

Cliff shook his head. "It was the government's idea that we handle it," he said. "Particularly after the gang got in touch with us rather than with the museum. The advance publicity on the two million dollars' insurance policy, of course …"

"Most unfortunate," Balch said. "Most unfortunate. It merely let them know that we were available to make a payoff." He stood up and circled the desk.

"Well," he said, "it's too late for regrets. I just hope we are doing the right thing. I hope we are not throwing good money after bad. In any case, take care of yourself, son, and take no unnecessary risks. We must have that picture back. Without fail." He held out his hand, and Cliff took it. "Get in touch with us as soon as you can," he said.

Within a minute of the time Cliff left his office, Julius Balch spoke softly into the receiver of the private telephone on his desk.

"He has just left, Mr. Riley," he said. He listened a moment or two and then added, "No, he didn't tell me. Refused to divulge any information, and merely said he would be in touch." He listened again for a moment and then said, "I see, thank you," and hung up.

Richard Riley shrugged his wide shoulders and stepped away from the desk. He looked over at Deputy Inspector Gotterman, who slouched in a large leather chair at the other side of the desk.

"He's leaving the building now," he said. "He has the cashier's checks, made out to himself. One million dollars' worth. But at least for the time being it is safe enough. Only Johns can cash them, but where he makes the exchange, and when, are something no one knows."

"Somebody knows," Gotterman said dryly. "The ones who have been in touch with him know." He hesitated, staring at the dead cigar butt in his hand. "And maybe Johns knows," he added after a moment, looking up from under his eyebrows at the FBI man.

"Exactly," Riley said. "Maybe Johns does know—has known all along. I tell you, from the very beginning it struck me as just a little bit odd that the ransom note specified that the go-between had to be someone from the insurance company. Of course the same thought occurred to us as must have occurred to you people. Johns could be in on it. Lord knows he had enough inside knowledge. He was with the Botticelli from the very beginning. But we have made every check humanly possible, and so far there is absolutely nothing to tie him to the gang in any way. His background holds up, his Army record, his record with the company, everything. Certainly, we shall continue to have him followed. If there is anything fishy about him, we are bound to find it out. On the other hand, even if, as we are now convinced, Johns is in the clear, I still don't believe we are taking too great a risk. We are taking every precaution to see that neither Johns himself nor anyone he might be meeting will be aware that he is under surveillance."

Gotterman looked skeptical. "There's a risk all right," he said. "If Johns is on the up and up, and the gang learns that we are watching him, it can very well botch up the negotiations. They could live up to their threat and destroy the painting. If that should happen—"

"I don't even want to think about it," Riley said. "My instructions were to do absolutely nothing which would endanger the safe return of that painting. But I'm still a little too much of a detective, and I hope too good a one, to sit idly by."

"I only hope those operatives of yours are good," Gotterman said, his voice unhappy.

"They are the best," Riley said. "And they have their instructions.

At the first sign of any danger of discovery, they are to drop the tail and permit Johns to carry on alone. We want to live up to our promise not to interfere until the picture is safely returned, but at the same time, we are going to end up sooner or later with a crime to solve and we want to do what we can to make that solution possible."

Gotterman got up and crossed the room and stared out the window. "I would feel a lot better about things if we had a professional— either one of your people or one of our own—handling the exchange," he said.

"I would myself," Riley said. "But you can be sure that the reason the gang specified someone from the insurance company was because they did not want to deal through a professional. They know as well as we do that a police officer would be a lot more dangerous, particularly from the standpoint of what he might observe and use later on. No, they were smart. They wanted an amateur. That is, of course, assuming that Johns is not actually a member of the mob himself."

Gotterman shook his head and turned back from the window. "The fact he looked up that girl, found out who she was, makes me doubt it," he said. "He wouldn't have had to have gone to all that trouble if he were connected with the mob. After all, the thieves have the girl. He would have known without all that smart amateur detective work of his—putting in his nose where he was not wanted. No, the more I think about it, the more I doubt if he is involved.

"By the way, what do you make of Johns' story about the Donahue woman?" Gotterman asked. "It seemed to me that he was awfully cagey when we asked about her. He certainly seemed convinced that she is being held against her will and that she is in danger; yet she apparently hasn't been harmed in any way. I don't like his reluctance to tell us exactly what did take place when he had his meeting with the gang. We still have to consider the possibility that the girl is now involved with the gang."

"Right," Riley agreed. "And we also have to consider the much stronger possibility that Johns is right—that the girl, and her infant, are in grave danger. It's because of them that I hate this pussyfooting. I don't like playing around with human lives."

Gotterman nodded in agreement. "One thing we must take into consideration," he said. "The gang probably didn't want the girl any more than she wanted to be with them. Stealing a picture is one thing; murder, or kidnapping, is something else again. There is a reasonable chance that once they've collected the ransom for the picture, they will let the girl go and run for it. That way, if they do get picked up eventually, they'll have a chance of beating a life sentence or the chair. It would probably mitigate in their favor in front of a jury. If they harm the girl, they are dead pigeons. I think the kind of criminal mentality involved in this job might well take that into consideration."

"Perhaps. But they might also take into consideration the fact that a dead witness is no witness at all," Riley said. "And that is what makes the whole thing so infuriating. The museum people, the insurance company, even certain people down in Washington seem totally unconcerned about the girl and her child. Their interest is exclusively the return of the Botticelli. Well, perhaps they are right. Certainly I don't underestimate the damage to this nation if the loss of the painting were made public knowledge. On the other hand, the protection of human life is more important to me than the protection of property."

"True enough," the Inspector agreed. "The trouble here is that when it comes to property, we have an established crime. When it comes to the woman and her child, we can't even prove that a crime exists. They didn't force her in that car. They have made no ransom demands for her safe return. The girl herself, when she was able to talk with our intermediary, apparently was unharmed and, according to what Johns has told us, did not say she was being held against her will. And no one has come forward to report her missing."

Riley shrugged and tapped out his pipe in the ashtray on the table. "Well," he said, "it wouldn't make too much difference at this point in any case. There is nothing we could do at the moment. We have to play along according to their rules. The one thing this department has discovered is that the most dangerous thing you can do with a kidnapper is to throw him into a panic by letting him know that the dogs are snapping at his heels. When kidnappers panic, they kill— the old business of getting rid of the evidence when they are on the run. And getting rid of the evidence always means knocking off the victim. No, there isn't a thing we can do but play it their way—that's the most infuriating thing about cases of this type."

Gotterman reached for his hat and fingered the brim. "I've got to be getting back downtown," he said. "Of course you're right. We just have to take it on faith for the time being. But at least while Johns is changing those checks for cash, we may be able to get some serial numbers. We probably won't be given much time, but every bank in the East has been alerted and instructed to take down serial numbers on all large bills currently on hand. Everything from twenties on up. Of course we had to give them a story, as we didn't want anyone to let anything out or start any rumors. But it may help if your men are around when Johns makes the switch."

"They'll be around unless Johns is a lot smarter than I think he is," Riley said. "We're going to follow through that far. Of course, if Johns should start boarding a transatlantic jet for South America or something, we'll follow through a lot further. Otherwise, we'll give him a clear field and just keep our fingers crossed."

Gotterman said nothing but held out his hand, and the two shook briefly.

"One thing we have accomplished, at least temporarily," Riley said, as the Inspector prepared to leave. "We've managed to get the newspaper boys off our tails. The story the Commissioner released about the Washington Gallery needing a couple of extra weeks to make emergency repairs in the heating plant seems to have done the trick."

"It must have taken a good deal of pull in the Capitol to have managed it," Gotterman said.

Riley nodded. "No doubt. Well, I'll keep you informed."

CHAPTER EIGHT

1.

The hardest part was the waiting.

He had checked into the small, theatrical hotel in the West Forties on Monday afternoon, and now more than forty hours had passed. He'd sent down for his meals and, aside from that single trip to the corner newsstand that morning, had never left the premises.

The ad was in the classified section of that morning's *New York Times* and he'd read it carefully, but then later, when he'd tried to read the other sections of the paper, he'd found it was impossible to concentrate. He had too many things on his mind.

Looking at his wristwatch, he saw that it was almost ten o'clock. He was sitting at the writing desk, sketching on a piece of art paper with the soft piece of charcoal he always carried with him.

He'd been drawing the head of a girl and now, looking at the drawing, he realized what he'd done. It was the face of the girl he had talked with several days before at the hideout. The face of Mary Donahue.

Cliff Johns had tried to put her out of his mind, tried not to think of those frightened eyes. He knew how happy those large, beautiful eyes could look, because he still carried the photographs he'd obtained from Mrs. Finkle. But these were not the eyes he had drawn. He'd drawn them as he had last seen her, when Mary'd whispered, "Please help me."

Help her? Yes, he'd be helping her all right. Helping to get her killed, most likely. Soon that phone would ring and he'd be given his instructions, and then, sooner or later, the exchange would be made, and they would have the money and he would have the picture. If all went well and he was lucky. But what would Mary Donahue and her newly born baby have?

He slammed the charcoal down and tore the sheet from the art pad, crumpling it.

He'd thought it all over—considered the possibility of holding out for her freedom and the child's freedom as part of the price. There was, of course, the possibility that the gang would go for it. But there was an equally strong possibility that they wouldn't. It was obvious that she would be able to identify them—obvious that, alive, she would always present a threat.

There was the other angle. His instructions had been to trade the money for the Botticelli. His firm had not insured the life of this one girl. Did he have the right, as a representative of his company, to bargain for her with their money? Could—?

But he didn't have to ask himself this question. He would take that right if he had to. There was nothing else he could do.

He reached for the picture and straightened it out. It was strange how this girl haunted him. He began to wonder if he could have fallen in love with someone he had seen but once for a few brief moments. He knew nothing of her.

But yes, he knew something. Several things. She was beautiful and she was frightened and she needed help. Needed help desperately. And there was no one else to help her.

Using his finger, he smudged the lines at the side of the delicate jaw line and twisted his head to observe the effect. God, but he would like to paint her. There had been some subtle quality about her, something in her expression, something beyond and above that startling beauty and loveliness....

He threw the picture across the room and cursed.

He must have time, must think it out. He couldn't let himself be the instrument for her destruction.

The telephone rang.

In spite of himself, his hand was shaking as he reached for the receiver.

"Yes?"

"You the party who advertised a Wills-St. Clair in this morning's newspaper?"

It was a thin, high-pitched voice and it cracked in the middle of the sentence. It was a voice he had never heard before. He hesitated only a second.

"Why yes, yes, I did."

"You don't mean to say you have an honest-to-God old Wills-St. Claire, Mister?"

"That's what I advertised," Cliff said softly. "That's right, a Wills-St. Claire."

"It doesn't seem likely," the voice said. "I seen one once in a museum out on Long Island, and I read an article in *Road and Track*, but I sure find it hard to believe. Say, Mister, could I see the car? And how much—?"

Cliff found himself at a loss for words. "Who is this calling?" he asked at last.

"Why, this is Johnny, Johnny Farbstein. I live out in Queens and I saw your ad and I'm sort of a nut on old cars and I thought maybe ..."

"How old are you, Johnny?"

"I'm fourteen," the voice said and it wavered just slightly, then hurried on. "But I have a hundred dollars saved up from mowing lawns, and if I could see the car, well, maybe ..."

Cliff sighed. "I'm sorry, son," he said. "The fact is you called just a little too late. I sold the car about an hour ago."

He replaced the receiver as he heard the sound of an indrawn breath at the other end of the line.

"Now who would ever have believed?" he began, half aloud, and then he laughed in relief. At least he'd know where to advertise if he ever ran across an old Wills-St. Claire!

Crossing the room, he poured a cup of coffee from the silver thermos bottle he'd ordered with his breakfast. He had already used up the cream on his first cup, so he drank it black. It was almost cold. He was thinking of calling room service and ordering a fresh pot when the telephone again rang.

This time there was no question about it.

"You recognize my voice?"

He didn't hesitate. He recognized that voice only too well. "I do," he said.

"Where are you?"

"A small hotel on West Forty-eighth, just off Sixth," Cliff said. "I'm in room—"

"Listen closely," the voice said. "Leave immediately. Go to the pawnshop on Sixth Avenue, midway between Forty-fourth and Forty-fifth. The east side of the street. Purchase two large secondhand suitcases. Take a cab and go to the Chemical National Bank, the main office down on Wall Street. See the manager of the foreign exchange department. Arrange to exchange the checks for Swiss francs, West German Deutsch marks, Belgium francs, and English pounds. Small denominations. You will be given exactly one hour to do this. When you leave the bank, take a subway to Grand Central. Get out and walk back to the bar on the southwest corner of Fortieth Street and Lexington Avenue. Sit at the bar and order a drink. This is the only opportunity you will have to obtain the item you advertised for. You must be at that bar between twelve-fifteen and twelve-thirty, or the deal is off."

The line went dead.

Hurrying from the hotel and starting down Sixth Avenue, Cliff thought: They're clever. Damned clever. So that was the gimmick—foreign currency. They had guessed that all large bills in the metropolitan banks would be listed. Had known that it would be too risky to cash them. But foreign currency? Yes, that would be safe or at least relatively safe. No one would have thought to have had the serial numbers on foreign money listed. It was doubtful if the banks themselves ever went to the trouble of writing down the numbers. The tax people weren't interested in large foreign bills.

And there would never be time to list more than the smallest fraction of the bills once he was in the bank if he were to keep his schedule and be uptown again shortly after noon. It was a clever plan and almost a foolproof one.

They'd smuggle the money out of the country and then, later on, cash it in abroad. South America or almost anywhere in the world would be safe. They were taking no chances on being traced, once they'd collected the ransom.

2.

Looking across the gleaming mahogany of his wide desk at Cliff Johns, the bank executive opened his eyes wide in surprise and for a brief moment regretted that he had acceded to his visitor's request and sent his secretary out of the room, leaving the two of them alone.

"Did I understand you right, sir?" he asked, disbelief in his tone. "Did I understand you to say a million dollars, Mr. Johns? A *million* dollars?" His eyes went from Johns to the suitcases on the floor and then traveled to the letter of introduction he held in his hand.

Cliff nodded.

"That's right," he said. "A million dollars. I would suggest you call Mr. Balch at Continental Assurance if there is some doubt in your mind. I believe he can explain...."

The banker nodded. He spoke in a soothing voice, as though he were talking to a slightly deranged stranger whom he didn't wish to offend.

"Perhaps," he said, "perhaps that would be best."

He reached for the telephone, not taking his eyes off Cliff as he spoke into the mouthpiece.

"Would you get me a Mr. Julius Balch?" he asked. "The executive vice president of Continental Assurance, up on East Forty-second."

He watched Cliff closely as he waited and then after a moment spoke into the receiver. He identified himself and started to say something, but then hesitated and listened. He nodded several times and then handed the instrument to Johns.

"This is Clifford Johns," Cliff said. "I am down at the Chemical National and I ..."

He hesitated and then listened for a moment and nodded. He handed the instrument back across the desk.

Again the banker listened for several moments, still looking mystified.

"Yes—yes," he said at last. "Yes, we will take care of it. And of course you may rest assured that we will keep the matter in the utmost confidence. Yes, you may be quite sure. Only it is a bit unusual. I just hope we have enough on hand to ..."

Again he hesitated a moment and then again nodded and put the receiver back.

He turned to Cliff, and although he was still thoroughly bewildered, he no longer looked quite so ready to cope with a madman.

"It will take a few minutes, Mr. Johns," he said. "Would you like to wait here?"

Cliff nodded. He pointed to the suitcases. "If you could have it placed in the bags," he began.

The banker nodded. "We can try," he said, and almost smiled. "I'm afraid it will have to be largely in Swiss francs, however. We don't make it a practice …"

He stood up and started for the door and then, remembering the suitcases, turned and picked them up.

"If you would care to have one of our security people accompany you when you leave …"

Cliff shook his head. "No," he said. "No. I'm quite sure I'll be all right alone. But time is of the essence and—"

"We'll handle it as quickly as possible. But it may take a bit of doing. We'll probably have to send out around the neighborhood. It is a rather staggering amount."

"Quite," Cliff said.

Three quarters of an hour later, bowed under the combined weight of the two suitcases as he moved down the steps of the bank, Cliff realized that staggering was a very appropriate word. A million dollars weighs a lot in any language.

It was twelve-forty-five when he entered the bar on Fortieth Street. He had hurried, but he hadn't been able to make it on time, and he was worried as he found a spot at the end of the bar and placed the two suitcases on the floor at his feet. He ordered Scotch and soda from the bartender and was about to raise the glass to his mouth when the slender, sharp-faced man he had passed in the doorway approached.

"Your name Johns?"

Cliff nodded.

The man held out an envelope. "I'm the manager," he said. "Some guy left this for you about an hour ago. Said a guy would be along carrying two suitcases and that if his name was Johns I was to give him this."

Cliff reached for the envelope. "What did the man look like?" he asked.

The sharp-faced man looked bored. "How would I know, brother?

They come and go. All kinds. I never look at 'em, just serve 'em." He shrugged and turned away. It was lunch hour and he was busy.

Cliff opened the envelope.

3.

Nick Dekota selected the Lincoln convertible and drove himself. The car carried New Mexico license plates and was registered in a fictitious name. He only used it on those occasions when he wanted to be very sure that if the car should be seen or its license plates remembered, there would be no chance it could be traced to him.

He left the Fort Lee house around ten-thirty in the morning and ducked the heaviest part of the commuting traffic. He took the George Washington Bridge, crossed into Manhattan, and then over to the Triborough, where he picked up the Long Island Expressway. He made very good time, although he was careful to stay within the speed limits. He reached the turnoff in a little over an hour.

Although Nick had never been to the hideout and wasn't too familiar with the secondary roads, he found it without being forced to ask questions. When he reached the gates of the old Asher place, he stopped, getting out to open them.

A patrol car was approaching from the opposite direction and beginning to slow down. Across the tree-lined road a station wagon had pulled up and a man in a brown tweed jacket and wearing steel-rimmed glasses was inserting a handful of mail into a box at the side of the roadway. Nick carefully concealed his face with one arm, as he swung back the gate. He had his hat pulled low over his forehead. As the patrol car came to a stop, he started up the driveway, not bothering to close the gates behind him.

Morry Shine wordlessly climbed into the front seat as Nick stopped at the front entrance. Morry gestured toward the opened doors of the four-car garage at the side of the house.

Nick drove in and cut the ignition. He spoke for the first time, and his voice was tense with controlled fury.

"All right," he said. "All right, now what's it all about? Why did you call?"

"Well," Morry started, his voice hesitant, "well, boss, I thought you should get out here. I didn't wanta talk over the phone and I thought you should—"

"I know what you thought, stupid," Nick said. "You don't have to tell me what you thought. All I'm asking is why you wanted me to get out here. What's gone wrong?"

"It's Judy," Morry said.

"Judy?" Nick looked at the other man sharply. "What do you mean, Judy? What's with Judy? Ain't she here?"

"She's here all right, but maybe it would be a good idea if she wasn't. You told me to keep my eyes open and that's just what I been doing. She and Reason ..."

Nick grabbed the other man by the front of his shirt. "What about her and Reason?"

Morry avoided his eyes as he spoke. "I walked in on 'em last night. They was in a clinch. But that ain't all of it!"

"No? That's plenty. I should have known—"

"The thing is Judy has gone nuts over that baby. She acts like it was her own. And the old man, well he's almost as bad. All of 'em, they treat that dame as though she was something special. Couple of days ago, I came in on her, the dame, and she was out of her room and in the living room where the phone is and I got there just in time. She was starting for the phone. I grabbed her, and I was going to give her a working-over. We almost had a blowup right then. That big spade stepped into it and what happened was they just bawled her out and let it go at that. Well, when they wouldn't let me go to work on her, I tol' her I'd strangle that brat if she got out of line again, and that's when Judy cuts in and says no one is going to touch the kid. How the hell can we keep her in line if I can't knock her around and can't even threaten the kid? I ask you."

Nick took his hand from Morry's shirt and slowly blew out a mouthful of cigar smoke. "So they're getting sentimental about the dame and the kid," he said. "I should have guessed it. It's what we get for messing around with a bunch of amateurs. But I can handle that all right. They may be kidding themselves but they know what's got to be done about the girl. The baby don't count. We can leave it on any doorstep. Anyway, let's have it about Judy and Reason. Just what's going on? You think it might be more than just climbing into the sack together? You think maybe they're setting up a double-cross?"

Morry scowled. "Maybe yes, maybe no," he said. "All I know is if Judy is playing around with Reason, then she's on their side and not on yours, boss. You know—in case anything should come up. Anyway, you told me to keep an eye on things and that's what I been doing. A course, when I walked in on 'em, I should of taken care of Reason and I could of slapped her around good. But I didn't want to do anything before I talked with you."

"You did right."

"Well, you know, boss—"

"Shut up," Nick said. "I'm thinking."

For several minutes he sat, staring at the dashboard. Finally he sighed and again spoke.

"This is the day," he said. "Tonight we either get it or we don't. I'm staying until it's over. Who's in the place now?"

"There's Judy and there's the old man and there's the black boy. Reason left early and he took the big car."

Nick nodded.

"An' of course there's the dame and the baby."

"Yeah—yeah. I know that, stupid. I didn't expect they'd be out taking a walk."

He was quiet again and thought for a long time. At last he turned toward Morry and his eyes half closed.

"You been through their stuff? You know what kind of iron they're carrying?"

"I been watching everything boss. Reason, he don't carry nothing. Not even a pocket knife. The old man had a blackjack in his suitcase the first time I looked, and then when I checked up again, it was gone. I found it in that big black boy's room. Nothing else. I don't think there's a gun among the bunch of them."

"And Judy?"

Morry looked at him in surprise. "Why nothing, boss. Nothing at all. But one thing I did notice. She's got some sort of phony passport and it ain't in her name. She got it after she came here, only a few days ago. I don't know where it came from, and I didn't ask her. It looks like the ones those others have, and they also are made out in phony names. All I can figure is they are all planning to blow together. I was suspicious when I seen that passport in Judy's room and that's when I started watching her close. How I happened to sneak up on her and Reason when they were in that clinch I told you about."

"The little bitch," Nick said. "Why the dirty—"

"You want I should go in and start?"

Nick shook his head. "No," he said. "That can wait. We have time. I don't want to do a thing until we get our hands on the dough. Not one thing. We go inside, but we say nothing. Keep a straight face. I don't want her to think I suspect a thing. We have to play this one smart. When it's over, then I'll clean up the details. So far as Judy goes, she's had it. No one double-crosses Nick Dekota."

He turned to his companion and smiled; it was not a pleasant smile.

"You always had a yen for that dame, Morry," he said. "You always drooled every time she was around. So I tell you what I'll do. I'm going to give her to you. When it's all over and I got the dough, I'll let you have Judy. You can do anything you want with her—just so long as you end up doing what I want you to with her. Understand?"

"Whatever you say," Morry said. "I'll be having my hands full. Two of 'em to take care of."

"You should enjoy the work," Nick said.

"After about a month out here without a dame? I should say I will," Morry said.

"Well, don't let it throw you. Just be damned sure you don't tip your hand. We're going inside now and be careful around old Liebman. He's smart as a whip, and I don't want him to think anything is wrong. As far as Reason is concerned—well, we'll take care of that too when the time comes. I don't like punks moving in on my territory."

He reached for the door handle and stepped to the ground.

"Close the garage doors," he said. "This load is going to be here for a few hours."

4.

It was late afternoon, and the four of them sat in the room with the blinds drawn. Three shaded lamps cast isolated islands of lights so that the corners of the room were in shadows. There were the four of them and the infant, of course. Each was buried deep in his own private thoughts.

Mary Donahue could feel the tension. It was almost a physical thing. She had sensed it all day, this odd feeling that something was about to happen. She couldn't understand it but she knew it existed. It was as though some disaster was moving inexorably closer and she was powerless to do anything about it.

Her eyes lifted and she looked at the couch where the huge black man sat, holding the infant against his shoulder. The baby had belched, closed his eyes, and fallen asleep. The black man sat motionless, and there was something wonderfully gentle about the way he held the child against his tremendous shoulder.

Her baby was so small. Oh God, he was so small. So helpless.

She, she and her newly born son, were prisoners and this she understood. The black man was one of the gang. But she didn't object when he smiled at her and asked if he could hold her son. He was one of them, but she didn't mind: she could sense his love for the child.

It was strange, but she couldn't bear to have the girl hold her baby.

The girl also crooned over the infant and talked to him and admired him and wanted to pet him. But Mary hated it when the girl held him in her arms.

It was hard to think that any of them could hurt him, hard to think that they might hurt her. But somehow or other she had this strange feeling of doom. They wouldn't talk to her, wouldn't answer her questions. And now today, she knew that it was coming to a head. It was in the air. Something had to happen. Now with the four of them sitting in the room, she could almost feel them waiting. Waiting for whatever was going to happen. When the girl Judy had returned a few minutes ago, wordlessly, and gone over and sat by the shade-covered window and stared sightlessly at the floor, she had felt the tension all over again. It wasn't like the girl to be silent.

Her eyes moved and she looked at Judy more closely, and noticed her bruised mouth. She observed the black and blue marks on the slender arms, the lackluster expression, and the way she half slumped in the chair. Judy looked like a slightly disreputable rag doll who had been tossed in a corner.

Judy buried herself deep in the upholstered chair, oblivious to the other girl's watching her. She was busy with her own thoughts.

The bastard. There was no need for him to have been so brutal. No need for him to have hurt her so. God knows, Nick Dekota had never been tender and had never had any particular finesse. He had used her when he had needed her or wanted her, and at best his treatment had been cold and casual. But it had never been like this.

She had known from the minute he walked in with Morry that something was wrong. It wasn't hard to guess the trouble. Morry had seen her and Jack together; he'd walked in on them that evening a couple of days ago, and she had been sure that although they had quickly stepped away from each other, Morry had known what was going on. So he'd called Nick.

But why hadn't Nick come in storming, why hadn't he started right out slapping her around? It wasn't like Nick to be subtle. When somebody moved in on him, he didn't take it lying down.

He'd been almost polite. Had called her "kid" and asked how she was and he'd seemed to mean it. Later, he'd dismissed Morry, and the two had been alone together. He'd even said he'd sort of missed her. It had been then that it started. When he'd pushed her over to the bed and started tearing at her clothes. It hadn't been passion; it had been cold fury. The cruel hands, hard and vicious on her body. She'd known at once that he was deliberately hurting her, waiting for her to cry out, waiting for her to say something, to beg him to stop what he was doing to her.

But she hadn't cried and hadn't begged and he'd explained nothing, merely done what he was doing deliberately and systematically. Hurt her physically in a way that only he knew.

He had guessed about her and Jack and he was punishing her in a way which he could be sure Jack would also know and understand.

Sitting in the dusk of the room, her body bruised and aching, Judy thought of only one thing. She would somehow or other have to warn Jack when he got back. Put him on his guard. Nick wasn't going to let it go at merely punishing her. He wasn't through. The showdown would come when the money came.

She lifted her head and looked over at the others. At Neddie, the great hulking colored man who was Jack's friend. At old Liebman, who was also Jack's friend. She wondered what would happen, how much Jack could count on them in a pinch.

Neddie took the infant from his shoulder and carried him back to his mother and then moved off and stood by the fireplace, slowly packing tobacco in a stubby, blackened pipe. He was glad it was about over. He wanted to get back to his family. He wanted to get it done with.

It was a lot of money, and although his cut would be small in comparison to the others, still he would be satisfied. But he'd like to get it finished. Those others, Morry and that one who had arrived earlier in the day, bothered him. They were the kind he'd always stayed clear of. Trouble. That kind always spelled trouble. Well, he'd just keep his eyes open and see what happened. He had confidence in Reason and old Liebman, and he was sure that they could handle anything that came up. But still and all, he'd just keep his eyes open and be on guard.

Mark Liebman sat low in his chair, his eyes half closed as though he were dozing. Now and then he looked up and stared at Judy. He'd known the moment that she walked into the room that something had happened. He could tell by the way she walked, almost as though she were stepping on eggs. The way she held herself, as she had let her body sink into the chair. She'd been hurt, badly hurt.

Liebman had been surprised when Nick Dekota had shown up, but he had kept his feelings to himself. Nick had spoken only a dozen or so words to him, merely said that he thought he'd drop out just to see that things went all right during the cleanup. There had been nothing odd about it, nothing overt to make him suspicious. But Liebman had known something was wrong.

Later, Nick and Judy had spent several hours together upstairs in one of the bedrooms, and then a half hour or so ago, the girl had come downstairs and joined them. And he had known at once that something had happened.

Damn it, it served her right. She and Jack had been fools to get mixed up. They should have known that Morry would have suspected something and would have gotten in touch with his boss. She'd asked for trouble and trouble had arrived.

Dekota hadn't come out because he was merely interested in being on the scene when the money arrived. Morry was there to protect his interests on that. Dekota wasn't worried that they'd try to chisel him out of his cut. No, it was more than that. Dekota was there because he knew what had been going on between Jack and his girl.

Liebman cursed under his breath. Well, what would happen would happen. After all, it was none of his worry. His worry was seeing that he got his cut of the ransom money and made his getaway. If the others, Jack and the girl, asked for trouble, they'd get trouble. But he, Mark Liebman, wanted no part of that. All he wanted was his slice and a chance to get away from all of them.

Pulling the old-fashioned gold watch from the pocket of his vest, he turned the face of it toward the light and saw that it was shortly after seven-thirty.

If everything was going according to schedule, Reason should be making the meet at the movie house over in Port Washington, not more than a dozen miles away.

It wouldn't be long now.

The door opened and Morry Shine sidled into the room.

"You," he said, looking down at Judy, "get that dame and her brat upstairs. Take Neddie with you. Mister"—he hesitated a moment, looking at old Liebman—"he's coming in to join us while we wait."

CHAPTER NINE

1.

The instructions were concise, and the note started out with a warning. Johns was told that every move he made would be observed and that he must follow the directions exactly. The slightest deviation would cancel any possibility of an ultimate contact.

When the rental limousine from Carey Cadillac arrived following his telephone call to the office in Grand Central Station, he gave the driver the address of the yacht basin in Mamaroneck, up in Westchester County on Long Island Sound. Seated in the back of the car he unfolded the note and again read the directions.

"The Bayside Yacht Livery," the note read. "The boat is a 28-foot, drive-it-yourself Chris-Craft, and it has been chartered in the name of Gerald Smith for three days. You are to pick it up no later than four o'clock. Contact no one, make no telephone calls, talk with no one. The people at the livery have been told you will be going to Old Saybrook, Conn., and have supplied you with the proper charts. The boat has been gassed up and supplies are on board.

"Get on the boat at once and follow the channel markers until you have left the basin and are out in the Sound. Go as far as the No. 10 red buoy."

And it ended there.

Leaning back in the deep upholstery of the car, Cliff slowly refolded the note and put it in his pocket.

They know a lot about me, he thought. They have done their research well. They knew I can handle a boat by myself and I am able to read a chart. Well, it probably hadn't been difficult for them. They'd had plenty of time to work on it. They must have seen my picture in the papers at the time the Botticelli was getting all the publicity when the painting first arrived. Any one of them could have been at the museum, could have seen me around the place. Thousands of persons had passed the picture and I was always there.

And then, later on, after they had made it clear that the intermediary must be someone from the insurance company, they had found out where I lived. They could have checked the doorman at the apartment, could have found out things about me with no trouble at all. They had planned it with care and precision.

Again he thought of the note.

Buoy number ten. And he was to pick up the boat at four o'clock. That would put him at buoy ten around four-thirty, as he remembered the harbor off Mamaroneck.

And what would happen then? Would another boat suddenly show up? Was it possible they would zero in with a small seaplane? Or would they have someone planted on the Chris-Craft who would make his presence known once they had left the harbor?

Looking down at the two suitcases which held the money, Cliff unconsciously reached over with his right hand and felt the slight bulge made by the thirty-eight, short-nosed police special he had strapped under his left armpit. He was very glad that he had decided to take it along.

He decided that it was doubtful they would have anyone planted on the boat. Certainly they would not have the Botticelli on the vessel, ready to be traded for the money in the suitcases. They were too smart to take chances like that. No, the boat would be merely a means of guaranteeing that he wasn't tailed.

He began to wonder just how they were going to manage it.

One thing was sure. If they had left word at the yacht livery that this Mr. Smith who was picking up the boat would be going to Old Saybrook, that would be the very last place he could expect to go. The note said that the boat was chartered for three days. There were a lot of places a fast cruiser could go in three days.

The car was on the East River Drive now and the traffic was getting heavy. The driver turned and spoke over his shoulder.

"Will you be taking the car back, sir," he asked, "or will you be staying over?"

"Staying," Cliff said.

He stared at the man's back, wondering for a moment if he had been a plant. Wondering if Riley, the FBI man, or Inspector Gotterman were keeping their word.

He decided after further thought that it was impossible for the man to be connected in any way. No one but the writer of the note in his pocket and Cliff himself had known he would call the car rental agency. The phone couldn't have been tapped. And the car itself had arrived within minutes. No, if he were being tailed it would have had to be some other way.

At ten minutes to four, Cliff stood in front of the desk at the Bayside

Yacht Livery and the leathery-faced man wearing a blue blazer and a peaked fishing cap smiled and nodded.

"Been expecting you, Mr. Smith," he said. "We have everything ready."

"Very good. Then if I may, I guess I'll be getting aboard," Cliff said.

The man nodded. "I'll have one of the boys take your luggage," he said. "You're alone?"

Cliff nodded.

"If you'd like I can have you briefed in before you take her out. Of course your secretary said you were familiar with the craft, but sometimes …"

"Oh, I don't think that will be necessary." Cliff smiled. "I've handled similar boats."

"Of course, sir," He motioned to a slender youth in stained white ducks and indicated the two suitcases.

"Understand you are heading up for Connecticut—Old Saybrook?" Cliff said that he was.

"Well, you have nice weather for it," he said. "I doubt though if you can get up there until well after dark. Do you know the course?"

"I probably won't try to make it tonight," Cliff said. "I'll cut in at Stamford or someplace up the line before dark."

"That would be wise," the man said. "Some of those harbors are pretty tricky after dark."

The boy picked up the suitcases. "Gas tanks are full, sir, and she's been iced and the supplies you ordered are stowed," he said.

Cliff thanked him and followed his guide down the dock.

She was a trunk-deck cabin cruiser with a single screw, probably a couple of years old. She had been well kept up and looked efficient.

The boy put the bags below, opened the icebox to show Cliff that he had put a hundred pounds of block ice inside and where he had placed the cans of beer and the small supply of groceries. He asked Cliff if he wanted him to unpack the bags and stow his clothes, and Cliff very quickly shook his head, saying he'd take care of it later.

The boy watched as he turned the ignition key and warmed up the engine, and then, after Cliff had tipped him, he climbed back to the dock and freed the mooring lines.

Cliff coiled them as the engine idled and then went back to the wheel. There was an open-deck sea skiff pulling in for a landing as he eased off the dock. It was five minutes after four.

He waited until he had passed the small fleet of craft anchored in the inner harbor before he pushed the throttle forward to pick up a couple of knots. And then he reached for the rolled-up chart which had been left between the wheel and the windshield.

The sealed note dropped out as he opened the chart. Again the instructions were very clear. He was to pass buoy number ten to the port, and then head twenty-two degrees south of due east. He was to continue on that course for exactly sixty minutes, keeping his throttle set so that the engine would be turning at seventeen hundred RPM.

Cliff made a rapid calculation and realized it would put him almost in the dead center of Long Island Sound, approximately off Stamford.

He was instructed to make observations at that point, and if there was no other vessel in sight, and no planes in the sky, he was to turn sharply to the south and follow the course marked on the chart which would take him into the harbor off Port Washington, Long Island. Should there be any other craft in the vicinity, he was to proceed until he was completely alone on the water, and then make his change in course.

It would be up to him to be sure he was not observed. Cliff smiled grimly.

They were taking no chances—no chances at all.

He moved the throttle forward, picking up speed. His eyes went to the tachometer as the swells pushed against the hull and the bow rose. And then suddenly he smiled.

They had finally made a mistake. His eyes had stopped when they rested on the ship-to-shore radio dials which were just to the left of the wheel.

Yes, they had finally slipped up.

Not that he would use the instrument; he was as anxious as they were to be sure no one followed him, that no one knew where he was headed. But they had slipped up. Had he wanted to, he could contact the shore.

His hand reached out and he turned the dial.

After several minutes, he again smiled grimly. They hadn't missed after all. The radio was dead and Cliff knew that whoever had chartered the boat and put those supplies aboard for him had also fixed the set so that it wouldn't function—probably by doing something as simple as removing a tube and throwing it away.

It wasn't until more than three and a quarter hours later, as the dockmaster took the lines Cliff handed him and made them fast at the marina where he had been ordered to tie up, that Cliff drew a real breath of relief.

It hadn't happened as he had thought it would. No fast speedboat had pulled alongside. No seaplane had made a landing in the water nearby. They hadn't done what he'd been almost sure they had planned to do. No one had boarded him; no attempt had been made to hijack the money.

And this sudden relief was not because he had been afraid that they would merely board him and grab the ransom. He had been prepared for that. He would have given them a fight for that. No, it wasn't this which had kept him on edge. It was the thought of what would happen to that girl and her child should they have decided to intercept him and try to take the ransom by force.

The dockmaster looked up after making the lines fast and smiled. "Mr. Smith?"

Cliff nodded.

"We've been expecting you," he said. "The cab is waiting. This envelope was left for you."

2.

Jack Reason took the binoculars from his eyes and carefully replaced them in the leather case which hung from his shoulders. He moved down the rail a few feet, one hand pushing the yachting cap back on his forehead. He smiled thinly and flicked the cigarette over the railing; it struck the water and fizzled for a moment like a tiny dud firecracker.

The Chris-Craft moved in cautiously and Jack watched as the dockmaster directed it over to the starboard side of the landing dock.

Looking at his wristwatch, Jack nodded and muttered under his breath. "Right on the button."

He was but one of a dozen or more people who leaned on the rail and watched as the boat was tied up. He watched as Cliff took the two heavy suitcases and put them on the dock and then stepped off the boat. The dockmaster said something, but Jack was unable to hear it. He waited, watching, as Johns stood by the bags. The dockmaster left and Johns stood alone. Several minutes passed, and then a man in a leather jacket and a cap moved down the dock and picked up the bags.

Johns followed him as he started for the shore.

Jack grunted, satisfied.

It was going according to plan.

He didn't hurry, but he managed to reach the Cadillac limousine in the parking lot as Johns was stepping into the cab a hundred feet away. He waited until the cab pulled out and then quickly put the Caddie into gear. A block from the marina, he passed the cab, going fast.

He didn't stop when he came to the theater but continued on to the next corner and made a left-hand turn. He parked several yards down the darkened street and pulled the keys from the ignition. He was back, standing across the street in the shadows of a doorway, when the cab came to a halt. Johns got out and handed the driver a bill and didn't wait for his change.

It was an old motion picture house which, along with thousands of others around the country, had failed when television became popular. Recently an enterprising but misguided entrepreneur had remodeled it into an art theater and contracted with distributors to show foreign pictures. The idea had worked in many places, but it was a dud in this particular neighborhood, and as a result the pictures were playing to no more than a couple of dozen persons nightly.

There was no one in line when Cliff Johns purchased his ticket.

Reason walked quickly across the street and was at the ticket booth as Johns struggled through the door with his two suitcases.

The rest rooms were down a flight of stairs, off a rather fancy lobby decorated with original paintings, all of which were for sale. Free coffee was served in the lobby, but the room was empty as Cliff passed through.

Reason followed him downstairs and lingered until he was sure that Johns had gone through the door marked "Gentlemen."

He went to the automatic coffee urn, drew a small cup of black coffee, and toyed with it for a couple of minutes. Then he put the cup on the side table and followed Cliff through the door.

It was a small, square room, about twelve by fifteen. Twin urinals and a pair of sinks lined one wall. Opposite were the two booths, and the door of one was closed. No one was in the washroom.

Jack softly closed the door and moved to the empty booth, entering it and locking the door. As he sat down he could see a single foot through the open space under the partition.

He cleared his throat. "Do you have it, Mister?"

There was a moment of silence and then Cliff Johns answered. "I have it."

"Good. I am leaving now. Give me two minutes, then come out. When you leave the theater, turn right. Go to the end of the block. Turn left. Get in the car parked thirty feet down the street. A black Cadillac."

Cliff said, "And then what?"

"You will be driven to where the picture is. You take the picture, we take the money."

There was a silence for several seconds and Cliff again spoke. "No," he said.

"What?"

"No."

It took him a second to understand. "What do you mean no? I thought …"

"You get the money," Cliff said quickly, still keeping his voice down, "but I want something beside the picture. I want the girl you are holding. The girl and her baby."

Again for several moments there was silence.

"All right," Jack Reason said at last, his voice tight with anger. "All right. The girl and her baby—and the picture. Now do as I say. Leave and get in the car."

Again there was a sound of shuffling from the next booth, and again Cliff spoke.

"It won't do," he said. "Once I get in the car and we get to where we are going, you'll have the money, but you'll have the picture and the girl and her baby—and me as well."

"We don't want you. All we want is the money."

"I know," Cliff said. "I haven't seen you, I couldn't identify you. The girl could."

Again for several moments there was a silence.

Reason, fighting back his anger, opened his mouth to speak, but as he did, there was the sound of someone at the door. For a moment he looked alarmed and then quickly he stood up.

"Stay here," he said.

A moment later Cliff heard the door open and there were sounds as someone came in. Again the booth next to him was occupied, but he couldn't tell who it was. Someone was running water in one of the basins against the opposite wall. A couple of minutes and the outer door again slammed.

Stepping back into the booth, Jack spoke in a quick voice. "Mister," he said, "you are missing your only chance of getting the painting back."

"And you," Cliff said, "are missing your only chance of getting the money. I want the girl."

"But you can have her. I've told you …"

"It won't do," Cliff said. "Bring the girl and her baby to me and keep the picture. Then I will get in the car and go with you—wherever you want. Take me back to where I was before—where you have the picture. You can then have the money and I'll take the painting."

"Maybe the girl doesn't want to come," Jack said. "How do you know that she—?"

"I know," Cliff said. "It's the only way it can be done. Let me see that the girl and her baby are safe, and then I'll go with you and turn over the money. I can't double-cross you. You'll still have the picture."

There was a silence for several minutes and at last Jack spoke.

"We can't stay here any longer," he said. "And I can't make the decision. I'll have to telephone. I'll leave first. Give me a minute or two and then you come out. Stay in the lobby outside for twenty minutes. Make no phone calls, talk to no one. Then come back in here. In exactly twenty minutes. When I return, I'll drop an unlighted cigarette on the floor so you'll know you are talking to the right guy."

A moment later the outer door slammed.

Cliff sucked in a long breath and slowly stood up. It was a little tricky, maneuvering to get the bags out of the booth.

3.

Liebman put his hand over the mouthpiece of the telephone and turned to Nick Dekota.

"There's a jam-up," he said in a husky voice. "Jack's on the phone. There's a hitch. They want the girl and her baby as well as the picture."

Nick crossed the room quickly and snatched the phone from the old man. "Goddamn it," he said, "what is this?"

He listened for several moments and then spoke quickly. "You're sure—sure he won't give?"

He listened again for a second and then said, "All right, shut up a minute and let me think."

He stood, the receiver in his hand, staring at the floor. Suddenly his face brightened. "Jack?"

"Yes?"

"Tell him we agree," he said. "He can have the broad and her kid. Is he still at the theater?"

"Yeah."

"Is there a phone booth there?"

"Yeah."

"All right, tell him the girl will call him back in twenty-five minutes and say that she is away and safe—her and the kid. Then he can come on out with you."

"It won't work," Reason said. "The guy's too cagey, Nick. He insists on seeing the girl and the baby, and it has to be someplace where he knows she'll be safe."

"All right, let me have another minute."

Again he stood staring at the floor. At last he nodded to himself. "You remember that motel about four miles up the line from Syosset on Jericho Turnpike?" he asked. "The place you met Morry when you picked him up the day he came out to the Island?"

"Yes."

"Well, that should be safe enough." Nick said. "I'm going to call and reserve a room, under the name he used for the boat. He's to go there at once and check in. You call back in three minutes and I'll give you the room number. Follow him and see that he goes directly to the room. Tell him that in one hour the girl will walk into his room, with the kid. Then he can leave her there—there are dozens of people around—and he can come with you. That should satisfy him, shouldn't it?"

"Yeah, I guess so, Nick. But do you really mean—?"

"Shut up and listen, stupid," Nick said. "Just do what I tell you. Get him to agree, follow him to the place, and be sure he checks in. Then come out here as quick as you can. Got it?"

"I got it."

"All right. Give me five minutes to make the reservation. Then call me back. Go to a different telephone."

Nick had no difficulty in making the reservation, but he was impatient as he waited for Reason to call him back. While he waited, he turned to Liebman.

"Go upstairs and get the rest of 'em," he said. "I want them all down here. Right now."

"All of them?" the old man asked.

"Yeah, all of them?"

"Who stays with the girl?"

Nick Dekota smiled grimly. "When I say all, I mean all," he said. "The girl, too. The girl and her baby."

"But—"

"Do what I tell you, old man," Nick said. "From now on, I'm taking over. You boy scouts have been in charge long enough. Now go on and get them. All of them!"

The phone rang again as he finished speaking.

4.

Riley sat in one corner of the room, off by himself. Dr. Dangleader and Charleton Manners stood by the window, attempting to conceal their nervousness as they waited. Julius Balch, vice president of Continental Assurance Company, made no effort to conceal his nervousness. After all, it was his money, or at least his firm's money.

The Deputy Inspector sat at the desk and glared at the silent telephone in front of him. Finally he looked at the clock on the wall and spoke.

"Ten-thirty," he said. "Ten-thirty and not a damn word."

Riley unconsciously checked his own watch. "Eight and a half hours," he said. "Eight and a half hours since he left the bar on Fortieth Street."

Balch glared at the other man. "I can't understand how you people happened to lose him," he said. "After all ..."

Manners swung to the others, frowning. "And I can't understand why you broke your word and attempted to follow him in the first place," he said. "You did promise to give him a free hand. I believe it was agreed nothing would be done to jeopardize the return of the painting. Now if something has happened ..."

"If anything has happened," the Inspector cut in, "you may rest assured that it had nothing to do with our keeping a tail on young Johns. If any mistake was made, it was made in the very beginning—when it was decided that we would make a deal with the criminals rather than treat this like any other official case."

"We had no option," Riley said. "But I agree with you, Inspector, that if something has happened, our putting a tail on Johns certainly had nothing to do with it. I am only sorry we didn't assign more men to the case. If we'd had a few more operatives, we would never have lost sight of that Carey Cadillac after it left the midtown zone."

"Doesn't matter in any case," the Inspector said. "We got the license and we've traced it. We know that the driver took him up to Mamaroneck. We know that he went out on that rented Chris-Craft. But, damn it, that's all we do know."

Julius Balch snorted. "We know that there's a million dollars of our money floating around somewhere," he said coldly. "Twelve hours ago we were in for two million dollars. As of the moment, we are still liable for that amount, and now we have another million at stake."

Dr. Dangleader moved away from his companion. "Yes," he said. "And there is another factor. We now have another life on the line. You gentlemen who are worrying so much about the money are seeming to forget that Johns' life may very well be at stake right at this moment. So far as we know, he could have gone out in the Sound and been hijacked—"

The Inspector slammed his fist down on the table. "Gentlemen," he said, "this discussion is pointless. We are doing what we can. We are trying to find that boat, and we will find it unless it's at the bottom of Long Island Sound. Please remember that we have only known about the boat for a very short period of time. Also, we have no idea of how long it was supposed to take Johns to make his contact. My suggestion is that with the exception of Mr. Riley, the rest of you leave and get some sleep. The moment we have any word at all, we will get in touch with you."

"Well, we better have something pretty soon," Dr. Dangleader said. "The newspapers are beginning to give me a hard time. I think they suspect something. That story about all the extra time needed to repair the gallery's heating system was a little thin. They want to know why the picture is still not on exhibition in the capital. And the foreign press is asking the same question. Sooner or later the Vatican will be asking too. When they do—well, when they do, I'm going to have to issue a statement. I don't think we can stall around much longer."

"I am confident that our man will have the picture back," Mr. Balch said. "That is, if he isn't, well, he isn't already ..." His voice trailed off and the others stared at him. Each man in the room knew exactly what the end of that sentence would have been if he had finished it.

It would have been "if he isn't already dead."

5.

Sitting alone in the unlighted room, the two suitcases firmly wedged between his legs as he leaned forward in the straight-backed chair, Cliff Johns reviewed the events of the last hour—the hour which must already be up, but about which he wasn't sure, as he was following instructions and showing no light.

When he had left the theater and walked across the street and climbed into the back of the limousine which stood with its engine purring softly, he had, for the first time, actually seen the other man. Cliff had been cautious, making sure that no one else was in the car or nearby. The driver sat hunched over the steering wheel, his head turned so that Cliff could see only part of his profile.

The moment Cliff had seated himself, he'd dropped the suitcases on the floor and snapped the locks on each door. Then, before putting on the almost opaque dark glasses which lay on the seat beside him and which he had been instructed to wear, he'd reached up with his right hand and carefully loosened the thirty-eight in its holster. He was taking no chances on an ambush.

The man in the front seat wore a yachting cap and he had it pulled well down over his brow. He was a tall, slender man with wide shoulders. In the dim light, he was featureless and he was careful to keep his eyes straight ahead as he drove.

It took less than a half hour to pass Syosset and reach the motel. It was one of the newer, fancier places, with an Olympic-sized swimming pool, a well-lighted patio with deck chairs and beach umbrellas, in front of a cocktail lounge and restaurant. There was a lobby facing the circular drive. Two long, double-story wings stretched out from each side, and they were fronted by well-landscaped walks and wide lawns.

The driver stopped in front of the main entrance but didn't shut off his engine. He muttered, "Wait."

Three minutes later he returned with the key. He backhanded it to Johns as he got behind the wheel.

"Number twenty-nine," he said. "I'll stop in front, and you get out and go inside. Don't try to look at me. Do just as you have been told to do. It will be less than an hour. And remember one thing. You'll get the girl and her child as I've promised. But at the slightest sign of a double-cross, that picture will be destroyed. There will be no possible second chances."

He pulled up in front of number twenty-nine and stopped, turning his head away as Cliff got out of the car.

"Leave the glasses on until you are inside," he said.

Cliff stumbled at the single step leading up to the door. He put one suitcase down and found the keyhole.

It was a large, luxurious room, with a full tiled bath at one side and two large clothes closets at the other. There was a telephone on a desk next to the double bed.

For one brief second he was tempted. He would have time. He could put the call in, let them know where he was. But at once he dismissed the thought. There was no way of knowing who might be in on the thing. The motel could have been part of the plan from the beginning. The phone might just possibly be tapped. Even the person sitting at the switchboard could be an accomplice.

In any case, his sinister companion had figured it right. If he wanted the painting he had to play ball. Call the cops in now and maybe they would be able to pick the man up when he returned. But it wouldn't get them the Botticelli. And it might very well cost the girl and her child their lives, if the phone were tapped and he were to use it.

The thin, wide-shouldered man had not been taking any chances at all.

Cliff did as he was instructed to do. He placed the chair in the center of the room and then made sure all the blinds were drawn. He checked the door to see that it wasn't locked.

And now he was sitting in the chair, in the dark, waiting. He sat with his back to the door, as he had been instructed. Bags between his feet, he kept his right hand on the butt of the thirty-eight.

A dim light filtered between the venetian shutters and penetrated the heavy drapes so that now, without the dark glasses, he was barely able to make out the outlines of the bed over at one side of the room and the dressing table next to it. He had studied the room very carefully before he'd turned out the light and he'd memorized the location of the furniture. He was dying for a cigarette but he'd been told to light no matches. It must have been at least an hour and he was getting nervous. He was about to take a chance and snap his cigarette lighter long enough to check on the time when he heard the wheels of the car on the gravel outside the door. He could hear the car come to a stop and a moment later there was the slam of a car door.

They didn't knock.

He could feel the slight draft as the door opened, and his fist tightened on the thirty-eight and he half drew it from the holster. When he heard the gentle sound of the door being pushed closed, he hitched slightly and turned in his chair.

He could just barely make out their silhouettes: the tall, wide-shouldered one and a second figure, small and slender and oddly shaped. She must be holding the infant in her arms.

"We're here."

It was the voice he well remembered.

Cliff stood up and turned to face them. "You have the baby?" he asked.

The voice came in a moment and it was a thin whisper. A frightened whisper. "Yes."

"You are all right?"

"Yes."

"And you will stay right here until I return?"

"Yes."

He took a step forward and the woman moved and a hand came out and met his, a small, soft hand, and the minute it found his hand it squeezed and then lifted his hand, and in a moment he felt the back of his hand barely touch the soft moist face of the child. She dropped his hand then and stepped away from him, toward the bed.

"Pick up the suitcases," the man said in a husky voice. "We're going."

"Right."

Cliff reached down as he spoke. He was lifting a suitcase in his left hand as the man in front of him began to turn back toward the door.

Cliff lifted the suitcase clear from the floor, and as he did, his right hand came out of his jacket and he raised it high in the air. A second later the butt of the thirty-eight crashed into the side of the tall man's head.

For a moment he weaved in an odd way and then pitched to the floor.

The woman was opening her mouth to release the scream as Cliff dropped the gun on the carpet and his curved fingers reached her throat.

CHAPTER TEN

1.

They're going to kill me. In ten minutes, a half hour, perhaps an hour—they will kill me. One of them, probably the huge, apelike Morry will do it. He won't have to use a gun or knife or anything like that. Just one solid blow from that huge fist and my face will be smashed and I'll be dead.

Sitting on the sofa, her hand over the bruised eye which Nick had struck when she'd refused to give up the baby, Mary sat and tried not to cry. It wasn't the pain that bothered her; it wasn't even fear. It was just that shocking realization they were going to murder her in cold blood.

She knew. She had to know. It wasn't what they had said. It was just the fact that they had talked at all. Made no effort to keep anything from her. They talked as though she wasn't even there. As though she was already dead.

She wanted to cry but she wouldn't cry.

The other girl was gone now and the one called Jack was gone. But the others were all there in the room with her. The old man who had said almost nothing. The big colored man who had been kind to her and to her child. The huge, animal-like one who would kill her. And the one who had struck her in the face with the back of his hand and taken the child from her. He was the worst. He was the one who'd shown up only that day, but he was the worst. It was he who had made no bones about what he said in front of her.

It was strange that although he was the most sinister, it was because of him that in a way she didn't mind dying. It was he who had said, "What the hell is the difference? Give him the kid. Let him have the goddamned brat. Who cares. The kid can't talk. The kid can't hurt us."

So they had pried the child from her, and the other girl had taken it with her when she'd left. She knew whom they had been talking about.

It was the man who'd been brought into that room and whom she'd given the instructions about the money. Mary still didn't quite understand, but it was getting clearer all the time. He was the one, the one she'd talked to, who must be arranging the ransom for the picture. And he'd held out, wanting to be sure that she and the baby were safe first.

It had infuriated them.

She felt a sudden odd sense of warmth when she realized somebody had cared what happened to her. And so they had agreed to let him have the child. But not her. It was the other girl who'd gone with the baby to meet him. Mary wondered just how they were going to manage that.

But it no longer mattered. The baby was gone now, and as she remembered the lean-jawed man with the serious eyes, she was secretly glad that it would be he who would be given the baby. He'd make sure the baby would be all right.

She started to cry then, silently, but it still wasn't for herself.

Poor, poor little thing. First to be born without a father and now—now …

She clenched her hands tight to keep back the tears. Oh God, if only she hadn't written that letter to her own father and mother. If she'd only told them the truth. Sooner or later the child would turn up, but no one would really know who he was or where he belonged. But at least he would be safe. She just had to believe that.

The fat, bald one, the one who had struck her, stood up and looked at his watch.

"Over an hour and a half," he said. "Goddamn it, what's keeping them? Where are they? They should be here by now. Something must have gone wrong."

He looked at Mary and snarled, "Keep quiet. Keep quiet or I'll really give you something to make you blubber." He beckoned to Morry and started for the door.

Morry, silently, followed him out of the room.

Neddie raised his head and looked at Mark Liebman. "I don't like it," he said. "I don't like it one bit. I think we ought to be getting out of here."

Liebman stared at him, his face without expression. "Not yet," he said. "We have to wait for Jack. Jack and the money."

Neddie shook his great head. "I'm beginning not to care about the money," he said. "I'm beginning to just want to get out. I don't like this at all. I don't like what's going to happen—even with the money."

"We can't go without Jack," Liebman said. "You know that—we have to wait."

"Them two," Neddie said, gesturing toward the closed door. "They're up to something. I tell you, Pop. I don't trust 'em. I want to get away from here."

Liebman stared at him for a moment and then his eyes went to Mary. "And leave her with them?" he asked. "Leave her with them and go without waiting for Jack and the money?"

Neddie sank back on his seat and folded his hands between his legs. He shook his head back and forth slowly. "It's no good," he said, "no good at all."

Morry waited until they were out of earshot of the door before he spoke. "What do you think, boss?" he asked. "It's getting on—what do you think?"

Nick cursed. "Think? How the hell do I know what to think?"

"Maybe we been double-crossed, boss. Maybe ..."

"No," Nick said. "No—we still got the picture. They wouldn't settle for just the two of them. They want that picture and they want it bad. They know there is only one way to get it."

"I didn't mean that," Morry said slowly. "I mean Reason and Judy. Maybe they got the dough by now. You know, maybe they managed to get the money and they just took off."

Nick shook his head. "No," he said again. "I don't believe it. To begin with, neither of them were armed. You can bet that the guy the insurance company sent with the dough is no baby. You can bet he was carrying some kind of hardware. They wouldn't have been able to take him. Another thing, even though Judy would double-cross me in a second, Reason wouldn't walk out on the others. He wouldn't walk out on Neddie and the old man. I know his kind. And he'd be afraid to double-cross me on the dough. He knows that I'd catch up with him sooner or later. Not only that, he also knows his safest out is to see that the picture is returned. It's the only way he can take the heat off. No, there's no double-cross there. Later maybe, after this deal is over with, but not yet."

"Then what do you think?"

"How the hell do I know? Maybe the guy found out that Judy was the wrong broad. Maybe he didn't go for that business in the dark and insisted on seeing her as well as talking to her. Maybe he's dickering—how the hell would I know? The only thing we can do is wait."

"So we wait," Morry said. "In the meantime, why not let me clean up a few things here? There's that broad inside. Sooner or later ..."

"Sooner or later you can have her," Nick said. "But not yet. She's still insurance. Suppose they call back and the guy insists on talking to her before he does business? Don't you see, we got to keep her for a while yet. Until we get the money."

"Well then," Morry began, but before he was able to get further, there was the sound of the telephone from the other room. They turned quickly toward the door.

The old man was holding the receiver close to his ear, listening intently. For several seconds no one moved. Liebman stood frozen at the phone. Finally he took the receiver from his ear, holding one slender palm over the mouthpiece.

"It's Judy," he said. "It fell through and all hell busted loose. The guy knew at once it was the wrong girl. He knocked Jack cold with a pistol butt and now he's holding ..."

Nick whirled on Morry. "Get the car!" he yelled.

Liebman shook his head. "Wait a second," he said. "Wait a second. They aren't at the motel anymore. Judy's calling from a phone booth."

"Cops?" Nick gritted the word between his teeth.

"No cops," Liebman said. "Just the guy himself and Judy. He has a proposition."

"Proposition!" Nick cursed and reached out his hand. "Let me talk to that dumb bitch—"

"Better not," Liebman said. "Better stay out of it. The guy is right there with her, I said. He wants to make his proposition now."

He lifted the receiver again and said, "Put him on. We'll listen."

For several minutes he listened. Once or twice he started to interrupt to say something, but apparently the man at the other end of the wire was giving him no chance to talk.

At last he said, slowly, "I see."

Without another word he hung up the phone. He turned to the others in the room.

"He's got Jack and he has got Judy and he has the money," he said. "He still wants to do business. But I don't think you are going to like it."

2.

Cliff's hand moved from her throat and went up until it covered the scream which had started. He moved fast, whirling her around and holding both her and the child as he pushed her across the room. He found the light switch, and suddenly, as the room came ablaze, she ceased to struggle.

She fell back then, still holding the infant in her arms. He watched as she sank down on the edge of the bed.

Cliff moved quickly and picked up the gun from where it had fallen on the floor.

Judy, her mouth half open, looked over at Jack Reason where he lay sprawled on the carpet.

"You've killed him," she said dully.

Cliff shrugged. "I doubt it," he said. "But I couldn't care less. Put the baby down."

Judy laid the infant on the bed and took a couple of pillows, putting one on each side of him.

"All right, now take a sheet from the other bed. Start tearing it in strips."

He moved to the door and snapped the night lock. He watched the girl carefully as he tied the man's wrists and ankles. And then he examined the wound on his head which was bleeding slightly where the skin had been broken. Satisfied at last as the man began to mutter, he again turned to Judy.

"All right, sister," he said. "Give. Who are you? Where is the other one? Mary Donahue?"

"She's still at the hideout," Judy said.

"And you?"

Judy said nothing.

"It doesn't matter," Cliff said. "But tell me, did you really think I could be taken in that easily? That I wouldn't have recognized her?"

"Well, in the dark …"

"The dark made no difference," Cliff said. "I knew the second I touched your hand. But that doesn't matter. I want to know why you came. Why he"—his toe touched Jack who was beginning to moan—"why he didn't bring the right girl. You brought the baby—why not the girl?"

For several seconds Judy stared at him and then she slowly spoke. "The girl is all right," she said. "But they want the money first. They don't trust you and—"

Cliff laughed bitterly. "Don't trust me! What are you trying to give me? All they had to do is keep their bargain. Release the girl and the baby and I'd give them the money and they could turn over the picture. Now …"

"If they don't get the money," Judy said, "there will be no picture. If you and Jack are not back—"

"We'll go back," Cliff said. "Don't worry, sister, we'll go back. With a couple of wagon loads of cops."

Judy slowly shook her head. "No," she said. "No, you won't. Because you won't know where to go. And there isn't time for you to force either one of us to tell you. Because if you are not there within a very few minutes now, they will already have destroyed the picture and gotten rid of that girl. And have taken off. So you will end up with us and what good is that going to do you? What can you charge us with?"

"Plenty," Cliff said. "Kidnapping, robbery, possibly murder."

"Kidnapping? Where will your witness be? Robbery? Again, where is the evidence? Murder?"

Jack groaned and lifted his head, his eyes bleary. He saw Judy sitting on the edge of the bed and then his eyes slowly went to Cliff. He tried to sit up and for the first time realized he was tied hand and foot.

"Don't bother to move and don't make any noise," Cliff ordered. He turned back to Judy. "You say the girl is still all right?"

Judy looked at him closely for a moment and her eyes took on a shrewd expression. "You are the man from the insurance company, and you have the money, don't you?" she asked.

"I am and I have."

Judy nodded her head slowly. "And is the insurance company putting out a million bucks to get the girl back?" she asked.

"Shut up, kid," Jack muttered.

"I can handle this," Judy said. "This guy still has to get the painting and …"

Cliff stood up. "No," he said, "you got it wrong, sister. You have it all wrong. I'm the one who is handling things now. You people had your chance but you blew it. You tried a double-cross and you muffed it. Now you are going to play it my way."

"Yes?"

"Yes," Cliff said. "There's still someone at that hideout to take a phone call?"

"And suppose there is?"

"Well, the first thing we are going to do is to gag your friend here. Then you and I are going to take a little ride. To a phone booth. You're going to call that hideout, and when you get them, I'm going to do a little talking. This time it's going to be my way."

"And what way is that?"

Jack Reason raised his head and spoke in a thick voice. "Listen, Mister," he said. "We can still do business. We can—"

"Not with you, I can't," Cliff said. "I tried doing business with you once and it didn't work. This time we'll try it my way."

He picked up several strips of the torn sheet and moved toward the other man.

"Just so you won't be talking to yourself," he said as he tied the gag tight over his mouth.

When they left the room five minutes later, Cliff was carrying the infant. He held the gun in his pocket with his other hand and Judy was struggling with the two suitcases containing the money.

He was careful to turn the lights off before locking the door behind them. He had Judy drive the limousine.

They passed up the phone booths in the next town and drove on until they reached Huntington Station. At the edge of the village they came to an isolated glass telephone booth at the side of the road and pulled over. He left the infant sleeping in the back of the car as he stood in the half-opened door of the phone booth while Judy dialed the number. She spoke for several minutes and then wordlessly handed him the instrument.

Cliff crowded in next to her. "Listen closely," he said. "I am holding two of your mob. I still have the money. There is one way and one way only that you can get it. I am not going to dicker and I am not going to bargain. This time the shoe is on the other foot. This time you have to trust me."

He hesitated a moment and took a deep breath. He knew that what he had to say next might very well determine whether the Vatican would ever see the Botticelli again—and whether he would save a girl named Mary Donahue.

"It is now almost midnight. I don't know exactly where you are but I know you can't be more than two hours from Manhattan. In exactly two hours from now, I am going to telephone Deputy Chief Inspector Gotterman at Police Headquarters on Centre Street. If the girl you are holding, Mary Donahue, is not in his office at that time, and if she doesn't have the Botticelli with her, I am going to tell him everything I know and I am going to turn over to him the two people I am holding.

"On the other hand, if she is there with the painting when I call, and she is unharmed, I will keep my bargain and turn the money I have with me over to these two people. I will see that they have exactly an hour to make a getaway before I make a full report. If you do what I ask, you get your million dollars and your people will have a fair chance of getting away clean. If you don't—well, you figure it out."

He didn't wait for an answer but crashed the receiver back on the hook.

Judy stared up at his face in the light of the phone booth. She slowly shook her head. "They'll never—" she began.

"All right," Cliff said. "Then just give me the address and we can try it with the police. Do you want to do that?"

She shook her head. "Where to now?" she asked.

"Back to the motel," Cliff said. "I want you to be near the boyfriend. However, we'll take another room just in case of unexpected visitors."

Climbing into the car, Judy said, "And if the girl and the picture do turn up, you will give us the money and let us go?"

"I said I would."

Judy whistled under her breath. "And you'd gamble getting that picture back, gamble a million in cash for a girl you've only seen once in your life?" She asked it unbelievingly.

"I'm gambling that your friends will be willing to spare the girl to get the million," Cliff said.

"Mister," Judy said, "I just hope you are right. I really hope you are right. It's going to be a pretty interesting two hours."

Cliff didn't answer her. But he agreed with her. He hoped he was right, too—hoped as desperately as he had ever hoped for anything in his life.

The next two hours were to be the worst he would ever spend.

3.

"And that," the old man said, "is the way it is. Just as I have told it. He didn't let me get a word in. He hung up." For several seconds Nick Dekota was silent.

"Goddamn it," he said. "Goddamn it, get him back on the phone. Call him back right now."

Liebman shook his head. "They called from a phone booth," he said.

Slowly Nick sank back in his chair. "Crazy," he said. "This guy is plain nuts."

"It is crazy," Liebman said. "But what can you do? We play along and there is an outside chance ..."

"There's no chance," Nick said. "Are you stupid? You think once they got the girl and the picture, they're going to turn that dough loose? That they're going to let Judy and Reason get out of their hands? They'll hold them and they'll beat it out of them. Find out about you and all of us. That's what they'll do."

"So what's the option?" Liebman asked. His eye went over to Neddie who sat on the couch saying nothing. "What's the option? If we don't play along, they still got Reason and the girl. They can still beat it out of them. Maybe Jack can hold out, but Judy ..."

"Jack wouldn't hold out for five minutes," Nick growled. "As far as Judy is concerned, that double-crossing bitch would like to turn me in. Don't think I don't know what's been going on out here, old man. Don't think I don't know she and that partner of yours have been ..."

"None of that matters," Liebman said. "The thing is we have to go along, like it or not. One way we got a chance; the other way we got no chance. Reason is my partner, no matter what you think of your girl. If there is any chance to get him off the hook, let alone a chance at the dough, I want to take it."

"Yeah?" Nick looked up at the other man and the whites of his eyes showed. "Yeah? You want to get him off the hook, but how about the rest of us? Huh? How about Morry and me? This dame here"—he gestured over to where Mary sat white-faced—"this dame has seen me, me and Morry. She can identify us."

"She can identify all of us," Neddie said. "That can't be helped now."

"Shut up," Nick said. "I gotta think."

Yes, she could identify all of them. But particularly Nick Dekota. Suppose he did play along. Suppose, just for the hell of it, he played along and the other side did what they said they would do—turn over the dough and give Judy and Reason one hour to make a getaway.

They had a description of the car, probably had the license number. They would know who they were looking for. And the girl had a description of all of them. They wouldn't have a Chinaman's chance.

On the other hand, just suppose there was a chance. Suppose they released the girl and the picture and they played it fair and Judy and Reason got the million and that hour of grace. Would it do him, Nick Dekota, any good?

Why had he come out here in the first place? Because Morry had discovered Judy and Reason were double-crossing him. Planning to take off together after it was all over.

He'd lose either way. He had to lose. If Reason and Judy got that money, they wouldn't have time to make it back to the hideout even if they wanted to. And they wouldn't want to. Oh sure, he and the others could leave, and very likely Reason would get ahold of the old man and the black boy sooner or later and cut them in. But they wouldn't be cutting Nick in.

Anyway, the thing was crazy. No one paid out a million bucks when he didn't have to.

There was only one answer. Let the girl go and he was a dead pigeon.

The girl was the only real witness and the girl had to be taken care of.

The picture? He'd have to take the chance of keeping it. And hope he could still bargain for its return. Bury it away. If it was worth a million dollars today, it would still be worth a million dollars tomorrow.

Judy and Jack? He'd get a lawyer, as soon as he could get to a safe spot; he'd get a lawyer and have them sprung. After all, what could the charge be without a witness? Yeah, he'd try and get them out on bail before they cracked and talked. And then, once they were out, well, they would be easy to keep quiet. Very easy. And it would be a pleasure.

He'd been in tougher spots before. The trick was, just don't panic.

It was bad, very bad. But if he played it cool, laid low for a while until things sort of blew over …

He lifted his head and looked over at Morry. Morry was pretty dumb, but Morry had been with him a long time. He wouldn't have to spell it out to Morry.

"Morry," he said, "Morry take this here broad upstairs." Mary Donahue had not taken her eyes from his face from the time old Liebman replaced the receiver on the phone. She knew. She understood. It would be he who would make the decision—this fat, tubby, evil man with the dainty white hands and the highly polished black shoes.

Morry began to rise from the chair. His eyes had a strange glitter.

Mary opened her mouth and one hand went to her face as she screamed.

Neddie came out of his chair as though he were sitting on a coiled spring. "Now," he began, "now …"

Nick Dekota took the thirty-two automatic out of his side coat pocket and clicked off the safety.

"Sit down, black boy," he said.

Morry never wavered. He crossed in front of Neddie, and as Mary leaned far back on the couch, her eyes wide with fear, Neddie shot one foot out and pushed Morry from behind.

Morry threw up his arms to save himself, and as he did the gun in Nick's hand began spitting.

The first slug missed him, but the second two took Neddie in the stomach.

They didn't stop him.

He had the blackjack raised now, and as Nick kept pumping the bullets into him, he reached the fat man. The blackjack crashed down on the bald dome, powered by Neddie's terrific muscular strength.

The front of Nick's skull caved in like a broken egg, and his gun went sliding across the floor as he fell under the weight of Neddie's huge body.

Morry had regained his balance and he was turning now, a baffled expression on his dull, apelike face. He didn't seem quite to understand what had happened. All he could remember was the last order the boss had given him. Once more he moved toward Mary, who was crunched up in a ball in one corner of the sofa.

As Morry's arm went out to reach for her, Mark Liebman lifted the gun from where it had fallen on the floor.

It wasn't until he'd emptied the last three shots into the back of Morry's head and was dropping the gun that he realized that at least one of those slugs which had plowed through Neddie's body had found his own.

He looked down and saw the red spot spreading slowly on his white shirt, just below his right rib cage.

His face was white as he sank back in the chair and his eyes found those of the girl across the room.

She looked at him and she must have understood that he was wounded. She swallowed hard and spoke.

"I'll—I'll get a doctor," she said in a small, thin voice. The old man shook his head.

"Can you drive?" he managed at last.

She nodded. "Yes. Yes, but …"

"A doctor won't help me now," Liebman said. "I don't need a doctor. Get the car. There's one out in the garage."

He looked down at where Nick Dekota lay, half under Neddie.

"You'll probably find the keys in his pocket," he said.

"But … let me call a doctor. The police …"

"No police," Liebman said. "No police. Get the key and then get the picture. It's in the next room."

Mary stared at him. "But where—"

"We'll keep that appointment down at headquarters in New York," Liebman said. "We'll keep the appointment and maybe they'll live up to their end of the bargain. Now hurry. I'm not feeling very well. The keys, and then the picture, and then get the car."

CHAPTER ELEVEN

Joe McNulty, day city editor of the *New York Tab*, arrived in the city room at ten-thirty, exactly two and a half hours late. He was considerably hung over, red-eyed and unhappy. He had been playing poker for twelve straight hours and had lost the equivalent of three weeks' pay.

McNulty had been due to relieve Ed Milton, who handled the lobster shift. At least he'd called in to say that he would be late, and although Ed appreciated the call, it hadn't made him feel any better about spending the extra time on the job.

Normally, Joe would have picked up a morning paper just to get an idea of what had been going on overnight, but because of the poker game, he hadn't bothered. It wasn't until he had a container of black coffee in his hand and had muttered an apology for sticking Ed with the extra work that he asked what was new.

"We're using the Dekota story for the lead," Ed said.

Joe sighed. "Dekota? What happened in Dekota?"

"Not in Dakota," Ed said. "Nick Dekota. He got bumped off last night."

Joe looked up sharply. "Nick Dekota? The gambler? Bumped off? What happened? I hadn't heard about it. Did it—?"

"Out on Long Island," Ed said. "The cops found him dead on a private estate. Head smashed in. Along with two others. A guy named Morry Shine, who was a sort of chauffeur and bodyguard for Nick. He was shot to death. And a Negro named Washington. The colored man was also shot to death. Same gun that killed Shine. Nobody yet knows quite what happened. A local patrolman was called when someone heard shots. It could have been a gang bump off, but the cops are being awfully cagey about it. The homicide boys from Centre Street are handling it, and they just aren't talking. It should be good for the next edition, and maybe our Long Island man will have something new on it for later in the day."

Joe nodded. "Nick Dekota," he said. "Well it couldn't have happened to a nicer guy. Anything else local?"

"Well, yes. We have another Long Island story on the front page. Didn't like to double up on the Island, but this one's got a good angle. Our boy out there had a busy night."

"Yeah?"

"Yeah. Seems a couple of motorcycle cops smashed up and made the emergency ward."

Joe looked up, his expression sour. "So what makes that a story?"

"The way they did it. They were chasing a car out around International Airport. As near as we can find out, New York put out an alarm on the car. What makes it interesting is that someone in the car—one of the cops came to long enough to say that it was a woman—tossed out a couple of suitcases just as they were about to catch up with them. Apparently in what turned out to be a successful effort to wreck the motorcycles."

Joe McNulty grunted. "So I still don't see what makes it a story," he said.

"There was about a million dollars in the suitcases," Ed Milton said. "In foreign currency."

"Well, I'll be damned," Joe whistled. "A million bucks and they tossed it out to keep from getting a speeding ticket!" He was suddenly remembering the money he had dropped in the poker game.

"Whose dough was it?" he asked. "Where did it come from?"

Ed shrugged. "That's what makes it a story," he said. "Nobody seems to know. There have been no robberies reported, and if the police know anything about it, they certainly aren't talking. The motorcycle cops are going to be all right. When they hit the asphalt, the car was able to make a getaway."

Joe shook his head and took another sip of the coffee. "The way some people can be careless with money," he said. "Anyway, it sounds like the police are going to have a couple of tough ones on their hands. Well, if that's it …"

Ed Milton stood up and reached for his coat. "A sort of odd one came in from headquarters but our man hasn't been able to get anything much on it yet. A dame showed up down at Centre Street with a dead man riding in the car with her. An old buzzard who had a record, and he also had a bullet in him. We don't know what it was all about, but the girl must have had a pretty damned good story. The cops released her and some guy carrying a baby met her and they left in a taxi. But they weren't talking and we haven't been able to get a thing on it."

"They never do," NcNulty said. He moved behind the desk and sat down. "Thanks for covering me, Ed," he said. "I'll make it up to you."

"That's all right." Ed took his hat from the wastepaper basket and started to leave and then hesitated again for a moment.

"By the way," he said. "Something came in just before you got here. Remember that Botticelli painting that was on exhibition? The one they insured for a couple of million bucks? *Madonna and Infant*, I think it was."

"Yes?"

"We just got a message from the museum that exhibited it here. It was supposed to be shown in Washington, you know, but they kept postponing the showing down there. Anyway, they have decided to shoot it back to the Vatican. An armored car is delivering it to the boat this afternoon if you think it's worth doing anything about. Maybe a cameraman ..."

Joe McNulty shook his head. "That story's dead," he said. "Let the *Times* or the *Trib* have it. Who the hell is still interested in Botticelli?"

THE END

THE HOUSE ON K STREET

Lionel White

This book is for Mary Vernon Beale

CHAPTER ONE

1

The murderer used a Webley Target Special with a ten-inch barrel, designed to accommodate a .22 caliber lead slug, and he killed his victim with a single shot at a distance of some thirty feet. He shot from the front seat, after his car was at a complete stop at the curb directly opposite the opened window.

There were no witnesses.

Having observed his victim drop, Francis Blantz didn't bother to assure himself that his bullet had been fatal, but at once laid the Webley on the seat and covered it with a newspaper. He moved the shift stick into low, and the sports car started forward and away from the curb. The assassin's face was without expression as he put the car through its gears.

2

The victim's name was Joe and within the span of his relatively short life he had experienced many adventures in many countries; and had been the object of curiosity, affection, and love; had been pampered, petted, sheltered, and protected. He had been kidnapped from his mother before he had learned to speak. Later he had been smuggled aboard a tramp steamer by an alcoholic first mate and ultimately sold to the madam of a brothel in Marseilles, where he picked up a few bumbling words of French. Then he had been adopted by a retired British major from whom Joe acquired an English style with Cockney overtures.

The British major died of a stroke, and for the next few years Joe moved around with a succession of people. In the middle 1960s, an American high school teacher spending her sabbatical in Italy became enamored of him and took him to the States with her. But the schoolteacher had run out of money and so was happy when Mrs. Carolyn Margulies showed so much interest in Joe. For Mrs. Margulies, it was a case of love at first sight, and so, within an hour of their initial contact, Joe found himself accompanying his latest admirer to the old Georgian house on K Street.

Although it was crushed between two other brownstones, the small, three-story house was a gem, having been designed by Stanford White, who had been commissioned to create it by a Cabinet officer in Theodore Roosevelt's Administration, after that official had fallen in love with a similar place on the Upper East Side of Manhattan.

The house on K Street, like most of its neighbors, had ultimately been converted into floor-long apartments, but it had lost none of its charm in the transition. Mrs. Margulies, who had excellent taste, furnished her first-floor rooms with Early American antiques and fine reproductions.

The effect was lost on Joe, who had little feeling for aesthetic surroundings. But he was happy enough in the place and enchanted by the private walled garden behind the house, where he would spend a good deal of the time during the warm summer days. In the spring, while the weather was still a bit chilly—the sun didn't have much of a chance to strike the garden because of the height of the surrounding buildings—he stayed mostly in the front room, where he was able to watch life through the broad, plate-glass window which faced the street.

The front window was normally kept closed, but Carolyn Margulies had decided that the living room of her apartment needed airing, and, as it was an exceptionally warm evening for early May, she'd opened the window wide when she had returned home shortly after six o'clock.

Joe stared at her with one eye closed, whistled and said "Thank you." He repeated it three times, in a sarcastic voice. "Thank you—thank you—thank you!"

"You big fool," Carolyn said, her voice filled with affection. She took her pocketbook and turned to the door.

"A little fresh air won't hurt you a bit," she said. "I'm going to run down to the grocer for a few minutes and pick up some things we need. I won't be long. And you behave yourself while I'm gone."

She had left the Volkswagen parked in front of the building and no sooner had she pulled away from the curb than the other car, which had been waiting a half block down the street, moved forward and slowly approached the parking spot she had left vacant.

Mrs. Margulies shopped at a small delicatessen several blocks from her apartment and ordered two rolled beef sandwiches on kosher rye bread. She purchased a jar of new dill pickles, for which she had an inordinate fondness, a can of Sanka coffee, a carton of filtered cigarettes. She bought a banana for Joe.

Aside from the banana and the cigarettes, it was thrown-away money.

For seven years Carolyn Margulies had been the dietician for a chain of middle-class cafeterias located in Washington and in adjacent towns in Virginia and Maryland. One of the prerogatives of her position was that she could eat in any of the branches of the chain. But she liked to eat in the apartment, and she enjoyed Joe's company at breakfast and dinner. Joe was a fine companion, and, since they had been together, she had been a lot less lonely.

Carolyn Margulies was sixty years old, a slender, tall, well-preserved woman who dyed her hair an attractive blue gray and took excellent care of her youthful figure. Her husband had been killed in an automobile accident when she was in her early twenties and she had never remarried. She had no children, no living relatives to her knowledge. Her apartment—on which she had spent considerable money and a good deal of thought—her work, and Joe: these were her life. Over the years she had lived frugally and she had saved more than sixty thousand dollars which she had invested in A.T. & T. She could have retired but was far too smart to do so. Without her work she would have been utterly lost.

The sun was beginning to creep behind a low-hanging purple cloud as she paid for her purchases, and she looked out the store door with a slightly worried crease between her eyes. The rain might start at any moment—and she had left the window open. She quickly gathered up her purchases and hurried to the Volkswagen. Five minutes later and she was again parked in front of the house on K Street.

The sky was very dark now, but the rain had not begun, and so, when she entered the apartment, she went through the living room into the small kitchen which separated the front room from the bedroom. Not bothering to remove her hat, she dropped her large leather bag on the sideboard, put her sandwiches in the refrigerator, and took the banana from the paper bag. She peeled it, and then walked back into the living room.

She was speaking in her soft, pleasant voice, a voice filled with love, as she approached the window.

"Look, Joe," she said, "just you look what Mommy's got for her boy."

She reached toward the cage, holding the banana at arm's length.

And then she screamed.

3

The death of the mynah bird was the climax of a series of persecutions and disasters that had befallen Carolyn Margulies during the last three weeks. She had not yet recovered from the shock of two weeks ago when vandals had broken into her apartment and smashed a dozen beautiful pieces of Spode, poured the bottle of blue ink over the lovely handmade petit point which she had converted into a couch cover, pulled the fine leather-bound books from the shelves and torn handfuls of pages from the priceless volumes. They had not been out to steal—just to make a shambles of her lovely home. Even the police had been astonished when they had viewed the scene of senseless destruction.

Now, kneeling on the floor, Carolyn Margulies clutched the still warm, tiny black body and cried unabashedly.

She hadn't as yet found the lead slug which had taken the little bird's life, but Carolyn knew only too well what had happened. They—*they*—had deliberately murdered her pet: it was another in the series of insane persecutions. And it was by far and away the cruelest one yet.

Why were they doing this to her? What possible point was there to it? What did they want? Dear God, who could possibly hate her this much?

She'd racked her brains for the answer and there had been no answer. The police, the private investigator whom she had hired, her few friends in whom she had confided—none of them could figure the answer. If there were some psychopathic maniac loose in the neighborhood, some demented sadist, why had he chosen her and her alone as his victim? Paul Dabney, her top-floor neighbor, the two girls, Joan Harrington and Marty Eden, who lived above her on the second floor, had not been bothered. Only she, Carolyn Margulies.

It made no sense at all.

Three weeks ago. That's when it started. That's when the first telephone call had been made. Each time she thought of it, she flushed from the surge of shame. The words he had used were engraved in her memory. The vile, obscene, words, spoken in that faint but very clear voice. A cultured, almost gentle voice, but a voice reeking with filth.

The ivory white telephone on the night table beside her bed had started ringing shortly after midnight on a Monday night. She had retired, but the reading light had still been on. Her eyes had closed, and the paperback novel had fallen from her hand, before she could muster the energy to put out the light. The unexpected sound of the bell had jerked her eyes open, and she'd reached for the receiver, wondering who in the world could be calling at this hour. She remembered thinking that it was undoubtedly a wrong number, thanks to the new automation system.

But this time it hadn't been a wrong number.

"Mrs. Margulies?"

"Yes?"

And then it had started.

At first she hadn't really understood. The words he used, the things he said—she just couldn't believe she was hearing right. It had to be some ghastly mistake. But as the soft voice had continued on and on, not hesitating and obviously expecting no answer to the obscene questions and suggestions, she had come to her senses and taken the receiver from her ear, holding it away and staring blankly at it for a moment before slamming it back on the hook. She had started to cry, the hot tears pouring down her face.

She was reaching for the receiver, to call the police, when the phone had again rung. She was afraid to pick it up, and, after a minute or so, when the ringing continued, she had taken the phone off the hook and covered the receiver with a pillow.

In the morning she had gone directly to the precinct station and reported the incident. She had been too embarrassed to repeat the exact words the man had used, but the plainclothesman who took her complaint understood.

The second time it happened, the police advised her to try to make an appointment with the man. This might give them a chance to make an arrest. Or she might have some friend stay with her, so that if another call came, she could attempt to keep the man on the wire long enough for her friend to reach another phone and alert the police to trace the call.

They explained that this type of anonymous, obscene telephone call is not unusual. "This kind of nut," the detectives said, "usually isn't really dangerous. He gets his kicks out of shocking and frightening people. He rarely follows up with actual violence. On the other hand, it sometimes does happen. And so we don't like to take chances. You never can tell with a nut. We want to help you, but we would like you to help us. Now if you can only pretend to go along with his suggestions ..."

But she couldn't. She simply wouldn't be up to it. So the police did the next best thing and had her number transferred so that her calls were picked up by a policewoman; Mrs. Margulies was given a private, unlisted phone number.

Whoever her persecutor was, he was too smart to fall for the subterfuge. He made one more call and he must have sensed at once what had happened because the moment the policewoman answered the telephone and attempted to get him into a conversation, he slammed down his receiver and never called again.

4

It was Detective Lieutenant Majeska—Jan Majeska, working out of headquarters and attached to homicide—who picked up the small, misshapen lead pellet which had taken the bird's life. The reason he retrieved the pellet had absolutely nothing to do with the fact that he was attached to homicide or that he was in any official way involved in the case.

Paul Dabney, who lived on the top floor of the house on K Street and was the associate editor of *Klingmyer's Weekly Report*, one of Washington's better newsletters, had pointed out the slug.

On Monday nights Paul worked late because the newsletter went to press early Tuesday morning. As a result, he arrived home just after eight o'clock, and he had keyed his way into the front door and was walking through the downstairs hallway when he passed the open door of Mrs. Margulies' apartment. Under normal conditions, Paul would never have noticed the open door, nor have heard the muffled sobs coming from the living room.

At thirty-two, Paul Dabney was a preoccupied, studious man who made a point of avoiding involvement in the affairs of his neighbors and, in most cases, his friends.

Wharton Business School had given him a keen interest in economics and five years as the Washington correspondent for a Chicago newspaper had given him an interest in politics. He had left the Chicago paper to take the job with Klingmyer's and he never regretted the change. The position with the newsletter didn't pay as much money as the newspaper job, but it gave Paul two things he wanted.

Klingmyer's was a unique and powerful force in the capital. A combination political and financial tip sheet, it boasted a limited but highly influential circulation among top government officials and business leaders of the nation. As the associate editor, Paul was in a position to gain a good deal of very select and often important information not available to the average journalist.

The position also gave him more personal leisure than he'd had as a newspaper correspondent.

Paul needed the information as the background for the book which his added leisure was permitting him to write. The book itself was something he'd set his heart on doing a long time ago. It was going to be a major work; a significant volume which would reflect the knowledge he had gained during his years in the capital. It would be a sort of *Inside Washington*, emphasizing the tremendous importance of the business world in the policies of the country on both the national and international level.

He had been working on the project in his spare time now for more than eighteen months. But he wasn't to be rushed. If it took another year—two years—it wouldn't matter. It was to be an important book and it had to be done right.

Paul Dabney was thinking of the book and of his job as he passed Mrs. Margulies' door. It was really strange, that argument he'd had with Martin Klingmyer. Amazing that a man of Klingmyer's background and experience could be so naïve! The man had virtually cried with indignation when they had discussed the President's invitation to the Russian Premier.

"Stupid," he'd said, his voice high and thin. "Plain damned stupid: bringing him over here as an honored guest. God, it was bad enough when Eisenhower had Khrushchev go through that Camp David routine; let him have a Cook's tour of the country so he could see how we grow wheat and so forth. But to think that we can be childish enough to believe there can be any possible thing to gain in attempting a top-level meeting between the heads of state at this stage in the game, why …" He almost choked on his own indignation.

Paul himself was convinced that such a meeting would be significant, could well lead to a better and more open understanding. In fact, in his third chapter, where he'd reviewed that previous getting together of national leaders …

It was at this point that he became aware of the sounds coming from Mrs. Margulies' apartment. Instinctively he hesitated. There was no doubt about it. A woman was sobbing, just beyond the door.

Under normal conditions, Dabney might very well have ignored the matter and continued on up the stairs. Certainly a lot of people cried and certainly everyone had a perfect right to privacy in misery. It could be none of his business. And Mrs. Margulies, whom Paul knew only very slightly and who had always struck him as a woman of unusual self-sufficiency, would hardly be likely to welcome attention if she saw fit to …

But Mrs. Margulies was not the sort of woman to parade her feelings. And if Mrs. Margulies had something to sob about, it was hardly likely that she would leave her door open so that anyone might witness her grief.

Paul suddenly remembered the interview with the policeman after Mrs. Margulies' apartment had been broken into by vandals.

He turned and entered her living room.

She was sitting on the floor, holding the headless body of the mynah bird in her hand, her own head bowed.

She looked up at Paul as he stood in the doorway, staring at her in utter bewilderment.

"Somebody," she said, "somebody has murdered Joe." She hesitated a second, and he thought she was going to burst into sobs again. But she didn't. She said, "Dear God, what are they trying to do to me? What do they want? Can't somebody help me?"

Ten minutes later Paul made the telephone call from his own apartment. It took him some time to reach Majeska, who had gone off duty and was in his favorite restaurant just finishing dinner. It took him even longer to explain.

"A personal favor, Jan," he said. "The woman is really hysterical. The Lord knows, she has every right to be. Yes, I know. She already has seen the local police. They haven't been able to do a thing. Of course I know that you can't interfere in an official capacity, but I just thought as a sort of humanitarian gesture you might stop by and talk with her. And there has to be something behind it. Just too many coincidences. Too many things have happened. It doesn't make any sense, not any at all." Again he hesitated and listened for a minute.

"Yes," he said. "If you would I'd consider it a personal favor. Just listen to her story and try to advise her what to do."

So Detective Lieutenant Jan Majeska didn't bother with his brandy and coffee but cut his dinner short and drove directly to the house on K Street. He had no official right to interfere in the case, and certainly the entire thing was out of his province. But Paul Dabney was a friend and anyway ... well, it certainly was damned strange that anyone would systematically persecute, for no known reason, a perfectly respectable widow who apparently had never made an enemy in her life.

It took the lieutenant the better part of an hour to get all of the details, and twice he excused himself to go up to Paul's apartment and use the telephone. He wanted to check with the local precinct about the phone calls and the breaking into and wanton destruction of the apartment.

He did a very thorough job, and it speaks well for Mrs. Margulies' personal emotional control that she was able to cooperate as well as she did in answering his questions. Certainly a good many of the questions must have been exceedingly embarrassing, particularly those to do with any possible romantic connections in the present or past. Questions dealing with anyone she might have misused or injured. But she answered them all, and there could be no doubt of her complete frankness.

When it was all over, the lieutenant examined the cage, and it was then that they found the lead pellet. There were traces of blood on it.

Holding it in his hand, he said, "It just doesn't make sense. I simply cannot believe that these things which have happened are merely a series of unrelated incidents. There has to be a connection. Someone must hate you a good deal. Or else someone wants something from you. If that is so, sooner or later they will make known what they want."

"But what could they want?" Mrs. Margulies asked, helplessly.

Majeska shrugged.

"Who knows?"

"What am I to do? Must I just stay here and ..."

Majeska looked at her closely. Slowly he shook his head.

"No," he said. "No. I don't think you should stay here. I think the safest and the best thing you could do would be to go away for a while. Give up this apartment, and, if possible, take a leave from your job and go away. Take an ocean voyage, perhaps go to Florida or Southern California. Could you manage to get a leave of absence and would it be possible ...?"

"Yes, yes, I can get away all right. I think I really do need some sort of vacation."

"If you would like me to speak with the people you work for …"

"It won't be necessary." She smiled weakly. "I really don't need the money," she said, apologetically. "And I guess they wouldn't mind too much if I just stopped working. Somehow, after everything that has happened, I think I would be a lot happier in some other place. And so far as this terrible apartment is concerned …" Again she hesitated. "Of course I do have a lease, but perhaps I can find someone to take it over."

Twenty minutes later Paul Dabney and Majeska were having a drink in Paul's apartment on the top floor.

"Damndest thing I ever heard of," Paul said. "Why anyone should want to persecute that sweet old soul …"

Majeska shrugged.

"Well, you never know in these cases. Might be anyone at all. Maybe a neighbor. Maybe she plays her phonograph too loud late at night and the people upstairs are burned up and trying to get rid of her."

Dabney laughed.

"Hell," he said. "Two Government girls live over her. They are the ones with the damned record player. If anyone has a complaint …"

"Two girls?"

"Yes. Eden—Marty Eden and a Joan Harrington. I've met them a few times on the stairs and so forth. Perfectly respectable. In their twenties. I'm quite sure …"

"Do you suppose they are in now?"

"Could very well be. But I can assure you, Jan …"

"Oh, I'll take your word for it they are all right. But as you say, they live in the apartment above Mrs. Margulies. This whole thing intrigues me and I'd sort of like to know what it really is all about. It is just possible that your girls know something, might have seen someone hanging around, might possibly have some sort of information."

Paul shrugged.

"So—go down and talk with them," he suggested. "At least they are damned pretty, or that is to say one of them is."

"My wife is damned pretty," Majeska said. "You can come along and appreciate beauty; I'll just try to find out what they know—if anything."

CHAPTER TWO

1

As befitted a man who stood at the top of his profession, Marko demanded top dollar for his services. After twenty-five years in the business, he got it. He had also reached a position where he was able to choose and pick among those who sought his services, select the times and places he wished to work.

Marko was a perfectionist (he had to be to have lasted as long as he had) who took great emotional delight in the tasks he performed. It was his whole life.

Someday, of course, it would be his death.

The cheap, ready-made blue serge suit which draped his short, heavyset, almost truncated figure, the scuffed, down-at-the-heels brown shoes, the frayed gray-white shirt and stained striped tie, would give no indication of Marko's prominence. But a glance at the pale, beautifully kept hands which, in spite of the three packages of Turkish cigarettes he smoked each day, showed no trace of nicotine stain, and, even stranger, no sign of nervous activity, might have given a hint of his occupation, if not his professional competency. To suspect that, it would be necessary to observe his face. Especially his eyes.

Set far apart in the round, pasty face, the eyes themselves were almost perfect circles. The gold-flecked irises were completely surrounded by the white of the eyeball, and they gave a peculiarly opaque effect as though their owner were blind and there lay no mirror behind them to register what they observed.

The nose was a purple blob, and the thick bloodless lips perpetually pouted as though the entire face were about to collapse into tears. There was a negligible chin which fell off without definition into the thick neck.

It was a thoroughly unprepossessing face, the almost formless face of a newborn baby; it was a face that would look exactly the same an hour after its owner had died. It was a face devoid of human dignity, devoid of feeling or expression.

It was the face of an assassin.

Marko had to shave only two or three times a week at most, but he went through the ritual with fidelity each noon when he arose. It was what he was doing now, on this morning of May eleventh, as he stood in front of the mirror in the hotel bathroom, leaning slightly forward on his toes to get the best image of himself. He had lathered himself with soap, taking advantage of the bar supplied by the hotel, and he was using a straight razor. As usual he had nicked the lobe of his left ear, and the blood dripped mindlessly down his jowl. He wouldn't bother with a styptic pencil, but after he had dried his face he would stick a bit of toilet paper over the cut where it would stay until sometime later in the day when it would drop off of its own accord.

He didn't bother to wash the remains of the lather from his cheeks when he finished, but used a dry towel to wipe his face. At the same time he looked over at the fifteen-hundred-dollar Girard-Perregaux wristwatch which lay face up on the shelf under the mirror (a grateful South American dictator had given it to him for a service loyally rendered) and observed that he had better than an hour before his appointment.

It would take at least an hour for the limousine to drive in from the airport.

Ten minutes later he put a cigarette between the pouted lips and then, reaching for the solid-gold Dunhill lighter, clumsily twirled the roller. The lighter as usual failed to work, and he cursed and tossed it back on the bed and reached for a pack of matches.

He was never able to make the lighter work because he didn't understand the need to replace a worn flint. Yet this was a man who had the manual dexterity to take down and reassemble a Beretta nine-millimeter submachine gun in two minutes and a half flat, a man who could put together the delicate mechanisms of a time bomb with his eyes blindfolded, a man who could reload a machine pistol in less time than …

But it has already been established that he was a master at his own craft.

2

Gordon Franklin Minor was still in a foul mood when the private plane reached Newark Airport. One thought and one thought only kept going through his mind. He was still muttering about it as the pilot zeroed the plane in and the wheels of the big, four-engine ship touched the landing strip.

"Sixty million goddamned dollars—sixty million dollars, a string of hotels, a dozen insurance companies, oil wells on five frigging continents—and I still have to put up with a bunch of son of a bitching reporters! What kind of a goddamned country is this becoming when a respectable, honest citizen has to answer a lot of mother f....?"

The copilot, who had had far too much sense to have warned him to use the seat belt before the landing, approached to hand him the attaché case, but seeing the expression on the dour, aged face, quickly walked on toward the rear of the plane without speaking.

So the bastards must have gotten wind of something. Wanted to know if I'm a member of the Sons of Columbia. Why damn it to hell, I am the Sons of Columbia! Wonder what they'd make of that if they knew?

Had the guts to ask me if I didn't think the Sons were doing the country more harm than good. A lot of perverted Commies, that's what those reporters are. And no damned wonder. The press is owned by a bunch of Jew radicals so it's no wonder the people they employ should be out to ruin one of the few truly patriotic American groups which dares to oppose the left-wing intellectual fairies running the country from that cesspool in Washington.

He pulled the wide-brimmed white Stetson down over his leathery forehead so that it shaded the steel blue eyes and slowly shifted his lean six-foot-four frame in the soft, quarter-grained leather chair. The big ship turned slowly and moved down the long runway toward the private landing area. Several minutes later, the motors were cut.

The copilot returned from the rear of the plane and wordlessly handed him the attaché case. Minor grunted but said nothing.

A moment later and a landing platform arrived and was placed against the side of the plane.

The two men who had been sitting opposite each other at the far side of the ship got to their feet and, without looking at him, went to the door which they unlatched and opened. They were enough alike to be twins. Both were tall, broad-shouldered, in their early thirties. They had the build of professional football players, the hard, uncompromising facial expressions of guards at a Las Vegas gambling house. Which is exactly what they had been before Gordon Minor had pressed them into a more personal type of service.

The copilot preceded them down the landing ramp and Minor himself merely leaned against the back of the seat in which he had been sitting and stared at the floor.

Three minutes later Francis Blantz entered the plane and closed the door after himself. The two men who had gotten off the plane had followed him up the ladder and they waited outside, at the top of the platform.

Blantz approached with his hand outstretched. His thin lips were unsmiling.

Minor ignored the hand.

"You had to wait long?" Minor asked. The question was perfunctory.

"About an hour and a half," Blantz said. "Left Jackson a little after midnight."

"Well, I left Fort Worth at one o'clock and we ran into head winds. These damned propeller jobs are getting outdated. Going to turn this one in and get a jet."

"I managed a little sleep," Blantz said. His eyes went to the attaché case but quickly shifted. He didn't want to be obvious. Minor snorted.

"Hell, I was in a poker game that started at four yesterday afternoon. Played up till the plane took off. Won seventy-eight bucks." He grunted, satisfied.

Blantz smiled painfully, said, "Good." He couldn't help reflecting that Gordon Minor's net worth had probably increased some three or four thousand dollars while he sat in on the poker game.

"We had a triumph in Jackson," Blantz said. "Must have been at least four thousand people there. The Governor, Lieutenant Governor, a couple of big ..."

"Sure, I know," Minor said.

"A great night for the Sons of Columbia," Blantz continued, his voice proud. "Why even the networks picked up a part of my speech. Did you happen to tune in?"

"I did."

"Did you like ...?"

Minor lifted the Stetson from his forehead with a leathery finger and stared at his companion coldly.

"No," he said, his voice sour. "I didn't like it. Why did you want to waste your time on all that goddamned segregation stuff? You don't see the John Birchers making speeches like that. What the hell, let the little people worry about segregation. The motel owners, the hamburger joint guys. That's their department. We got real things to worry about. The Sons of Columbia is supposed to be fighting the Commies. Christ in a puddle, with half the damned cabinet, the Supreme Court, and Congress loaded with card carriers, who has time to worry about the nigras."

"But we know that the entire integration struggle is Communist-led. We know …"

"Don't tell me what we know. All I know is I'm putting up a half million bucks this year—maybe more—to see that the Sons of Columbia get out and fight the devil where the devil lives. Now if you want to go on headin' up the Sons …"

Blantz blazed with anger. "It happens, Mr. Minor," he said, coldly, "it just happens that I am the leader of the Sons of Columbia and the rank and file will follow me."

"Rank and file, my sweet butt. You sound like some sort of Commie yourself. I take away my backing from the Sons and, brother, you'll be just where I found you a couple of years ago. Running your outfit out of a furnished room and your lousy hat. I can dump you so fast it would make you plain dizzy."

"No offense meant," Blantz said quickly. "You know, of course, that I agree with you. It's just that in the South, it seemed to me a good idea to let our allies know that we have a deep sympathy for their private cause. That …"

"Sure, let 'em know, son. But also let 'em know what we stand for and what we are fighting for. You get those red bastards out of Washington, those give-the-money-away and tax-the-rich bastards, and our people will solve that integration problem right fast. Why if my own people in Dallas were running this country …"

The old man stopped and reached for the attaché case. "Did your man get in?"

"He's at the hotel now, waiting for me."

"Okay. Here it is. But it seems expensive to me. A hundred thousand bucks. Hell, I know boys back home who would massacre an entire Mexican village for one-hundredth of that kind of money."

Blantz said, "We aren't exactly thinking in terms of a Mexican village."

"I should hope not, at these prices," Minor said.

"The man I have lined up is the absolute tops …"

"Good God, don't go telling me about him. It's enough I get up the loot to pay the bastard. You know that I want to know nothing, nothing at all, about any details."

"Speaking of the money," Blantz said. "I don't suppose there is any possibility, in case of a slipup, that it could be traced?"

Minor shook his head, looking at his companion sadly. "You think I'm stupid? Of course not. Can't be traced to me or to the Sons of Columbia. We both got to keep officially out of this. This money is straight from Nevada. Right out of the till of one of the biggest clubs. Safe as churches."

Blantz nodded. "Well, I suppose I should be getting along. The press may have spotted your plane coming in and, if they did, they'll be swarming any minute now. It would be better if I wasn't seen getting off."

"A lot better," Minor said. He stood up and, as the other man turned to leave, spoke again.

"That boy I sent you, the young fella from the East, how's he working out?"

Blantz halted and turned his head.

"Just fine," he said. "I have him working directly under myself. By the way, was he supposed to go on the regular payroll? I wasn't sure so I ..."

Minor laughed without humor.

"He might use the dough," he said, "since his old man only left him about three million." He grunted and hitched up his belt.

"That boy has good stuff in him, even if he did go to a damned Eastern school," Minor continued. "He's working for the cause because he believes in it. You go offering him one of your measly little Sons of Columbia salaries and he'll probably hand you your testicles. Now get going and see that that money ends up where it is going to do the most good."

A moment later he stepped to the window and watched as Francis Blantz climbed into the private, chauffeur-driven limousine which had carried him to the side of the plane. His eyes shifted, and he observed the second car racing up with the sign "Press" in its windshield.

He gave a thin-lipped laugh.

"Sons of bitches," he said, under his breath. "That's one time I put it over on them. Shows how damn smart they are, falling for that phony flight log. They should of known I'd never let my pilot land on anything named after LaGuardia, even if he was a Republican."

Ten minutes later Gordon Franklin Minor's private, four-engine plane was circling to the West, heading back for Texas, its sole passenger stretched out on the couch in the main salon with a double shot of Jack Daniels in his right hand, a brown-paper, hand-rolled Bull Durham cigarette in his left.

3

Blantz had done the basic research, correlated the information and passed on all that he had been able to find out about the two girls. He had made suggestions, offered advice. But Jerry Townsend preferred to develop his own techniques and follow his own theories as to the best approach.

The fact that neither girl appeared to have a steady boyfriend gave him a certain freedom in making his selection, and a less astute—or more selfish—man would at once have chosen the small, pretty brunette as his target.

Jerry Townsend, however, was no ordinary man. Twenty-seven years old, handsome, and with a high degree of intelligence as well as wealth, he was more than adequately endowed for the task he had set himself.

Blantz's dossiers, of course, had been valuable.

Marty Eden, 22 years of age, 5'2", 108 lbs., employed for the last year and two months as a secretary in a nonsensitive Government office. Hometown Duluth, Minn., mother still living there. Graduate of public high school and two years of business college. Neither family nor intimate friends in Washington. Had taken the apartment at the house on K Street with the Harrington girl some six or seven months ago. Lived a quiet and thoroughly proper life. Had a normal amount of dates. Interested in sports, occasionally attended dances with friends from her office. No known bad habits. No political interests. Decidedly attractive, and believed to be intelligent. Lives within her salary. Approachable, but thoroughly conventional.

Joan Harrington, 25, 5'6", 124 lbs., blonde, blue eyes, good figure but a rather plain, colorless face. Gave the impression of being rather high-strung. Had had several sessions with a psychiatrist. Employed as a research assistant in the Library of Congress. A resident of Washington for the past two years and a native of a small town in upstate New York. Middle-class family background. Mother and father killed in car accident several years back. Educated in private schools. Graduate of Bennington. Appeared to live a rather lonely existence: no intimate friends and few dates. Enjoyed a small, supplementary income. No known hobbies. Extensive reader and frequently attended concerts, usually alone. No political interests.

The two girls had apparently not known each other before agreeing to share the apartment. They seemed to get along together well enough, but there was no indication of any deep friendship. They rarely double-dated and each seemed content to go her own way.

The telephone was listed under the Eden girl's name.

Townsend, of course, had secretly observed each of the girls before making his plans. The little one, the dark, pretty brunette with the friendly, sparkling eyes, was certainly the more attractive. She also seemed by far the more gregarious and lively of the two. On the surface it might have seemed that she would have been the better bet.

But Jerry Townsend made it a practice to look well beneath the surface.

Given time and given the opportunity to make a mistake, there is no doubt but what he would have made his pitch for the Eden girl. But he had little time and there could be no mistakes. No mistakes at all.

Blantz had been very insistent in his instructions.

"A casual friendship with the girl will not be enough," he'd explained. "Whichever girl you choose will be the key to the success of the entire operation. Only a complete seduction will do. And the girl must fall in love with you, be firmly under your domination. It is the only way you will be sure to know what will be going on in the house at all times. It will also make it possible for you to be on hand at the psychological moment so far as the Margulies woman is concerned."

And so it was Joan Harrington that he selected. The pickup had been so easy, it even surprised him a bit. He hadn't quite realized how vulnerable a typical, lonely Government girl in Washington might be.

The gambit had been a little crude, but it had worked. He had arranged so that the first contact was made in the cafeteria where Joan usually stopped for a quick breakfast on her way to work in the morning. Because the place was crowded, it had been relatively simple. A mere matter of bumping into her so that the tray she was carrying upset and the dishes had crashed to the floor.

There followed embarrassed apologies and his insistence on getting her a fresh breakfast. And then of course it was only polite that he should have offered to drive her to work in the green XKE he'd left parked at the curb.

Luck had been on his side, and within the very first few minutes it had turned out he'd known a man at Yale who was the brother of the girl who'd been her roommate in college.

There had been a bad moment when she had first learned he'd gone to school in New Haven. She had started asking questions, and for a flashing moment he'd almost forgotten, almost lost his temper and gone into one of those moods that always overtook him when he remembered the school from which he had failed to matriculate. Even today, years after it was all over and done with and forgotten, he still was consumed by fury when he remembered.

Of course he had beaten the charge and the thing had been hushed up. It had cost a great deal, but, fortunately, he had the money. Had enough to have it wiped off the record, pay off the girl's family. But they hadn't let him off on the other part of it. The going to the psychiatrist who had willingly taken his fee only to inform him that he was a latent homosexual and a sadist.

The fool hadn't even listened when he had tried to explain that the girl had needed beating and that he had acted only as an instrument of justice. But then, of course, the school hadn't understood either, nor had the authorities.

It had not been his fault that she had fought back, that he had been forced to cripple her. After all, he had not hurt any of the other girls with whom he'd had experiences at prep school and Yale.

He had managed to change the subject with Joan by explaining that he hated to talk about himself.

From that point on it had been clear sailing. Even before he'd let her out of the car in front of the Government building where she worked, it had been arranged that he would stop by at the house on K Street that evening to take her out to dinner. It was the least he could do to compensate her for the stained skirt which she must send to the cleaners and for which his planned clumsiness was responsible.

He knew he would have no trouble. He'd always been considered extraordinarily handsome, and he had all of the social graces. He danced well, could hold up his end of a conversation. He'd known instinctively that a ready ear is a much more valuable asset than a ready tongue and so could play the willing and sympathetic listener. He also realized that a plain, dull girl could be highly complimented by, and extremely vulnerable to, the attentions of an attractive man, especially when it was quite obvious that for some reason he might prefer her to a more alluring and enchanting creature.

Jerry made this obvious from the moment that Joan introduced him to her roommate.

It was even easier than he had thought it might be. Within a week from the time he had first arranged the pickup, Joan Harrington was in love with him. She was unable to figure out quite how or why it had happened, but there was no doubt about the depths of her feelings. And if she could believe the things that Jerry Townsend was telling her, these feelings were reciprocated.

If once or twice during the later part of that week, when she had tried to confide in her roommate, Marty had looked at her with just the slightest amount of skepticism and advised her to take it a little slow, she had been annoyed and showed irritation, it was soon forgotten.

After all she could understand Marty's attitude. Marty wasn't in love. And Marty was not being pursued by a tall, handsome, young man who seemed to have limitless sources of income and nothing in the world better to do than absorb every possible moment of her free time.

Jerry, of course, was more than pleased with his progress. The plan was proving successful and everything was going according to schedule. It couldn't have worked out better. There was only one slight annoyance. He was rapidly discovering that rather than being merely indifferent to the Harrington girl, he had an active and very distinct dislike for her.

It could very easily develop into hatred.

It was a peculiar thing, but from the very beginning, when he had first become involved in his current activities some three or four years back, he had discovered that he had less and less liking for women in general. Certainly he had no inclination to become romantically involved with any girl, least of all this faded, plain, colorless female with whom he found himself increasingly intimate. Even kissing her was becoming a chore.

The next step, the eventual sexual intimacy, would he positively painful. But he would manage. It was his job to manage.

4

When the knock came on the door, Joan Harrington was bringing in the steak from the charcoal hibachi which the two girls kept in the fireplace and used for special occasions. This particular special occasion was the steak itself, a fantastic, juicy, eight-pound, four-inch-thick slice supplied by the guest of the evening, who happened to be Jerry Townsend. It was the night of May seventh, and Jerry had known Joan Harrington exactly ten days.

Jerry was standing at the opened gateleg table, mixing the tossed salad, and Marty Eden was pouring the imported Heineken's beer into the iced shells which she had just removed from the freezing compartment of the refrigerator.

Marty said "Oh, damn!" put the bottle down on the table, and went to the door.

She recognized her upstairs neighbor, and the frown disappeared from her face.

Paul Dabney realized that the girls and their guest had been about to sit down to a late dinner, and he backed off, a quick apology on his lips.

But she would have none of it. In the relatively short time since Marty had met him, she knew enough about Jerry Townsend to understand that the interruption would annoy him and so some private devil of her own made her insist that Dabney and his companion come in and meet the others.

Joan Harrington was furious. She had taken an almost instantaneous dislike to the slender, studious man who lived on the floor above and had never been able to understand how he had been able to kindle the interest of her very attractive roommate. And now, just as they were about to sit down to the marvelous meal which Jerry had so generously supplied ...

The really strange thing was that Jerry Townsend, a stickler for form and timing, seemed not at all annoyed from the moment Dabney introduced his companion.

"Detective Lieutenant Majeska," Dabney said. "He would like to ask you a few very brief questions if you would be kind enough."

The lieutenant came to the point at once. "Are you acquainted with the woman who is living on the first floor?"

"Mrs. Margulies?" Marty asked. "Well, yes of course. There's nothing wrong is there?" Her eyes, suddenly worried, looked over quickly to Dabney.

"You knew about her place being broken into?"

Both girls nodded, but the lieutenant continued before they could elaborate. He had already read the local precinct reports and was familiar with their testimony.

"And did you know about the telephone calls?"

Neither girl did.

So the lieutenant explained about the obscene calls and then he told them about someone having killed the mynah bird.

"It would seem," he said, "as though all of these incidents are related. A rather vicious and sinister campaign of terror against the woman. Now I wonder ..." and he went into his questions.

When he had finished and when they had answered all of his questions and had proved of no help at all, it was Jerry Townsend who spoke up.

"Darndest thing I've ever heard of," he said. "You say she is planning to quit her job and leave the city? You don't suppose by any chance that it can be some crazy person who wants her job? Some minor employee where she works who hopes that if she leaves, he or she will be promoted?"

The lieutenant shook his head.

"Hardly likely," he said. "She's a dietician for a string of cafeterias, and if she is replaced it will be by another woman. Very likely an experienced, middle-aged woman. I can hardly believe that a middle-aged woman would break into and wreck an apartment. And the voice on the telephone was certainly not that of a woman."

Jerry shrugged.

"There has to be some reason," he said. He looked thoughtful for a moment or two and then spoke up again. "I know it is farfetched, but could it be that someone just wants her to move? You know, maybe the previous tenant in her apartment was a bank robber or something like that and stashed away his loot in a secret hiding place."

The lieutenant didn't smile.

"Mrs. Margulies has lived downstairs for at least a dozen years," he said. "Oh, I know, maybe the man has been in prison and just got out. But believe me, I really searched the place—both her apartment and the basement under it. There is nothing concealed in either place. No false panels or secret hiding places. That sort of thing happens only in suspense novels. Besides, when the men wrecked the apartment, they would have had all the time in the world to have retrieved any hidden loot. And certainly if they had been looking for something like concealed bank notes or jewelry, the last thing they would have done was make a lot of noise, deliberately breaking up dishes and furniture. No, I am afraid we have to look elsewhere for a motive, if there is one. Personally, I am inclined to believe we are dealing with a psychopathic personality who for some reason or another has selected this woman as the victim for his paranoia. Either that or quite unknowingly she may sometime in the past have injured someone who is seeking revenge."

The interview had taken a considerable amount of time as both Dabney and his detective friend had insisted that the others continue with their dinner as they talked. Majeska looked at his wristwatch and saw that it was almost twelve o'clock.

"Well," he said, "I'm sorry to have bothered you people and interrupted your dinner. I guess ..."

Jerry stood up. "You know, I feel sorry for that poor woman. You say she has a lease on the apartment? Don't you think that in view of everything that has happened she could legally break the lease? I don't know too much about the law, but it would seem to me ..."

"She didn't strike me as the sort who would attempt to break a contract, no matter what the reason," the police officer said. "I dare say, however, that she will be able to find someone to sublease the place. Of course, if anything should be made public, a lot of people might hesitate to move in, but ..."

Townsend looked thoughtful. "Look, you know what? I would be only too glad to relieve her of the lease. I'm living at the Shoreham temporarily and have been thinking of getting an apartment anyway. If this Mrs. Margulies really does want to move out and give up the place, I might possibly take it off her hands. At least," and he turned and looked with a certain significance at Joan Harrington, who was suddenly blushing deeply, "at least I'd feel a great deal better about the girls here if there was a man in the house."

"I haven't exactly taken up knitting as yet," Paul Dabney said dryly. He noticed that Majeska was looking at the youth very oddly.

A few minutes later, once again upstairs and having a nightcap, Majeska spoke. "That Townsend chap. He sort of goes for the Harrington girl, is that right?"

"It certainly looked that way tonight."

"Pretty farfetched, of course, but you don't suppose by any weird chance ..."

Paul Dabney shook his head.

"I would hardly think so," he said. "I must admit that for some reason or other I didn't exactly like him, but I would find it awfully hard to believe that he could be involved. The fact is, I was talking with the Eden girl only last evening—saw the XKE at the curb and made some sort of comment about it—and she told me it belonged to young Townsend who was her roommate's new boyfriend. Said that they had only met something like a week ago. This thing with Mrs. Margulies goes back three weeks or more, and so it just doesn't add up."

"Well Townsend can be checked out in a hurry," Majeska said. "I agree with you, however. There may be a housing shortage in Washington—there has been ever since we moved the capital here from Philadelphia—but no one goes to that much trouble to get someone to break a lease. No, it doesn't make any sort of sense."

"The only thing that makes sense is that you go home and get some sleep," Paul said. "Damn it, I shouldn't have dragged you in on this thing in the first place. But I did feel so sorry for that poor woman."

"I feel sorry for her myself," the lieutenant said. "Sorry—and worried. The sort of twisted mentality which would be capable of destroying someone's harmless pet ..."

He let the sentence drift into silence and several moments later was letting himself through the locked front door of the house. He noticed that the green XKE was no longer parked in front of the place and made a note to run a quick check on young Townsend as soon as he had a chance. He didn't expect it to do him much good, however.

Anyway, it wasn't his case in the first place and the woman was going to give up the apartment and leave town. Hell, she probably had a vacation coming her way. So far as the psychopath who was responsible was concerned—well that sort of nut comes and goes. Sooner or later he'd slip up and they'd have him.

He only hoped it would happen before he started killing people instead of mynah birds.

CHAPTER THREE

1

Martin Klingmyer softly closed the door of Paul Dabney's office and slouched into the red leather armchair next to the desk. He sighed, took a thin Havana cigar from a tooled Moroccan case and carefully clipped the end with his penknife. He didn't light the cigar but held it in the corner of his mouth as he spoke.

"I have spent the last two hours with the President's press secretary, Paul," he said. "Tomorrow, in his address to the nation, the President is going to confirm the date. It will be June fourth, a Monday. They are going to give him the full treatment. The decision has been made in the face of warnings from both the heads of Security as well as top military brass."

"Do you think we should run …?"

Klingmyer shook his head.

"Nothing," he said. "Not one damned word. The newspapers and TV people will beat us to the punch on the news angle, and I've been asked to play down any possible indications of a difference of opinion between the executive branch and the Security people. They are going ahead with the thing as it was originally planned some months ago.

"The Russian plane carrying the Premier will arrive early Saturday morning at Kennedy International Airport. The Soviet ambassador will meet the plane along with the Secretary of State and our own ambassador. The party will be driven directly to the United Nations where the Premier will make his address. The Russians will spend Saturday night, Sunday, and Sunday night in New York, and on Monday morning, contrary to good sense and certainly contrary to the advice of our Security people, they will entrain from Grand Central for Washington. The Premier insists on taking a train: he says he wants to sightsee!

"A motorcade will pick them up and they will make the usual ceremonial drive up Pennsylvania Avenue. The President will welcome him formally at the White House. Later, the Premier will be installed in Blair House, which will be his official residence for the five days he will be in the capital. He will be in the country for two weeks, but nothing official has been released about the routine for the remainder of his stay."

"If there are going to be any demonstrations, or incidents," Paul said, "I should imagine the danger spot would be New York. Either at the airport or at the United Nations."

Klingmyer shook his head.

"Security doesn't think so," he said. "What has them worried is the parade here in Washington. But they are planning every possible precaution."

"It seems a little foolish to have released the details of the route and time in advance," Paul said. "Just why …"

"I'll tell you why," Klingmyer said. "It is because the President wants it that way. He feels that a first-class public reception with a really big turnout—despite the pickets—will have a tremendous influence toward easing international tensions.

"The President is aware of the danger. He knows that if anything happens to the Premier while he is in the country, the CIA will be accused of having masterminded the thing. We could expect the missiles to arrive within minutes. The situation is exactly what certain groups in this country are looking for. An excuse to retaliate, an excuse to make a massive, all-out counterattack.

"But he feels that the risk is too remote. As I have said, Security disagrees with him and were it a case of his own safety, the opinions of Security would be the deciding factor. But this is a matter of policy, and in this case the President's own wishes take precedence."

Dabney stood up and crossed to the window and then turned to the other man.

"Martin," he said, "why don't we run a paragraph or two and point this out. You can be sure it would be picked up by the press and the TV commentators, and it might just possibly generate enough feeling so that the Administration would be forced to make a change in plans. Certainly we ourselves carry sufficient influence …"

Klingmyer took the cigar from his mouth and again shook his head.

"No," he said. "No, Paul, and I'll tell you why. I have had the complete confidence of the last four men who have lived in the White House. You may think it is some sort of hat trick, being on intimate and even personally friendly terms with four Presidents who have represented four completely different points of view and two different political parties. It wasn't as difficult as you may think. I have been able to maintain this position because each of those four men knew that he could trust me. It wasn't a case of bootlicking; it was merely a case of integrity.

"When a President personally confided in me and asked me to support his position, I have done so and I shall continue to do so. The continuing strength of *Klingmyer's Weekly Report* lies in this fact. I have supported the policies of each Administration, once it is established in office. In return, I have been granted favors time and time again, have been given certain news releases way in advance of their general publication. No, no matter what my personal convictions may be, the policy of the *Report* will coincide with the official policy of the Administration. The function of *Klingmyer's Report* is not to assume an editorial position, or offer advice. It is to give its readers the significant news of the moment, in advance of the general dispersing of that news. We may interpret that news and draw conclusions from those interpretations, but we are not going to attempt to advise. We advise our readers, but we will not advise those people and institutions that supply the facts. I will leave that function to such pundits as Walter Lippmann—or Walter Winchell."

Klingmyer smiled wryly as he finished speaking. He stood up and tossed the unsmoked cigar into the wastebasket.

"Get your hat, Paul," he said. "I'll buy you lunch."

"The Press Club?" Paul Dabney suggested.

"Hell, no. Harvey's. I want to eat my lunch, not drink it."

2

Mrs. Margulies was lucky. There had been the problem of storing the furniture, or possibly selling it. She didn't really want to sell it because she knew that when she returned from the Hawaiian trip she would take another apartment.

But the few pieces she owned were things she had had for years. Each one had been chosen with a great deal of thought. Carolyn Margulies was a woman who hated to part with anything which she had grown to love.

But she was convinced that the people who worked in the warehouses were careless and that her rare and valuable pieces would suffer damage. Just lying around in cold storage certainly would do them no good, and she could visualize the glue drying out and legs falling off her chairs. Or dampness getting into the wood and spoiling the lovely finishes.

And so when that very nice young man, that Mr. Townsend, the friend of the young girl upstairs—when he suggested that perhaps she would like to sublease her apartment furnished and had promised that anytime she wanted her furniture back he would give it to her, well she had agreed at once.

The people who ran the building agreed to permit her to sublease the apartment and then, which was really most fortunate, had told her they would have no objection to her storing a trunk and some cartons in the basement. They had been most kind about it. It solved the immediate problem of what to do with her extra clothes and various bits of valuable bric-a-brac which she hated to leave lying around loose.

It was really amazing how much she could accomplish in almost no time at all. Here it was only Thursday, barely forty-eight hours from the time that she had made the decision that was to create such a complete change in her life, and already it was as though she were living in a different world.

The sublease had been signed; her personal possessions stored in the basement of the house on K Street. The round-trip ticket for Honolulu had been purchased and was safely folded away in her pocketbook. She had spent the last two nights in a pleasant room at the Statler, and planned to remain there a few more days until her plane left for San Francisco, where she was to board the steamship.

The people at the office had been truly wonderful. They didn't even want to listen to her reasons for leaving. Just told her that anytime, anytime at all she should ever wish to come back, there would always be a place for her. And then, to cap it all, they had presented her with a matched set of luggage at the luncheon in her honor.

Mr. Clarence himself had slipped her the envelope. The envelope in which was the check for a thousand dollars! He had said that the company was giving it to her in appreciation for her years of loyal and honest service, and she had been unable to hold back her grateful tears.

He had then proceeded to kiss her on the cheek, right in front of everyone. It was really strange how something that had started as a tragedy could so suddenly turn into something so nice. Well, another five days and she would be off. Odd how everything was really working out so very well at last.

Mrs. Margulies was already getting over her grief at the death of

Joe. She would never forget him, of course, and certainly she could never attempt to replace him. But sometime after she returned and found a new apartment, she would perhaps get a parrot. Or possibly a toucan. They were such beautifully ugly birds with those great purple and red beaks.

Thinking of Joe reminded her of one thing she still had to do and she was thankful that she'd remembered it. She must make one more trip back to the house on K Street. She still had her key to the outside door as she had neglected to leave it when she turned over the other keys to the new tenant. And when she took it back, she must remember to go down to the basement where she had stored her trunks. She had forgotten and put the photographs in the trunk before she'd locked it. The snapshots she'd taken of Joe last spring.

She knew that his death was too recent for her to be able to look at the pictures just yet. But she did want them with her and sometime, perhaps after she was over in the islands and had rested up and was feeling happier, she'd take them out and have them framed so that she could keep them on her dressing table.

Yes, she'd stop by the place the following Monday. She wouldn't have to bother young Mr. Townsend, even assuming he might be at home. In fact, she wouldn't have to go into the apartment at all. Just open the front door and go directly down to the basement. And then she could leave the key on the library table in the hallway as she departed.

She would not be needing it again.

<h3 style="text-align:center">3</h3>

Francis Blantz waited until the limousine had left the tunnel and arrived in Manhattan before he picked up the telephone that permitted him to speak to the chauffeur.

"I would like to make a stop before going to the hotel," he said. "It will only take a few moments. I'd like to stop at the Chase Manhattan Bank, Forty-fourth and Fifth Avenue."

"Yes, sir."

He looked at his watch. It was ten to ten and he knew that the bank would be open when they arrived there. Holding the attaché case on his lap, he clicked it open and lifted the lid a few inches. Making sure that he was not being observed through the rear-vision mirror, he slipped his hand into the bag and took out a sheaf of bills bound by a paper band.

A quick glance showed him the figure $10,000 printed on the band, and he knew that the bills were hundreds. He slipped it into the inside pocket of his jacket. The two others went into his outside jacket pockets. He was not happy with the arrangement, but it was the best he was able to do, as three packages were too bulky for a single pocket.

The attaché case was then closed and put back on the seat at his side.

The chauffeur was lucky. He found a place a few yards from the corner, directly under the "no parking" sign. The sign didn't bother him in the slightest. He was driving a Carey Cadillac, and he knew that any passing traffic cop would recognize the car as belonging to the rental service. So he didn't worry about a ticket.

Apparently the "no parking" sign also held no threats for the driver of the taxi that pulled up a moment later, just behind the Carey Cadillac. The cab waited while the passengers observed Blantz enter the bank. Then the passengers got out. They were wearing dark, opaque glasses and wide-brimmed, gray felt hats slanted down over their foreheads. They were wide-shouldered, muscular men with the bodies of football players. Their eyes had the typical expression of Las Vegas gambling house guards.

It took Blantz less than three minutes to make out the deposit slips and hand the thirty thousand dollars in bills to the amazed and slightly incredulous teller. And then he was back in the limousine and the car was heading across town.

Blantz knew that he was going to be very late for his appointment with the fat man. But it couldn't be helped. The plane had been late and he had had to make that unscheduled stop, of course. But the fat man would wait. Anyone expecting a fifty percent installment on seventy thousand dollars would wait.

The cab which had pulled in behind the limousine also departed after a few minutes. But it departed without its former passengers who had been content to pay off the driver, giving him a ten-dollar tip for excellent services rendered.

Gordon Franklin Minor received the telephone call shortly after four o'clock that same afternoon. He took it over the wire at his ranch, some fifty-two miles northeast of Dallas. He was in the billiard room at the time, playing three-cushion with his Japanese houseboy, who was beating him badly.

The old man was tired and wanted to get to bed and get some sleep, but he was staying up until the call came in.

The message was brief and to the point. "Chase Manhattan Bank, Fifth Avenue and Forty-fourth Street branch. I would guess somewhere between twenty and thirty thousand. He used a checking account deposit slip. Under his own name. I heard the teller speak it. I didn't take a chance of getting close enough to make sure of the sum, but he had either two or three of the packages."

Minor grunted, said nothing.

"You want me to bring him back?"

"No," the old man said. "Don't do anything. Nothing at all. Just let me know when he gets to Washington, and stand by. We'll handle him later. You keep in touch."

He replaced the receiver without saying goodbye.

"What do I owe you now, Tashi?" he asked, picking up his cue.

"One hundred and fifty, boss."

"I'm going to bed," the old man said. "We'll play it off in the morning."

4

The legend in the lower-right-hand corner of the blueprint read: "Department of Public Works, District of Columbia. Official Survey; sewage lines of present system laid between 1889 and 1910 with certain variations. Survey completed in 1912. Not to be removed from the files of the City Engineer."

The blueprint had been thumbtacked by four corners to the drawing board, and Blantz had circled the area encompassing the block on K Street. A red-penciled line indicated the sewer pipe that passed under the approximate center of the street.

Blantz pointed to the line with a ruler as he spoke.

"As near as I can figure it, the pipe is approximately twenty-two feet from the edge of the sidewalk. The basement of the house extends to a spot almost paralleling the edge of the street curb which in turn is the outer edge of the sidewalk itself. It is probably five feet beneath the surface.

"We want to tunnel so that we just miss it. I should say with two men working in alternate four-hour shifts we can make it in no longer than seven days at the most."

He shifted his position, and his ruler traced a line from the house to the street.

"I will make an examination of the basement on Monday," he said, "but I have already talked with Townsend. It appears that the outlet from the house is a six-inch tile pipe. We will plan to use that as our focal point and follow it out to the sewer, but we will have to be extremely careful not to crack the pipe. We can't afford to interfere with the disposal from the house itself, or one of the tenants on the other floors will call a plumber.

"We will not be able to work from five o'clock in the morning until after everyone has left the premises. That will give us approximately eight or nine hours during the daytime. We can work after midnight for at least three to four hours but will have to be careful about making any noise. Townsend, of course, will be upstairs, and we are arranging an alarm system just in case."

"These others who live in the house," Marko said, "what of them? Suppose they do hear strange noises, do become suspicious?"

"We have protected ourselves by planting Townsend in the house," Blantz explained. "He has gone to considerable trouble to establish a close relationship with one of the girls who lives on the second floor. They are already lovers. She, of course, knows nothing of our plans, but she is completely under his influence and through her he will know if trouble should develop. There is only the other girl who is her roommate and the man who lives on the top floor. He will present no problem so long as we are careful and so long as Townsend is alert. We will take every precaution. Even the dirt we remove will be stored as it will be too dangerous to take it from the premises."

Marko lifted his eyes from the map and stared at the other man, blinking rapidly.

"The dirt we remove?" he said, a question in his voice. "No—no, I do no digging. That part is up to you. I supervise. I supply the materials and make the bomb. I plant the bomb. I detonate it at the proper time. That is all. And who is the man Townsend?"

"Townsend is one of my principal lieutenants in the Sons of Columbia," Blantz said. "Completely trustworthy, completely reliable."

Marko shrugged his thick shoulders.

"I should hope so," he said. "I have no great faith in these dedicated maniacs with their bizarre causes, but that is no concern of mine. Just so he is reliable—and follows orders. My orders."

Blantz looked at the fat man coldly and started to say something, but then thought better of it.

"So who will dig?" Marko asked.

"We have recruited volunteers from the membership," Blantz said. "Dedicated men—trustworthy men. You will not have to worry about them."

"I worry about everyone," Marko said. "They are not to know my name, not to know what I will do. It might even be best if they were to be left in the tunnel at the time...."

Blantz stared at his companion, his mouth suddenly dropping.

"Good God, man," he began, but the fat man waved his comment aside.

"Merely a suggestion," he said. "I have found it is never good to leave witnesses. They have a bad way of turning up when least expected. But have it your own way. I only hope that you can be sure ..."

"I am positive of these people," Blantz said. "They come from the hard core of our most trusted members. They are willing to sacrifice their lives."

"Which is exactly what I suggested they do," Marko finished for him. "But arrange it any way you wish. I have no interest in the politics of this matter. I am merely a professional hired to do a job of work. But there must be no repercussions. The work will be my responsibility; the results will be yours."

Blantz nodded and began to untack the map and take it from the drawing board.

"Townsend has a duplicate of this map," he said. "He has arranged for the proper tools and equipment; I suggest that following your initial visit, you stay away from the place as much as possible. The less traffic going in and out of the building, the better it will be. Here is your address in Washington. You are familiar with the city?"

Marko nodded.

"Yes, I am familiar with the city," he said.

Blantz finished rolling up the blueprint and reached for his hat.

"Well, check in with Townsend then, and if you should need anything, feel lonely or ..."

"I will need nothing and I am always lonely," Marko said coldly. "The only need I ever have is money, and money you have already given to me. Soon it will be on its way to a numbered account in a Swiss bank. The less I see of anyone and the less they see of me, the better for all of us."

The two men did not shake hands as they parted.

The fat man went directly to the airport where he boarded the

Washington plane. Blantz got his car from a Midtown parking lot and started out for Long Island. He was due to address a protest meeting being staged by a Nassau branch of the Sons of Columbia that same evening. The meeting was being held in an American Legion hall, donated by the latter organization as a patriotic gesture.

Blantz was expecting a pretty good turnout and it promised to be an interesting occasion. The meeting had been called to protest the announced arrival, early next month, of the Soviet Premier. At the same time, Blantz was keying his speech around America's continued participation in the United Nations, a participation which he was prepared to prove was inspired solely by certain highly placed officials who were following the Communist Party line.

A number of left-wing organizations had announced that they would be picketing the meeting and there would without doubt be quite a bit of action. But Blantz was not worried about the outcome. He would have a corps of his special Brown Shirt Elite on hand to see that the pickets got all and more than they came for.

Yes there would be a little action and without doubt Gordon Franklin Minor would read about it in the morning papers out in Texas and he would be pleased. He should be. Francis Blantz was putting his neck on the line, and Minor was merely putting up money. God knows he had plenty of that.

5

Marty Eden cocked her small dark head, and her mouth twisted into a wry smile. She lifted the slender-stemmed wineglass, said, "Skol." She sipped the sherry and then put the glass back on the table.

"It's silly," she said.

Paul Dabney watched her, his face serious.

"What's silly?"

"Us," Marty said. "Here we are, having dinner together the third time in a week, and we hardly even know each other. I don't know what in the world they would think of me back in Duluth."

Paul's face crinkled into a smile.

"This is Washington, not Duluth," he said. "Anyway, we really have known each other longer than a week, even if we hadn't formally met. After all, we've been living in the same house now for almost six months. We've been sleeping not more than thirty-five or forty feet from each other."

"Don't be vulgar," Marty said and laughed. "What would anyone think if they were to hear you? Anyway, I can't get over it. I've been in Washington now for over a year, and until you and that detective friend of yours stopped by and asked us all those questions—well, this is the first time I've had three dates in the same week, let alone with the same man. This is the loneliest town I've ever been in, and these have been the loneliest months."

"I know," Paul said. "It's been a lonely town for me, too. But I should think a girl like you, young, beautiful, talented …"

"Listen to the man! I really do believe you're giving me a line. Oh, of course I could have kept busy. There are a few creeps around that office where I work—but you know how it is. The nice ones are married and the others … well, unmarried available men in Washington leave a good deal to be desired. Or at least that's my …"

"I'm an unmarried, available man around Washington," Paul said smiling.

She looked up at him quickly and blushed.

"You're different," she said. "And I tell you, I don't quite know what I might have done if you hadn't sort of come along when you did."

Paul looked up, his eyes curious.

"Joan and I never did hit it off too well," Marty said. "It started as just one of those things—two can rent an apartment cheaper than one. Oh, I guess we got along all right, but in all honesty I can't say we found a lot in common. You'll probably think I am being vain, but I have always had the feeling that Joan resented my having dates, that in some odd way she was jealous of me. It isn't anything that she's ever said or done really, but somehow, every now and then, I have had a weird feeling that she really hates me."

"If you really feel that way," Paul said, "maybe you should think about changing roommates. For instance, there's me …"

"I'm serious," Marty said. "And now, since she seems to have completely fallen for this all-American hero who's taken over the first floor …"

"It happened sort of fast, didn't it?" Paul asked.

Marty looked thoughtful. "Almost too fast," she said at last. "Honestly, I just can't understand it. Oh, I know what Joan sees in him, what with his hot ol' Jag, his Ivy League clothes, and the rest of it. Undoubtedly all the money in the world and he's certainly giving her the rush act. But in all honesty, I just can't understand his type of guy falling for her. I'm not being catty, but she isn't exactly a glamor girl. Joan is just an average girl, neither awfully bright nor anything particularly unusual. There are thousands of us here in Washington and everywhere else. So   …"

"You are certainly not just an average girl," Paul said quickly. "I suspect you are very bright, and I may be just a doddering old fuddy-duddy, but when it comes to glamor …"

"Just listen to the man," Marty said. "Anyway, we are not talking about me. We're discussing my wayward roommate. What I'm saying is, the thing seems very strange. This Townsend character seems to have completely flipped for her. He's actually hinted that he'd be happy if I moved. God knows, if you hadn't come along and taken me out, I would have been walking the streets …"

"The District police don't approve of streetwalkers," Paul said.

"The man has a positively vulgar streak," Marty said. "Oh, well. But to get back to Joan and her flaming knight. As I say, it just doesn't figure. This guy is loaded, he …"

"Exactly what does he do, by the way?" Paul asked. "He never seems to leave the house, and his car is always in front when I leave and when I get home nights. Twice I've stopped by in the middle of the day to pick up something or other, and he was even home then."

"From what Joan says, he's mixed up with the Sons of Columbia. He's some sort of organizer or something. And even that is a little odd. He told her about it, but he was very careful to make her promise not to mention it to me or to anyone else. What sort of a job …?"

Paul Dabney looked up quickly. "Sons of Columbia?"

"Why, yes. Do you know what they are?"

"Do you?"

Marty shrugged. "Oh, I've heard of them. One of those weird fringe groups. Something like the John Birch Society, isn't it?" she asked.

"Not entirely," Paul said. "They make the John Birch Society look like a bunch of Socialists. They go beyond being just right-wing; they're out and out fascist. Professional patriots who have adopted their philosophy right out of *Mein Kampf*. Even go in for the brown shirts and the rest of the rigamarole. I must say I'm surprised that young Townsend is mixed up with them."

"Well, I don't really know how much he really is. From what Joan says, he has an independent income and actually doesn't really work for them on a regular basis. She just says that he told her he did organizing for them. Anyway, let's not talk anymore about either of them. Since they've suddenly discovered true love, or perhaps I should say sex, I'm finding both of them quite painful."

"Right," Paul said. "The hell with both of them. Let's talk about us. For instance, I have to finish some work tonight, so I'm not going to be able to do what I'd like to do, which is to take you to a show, or dancing, or just about anywhere you'd like to go. I'll drop you off at the house on my way back to the office, but how about tomorrow evening?"

Marty reached across the table and put her hand over his. She looked into his face, her eyes suddenly serious.

"Paul," she said. "Paul, I don't want to hurt your feelings or have you think I'm ungrateful or anything like that. But don't you think we're rushing things just a little bit? After all, we really have only known each other for a week. And here we are seeing each other almost every ...".

Dabney turned his hand over so that he was holding hers. "You said that this has been the loneliest six months of your life," he said. "Well, most all of my life has been lonely. And now, for the first time, I've found someone I really want to be with. No—I don't think we are seeing too much of each other. After all, that's how people get to really know one another." He stammered and suddenly stopped.

"Of course," he said at last, "If I'm taking up too much of your time ... if you would rather ...".

She quickly squeezed his hand and interrupted.

"You know I like being with you," she said. "It's only—well—like I said about Joan and that Townsend boy. Somehow or other, just suddenly rushing into things ...".

"We're not rushing into anything," Dabney said. "And I don't ever want to rush you into something. Certainly not something you wouldn't want. But it does seem silly, as long as we're each alone, each just going back to a sterile, vacant room ...".

"Consider the point as proved," Marty said and she laughed. "The argument is irrefutable. Tomorrow night it is, but there will be just one change. If my home were my own castle, instead of the love nest of my roommate and her amorata, I would invite you in for a home-cooked meal. As it is, I shall invite myself to your apartment, but I'm bringing the food and I'm doing the cooking. Now what will it be? Steak? Lamb chops? Veal scallopini? You name it and I'll cook it."

"It sounds great," Paul said. "I'll even do the dirty dishes before I go to bed tonight so that you'll have a spotless laboratory in which to create. And make it whatever you wish. I like to be surprised."

"You'll probably be surprised if you don't die of indigestion," she said. "And now, if you really must get back to work, we'd better take off. But don't drop me at the house. I think I'll take in a movie and give the lovebirds a clear field for a couple of more hours."

"Good God, can't they go downstairs to his apartment?" Paul asked. Marty shook her head.

"Seems some fellow members of Townsend's Sons of Columbia are using his place these few days to do a little party work," Marty said. "Undoubtedly conspiring to overthrow the Government and set up a dictatorship or a monarchy."

"Undoubtedly," Paul agreed, taking her arm and steering her out to the sidewalk and the cab waiting at the curb.

CHAPTER FOUR

1

Jerry Townsend had moved into the first-floor apartment of the house on K Street on Wednesday morning, May ninth. He arrived in the XKE and took a large suitcase, a briefcase, two airplane zipper bags, and a portable Hermes typewriter out of the storage space and carried them into the house.

An hour after he had installed himself, a half-ton black delivery truck, with no legend on its sides, drove up and stopped. The driver and a leather-jacketed man sitting next to him alighted. They carried a large steamer trunk into the house. This was followed by two surplus canvas army bags, some four feet square. They were extremely heavy and the men had difficulty horsing them up the stairs and into the hallway.

At two o'clock a representative of the real-estate company who handled the building for its absentee owner arrived and Townsend signed a sublease on the apartment for one year. The man from the real-estate company waited until two friends of Mrs. Margulies showed up and moved the things she had packed into a station wagon. They carried her trunk and several cartons which she wished stored temporarily down into the basement, and the man from the real-estate firm explained to Townsend that the basement held several storage bins in case he might have something he wished to put downstairs.

"Used to keep a janitor for the building," he said, "but we found it wasn't really necessary. Changed over to automatic gas heat and everything these days is automatic. There's a cleaning woman comes in once a week and she does the stairs and hallways, and of course the trash is collected regularly.

"Use the incinerator for your garbage, but try not to toss any bottles or cans into it. It fires up automatically; a man comes in the first of every month to clean out the ashes. Does it from outside. There's a bit of garden out in back, and you, as the first-floor tenant, have exclusive rights to it. The other tenants all have keys to the outside door and we try to keep it locked at all times. Basement door is kept locked also, but I'll show you where the key is hung in case you have to go downstairs for anything. You can mail your check in the first of each month. Anything you want, just let us know."

He left a card and was gone.

Jerry waited for a half hour or so, and then he went out to the hallway outside the front door and rang the bells first of the second-floor apartment and then the third. No one answered. Returning he found the key to the basement where it was hanging next to the cellar door, at the far end of the first-floor hallway. The light switch was at the top of the stairs.

He took his time and made a thorough investigation of the basement. The house had originally been heated with coal, and the coal bin had now been made into storage lockers and was at the front of the building. The back part held what had at one time been a one-room apartment. There was a small bath attached to it, but the fixtures had been removed. Two windows which opened high in the wall onto the yard were covered by a heavy wire mesh screen as well as iron bars. Dirt and cobwebs made them all but opaque.

At four o'clock the man from the telephone company arrived and changed over the phone. He was followed in rapid succession by the meter reader from the gas company and a man from the electric company.

Jerry substituted a calling card in the slot over the doorbell, removing Mrs. Margulies' name. By five o'clock he was firmly in possession.

Looking at his wristwatch, he frowned.

Joan Harrington would be arriving home from work within forty-five minutes.

Thinking about her, his mouth went sour and he muttered under his breath.

He had known her for a little over two weeks. He had been sleeping with her for a week. She had been a virgin on the initial occasion. She was completely inept and had improved not the slightest since her first contact with him. It had been not only the easiest seduction he had ever made—it had been the least attractive.

He was unable to understand how a girl who so obviously suffered, both physically and emotionally, while undergoing the act of love, should have such an overpowering desire to repeat the process.

She undoubtedly believed that she was pleasing him, in spite of her own private agony. He really must be a superb actor. Well, it wouldn't have to go on too much longer. And if she was so enchanted by pain, he'd make quite sure that she had her fill of it before he was through with her.

It was really too damned bad it had had to be the blonde instead of the little brunette. Although Jerry had never really enjoyed sex, with her it might have been different.

Tonight in any case, he would be free of the necessity to perform. Tonight Blantz was arriving and he would have to make his excuses to the girl upstairs.

It would be a real pleasure at last to get down to the final planning. It would be a pleasure to work with the fat man. Francis Blantz was all right, of course, as far as he went. But the trouble with Blantz was that the man was not really equipped for the work he was doing. Too soft. Too cautious. He had handled the business about the old lady all right, of course. Getting her out of the apartment and all that. But he had been foolish about the others in the building. It had been Blantz's idea that he make that girl upstairs, ingratiate himself with her so he would have free access to their apartment and be able to keep an eye on them.

Jerry was sure they would cause no trouble at all. As to the character on the top floor, hell he didn't look as though he knew he was alive. They could hold a lynching party in the hallways and he wouldn't know what was going on.

That detective, of course, had been something else. Why he should have become interested, Townsend couldn't guess. Just nosey, like all cops, very likely.

But the woman had moved, and of course the persecutions would stop and everyone would forget about it. In any case, in another three weeks, plus a few days, what was going to happen would be so big, so completely and overwhelmingly significant, that there wouldn't be a cop in the entire country who would be worrying about anything as simple as a single isolated crime, no matter how fantastic or terrible that crime might be. In fact, if things went off according to schedule …

The sound of the doorbell interrupted his thoughts.

2

Colonel Edwin D. Hauser, attached to Secret Service, was speaking, and from the tone of his voice there was no question that he was annoyed.

"Actually," he said, "it is not our affair. Our duties start and end with protecting the body of the Chief Executive. But we have been called in on this and we will cooperate."

The man from State shrugged his shoulders. "It's no one's affair and everyone's," he said. "So far as State is concerned, we may disagree on the techniques used but we are inclined to go along on the overall plan, since we feel the meeting will do a great deal to ease tensions."

Carter, the FBI man, in whose office the discussion was taking place, felt that things were getting a little out of hand. "The possible advantages or disadvantages, the diplomatic significance of the meeting is not under discussion," he said coldly. "We are here to discuss security measures."

Chief Deputy Inspector Cordovan of the New York Police realized it was time he took a part in the proceedings. Most of the responsibility, at least during those first couple of days of the Premier's visit to the UN, would rest with him.

"We are arranging that Kennedy Airport be completely closed off for two hours before and after the arrival of the Russians," he said. "Neither private nor commercial planes will be allowed to land, and all air traffic will be diverted to LaGuardia, Newark, or other appropriate points. The route into Manhattan from the airport is being kept secret. Even the chauffeurs driving the limousines will not receive their instructions until they are ready to start. The police escort will be the largest ever used. We are going to see to it that nothing can possibly happen. After all, New York is hardly Dallas."

Carter, who happened to be a Texan, looked up angrily. "New York

City's crime rate is a disgrace to the nation," he began, but Colonel Hauser quickly interrupted, sensing what was about to come.

"I feel confident the New York Police Department will do a first-class job," he said. "The fact that there will be no advance publicity about plans up until the time of the arrival of the party in Washington should be of much assistance. Certainly there is little danger of anything taking place until the party arrives at Union Station in this city. As I understand it, a pilot train will precede the special train carrying the Premier. What worries us is the motorcade from Union Station to the White House. Of course, were the President to meet the Premier at the station and ride down Pennsylvania Avenue with him, it would be a good deal more desirable. In that case, at least both men would be in equal jeopardy ..."

But he wasn't allowed to continue.

Brigadier General Harry Measure was on his feet and his face was choleric.

"By God, sir," he yelled, "that is the most unpatriotic damned suggestion I have ever heard! I am not sure but what it is out-and-out treason. Are you suggesting that you think it would be a good idea for the President of these United States to be the subject of an assassination attempt?"

"My dear man, please control yourself."

The State Department representative raised his hands in protest. "You completely fail to understand the issue. You must realize the delicacy of the situation, the possible implications. Why, should the Russian Premier be assassinated while an honored visitor in this country, God forbid"—The blood rushed again to the General's face—"it could precipitate a shooting war between our countries. And don't think a lot of people wouldn't like that, including certain of your compatriots in the Pentagon. The Chinese would like nothing better. So would certain elements in Russia, as well as some of our own lunatic fringe. The Birchers ..."

The general, whose younger brother was a guiding spirit in the society, had had enough. He stalked from the room. He would damned well see his Senator. It was time there was another full-scale investigation into the State Department. If they were harboring obvious Communists ...

Carter, from FBI, ignored the entire interruption. "We all understand the danger inherent in an incident," he said. "I can assure you gentlemen that once the Premier and his party reach Washington, every precaution will be taken. Even now, almost a month ahead of time, we have Union Station under twenty-four-hour surveillance. We have checked every single building along the route the motorcade will travel. On the day of the parade from the railway depot to the White House, there will be a man stationed every three feet on both sides of the street. Some will be District police, others are being drafted from several security agencies.

"There will be men stationed on rooftops along the entire route. Helicopters will hover directly over the motorcade itself."

Colonel Hauser nodded and spoke up. "Secret Service will supply exactly the same guards to ride in the Premier's limousine that they would supply a Presidential party," he said. "This is being done at the request of the President himself. The people will be able to see the Premier but he will be protected by the plastic dome. And it will take a lot more than the average rifle bullet to penetrate that dome."

He picked up a long pointer from the table and began tracing the route.

"The party will leave the station by a special ramp on First Street. They will proceed north as far as K Street, where they will take a left-hand turn. They will then proceed due west on K until they reach Sixth Street, where they turn south. Sixth will be lined by a good many people, but not until the party turns into Pennsylvania Avenue will you find the bulk of the sightseers.

"Pennsylvania will be lined a dozen deep, we expect, and it is here we may very possibly run into an incident if there is to be one.

"Naturally we cannot search everybody lining the sidewalks. But plainclothesmen, FBI agents, Secret Service personnel, and local police officers will be mingling with the crowd. Known agitators and troublemakers will be weeded out as soon as they are spotted. We are going to pay special attention to the pickets."

When the meeting ended, the man from State lingered on for a few minutes to speak with Carter. He realized that the general would undoubtedly lodge a personal complaint against him and that sooner or later the FBI would be asked to reinvestigate his background. It wouldn't hurt to have a friend at court.

"The military mentality is fantastic," the man from State said. "Can't seem to grasp the most fundamental points. They don't seem to realize that we are duty bound to give every possible protection to our Communist guests. The most unpatriotic thing we could possibly do would be to place them in a position of jeopardy."

"My department doesn't operate at the policy-making level," Carter said coldly. "All I know is that we have been ordered to see that nothing happens to the Premier while he is in this country, and we are going to follow orders."

The man from State, realizing he had a slightly unsympathetic audience, retrieved his hat and muttered a goodbye and left. One trouble with a democracy, he reflected, was the rather shoddy caliber of intellect of the people who were drafted to serve their government. At least in State they formed the policy, and, even if they missed once in a while, they were not forced to implement someone else's mistakes.

3

The digging started in the basement of the house on K Street shortly after ten o'clock on Thursday morning, May tenth. At twenty minutes to ten, the two men arrived. They looked enough alike to be brothers. In their early thirties, they were big, blond men, with broad shoulders and cold, rather blank, pale-blue eyes.

They were not related, had not in fact ever seen each other until two days before.

The slightly taller one, Karl Detrie, was a steelworker from Pittsburgh, a health food faddist, a onetime semipro football player, and an ardent racist. He hated all colored people, but he also hated Jews, Catholics (his mother and father had been Catholic), Puerto Ricans, Italians, and in fact members of all minority groups. He had been a member of the National Guard, but was court-martialed out after he had beaten up a second lieutenant who happened to be of Spanish descent.

The army had refused to take him, and so because of his passion for wearing uniforms he had been attracted to the Sons of Columbia.

Karl had an IQ of around eighty-five. He neither drank nor smoked and was an inveterate reader of comic books. When he wasn't reading comic books, he watched television.

During the drive to the house on K Street, Karl hadn't shown the slightest curiosity as to where the house was or even as to its city. All he knew was that the leader of his group had told him there was a job to do, and he was prepared to do it. When the job was done, he would be driven back to Pittsburgh and receive his reward: he would be given a full storm trooper's uniform. There would even be a ceremonial sword for special occasions.

The man who had picked Karl Detrie up in Pittsburgh and had driven him to Washington was the other one who would be doing the digging.

Despite their resemblance, Robert Marschalk was so different from Karl Detrie that the two could have been spawned on separate planets.

Reform school graduate, ex-con (auto theft, forgery, statutory rape) Marschalk had been attracted to the Sons of Columbia because he was sure the organization would give him a cover for certain illegal activities: he had an unerring instinct about organizations.

He had neither any interest in the political and economical philosophies of the organization nor any ambition to be a super-patriot, or in fact any kind of patriot.

Marschalk made rapid progress in the ranks of the Sons, largely because he was intelligent, capable of hard work when necessary, and perfectly willing to volunteer for difficult and dangerous tasks if by so doing he would advance his standing in the organization. Having no convictions of his own, he found it easy to pay lip service to those of others.

Marschalk soon came to the attention of Francis Blantz, the nominal leader. The moment they met each other, each recognized the true character of the other man.

Marschalk considered Blantz essentially an opportunist who was using the organization in order to gain personal power and to line his own pockets. Blantz in turn was convinced that Marschalk was only in the movement for what he personally could get out of it.

Nevertheless, Marschalk was a perfect man for the house on K Street. For the hundred dollars a day and expenses he was promised, he would follow directions, work like a horse, and keep his mouth shut. Like Detrie, he did not have to know the full details of the plan. Should he figure it all out afterward, assuming he was around to do so, it really wouldn't matter. He would be in no position to do anything about it. In fact, he would be only too anxious to forget any part he played in the scheme of things.

It took several hours, on that first day, for the two men to penetrate the heavy concrete wall at the back of the old coal storage room which separated the basement of the house from the dirt on the street side.

They didn't dare use air hammers as they would have made too much noise: as it was, Townsend kept his hi-fi stereo going full blast to cover the sounds made as they broke the large hole in the concrete. Halfway through the job, Marschalk wiped the perspiration from his forehead and went upstairs.

"It's a sustaining wall," he explained. "We are going to have to shore it up. Otherwise, the whole damned front of the house is going to start to cave in. Means you are going to have to get me some timbers. A couple of four by sixes, at least eight feet long. Another four by six to go over the top of them for the sill to rest on."

Townsend shook his head.

"Isn't there anything down in the basement that will do?"

"Nothing," Marschalk said.

"Well, it's too late today to try to bring in anything. I don't want to take a chance on having one of the other tenants arrive as the material is being moved in. Perhaps it would be best if you handle it Monday morning. Rent a small pickup truck and buy the stuff at a lumberyard. Try to get it here between ten and noon. Call from nearby just before you are ready to deliver, just in case."

Marschalk nodded. "We won't go any further for the time being then," he said. "You better go down and talk to that cretin I'm working with. Have him take the debris to the back of the basement and get it out of the way. I'll change my clothes and clean up. You sure you want me to pick up the truck and the materials, instead of doing it yourself?"

Townsend shrugged and spoke over his shoulder.

"I'm in charge of the job at this end," he said. "If I tell you to go out and get the stuff, then all you have to do is follow instructions."

"Sure, boss," Marschalk said, his tone sarcastic. "Only be sure and get up the money for the pickup truck and the lumber."

Marschalk cleaned up in Townsend's bathroom and changed into his street clothes. A few minutes later the cab he had ordered arrived and he left.

Detrie was to spend his entire time at the apartment, sharing a pair of twin beds in the back bedroom with Jerry. Blantz was afraid that, because of his innate stupidity, Detrie might say the wrong thing to the wrong person if left free in the city.

Detrie was expendable: when the job was over, plans had been made for his disposal. He would have served his purpose.

Townsend found the arrangements to his liking. Having Detrie as his house guest for a couple of weeks gave him a perfect excuse not to entertain the Harrington girl in his apartment. He could maintain his privacy and spend only what time might be necessary in the girl's quarters on the second floor.

Blantz had not taken young Townsend into his confidence so far as the ultimate disposal of Detrie was concerned. It hadn't been necessary. Blantz understood the youth's mentality and had realized from the very beginning that Townsend was convinced that once the deed they conspired to commit had been accomplished, he, Townsend, would be in the clear.

It wasn't that Townsend was too stupid or dull to realize that the crime might be traced to him; in fact it was almost sure to be. No, Townsend, the dedicated fanatic, was firmly convinced that in the long run he would be considered a hero. He fully realized that he might also be a martyr, but he was prepared to take that risk.

But he was not anxious to play the martyr role, and so he had made his plans carefully. He would disappear for a while, for weeks or months as the case may be. But once the role he had played was fully understood, there could be no question as to the right or wrong of what he had done. After all, a soldier is always justified in killing the enemy. And if the soldier must take a certain personal risk, it merely means that he is that much more a hero.

In Townsend's mind, the real inconvenience lay in the fact that for the present he must work undercover. The day would come, however, when he would be able to come out in the open and then the country, the entire world, would know him for what he was: the man who had sparked the incident that would lead to the termination of the international Communist conspiracy.

The honor justified any personal chances he must take, justified any deed which he must perform.

Marschalk took the taxi only as far as the lot where he had parked his car. He had dropped Detrie at the house on K Street that morning, but had not thought it advisable to leave his automobile in the vicinity. He had no idea as yet as to why he had been enlisted for the work in the basement, but he was sure of one thing. It was illegal. And since the plates on his car were legitimate and in his own name, he was cautious.

Blantz had only told him that he was to dig a tunnel. Nothing else. But when he had dropped off Detrie, he had carefully scouted the immediate neighborhood. Later he had circled the block, looking for a bank or a jewelry store but had found none. After all, a tunnel suggested a robbery, and yet there was nothing in the neighborhood that would justify so elaborate a plan.

It then occurred to him that perhaps this was a scheme to steal papers or documents from a foreign embassy, but there was no building adjacent to the K Street house that would possibly have housed an embassy.

Marschalk was baffled. But he wasn't worried. He knew that sooner or later he would figure it out. It was just possible that the tunnel was being dug so that the Sons of Columbia could secretly store arms or something of the sort. That theory didn't make too much sense either, though. The organization apparently had plenty of money in back of it—not Blantz's money certainly—and it would hardly have used the basement under a rented apartment for such a purpose. On the other hand, who could tell what a lot of nuts might do?

Well, it really didn't matter. He'd know sooner or later. In the meantime, he would return to the hotel in Alexandria where he had taken a room. He had the next forty-eight hours free and he might as well make good use of them.

That bellboy who took his bags upstairs had seemed a smart cookie. He'd know where the action was.

CHAPTER FIVE

1

The first place, the room out of which he would eventually operate and where he would be spending a few hours each night while he slept, was in a shoddy, rundown hotel not far from the railway station. Blantz had found it for the fat man, made the reservation, and paid three weeks' rent in advance.

It hadn't been easy. Marko had been very definite about its qualifications.

"Under no conditions," he had said, "can it be more than six blocks away from the house on K Street. This is vital. And it must be at least one block from the house. This too is of absolute necessity. There must be no large steel structures between the two locations. Small buildings are all right. But nothing huge.

"There must be a telephone in the room. I could, of course, have a private phone installed, but that would look suspicious, especially in a second-class hotel. Police would suspect bookmaking. Yes, there must be a hotel switchboard and a telephone in the room. It must be the sort of place where people mind their own business. I must have privacy. Comfort is desirable, but not of first importance.

"The room must be as high up as possible. At least four or five stories above the street. There must be no power stations in the immediate vicinity. You will make those arrangements, and I will take care of the second place."

"If it would help," Blantz had said, "I could probably find that for you as well."

Marko smiled.

"Only you are to know where the hotel room is," he had said. "And only I am to know where the other place is. Any contact I have will be at the house on K Street. No one, no one at all, is to come to the hotel or telephone me there."

"You tell me you don't drive," Blantz said. "We can supply you with a car and chauffeur if you wish."

Marko shook his head. "I take buses and streetcars and trains. I rarely use private automobiles or taxis. A public conveyance is always the best and safest. Where there are dozens of witnesses, there are no witnesses."

And so Blantz had found him the hotel room, and Marko had found the second place himself. He had visited the house on K Street Sunday, when he arrived in town, and finding only Townsend and Detrie there, had spoken privately with Jerry for a few minutes, learning about the delay in the tunneling. He shrugged his shoulders; Blantz would be there the following day and the affair was in his hands. He had left almost at once.

Sunday was a perfect day for his purposes. Instead of returning to the hotel, he took a Greyhound bus to Baltimore, arriving shortly before noon. He checked into a downtown hotel under an assumed name, registering himself as Professor Igor Ramnoff of Chicago. As soon as the bellboy had carried his worn pigskin valise up to the room, opened the window a crack and received his tip, Marko found the Yellow Pages of the phone book and started making his calls.

He called only those real-estate agents who had display ads in the book, figuring they would be the most enterprising and so likely would be open on Sundays.

He was very precise concerning his needs.

"A small, private, furnished house. I must have it for one month and am willing to pay accordingly. It must be in a quiet neighborhood away from the noise of passing traffic. There must be public transportation within a reasonable distance as I do not drive a car. Not too far from a shopping district where I may obtain simple supplies."

He explained that he was a visiting professor, doing special work at the university for one month. He didn't explain which university and no one thought to ask. He hinted that the work was highly sensitive and indicated that the Federal Government was behind the project. He said that he was prepared to pay in advance, but he must have access to the place at once.

He offered to give references, but no one bothered to ask what they were.

In all he called six real-estate firms. Three of them were unable to help him at all; one had a place which they were prepared to show him that afternoon; and the two others called back within minutes, also to make an appointment to show him properties.

He took the second place he saw and paid for it in cash. It was a small, five-room house in a residential section off Druid Hill Park. The house was on a hundred by hundred and twenty-five foot lot, surrounded by lawns and shrubbery which gave it complete privacy. It was comfortably furnished and the owners were in Europe. There was a garage.

Marko could move in the following day. The real-estate people would see that the electricity and gas were turned on and would take care of other essential details. If he wished, they would find a cleaning woman for him.

He thanked them, but said not to bother. He would hire a service. He didn't want anyone bothering him while he was working on his project.

They gave him the key and he returned to Washington, stopping back at the Baltimore hotel only long enough to pick up the pigskin bag and check out.

On Monday morning, he again traveled to Baltimore, this time leaving the pigskin bag in the hotel near Washington's Union Station, and carrying a large airplane suitcase. He handled the suitcase with the utmost care, carrying it on his lap at all times.

This time he violated his own rule. He took a cab from the hotel to

Dulles Airport and dismissed the driver. He waited for a half hour and then found a second cab and took it to Baltimore. He got off at a hotel in midtown and again waited for a few minutes and finally took a third cab to the house off Druid Hill Park.

Each time he made a special request that the driver be very careful of jarring him. He explained that the suitcase held several pieces of priceless porcelain.

What the suitcase held was twenty-four, sixteen-ounce flasks of pure nitroglycerin, carefully wrapped in cotton batting which in turn was encased in corrugated cardboard.

The representative from the real-estate firm was just leaving as he arrived. He told him that everything was in readiness and that the man from the electric company had just left. He wished to know if the professor wished him to arrange to have the telephone put in his name temporarily. It had been discontinued during the absence of the owners.

Marko explained that because of the concentration needed for his work, he didn't care to be bothered with the phone. If he found it necessary to make calls, he would go to the drugstore a couple of blocks away. The real-estate man departed after the fat man further explained that the rest of his luggage would be arriving by express the following day.

He carefully deposited the suitcase under the bed in the master bedroom and then left the house. He found a hardware store several blocks away and purchased a pair of heavy hinged hasps, a dozen long bolts and nuts, and a pair of Yale padlocks. Back at the bungalow, he at once bolted one of the hasps to the inside of the back door and snapped on the lock. He repeated the process on the outside of the front door. He wanted to be sure that no one from the real-estate firm could possibly enter the place.

Later he checked every window to make sure it was secure.

By noontime he was back downtown, beginning the shopping tour which would consume most of his time for the next three days.

His initial purchase was made in a shop that specialized in hi-fi components, tape recorders, and general electronic equipment. He bought two citizens band transistor radios that operated off dry cell batteries. Later there would be further purchases, but of much more sophisticated electronic devices.

2

Robert Marschalk had an exhausting weekend. His hunch about the bellhop had been only too right. He certainly had known where the action was. The action consisted of a seventeen-year-old girl. They never left the hotel room.

Between the two of them they killed three quarts of Bourbon, drinking it straight with water chasers. Several times they sent down to room service for sandwiches and coffee, but they didn't bother with the coffee. The girl, whose name was Renee, or at least that is what she told Marschalk, left after midnight Sunday—fresh as a daisy. Dripping wet, she didn't weigh in at more than a hundred pounds. Yet she had performed the burden of the work during their sexual exercises and taught Marschalk things that even he hadn't known about the subtleties of lovemaking.

She departed carrying a hundred dollars in cash over and above what she arrived with, a dozen sets of teeth marks on her neck and back, a few casual black and blue marks, and with absolutely no feeling of either affection or respect for her partner in lust.

Marschalk himself left the hotel at eight o'clock on Monday morning. He was thankful that he would not be returning to the house on K Street and resuming digging operations for at least a few hours. His back felt as though it was broken; he was suffering from a severe case of morning sickness, and he had the shakes. The two double bromos hadn't helped much.

He wasn't thinking too clearly.

If Marschalk had been himself, he wouldn't have made the mistakes.

The first was in going to the U-Drive-It Company to arrange for the vehicle. He should have remembered that they would want to see his driving license before releasing the truck, whereas any of a dozen third-rate outfits would have been happy to take his money and ask no questions.

But Marschalk had passed them up and gone directly to the U-Drive-It people after checking the Yellow Pages of the phone book.

His second mistake was in showing them his legitimate driving license. After all, he had a second one, made out to a false name and address, in a secret compartment of his wallet. It was to be used for occasions exactly like the present one—or in case he ever was stopped in a hot car. It had also proved useful once or twice in establishing identity when he was cashing a bad check.

Later, driving away with the rented pickup truck, he cursed himself for a fool, but shrugged it off. It probably wouldn't make any difference in the long run.

He had told the clerk at the U-Drive-It place that he would only be needing the truck for one day. He'd left a deposit and that was that.

The lumberyard told him the four by sixes came in sixteen-foot lengths and offered to saw them in two to make it easier for him to carry them. Normally he would have waited and had them do it, but the big power saw was being used, and it would take a half hour before they could accommodate him. So he merely purchased two pieces, each sixteen feet long, and put them in the pickup. They extended out several feet, and he tied them down so that they were secure.

As he was leaving the yard, the foreman yelled something after him, but Marschalk was anxious to get to a drugstore for something for his headache, and so he didn't hear the foreman's warning to tie red rags on the end of the planks.

It wasn't until he had turned into K Street that a passing patrol car spotted him and pulled him to the curb. Even then, had he been feeling right, he would have been able to talk himself out of it. As it was, he was surly and ended up with a ticket for the minor infraction. The patrolman naturally wrote down not only the license number on the rented truck but that on his driver's license as well.

He forgot about making the telephone call to Townsend to warn him of his arrival, but it really wasn't necessary. The other tenants had left the building by the time he pulled up in front of it at half-past ten.

The planks were too long to carry in, and so he had to get the handsaw from the basement and cut them in two on the street. Detrie helped him carry them into the basement, and, while they were taking the last one down the cellar stairway, Francis Blantz arrived.

Blantz, seeing the U-Drive-It truck in front of the place, was furious. He stopped at the first floor only long enough to talk for a moment with Townsend and find out what was going on, before heading for the cellar. He wanted Marschalk to get rid of the truck at once. The less activity observed around the house on K Street, the better for everyone.

3

The plane was leaving at four-thirty and the limousine would get her to the airport at four-fifteen, so that there was no need to worry about a thing. It would be the first time she had ever flown, but she was not the slightest bit frightened. She looked forward to it as a new experience.

It was hard to believe that she would be having dinner in San Francisco this very evening. Of course there was the time difference, but still and all, the jet would make the journey faster than it used to take her to get from Washington to Cape May, where she spent her summer vacations.

There would be a day's layover in San Francisco and then she would board the liner for Hawaii. Twenty-four hours was just about long enough to spend in a strange city. It had been very kind of Mr. Clarence, her ex-employer, to have written his sister to expect her.

"Can't have you just arriving in a strange city with nothing to do for a whole day," he had said. "Alice will be only too happy to show you the sights. She loves nothing better than getting a visitor in tow and showing off the town."

Carolyn Margulies had protested, but she had been secretly pleased and gratified. It really was going to be nice to be met at the airport even if it was by a stranger. So there had been an exchange of wires, and the arrangements completed.

Her luggage, aside from the small airline suitcase she was to carry with her, had been sent ahead, and she had already notified the hotel clerk that she would be checking out. The checkout time was noon, but they had been most considerate. They knew when the limousine was picking her up and had told her that she could use the room until she was ready to leave.

Everything had been taken care of. Last goodbyes had been said, and Mrs. Margulies found herself with time on her hands. And then she remembered about the key and about Joe's picture, packed away in the trunk in the basement of the house on K Street.

Had it been only the key, she would probably have mailed it to the managers of the building. But she did want that picture, and so at ten o'clock on Monday morning she decided that the walk would probably do her good.

Before leaving the hotel, she took the key out of her bag and attached one of her calling cards to it, using a bent paper clip. On the back of the card she wrote: "Key for first-floor apartment."

She noticed the U-Haul-It truck parked in front of the house, but she saw no one as she climbed the front steps and reached the door. She took the key from her bag and opened the front door.

Passing down the hallway, she thought she heard footsteps in her old apartment and for a second hesitated, but then continued on. The new tenant was probably home, but there really was no point in disturbing him. She would just leave the key on the small table in the hallway where it would be discovered sooner or later. After all, it was an extra key, and Mr. Townsend already had his own.

She was surprised when she reached the end of the hallway and put her hand up to where the cellar door key usually hung from the hook next to the jamb. The key was not there.

She frowned, quite unconsciously, and shook her head. Someone must have failed to replace it. For a second she hesitated, and then started to turn away. It was a shame; she really had wanted those snapshots of Joe.

It suddenly occurred to her that if someone had used the key and failed to put it back, they had very likely left the door unlocked. She smiled and turned back, reaching for the knob. She was right, of course. The door had been left unlocked.

As she opened the door, she noticed the light at the bottom of the steps, and heard voices coming up from below. That was why the key had not been in its usual position; someone was in the basement. So much the better—should there be any difficulty in getting at her trunk, there would be help available.

She felt her way down the stairs and, having reached the bottom, turned and started for the storage bin at the front where she knew they had put her trunk. She was dimly conscious that the hall was very dirty and that there was a trail of mud on the floor.

The light was on in the storage bin, and she realized that several people were in the room, talking. A moment later she entered the area and then stopped, her mouth half opened in surprise.

Two men, young blond giants, one stripped naked to the waist, were doing something with a long piece of timber. A third man, middle-aged, well-dressed, and smoking a cigarette, leaned against the wall, watching them.

Her eyes went with horror to the great gaping hole in the cement wall at the end of the storage bin. And then she saw her trunk, pulled to one side and lying at an odd angle against the wall. Someone had dropped a heavy piece of concrete on it and the top was split open, exposing its contents.

At this moment the man leaning against the wall, smoking the cigarette, became aware of her, and the two young giants froze in their tracks as they saw her standing in the doorway.

Indignantly, she pointed to the violated trunk.

"That," she said, "*that* is my trunk!"

For the space of several heartbeats, there was a dead silence. It was Robert Marschalk who was the first to respond—still suffering from his hangover.

"And just who are you?" he asked.

She swung around and glared at him.

"I am Mrs. Margulies," she said in a clear, precise voice. "Mrs. Carolyn Margulies and I live on the first floor. Or at least I did live there until last week. But that is beside the point. Who dropped that slab of stone on my trunk? What are you doing here in the first place, and what right do you have to move …?"

Marschalk started to say something, still holding the timber, but Francis Blantz had suddenly come to.

It was the worst of possible luck, but there was still a chance to save things if he thought fast enough. But he must do something and quickly.

He remembered that young Townsend had told him that she was leaving this week for Hawaii. As he recalled, she was supposed to leave this very afternoon. If he could only solve the immediate situation, she would be off and gone and there would be no harm done. Perhaps, months later, she might remember and put two and two together, but that was not the problem at the moment.

The thing was to get rid of her.

His voice was soft and apologetic. "I am sorry," he said, "but you see, there has been an accident. The wall suddenly caved in and a piece of it must have landed on your trunk and smashed it. We have been called in to replace the damage, and these men right now are making the needed repairs. I've been told by the owners to inform the tenants—and of course you as a former tenant—that the owners are prepared and happy to compensate anyone for any possible damage."

He noticed as he ceased speaking that her face had suddenly lost its look of anger. She was staring at him in an odd fashion, and he assumed she was still suffering from surprise. He continued talking.

"Unfortunately," he said, "until we get this wall shored up, there is a certain danger in being down here. That is why the firm has sent me to supervise the job personally. You can, of course, make an inspection of your property, but I would strongly suggest that you postpone it for the time being."

He looked over at the trunk.

"Undoubtedly some damage," he said, "but believe me it will be made good. I don't wish to rush you, but I really do suggest you return later after we've had a chance to make the area safe. You may rest assured we will remove the trunk to another part of the basement, cover it with canvas, and take every precaution to see that there is no further damage."

Even as he had finished his sentence, he observed that the woman was slowly backing out of the room. He saw that her face had gone dead pale, and that she was shaking badly.

Blantz congratulated himself on his fast thinking. Hell, she wasn't even worrying about the broken trunk anymore. He really must be pretty good. The story about the danger of the room collapsing had really reached her. Scared her stiff. She couldn't wait to get out of the place. Yes, he'd handled it perfectly.

By now she had reached the hallway, and wordlessly she turned and darted for the stairway. Her anxiety to leave the scene was almost comical.

It wasn't until she had run up the stairs and was in the hallway leading to the front door that Carolyn Margulies fully realized what it was that had so completely shocked and frightened her. At first, when he had begun to speak, it had only been a sort of vague, unconscious thing. A subtle sense of fear, of remembrance.

She had moved because of sheer instinct. Backed up, turned, and run up the stairs. But now she knew. Knew definitely and for sure.

She had to get to a phone. As fast as possible.

In her excitement, she hadn't realized that the door to her left, in front of her, had suddenly opened, and it wasn't until she ran full tilt into the man emerging that she realized that the youth who had subleased her apartment was in the process of leaving his new quarters.

They pulled apart and Townsend recognized her.

She still hadn't regained her breath, and so she acted rather than spoke. Without a second thought, she grabbed him by the right arm and literally pulled him back into the apartment, slamming the door after them.

He stood staring at her and at last she was able to gasp out a few words.

"A phone," she said. "I must use the phone!"

Townsend shook his head to clear it. It wasn't making any sense at all. What in the hell was the woman doing here?

"He's here," she said. "Don't you understand? He's here! Right in this very building. Now. Down in the basement! I would recognize that voice anywhere."

She started toward the bedroom where the telephone had been installed when she was a tenant.

"I must call the police at once," she said.

Jerry Townsend still didn't have the faintest idea of what it was all about. But two things had suddenly alerted him to danger. She had said something about the basement, and now she was saying something about calling the police.

His hand reached for her arm, as though to steady her.

"My dear Mrs. Margulies," he said. "Please. Please calm yourself. Tell me just what has happened. What man is in the basement and how ...?"

"The man who telephoned me," she said, turning back to him. The fear was leaving her slightly. After all, she was no longer alone. There was this tall, handsome youth with her, and there would soon be help on the way.

"Downstairs—I was down there to see about my trunk and he was there. There were three of them and they were doing something to the wall of the basement. Tearing it apart it seems. Anyway, I asked what it was all about and he started talking. I would have recognized that voice anywhere. It was the voice of that filthy beast who made those vile telephone calls. I cannot possibly be mistaken. I don't know who he is or what he's doing in our basement, but there is no doubt about it at all."

She stopped talking and swayed slightly. Townsend quickly steered her to a small upholstered armchair.

"You must try to control yourself," he said. "Now just sit quietly and then tell me all about it. How you happened to be here, what you were doing in the basement...."

She looked up at him, her face pale and fatigued.

"But we should call the police at once," she said. "Call them while the man is still downstairs. Any moment now he might ..."

He smiled at her gently. "Yes," he said, "of course you are right. But you stay right where you are. I'll go in and make the call. You just take it easy. Nothing can hurt you now, and the police will be here in no time. You've had a very bad shock, so just lie back and rest. Close your eyes and rest. I'll get the police immediately."

Mrs. Margulies looked up at him gratefully. It was amazing how kind and decent people really are. Always it seemed, always when things looked the blackest, someone really good showed up on the scene. It was strange how this particular young man had arrived twice now at the psychological moment. First to take the apartment off her hands and now to stand by her when she so desperately needed help.

She took his advice, leaned back and closed her eyes. She could hear his footsteps as they receded toward the bedroom to make the telephone call.

Dear God, the things that had happened to her in this terrible house during these last wretched weeks. Why had she ever returned? Nothing, nothing was worth it. Slowly her mind began to review the various incidents that had occurred since the first telephone call almost a month ago. It seemed she had lived a lifetime in these four ghastly weeks. But thank the Lord they would soon be over at last. The police would come and arrest the man, and she would be on her way to the Pacific and the rest and peace she so desperately needed. Yes, peace at last.

She drew a long sigh and slowly let out her breath.

How strangely silent it was in the room. Odd, she hadn't remembered hearing the bedroom door close behind him when he'd left, and yet there was no sound at all coming from the other room. Could he have made that call to the police without her having heard him? It hardly seemed likely.

And why was he being so long about it?

What was he doing?

Quietly she got out of the chair and walked to the door. She heard no sound from the other room.

Her hand reached for the knob and she twisted it.

He was standing by the table which held the telephone, but he wasn't using it. He was pouring whiskey from a decanter into two small glasses.

He looked up sharply as she stepped into the room.

"It will calm you," he said, holding out one of the glasses.

She shook her head.

"Have you called …?"

"Please take it," he said. "It will make you feel better. And I have been thinking about it. Are you really sure that you are right? That you have the right man? Voices are very deceiving."

"But I am sure," Mrs. Margulies said. There was a note of irritation in her voice. "Don't you understand? This man is downstairs and the police …"

He shook his head and again held out the glass.

"Really," he said, "even if you are right, and there is certainly no way of proving so, it would be a mistake. You are all ready to leave and, if we bring the police in, it will delay your trip unnecessarily. If you should be wrong, you will be open to lawsuits. And even if by any chance you are right, the thing will have to come up in court and that could prove extremely embarrassing for you. Don't you really think it would be best just to leave? Certainly the man will never bother you again, and I am sure...."

But she knew she was right: that was the man who had telephoned her. The man who had killed her bird and caused all of her troubles. Just thinking about it again turned her, from fear to anger. It might not be important to this young man, but it was to her.

Almost rudely she brushed past him, and her hand went to the telephone. She lifted the receiver. Her finger dialed the O for Operator.

For a moment he stared at her, and then he quickly put down his glass and he reached over and pressed his finger on the instrument, cutting off the connection.

"No," he said, "you must stop and think."

He felt a sudden surge of fury. Good God, what was wrong with the woman? Why wouldn't she just be satisfied to leave quietly? Why must she make trouble? If the police were to come now they would see what was happening in the basement. They would guess. And all of the carefully laid plans would be destroyed.

"Please," he said, "Please just leave. Let me handle it. I will …"

"Young man, take your hand off that phone."

She tried to brush his arm away as she spoke, and instinctively he pushed her away from the instrument. He reached out then and took her by both arms. He was having difficulty controlling himself and felt the blood surging into his neck and face.

"But I tell you," he began, "I tell you it would be best …"

She jerked her right arm loose and, without planning it, her hand swung and she slapped him hard on the left cheek. "Don't you dare lay hands …"

Her voice was high and thin, almost a scream, and quickly he jerked her toward him and put his hand over her mouth.

She struggled to free herself, and he hurled her to the floor. He followed her body down, and, as she again began to open her mouth in a scream, his hands found her throat.

4

"It will have to be the trunk," Blantz said. "It's the only thing large enough to hold her."

Townsend looked at the broken top.

Marschalk, following his gaze, shrugged. "We can fix that," he said. "At least enough so that it will hold for the time being. But I think it is too dangerous to start moving it out in the daytime. We should wait until after dark."

Blantz shook his head. "No, we must do it at once. Before any of the others get home from work. Passersby on the street, seeing a trunk being taken out of a house and put in a truck, will think nothing of it. But should that man Dabney or either of the girls see the trunk, they might recognize it as belonging to the woman. And if they know she stored it in the basement, they would wonder why it is being moved. The only safe thing is to get it out of the place now."

Marschalk pulled the trunk around and lifted the broken lid. He turned to Detrie.

"Start dumping this junk out," he said. "Try and keep it together in a pile, and we'll put it under the dirt in the back later. I'll get a hammer and some nails and see what I can do about a quick patch job. In the meantime, you two had better start bringing her down."

Jerry looked at him with distaste.

"Bring the trunk up when you have it ready," he said. "It will be easier."

Marschalk shrugged.

"Who drives the pickup?" he asked. "It's Townsend's job—let him get rid …"

"No, I don't think so," Blantz said. "He wouldn't begin to know how to do it. In any case, you rented the truck and, if you should be stopped for any reason, you have the proper papers. There will be no danger."

"The hell there will be no danger," Marschalk said. "There is always danger driving around with a corpse. I contracted to dig a tunnel, not get rid of a body, mister."

"If you are a loyal Son of Columbia …"

Marschalk said a vulgar word. The others were out of earshot, and so he spoke without pulling his punches.

"Don't bother to snow me, buster," he said. "You can con those boy scouts and lunatics, but don't waste it on me. I don't quite know what your angle is and I don't care too much. Right now, however, I know that you have a stiff on your hands and someone has to get rid of it. Well, if I'm elected, all fine and good. But this kind of work comes high."

"How high?" Blantz asked, cautiously.

"One thousand dollars high," Marschalk said.

"That's a little steep."

"One thousand dollars and a handwritten letter, signed by Townsend, before I leave—just in case I am stopped before I get rid of the body. Townsend is to admit committing the murder and say that I merely agreed to dispose of the evidence. The letter can be witnessed by that half-wit who is getting rid of the contents of the trunk. When I return, if I return safely, Townsend gets the letter back."

"I don't know if he will sign...."

"Then let him get rid of his own body."

Townsend didn't hesitate to sign the paper. He also paid the thousand dollars.

Twenty-five minutes later, Detrie and Marschalk carried the trunk out to the pickup truck.

As Marschalk threw the car into gear, he leaned out of the cab. "Tell them I won't be back until morning," he said.

5

Marty Eden returned to the house on K Street at a quarter to six on Monday evening. She was a little later than usual, having stopped to pick up her laundry, but she still managed to get home fifteen minutes before her roommate was to arrive and an hour and a half before Dabney got there. As usual on Monday nights, Paul Dabney had to work late.

It had been the custom of the house for the first person returning from work in the evenings to open the mailbox. Any letters not his own would then be placed on the small library table in the hallway for the other tenants.

Marty was not particularly disappointed to discover there were no letters for her. At least there were no bills. She saw that there were two letters for Paul Dabney and something which looked like a notice from the telephone company, addressed to Jerry Townsend.

She walked to the library table and, shifting her bundle of laundry, dropped the letter addressed to Townsend and the two addressed to Dabney. She was about to turn away when something caught her eye. It appeared to be a calling card.

She leaned over and picked it up and saw that there was a key attached to it. She recognized it at once as a key to the front door of the house.

Curious, she turned the card over and held it up so that the light from the overhead fixture fell on it.

She read the name: Mrs. Carolyn Margulies.

She was quite positive that neither the card nor the key had been there when she had passed through the hallway that morning. She clearly remembered stopping on her way out to check her face in the mirror over the library table for smeared lipstick after her hurried breakfast. The table had been completely bare at that time.

The key had been left there sometime during the day—undoubtedly by Mrs. Margulies herself.

Marty smiled, put the key back on the table. The sweet old soul, she thought. It was just like her. Thoughtful. She would never dream of not returning a key she had kept unthinkingly.

Marty was sorry she couldn't have been home when the woman had returned. She would have liked to have said goodbye to her.

CHAPTER SIX

1

Had Mrs. Alice Hopper not taken her obligations seriously, it is quite possible the Washington, D.C., Missing Persons Bureau never would have received the report.

But Mrs. Hopper was conscientious and so, when she arrived at the airport to meet Flight 236 directly out of the nation's capital and discovered that there was no Carolyn Margulies aboard, she was disturbed. Of course it was possible the woman had missed the plane, but it didn't seem likely. Elderly ladies, on the first lap of a planned vacation trip, rarely missed planes. But just to make sure, she waited until the next flight arrived. But the woman still was not aboard.

It was most strange.

There was the possibility that this Mrs. Margulies might have changed her plans, might have decided to cancel her flight and take a train. However, a check with the airline established that her ticket had not been canceled. A further check by long-distance phone assured Mrs. Hopper that no Mrs. Margulies boarded the plane in Washington.

Mrs. Hopper telephoned her brother.

Henry Clarence was astonished. He had gone to considerable personal trouble to see that his former employee would be greeted in San Francisco by his sister when she arrived. He simply couldn't believe that she would be inconsiderate enough to have accepted his invitation and then have changed her plan without letting them know about it.

It wasn't like Henry Clarence to misjudge anyone, certainly not anyone he had known for so long. Something must have happened, something so unexpected that she simply had had no opportunity to forewarn them.

Late Monday night, Mr. Clarence called the hotel where Mrs. Margulies had been staying. He discovered that she had checked out before noon on Monday. A call to the local airport established that she had never arrived and checked her luggage through, had never picked up her reservation and boarded the plane.

The whole thing was disturbing, and when he finally retired he found he had difficulty falling asleep. In the morning, after a restless night, he decided to stop by the hotel before going to his office. He had some sort of vague idea of trying to find out if she had called a cab to take her to the airport, or if the airline limousine had stopped by to pick her up. It was then that he learned she had left her suitcase, saying she would return for it, but had failed to do so. The suitcase was still there.

Mr. Clarence identified himself to the hotel detective who took him to the manager's office where he used the telephone. A completely efficient man, Mr. Clarence didn't waste time calling hospitals or morgues. He called the police department and explained the situation. It took them almost an hour before they telephoned back. No woman answering Mrs. Margulies' description had turned up either in an accident ward or at the morgue.

Carolyn Margulies had left the hotel sometime before noon and simply disappeared.

Mr. Clarence took a cab to police headquarters and went directly to missing persons. By noon on Tuesday, the report was on the teletype.

The police did not seem overly concerned. They had been able to determine that the woman had made no large withdrawals from her bank account, had not been carrying or wearing expensive jewelry. So far as they could find out, she merely had a few hundred dollars in traveler's checks in her bag when last seen. They doubted very much if she had been a victim of muggers in broad daylight. She had apparently been in excellent health, but of course there was always the possibility of a sudden heart attack or amnesia. The police were rather skeptical about the latter. They were quite sure she would turn up.

The legmen for the newspapers who happened to read the Missing Persons report saw nothing in it to justify a paragraph in the afternoon papers. The missing woman had neither social connections nor great wealth; there was no picture of her available, but it was a safe bet in view of her age that she was no glamour girl.

The fact is, that until Henry Clarence put the ad in the personal columns of the newspapers a few days later, no one, aside from a few bored police officials and of course the persons directly involved, was even aware that Carolyn Margulies was missing.

2

Robert Marschalk returned the U-Drive-It pickup truck to the agency on Tuesday at twelve-thirty. A check of the speedometer showed that he had driven the vehicle a total of two hundred and forty-seven miles. The manager of the agency was annoyed; he had been expecting the truck back at least fifteen hours earlier and had, in fact, promised it to another customer.

The body of the machine was covered with mud and a quick inspection established that the entire undercarriage was encased in muck, the steering rod badly bent, and one fender dented. There was considerable argument about the cost of repairs, but, in the end, Marschalk paid up and departed.

He was dead on his feet when he returned to the house on K Street, but nevertheless joined Detrie in the basement and began working on the tunnel. While he had been gone, Blantz had prevailed upon Townsend to help out with the work so they would not fall behind in their schedule.

Blantz was curious to learn how Marschalk had disposed of the trunk, but he hesitated to ask. In a way it would perhaps be best if he didn't know. But he realized that the broad-shouldered young blond was now in a position to put them all in danger. It was at this time he considered a slight change in his plans.

That afternoon Blantz stayed up in Townsend's apartment while the other three worked at the digging. They made considerable progress. Detrie and Marschalk did most of the shovel work, and Jerry, stripped to the waist, propelled the loaded wheelbarrow back and forth, picking up the dirt at the mouth of the tunnel and taking it to the back of the basement and dumping it.

By the time Townsend knocked off at five minutes to five, he was dead on his feet and every muscle in his body ached. After he had gone upstairs and taken a shower, he could have hit the sack for twelve hours.

The only trouble was that when he was through with the shower, it was almost time for him to meet Joan. She had told him that her roommate had a date that evening, and so she and Townsend would have the apartment to themselves. Joan was going to pick up some chops and other odds and ends for their dinner together.

The thought of the evening ahead infuriated Jerry Townsend. He knew exactly what would happen.

He would sit there while she made dinner, prattling away, overly anxious to please him and impatient for her roommate to get dressed and leave. The stereo would be going full blast with the corny folk music she adored, but even that wouldn't stop her incessant chatter.

Her roommate, Marty, would get dressed and go out as fast as possible. It was quite obvious that she disliked him.

Joan would want him to make love the second they were alone, whether dinner was ready or not. It was fantastic, but the girl was insatiable. She couldn't even wait until they got into bed. It was incredible how these respectable, quiet types always seemed to be the ones who were so terribly oversexed once they were aroused.

The girl had absolutely no modesty at all. She did everything but tear his clothes off and rape him.

Satisfying her was becoming more and more difficult. In the beginning, when he had been under the illusion that it was he who was doing the seducing, he had felt a certain desire, a certain sense of lust. But it hadn't lasted for long.

Still, had it been solely a matter of handling the sexual byplay, it wouldn't have been so bad. He could have managed that. The trouble was, it was essential to keep her under the impression that he had fallen in love with her, that he desired her above all else.

And so he found himself in the extremely difficult, not to say embarrassing, position of having to make verbal love to her and at the same time attempt to control her own passionate responses to that love. But it was the one way to ensure her loyalty to him, to guarantee that she would do what he might wish her to do when the time came. Besides, through her, he could be kept aware of her roommate's activities and even of Dabney's. And it was essential for the plan that he have control over the whole building.

His relationship with the Harrington girl was an arduous and boring task, but then everything to do with the plan was difficult. Difficult and dangerous. One doesn't go about planning an assassination, planning a deed that would lead to the wiping out of the enemy, without encountering certain difficulties.

3

Paul Dabney hesitated as they reached the second floor.

"The polite thing," he said, smiling down at Marty, "would be to invite me in for a nightcap. After all, having spent a staggering sum on your dinner and a double feature at the local cinema emporium, I feel that I'm entitled to at least a small token of your deep and sincere ..."

Marty laughed and squeezed his arm.

"I would invite you in for the whole bottle," she said. "For the last of the big spenders, nothing would be too much. However, seeing that the apartment downstairs is dark and that the lights are still on in our place, it occurs to me that our lovebirds are still at it. Why don't I just step in and grab the bottle, and we can go up to your apartment for a nightcap. Unless, of course, you relish the prospect of joining our gay companions."

"Let us silently and swiftly pass on," Dabney said. "We'll use my bottle. I'm beginning to think the kindest thing I can do is marry you and move you upstairs permanently."

Five minutes later they were sitting on the couch in Paul's apartment in front of the coffee table, drinks in their hands. Marty was talking and her voice was serious.

"I simply am unable to understand it," she said. "I could have sworn the girl is frigid. Yet it's been only two or three weeks since she met him, and I'm probably being a bitch, but I know she's sleeping with him. She's crazy about him. And according to Joan, he's just as much in love with her."

"Well there's no accounting ..."

"Oh, he's handsome enough," Marty said. "And rich too, as far as that goes. But that's just the point. There's something wrong with the whole picture. What is he after?"

"Well, according to what you've been saying, that seems rather obvious."

"Don't be vulgar, Paul. It's a little more than straight sex. I'm not supposed to tell anyone, but Jerry has asked her to marry him. He's already made her promise to quit her job at the end of the month. He's told her he wants them to be married during the first week in June and that he wants to take her on a honeymoon to South America."

"Well, I can't say I like him or even understand him," Paul said, "but maybe the guy is in love with her. It does happen, you know."

"But why all the secrecy, then?" Marty asked. "Anyway, there are a lot of funny things about him. Queer people who visit him and use his apartment, which is why he and Joan spend their time at our place. He never takes her out. Apparently he has all the money he needs: he doesn't have to work or anything. So why is he living here in the first place? Why did he move here? Why would a guy with all his money just hang around his girl's apartment? And these oddball friends of his—why he hasn't even introduced Joan to them. Anyway a man who's mixed up with anything as crazy as that Sons of Columbia outfit ..."

"Not exactly crazy," Paul said, soberly. "I would be inclined to say dangerous rather than crazy. Of course, it isn't too unusual for rich young playboys to go overboard for ..."

"That's another thing," Marty cut in. "He's now told Joan that he's decided to get out of the organization. He's made her promise she won't mention his connection with it to anyone anymore. Quite a turnabout, if you ask me."

"Perhaps a good woman's influence …"

"I'm afraid our Joan isn't being such a good woman anymore," Marty said. "I know it's none of my business, but—"

"But you should keep it none of your business then," Paul said. "Anyway, from what I hear around, not being a good woman is supposed to be rather fun. Now if you would like to try …"

Marty turned quickly and looked up at him.

"Why, Mister Dabney," she said, "am I about to be propositioned?"

Quickly, he leaned toward her and his mouth met hers. "You're terribly perceptive," he said.

"Why …"

"My intentions are strictly dishonorable," Paul said, placing his arm around her and drawing her to him.

4

For Marko it had been a busy week. Each evening at around nine o'clock he would leave the cottage in Baltimore, walk a dozen blocks and board a bus that took him into the center of town. He would then go to the Greyhound station for a bus to Washington. From the Washington depot, he would take a taxi to the hotel. He would go immediately to his room and stay there until the following morning. He never ate in the hotel but took his breakfast in small restaurants in or near the bus depot. He didn't bother with lunch and made his dinners when he was back in the cottage.

Four or five times he made trips into town, visiting various electrical radio shops. It took him awhile to gather all of the materials he needed and considerably longer to assemble them.

By the following Sunday he was almost done. Late that evening he once again snapped the padlock on the door, and this time he stopped to make a phone call on his way to the downtown bus.

Francis Blantz answered on the third ring.

An hour and twenty minutes later Blantz's car pulled up at the side entrance of the Baltimore railway depot and the fat man stepped out of the shadows and opened the door.

It wasn't until they had left the city, heading east on Route 2, that either man spoke. Marko broke the silence.

"And where do we go?"

"Place down in Anne Arundel County," Blantz said. "On Route 301. Sort of a nightclub. Very discreet. But it has everything."

Marko grunted, said nothing.

"I have ordered a private room and we can talk without interruption. Later—well you can have what you want. There are girls. Gambling if you prefer, dice, roulette, slots. And other things, should you be interested. Aside from the girls and the gambling. The food is damn good, especially if you like seafood."

"I can eat," Marko said. "The others, no. I don't mix business with pleasure."

Blantz shrugged.

"As you wish," he said, indifferently. "Incidentally, just how is business? What progress …?"

"It's time I paid a visit to the house," Marko said. "What is with the tunnel?"

"Another two days," Blantz said. "We're almost to the center of the street. But there have been complications. Pipes, underground electric lines, mains. And we've had to put in additional shoring. It's been complicated."

"I expected it would be," Marko said.

They didn't speak again until they were settled in the small, private dining room at the roadhouse and had placed their orders. Even then Marko waited until the waiter had served their food and left before answering Blantz's questions.

"It would be too difficult to explain in detail," he said. "You must trust me. I am a professional and I do not fail. I can explain this much. The basic idea is simple in theory, complicated in execution. But that is what I'm being paid for.

"The nitro is set off by a dynamite cap which in turn is sparked electronically. But no wires, no plunger switch as such. You understand the principle of a ship-to-shore radio? A citizens band transmitter system? A walkie-talkie? It is something of the same sort of thing I will be using. It is in essence a modification of the device used to control guided missiles by radio waves after they are launched into space. A very high frequency beam, except I will not be speaking into a microphone. I will be pressing a button on a switch which will in turn activate a second switch which will be located in the tunnel. This switch will close a circuit and thereby trigger the mechanism which will explode the dynamite cap. A split second the nitro will go off and then—poof!"

The fat man's dainty hands went out to his side; he shrugged his shoulders, and for the first time a thin, sickly smile lit up his pudgy face.

"It is really quite simple. But I must be most careful about every detail. Must make absolutely sure that there is no danger of possible interference by another transmitting device. Make certain that each component is perfect. It need only work once, but then it must work without fail. You may be confident it will."

Blantz stared at his companion for a moment before speaking.

"Seems awfully complicated to me," he said at last. "I can't understand why it wouldn't be simpler just to wire the thing directly and when the car arrives, handle it from the house."

"I have already explained that," Marko said. "You wish to be absolutely sure that the device does what you wish it to do. That there be no failure. This means that it can't be a simple explosion. A simple explosion would certainly destroy the car and blow a tremendous hole in the street under it. But it would not absolutely guarantee death. And so it must be a truly gigantic explosion."

"Well ..."

"Enough of an explosion so that the very house will crash in ruins. I do not care to be in that house at the time."

"You could be in a car parked nearby. Or perhaps at the rear of the house."

"Don't be a fool. The police will hardly pass up any suspicious cars parked in the immediate neighborhood. And within seconds after that explosion, you may be sure that the streets will start being blocked off, as the police close in. I want to be at least four blocks away at the time."

"But how will you know exactly when to activate the explosion if you are four blocks away? You will hardly be able to see exactly when the car is passing...."

Marko smiled. "Quite true," he said. "And that's why I insisted on a hotel room with a telephone. You see, several minutes, ten or fifteen perhaps, before the car is due at the spot, you will have someone at the house telephone me at the hotel. Ask for the room number. A reason I insisted on a hotel with a switchboard. There is bound to be an open trunk line.

"This person who telephones will be watching out of the window. He will give me the countdown. And at the right moment—well as I have said—poof!"

For a moment Blantz stared at him, his eyes suddenly wide. "And this person at the window," he said at last. "How about him? What happens when, as you say, poof?"

Marko shrugged.

"What happens? Why I suppose he is shaken. Shaken up a bit badly perhaps."

"You mean killed—and probably not perhaps," Blantz said, his voice suddenly high and thin. "How can you expect me to ask anyone ...?"

He choked suddenly, his face red. Recovering, he spoke again, his voice tense with anger. "You have made a bargain and I have paid you," he said. "You have accepted money and agreed to do a certain thing. There was nothing said about our supplying a sacrificial goat as well as the money."

Marko looked at him blandly. "Your sacrificial goat does not have to know," he said. "It is not necessary to take him into your confidence. Certainly in your vast organization"—his voice was suddenly heavy with sarcasm—"certainly you must have someone with whom you could dispense for so great a cause."

Blantz stared at him with mild horror. "You are a cold-blooded bastard," he said.

Marko again shrugged. "Cold-blooded? How about yourself? You are paying me so much money to kill a certain person. All well and good. Perhaps he needs killing, I wouldn't know. I am no different than any other public executioner. No different than the man at your Sing Sing who throws the switch, or perhaps the soldier who lifts the rifle. Not the judge. Only the paid executioner.

"Ah, but you. You pay me to kill one man, but you know very well that in order to do so I must probably kill another dozen. Two dozen, perhaps fifty. Perhaps even a hundred. You know this, you understand this, but it does not faze you. So what are you worrying about one more for? Why does one additional one make the slightest difference? Is it because it will be one of your own perhaps?"

Blantz shook his head helplessly. "You wouldn't understand," he said. "No—no it's not because it will be one of our own. God knows there are plenty of them we can spare. It's only ..."

He tossed up his hands and sighed.

"You amateurs are all alike," Marko said. "All alike. You are constantly killing, either because of stupidity, or greed, or avarice, or neglect. You think nothing at all of it.

"But I am a professional. I kill only for one reason. Because I am paid to do so. If I refused the job, someone else would take it. The victim would not be saved."

Blantz listened to the other's words, heard them and understood them. But the meaning didn't change his attitude. He stared at his companion as though he were observing a monster. He had, apparently, forgotten it was he, Francis Blantz, who had found and hired this man to do this job. Forgotten that it was he, Francis Blantz, who had already paid him part of his blood money in advance. Not only paid him, but held out some of that blood money for himself, cheating not only the assassin, but the assassin behind the assassin.

5

On Friday afternoon, May eighteenth, at four o'clock in the afternoon, the old man in Texas had his second heart attack. When Gordon Franklin Minor had suffered his first occlusion, some two years and six months previously, his lifelong friend, Dr. Harry Clark, had been brutally frank with him. He had, of course, waited until five weeks after Minor was released from the hospital and was back at the ranch, recovering.

"No more tobacco and that's flat," Dr. Clark had said. "No more boozing. One Bourbon, two ounces, with water, each evening before dinner. And that's all. No more whoring around. You want a woman, all right. Have one. Once, maybe even twice a week—but no more. Keep off those damned wild horses; get eight hours sleep a night."

There had been a lot more, including a reminder of his age and several comments about emotional disturbances.

"No damned reason a man worth a hundred million dollars should ever have to lose his temper," the doctor explained. "You think it's worth your life, why just go ahead and do it. And one more thing. You get a second one of these attacks, and it can very well be your last. The third one and there's no doubt. Out. Three strikes and out. And don't wait for three, because even if the second one doesn't kill you, it may make an invalid of you."

He'd run four three-cushion shots in a row and was just sighting in for his fifth one when it hit him. He was understandably excited at the time. Up until that afternoon, he had never in his life managed more than three successive shots and, by God, for a man in his late seventies to ...

He had the cue all the way back and was just moving forward to strike when the tip went suddenly high in the air and then dropped and dug into the green felt as he slumped and his great gaunt body crashed against the side of the polished mahogany and slipped to the cork-tiled floor.

The Japanese houseboy and two Mexicans who had been passing outside of the billiard room windows at the moment got him into the oak-paneled library and onto the leather couch. The Mexicans opened his shirt and removed his tie and riding boots while the houseboy rushed for the small vial of nitro tablets kept in the cabinet, and placed two of the pills under his tongue.

The old man's eyes were open and his jaw drawn tight; his leathery face was pale under his tan and the sweat stood out in great beads on his forehead. After the first minute or so, he regained consciousness. He wasn't able to speak, but he seemed to know what was happening.

Old Dr. Clark had died the previous year, but the Japanese houseboy was well trained. He put a blanket over the old man and then got on the phone. By the time the local doctor arrived from the nearest town, twenty miles away, Dallas had been notified; his secretary had arranged for a team of five of the top Dallas and Fort Worth physicians to be picked up by Minor's private plane; and a world-famous heart specialist in Boston was already on his way to an airport in that city.

It was while the young local doctor was ministering to him that Minor was first able to speak. He was in agonizing pain, and terribly weak, but he managed to make himself understood.

He was quite sure that old Doc Clark had been wrong. There would be no third chance. He opened his mouth and spoke in a whispering croak.

The doctor was unable to understand him and gestured, trying to keep him from speaking. But seeing the expression on the old man's face, he quickly figured it would be safest to pamper him.

He too was convinced the old man was dying; he just didn't want him to die until those older men from Dallas and Fort Worth arrived. He leaned down to hear the words.

"The telephone," the old man whispered. "Get on the phone."

The young doctor stared at him and then quickly nodded. There was no point in antagonizing him; any sudden anger and that could be it.

"General Merrivale. Hal Merrivale. You'll find his number in my book on the desk. Tell him I have to see him right now. To come by plane. Send mine in. Keep me alive until he gets here."

It didn't come out that clearly of course, but the doctor got the gist of it and understood. He knew who the general was, too. Lieutenant General Hal Merrivale, retired, had been a famous and controversial figure in his day. He was in his late sixties now, but he still made the news. They hadn't actually cashiered him out of the Air Force, but he'd been retired a couple of years before his time was up, after he and the top brass had disagreed on defense policy. Retirement had given him certain privileges that had been denied to him in the service. He was able to speak his mind publicly, and he had certainly not failed to take advantage of the opportunity.

A good many people disagreed with what the old general had to say, and some of them considered him rather dangerous and eccentric. But there were many other people who took him pretty seriously and went right down the line with him. Certainly there was no denying that he'd made a tremendous record in two world wars, was a patriot with an unblemished record for loyalty to his country.

He had a silver plate in his head from a crash in the First World War, wore a stainless-steel pin in his hip as a souvenir of the Second. He'd backed up old Billy Mitchell in the early days, been right more often than wrong so far as arguments with the chiefs of staff had been concerned. He was a real enough hero with medals and scars to prove it.

He also had a completely closed mind, a passionate distrust of all politicians, statesmen, and diplomats, a boundless faith in the United States Armed Forces, and an absolute conviction that the best way to win a war was to fight it, and the best way to fight it was to get in the first punch.

He was one of the few living men for whom Gordon Franklin Minor had genuine liking and respect.

The plane which picked up General Merrivale at his small ranch some twelve miles west of Fort Worth arrived at the old man's ranch some twenty minutes before the planeload of Texas physicians arrived, and it was lucky that it did. Otherwise the old general would never have been allowed to have his few private words with the oil and cattle baron.

The young doctor, under protest, left the two together. He knew better, but there didn't seem to be much he could do about it. He was afraid if he crossed the old man, it might be just enough to bring on the end.

The pain had eased off a little, and, by making an effort, Minor was able to turn his head and see the general seated next to the bed. He knew he wouldn't have long, and he wanted to get it over with as quickly as possible.

"Hal," he said, "what I got to say is mighty important. Lean close— I can't yell."

The general started to say something about maybe it would be better if he didn't try to talk just yet, but Minor quickly shut him up.

"That Russian fellow, the sonofabitch who's their leader—he's coming to this country in a couple of weeks," Minor said.

The general looked at him, a worried, concerned expression on his face. It wasn't making sense.

"I must know one thing," Minor continued, "and you're the man to give me the answer. What do you think would happen if he was shot in this country?"

The general leaned back, a shocked expression in his faded blue eyes.

"You mean, Gordon, if someone were to shoot the Russian Premier? Were to assassinate him while he's in this country?"

"That's exactly what I mean."

In his anxiety Minor tried to lift himself on his elbow, but the pain suddenly struck at him, and again the sweat broke out on his forehead; he had to slump back on the pillows. Still, his eyes remained open and riveted on his old friend.

"Why hell, Gordon, all goddamn blazes would break loose. Those damned Commies would just as likely as not send a bomb over.

"You really believe that, Hal?"

"Yep, I do believe it. They are just crazy enough to do it."

"And then what? What then, Hal?"

The old general's lips tightened and he squinted his eyes and his head began to nod slowly up and down.

"They might get one or two through, but that would be all," he said, his voice thin and sagacious. "Yes, that would be all. And in less than one hour it would be all over. There just plain wouldn't be any Russia left on the map. Why, by God, between our ICBMs and our bombers on the early warning patrol, plus our European and Asiatic installations, they wouldn't have a chance in hell. The whole damned miserable country would be wiped off the face of the earth before they could even surrender."

"You really believe that, Hal?"

"Believe it? I know damned well it's true!"

Minor hesitated for several seconds and then again spoke. "Well, why the hell haven't we done it already then?" he asked.

The general looked mad and shook his head.

"Damned politicians in Washington," he said. "Just like it was the last time. Afraid to make a damned move on their own. Like it took Pearl Harbor before the American people would get mad enough to do anything. It's the same thing all over again. We just have to wait until someone hits us first before we hit back. I've been saying that all along."

He looked down as he spoke, and he saw that the old man's eyes had closed and that his mouth was open and his breath was coming in gasps. At the same time he heard the sound of the approaching footsteps outside the door.

He was glad someone was coming.

CHAPTER SEVEN

1

Harrison Tillinghast, a seventy-two-year-old waterman living on Tilghman Island in Talbot County, on the Eastern Shore of Maryland, left his small cottage on Wednesday morning, May twenty-third, at six-thirty.

An hour later he was tending his trotlines a couple of hundred yards offshore on the bay side of the island. He had already taken care of one line, removed the few crabs eating the baits, placed them in a large wooden bucket, and rebaited the line with slightly aged chicken necks.

When he finished with the second trotline, he decided to quit for a while and do a little fishing. He'd heard there was an early school of rockfish in the area, and so he baited a hook with an eel and decided to give it a try. He'd get back to the trotlines later on.

If it had been a big eel, he'd have just let it float loose, but the eel was quite small and almost dead, so he weighted the line to deep troll. The line hadn't been out for three minutes when his reel started to sing.

The old man quickly cut his motor and grabbed his pole. He was an old hand, and he knew at once that this was no rockfish at the end of that line … no fish at all. His hook was snagged and snagged good.

He tried for half an hour to free his hook without success. A lesser man might have cut his line in disgust, but not he. He backed the boat until the line stood straight in the water, and then put his oar in to measure the depth. It was low tide, and his line was caught in something not more than four feet below the surface.

The old man took off his heavy rubber boots, stripped off his blue jeans. He rolled his shirt up under his armpits and then removed his socks and long underwear. A moment later and he was overboard. He was damned if he was going to lose a dollar's worth of tackle if it meant merely getting a little wet to salvage it.

Tillinghast didn't get his tackle back until an hour and a half later, when it was removed from where it had caught in the dead woman's body, just under the jawbone. A county coroner removed the hook, the eel still attached to it, in a private undertaker's parlor in St. Michaels, where the state troopers had brought it, after the Tidewater Fisheries had notified them of the finding of the body.

The coroner estimated that she had been dead, and in the water, for over a week.

The crabs had found her, of course, and they had made a mess of her face and throat. The flesh on her hands and arms was pretty well gone also, but there was one complete thumb and an index finger of the right hand. Enough skin left for two clear prints. The bottom teeth were mostly intact and there were a number of gold fillings. There was a full upper plate, still in position.

The body had been wrapped in a heavy, wrought-iron chain and this was what had kept it from rising to the surface. There was no mystery about the chain. It had been reported stolen by a construction firm doing some roadwork a few miles from where the body had been discovered. Just after dusk, a little over a week ago, a small colored boy had seen a car stop, and a man get out and take the chain, but the boy hadn't gotten the license number.

The body appeared to be that of a woman in her mid-sixties, 5'6½" tall, and weighing approximately 145 pounds. Her hair was blue gray and dyed.

There was no further identification.

An autopsy would be performed, but it wouldn't need an autopsy to reach the conclusion that a murder had been committed. Within a couple of hours, a seven-state alarm would go out over the teletype. Missing Persons Bureaus would automatically be given a full description, and the two fingerprints would be sent in to be checked against FBI files. Plastic molds would be taken of the teeth, both the legitimate lowers and the false uppers.

Sooner or later they would know who she was: if they were lucky, sooner or later they might learn why she had been murdered and who had killed her. It would then be merely a matter of time until they got the slayer.

If it turned out that the woman had been killed on the Eastern Shore, the chances are that the criminal investigation would be handled by the detective division of the Maryland State Police. On the other hand, if it were to develop that she was from some outlying city or state and that she may have been murdered there and brought to the Eastern Shore for disposal, well then the detective work would be done by the police department of that particular place.

2

Marschalk and his partner, Detrie, completed the tunnel on the afternoon of May twenty-third. It had been a long and laborious task, as they had not been permitted to use air hammers or other automatic tools. They finished at around three in the afternoon, and it was decided that Marko would come the next day and start rigging his equipment.

Shortly after three, Marschalk went upstairs to talk with Townsend, leaving Detrie in the basement to clean up. Townsend looked up from his magazine as Marschalk slumped into the chair across from the couch on which he was lounging. The blond giant wiped the sweat from his forehead with his finger and snapped it onto the floor. There was mud caked to his boots.

Townsend frowned in distaste.

"All done, thank God," Marschalk said. He took a cigarette from a crumpled pack and lit it, blowing out a mouthful of smoke. "I sure can use a day or two of rest," he said.

"That's about what you'll get before you start the refilling," Townsend said.

"Great!" Marschalk sighed deeply and then looked over at the other man. "You know what?" he said.

Townsend again looked up from his magazine. "What?" he asked.

"I've been thinking," Marschalk said. "You seem to be making time with that babe on the second floor. Well I happened to see her roommate a couple of times when she was coming and going. So how about you fix it up for me? I can use a little of that. We can pick up a couple of jugs, and you get it set up. We can go up and spend the night."

Townsend tossed the magazine aside.

"Really," he said. "I'm afraid you've been down in that hole too long. Must be getting a little stir crazy or something. I've been seeing the girl upstairs because it's part of my job to see her. It's your job to stay completely away from anyone who even lives in or near this house."

Marschalk snorted.

"Come off it, buster," he said. "What do you think I am, stupid or something? You think I'm blind? Hell, you've been humping that skinny one every night since I've been here. Don't try to kid me. You'd probably make the other if she'd let you. Well, buddy, just take me up there and give me an introduction and I'll show you exactly how an expert goes to work. It won't take me an hour before ..."

"What I do is my business," Townsend said coldly. He stood up and walked over to the fireplace, and when he turned his eyes were murderous.

"You are to keep completely away from either of those girls. Do I make myself clear? Don't go near them. If Blantz thought that you'd even entertain the idea ..."

"Blantz, crap," Marschalk said. "And what the hell are you getting so uppity about anyway. You forgetting that nice old lady you knocked off? You forgetting I had to clean up the mess for you? You know I might consider that you sort of owe me something of a favor."

"You have been paid."

"Sure, a lousy grand. One grand to be an accessory after a murder. Big deal."

Townsend stared at him for a second and then looked away. His voice was less distant when he spoke again.

"The fact is," he said, "I'm fed up with the girl. Only wish to God I *could* turn her over to you. To you or to anyone. I'll tell you what. As soon as this is over, I'll see that you do get to her. I'll even arrange it."

"The skinny blonde one?"

"Yes, of course. Joan is the one I ..."

"No thanks, chum," Marschalk said. "You keep her. I know those snotty, fishy-eyed types. You can have 'em. It's the little dark-haired one that interests me."

"Then let her interest you in a couple of weeks," Townsend said. "At the moment she happens to be off limits."

"You sound like a damned second lieutenant in the National Guard," Marschalk said. "Well, the hell with it. I'm getting cleaned up and getting out of here. You want to be a hog about your broads, go right ahead. I know where I can find what I'm looking for, brother."

"Find anything you like," Townsend said. "Only be sure to be back here no later than ten o'clock on Friday morning. We've got work ..."

Marschalk cut him short with a laugh.

"We?" he said. "Good God. What you mean, we? That creep downstairs and I are doing the work."

He left the house on K Street an hour later and headed across the river to Alexandria and the hotel where he still kept his room. He wasn't able to reach the 17-year-old girl when he called her number, but it didn't bother him a great deal.

The bellboy knew a girl who he claimed was only fifteen years old and almost a virgin. Marschalk wasn't quite sure what he meant by almost, but he didn't really care.

3

Contrary to the general opinion of the public, policemen are human beings. They eat, drink, make love, have problems (especially money problems), pay taxes, vote, live and die, just like everyone else. They have all of the normal virtues and all of the normal vices—the greeds, ambitions, desires, frustrations of the rest of us.

On the other hand, there are certain differences. A good policeman is not without sentiment and feeling, understanding and even kindness. On the other hand, if he is any sort of officer at all, it is essential that he develop a certain degree of professional callousness, a certain amount of skepticism, and a reticence.

These characteristics, however, do not mean that he doesn't go home at night—or whenever his tour of duty is finished—and talk shop with his wife.

Detective Lieutenant Jan Majeska was no exception. There were, of necessity, several things he could not discuss. But in general he did like to review the day's proceedings, and he often paid her the courtesy of asking her advice when he was faced with a particularly tough problem. As a homicide detective, it is possible that Majeska talked even more with his wife about his cases than did most cops. There was a very good reason for this. Majeska often worked overtime or on his own time, and it made it a little easier all around if he explained exactly what he had been doing.

On that evening when Majeska had spent a large part of it with Paul Dabney at the house on K Street, he had not hesitated to tell his wife exactly what had transpired after he returned home. It was the sort of thing that really interested her: it was, after all, a mystery, and she liked mysteries. During the following week, she thought about it often. Why should anyone wish to persecute a nice, harmless, elderly woman? Why should someone have made those obscene telephone calls, wrecked her apartment, killed her pet?

Several times since, she had asked her husband if there was anything new on the case, but, during those particular two weeks, Jan Majeska was involved in a particularly unpleasant murder investigation, and so his mind was preoccupied. Furthermore, the K Street woman had moved, had quit her position, and was planning a vacation out of the city and apparently had not been bothered further. He even had a little difficulty in remembering what his wife was asking about.

"That Mrs. Margulies," Carol Majeska would say, "don't you remember? Paul Dabney's friend whose mynah bird was murdered."

Her husband would merely grunt and mutter something about there being nothing new. He had to find a maniac who had recently raped and murdered a six-year-old child, and this was the sort of case he did not discuss with his wife.

It was while she was wrapping the garbage in the classified advertising section of the *Washington Star*, preparatory to putting it in the incinerator, that Carol Majeska came across the ad in the personal column. She wasn't actually reading the ad as such; it was merely that the name caught her eye. Carefully she leaned forward and read the entire paragraph. It read:

"MRS. CAROLYN MARGULIES—Will anyone knowing the whereabouts of Mrs. Carolyn Margulies please get in touch immediately with the address or telephone number listed below. Reward. This woman may be injured or suffering from amnesia."

There followed a rather lengthy physical description and an address and telephone number. At first Carol Majeska wanted to telephone her husband at once. But then she hesitated. It was quite possible that the woman had purposely disappeared in order to get away from whoever it was who had been persecuting her.

Besides, Jan hated to be bothered at headquarters unless it was really important, and, after all, this was no business of hers. The police probably knew of the ad, might even know the whereabouts of the woman.

In any event, it wasn't really Jan's case: he was on Homicide, not Missing Persons. Nevertheless, Carol cut the ad out of the paper and carefully put it away before sending the garbage down the chute.

Jan Majeska didn't get home until well after ten o'clock that evening, and he was dead on his feet. It had been a brutal day, the sort of day he didn't want to talk about.

They had picked up the man whom they were charging with the rape-slaying of the child. In the minds of the homicide squad, it was a clear-cut, open-and-shut case. There was only one trouble with it. The evidence was purely circumstantial: it would never hold up in court.

The man they had arrested knew this. He wouldn't talk.

It was one of those things that doesn't happen too often (although the public is convinced it happens all the time). A case where the police were sure beyond any reasonable doubt that they had the right man—but didn't have the evidence and weren't going to be able to get it without the cooperation of the man they wanted to charge with the crime. Of course, sooner or later, they might get a confession. But even a confession would hardly hold up if the criminal insisted it had been beaten out of him. Wouldn't hold up by itself, unless there was still that very definite legal evidence.

Well it had taken some seven hours, down in the shower room of an outlying precinct house, and in a way it had been almost as tough on the cops as it had been on the man they were working over. In the end they not only got their confession; they got the information they needed to obtain and correlate the evidence which the district attorney would later use to demand a death penalty. It hadn't been easy.

When Jan Majeska finally arrived home and sat down to a warmed-over dinner, there was only one thing on his mind. He was thinking that being a cop was lousy work and wondering why he stayed with it. As a result he didn't even hear what Carol said when she first mentioned the matter.

"The funniest thing," she said. "I saw it in the personal column of yesterday's paper. That Mrs. Margulies is missing and someone is advertising for her."

Her husband cut into his lamb chop.

She had to repeat it twice before she really got his full attention, and then she had to remind him exactly who Mrs. Margulies was. After that she showed him the newspaper clipping.

Lieutenant Majeska was on the telephone, talking with Missing Persons, before he had finished his dinner. Missing Persons didn't have to ask why someone from Homicide might be interested in a matter which was strictly in their province. They knew that all too often a case went from them directly to Homicide.

They had seen the ad and they had, of course, checked it at once. The ad was perfectly legitimate. There had been no answers so far.

Missing Persons had already learned about the woman's previous difficulties. They had done all of the usual things: checked her luggage, attempted to find relatives, and so on. They had absolutely no clues.

After he hung up on Missing Persons, Majeska telephoned Paul Dabney. The newsletter editor was completely mystified. He assured his friend that there was no possibility at all that the woman could have voluntarily gone into hiding.

"Why would she?" he asked. "After all she was only a couple of hours away from leaving for the Pacific Coast and her vacation. And certainly, if she had wanted to disappear, she would have taken her suitcase when she left the hotel. She would have cashed in her airline ticket."

The detective agreed.

Paul suggested possible amnesia; he realized that had she fallen ill or been injured, she would have turned up by now.

Majeska was skeptical. "Amnesia is merely another name for a disease suffered by men, or women, who happen to find someone more attractive temporarily than their current mates," he said.

"Are you suggesting foul play?" Paul asked, immediately embarrassed by his use of the cliché. He couldn't imagine a policeman using the term.

"Someone had been persecuting the woman," Majeska said. "Maybe they went just a step or two further."

"If that's so," Paul said, "it sort of destroys our theory that the only reason she was being bothered is because they wanted her to move. By the way, what did you ever find out about young Townsend, who took over her apartment? Remember, you were going to run a check on him?"

"We did," Majeska said. "No criminal record. Only thing we had was an FBI file. He joined the Sons of Columbia a couple of years ago, and he has been doing some recruiting for them. But that isn't considered a crime."

"It's a crime in my book," Dabney said.

"Matter of opinion, Paul. A man can't be arrested for his political convictions, no matter how far right or left they are, so long as he stays within the law."

They let it go at that, and the detective promised to let Paul know if there were any new developments.

When Paul saw Marty Eden the following day, he mentioned to her that Mrs. Margulies was reported missing. He didn't go into detail, didn't explain that she had last been seen on May fourteenth, the very same day that Marty had discovered the key to the first-floor apartment lying on the hallway table.

4

It took Marko a full day to make his installation. He showed up at the house on K Street just after dawn, arriving in a taxicab. The first package carried into the house contained vials of nitroglycerin, and this he handled himself, using extreme care. On his second trip he brought in the dynamite caps, while he allowed the cabdriver to handle the heavy cartons containing the electronic equipment, the long lengths of wire, and the materials he would need.

They dropped the stuff off in Townsend's apartment. Marko had picked up the taxi in Baltimore, and he had mumbled about some valuable art treasures he was delivering to a customer in Washington. The driver couldn't have been less interested.

Townsend offered Marko coffee and breakfast while they waited for the other tenants to vacate the building, but the fat man refused. He remained silent, avoiding conversation, until nine-fifteen when it was safe to go into the basement. Townsend asked if he needed Detrie to help him, but Marko said he preferred to handle things by himself. So Jerry led him down into the basement and left him to his own devices.

By two o'clock Marko had rigged the nitro bomb and attached the dynamite cap. The entire package had been placed on a small wooden platform, just above the large sewer pipe. Having made the bomb secure, he covered it with a tarpaulin and strung the doubly insulated wires down the length of the tunnel, bringing the ends into the basement proper. Then he returned upstairs.

"I will need your man now," he said to Townsend. "The bomb must be well covered with dirt. I would estimate at least two dozen wheelbarrow loads. The wires must be covered, too. What else you may wish to do is your affair."

"The charge is placed and ready?" Jerry asked.

"Placed but not ready," Marko said. "The wires which will connect it to the activating switch have been brought to the basement at the front of the house. The switch box will be concealed just within the basement proper. Should you replace the concrete foundation wall— and it is my understanding that Blantz wishes it replaced—it will not interfere with the high frequency reception."

"And it will be safe to have Detrie throw the dirt over the bomb? There will be no danger?"

"No danger at all if he follows my instructions. Until the switch box is finally connected to the wires, there is very little chance of an explosion. Of course, you must realize we are dealing with nitro and dynamite, and so there is always some danger. But until the switch box itself is connected ..."

"If the switch box is to be in the basement itself, and the concrete wall is to be replaced, what is to prevent the police finding the box when they investigate after the explosion?"

"Simple," Marko said. "You see, the force of the main explosion will be such that it will blow that wall down, will fill the basement itself with dirt and rubble. And in the switch box itself will be a second bomb, which will be activated a split second after the main charge goes off. It will be quite small but thoroughly adequate to completely demolish the box and its components."

Townsend looked at the other man skeptically.

"But won't the police discover parts, odds and ends of wire and so on? Won't they ...?"

"Perhaps," Marko answered. "But the conclusion they will draw is that the bomb itself scattered its own components. It is, of course, a calculated risk. I was told that you people were prepared to run that risk. The principle thing is that ..."

Townsend held his finger to his lips and indicated the closed bedroom door. He didn't want the conversation overheard by Detrie. He knew the plan called for Detrie to be in the house at the time of the explosion. Detrie was too stupid to figure out the calculated risk he would be taking, and there was no use warning him.

It took Detrie an hour and a half to pack enough dirt around the bomb to satisfy Marko, and, when he was through, he was sent upstairs with instructions to tell Jerry Townsend to come down to the basement.

Marko was rigging the switch box as Jerry entered what had been the storage room. It was a relatively small box, about eighteen inches by ten inches by four inches. The box itself fitted perfectly into a secondhand, well-used suitcase.

Townsend watched as he worked and, after ten or fifteen minutes, saw that Marko was returning the wooden switch box to the case. The twin wires which led down the tunnel were attached and came out of the back of the suitcase. Marko moved it over against the side wall.

"I shall assume no one will disturb it," he said.

"You may be damned sure no one will."

"Good. Then cover the wires with dirt and warn your people. I will return at the proper time and place the charge in the box. I will also put the tubes in the set which will receive the signal to set off the main charge. In the meantime, there is no danger. No danger if everyone keeps hands off things. You may replace the wall, fill the tunnel, do anything you care to do, but under no conditions disturb the wires, nor tamper with the box."

"And your work is now done?" Townsend asked, more to make conversation than for any other reason.

"Hardly. You are forgetting what I must do on the day of June fourth. There is much else to be done as well. Only part of the system is here; there are still arrangements to be made at the hotel. But if you wish information, ask Blantz. It's Blantz who hired me, Blantz who is in charge."

CHAPTER EIGHT

1

It took forty-eight hours for a positive identification, but this is not bad when one takes into consideration the fact that the woman's face was all but eaten away, that the FBI had no record of her fingerprints, that it takes days and sometimes weeks to make a positive identification through dental work.

The identification would have been made even sooner but for one human factor. The average person, asked to view the remains of a person killed by violence and in particular one whose features have been mostly destroyed, usually suffers from temporary shock and is unable to think very clearly.

The report reached the Washington Missing Persons Bureau by midafternoon on the day the body was found on the Eastern Shore of Maryland. It didn't take them long to realize that the general description fitted that of the missing Carolyn Margulies. Unfortunately there was no permanent address for the woman, no relatives listed in the initial report. Merely the man who made the report, a Mr. Clarence, her former employer.

Mr. Clarence was reached at his office and notified of the grisly find on the Eastern Shore, but when requested to accompany the police across the bay and make an identification, he pleaded the pressure of business, told the police that after all he had not been a personal friend of Mrs. Margulies and volunteered the service of a couple of his employees whom he said had known her well and long.

His selection was a trifle unfortunate as his secretary, who was his first choice, fainted upon being shown the remains, and upon recovery became hysterical when the police suggested she face the ordeal again.

His second choice was the treasurer of the company, an elderly bachelor, whose eyes had in twelve years never traveled below the neckline of the missing Mrs. Margulies, and as a result he was quite unable to identify the fragments left by the crabs. Both agreed however that it could have been their former fellow employee.

A search of the suitcase left behind when Mrs. Margulies disappeared turned up receipts for a recently purchased suit of clothes, and a little routine police work quickly established that the suit was similar to the one found on the dead woman.

The following day the police located Mrs. Margulies' dentist and took him to view the body. He recognized his own handiwork immediately.

On the strength of this evidence, the corpse was removed to Washington to await claim by whatever relative might be turned up, following a formal autopsy. The Maryland State Police were quite willing to assume that the woman was indeed the missing Mrs. Margulies and that she had been slain in the District of Columbia from whence she had disappeared. The case and all records were turned over to the Washington, D.C., homicide squad.

They received it officially on Friday afternoon, June twenty-fifth.

Detective Lieutenant Jan Majeska knew nothing at all about the matter until he read about it in the newspaper, while taking a tub bath on Sunday morning. He had been out of town for the last thirty-four hours, working on a possible arson murder, which had angles involving a witness being held by the New York City police on a vagrancy charge.

Ten minutes after he had dried his lean, muscular body with an oversize Turkish towel, he was on the phone to his office, the towel wrapped around his waist. He learned that no progress at all had been made in the case, and when he asked to be assigned to it, his superiors were only too happy to oblige.

They probably assumed he was beginning to go a little soft in the head. Nobody voluntarily takes on a loser.

A thorough, painstaking man, the lieutenant never went off half-cocked. He took his time dressing, had a substantial breakfast, and apologized to Carol for not taking her to the horse show down in Virginia, as he had promised. And then he drove to headquarters and got out the file on the Carolyn Margulies case.

It didn't take too long to go over it.

The woman's pocketbook had not been found with the body, but the suitcase she'd left at the hotel proved to hold her traveler's checks, steamship ticket from San Francisco to Hawaii, what few jewels she was known to possess, as well as six hundred dollars in cash. It certainly did not appear that robbery was the motive; in fact, the few people interviewed who had known her could not suggest any possible motive.

There was the original coroner's report, a statement from the Maryland State Police incorporating the information about the stolen iron chain found wrapped around her body. Her employer and fellow employees had been questioned. The people at the hotel where she had stayed verified their previous stories about her checking out and saying she would be returning shortly for her luggage.

A detective had stopped by her former apartment on K Street. The only person at home at the time was a Jerry Townsend, who had subleased the dead woman's apartment. He maintained that he had only met the woman a few times in his life and that his entire relationship with her had pertained solely to subleasing the apartment.

The detective had made a brief search of the apartment inasmuch as it still contained the dead woman's furniture. He turned up no personal belongings.

Townsend had volunteered the information that she had left a trunk containing personal possessions in the basement. He had been very surprised when she'd returned to the apartment the afternoon of the very day he'd moved in—May ninth—and said that she'd decided to put the trunk in storage after all. She had explained she was afraid that the dampness and muskiness of the basement would penetrate the trunk and spoil its contents, which, she explained, consisted mostly of old letters, personal mementos, and a few clothes.

Townsend said he had helped the cabdriver carry the trunk up from the basement and out to the car. He wasn't sure whether it was a local taxi or not.

Police had failed to turn up the cabdriver so far, and because of the weekend and the short time they had been investigating, had not been able to check out all the local warehouses.

It wasn't considered too important an angle—unless, of course, she had taken the cab to the home of a friend who may have been in close touch with her during the past few weeks.

There had been a safety deposit box key in her suitcase, and it would be checked out as soon as the banks opened on Monday. Mr. Clarence, her former employer, had told the police that she had been well off and that he believed she possessed around fifty or sixty thousand dollars in stocks and bonds. He told them the name of the lawyer who handled her investments. The man was out of town for the weekend.

And that was about all of it.

2

Carter, the FBI man, turned to his secretary and said, "Get hold of Colonel Ed Hauser, over at Secret Service, will you, honey. On the private wire."

He lit a cigarette while he waited, and, when the girl buzzed him back, he picked up the receiver.

"Colonel Hauser?"

"Yes, this is Colonel Hauser."

"Colonel, this is Carter, over at FBI. We've run into something rather odd over here, and I thought I'd better tell you about it. Probably doesn't mean a damned thing, but you know, with everyone as jittery as they are about this impending visit, we can't afford to miss any bets. Try it for size and let me know what you think. You ever hear of a man named Gordon Franklin Minor?"

"Who hasn't, Carter?" the colonel said. "You mean that Texas multimillionaire, don't you? Big oil and cattle."

"That's the one. I don't know whether you read about it in the papers the last few days or not, but he's supposed to be dying. Had a heart attack."

"Yes, so I hear."

"Well I've just heard from one of our field agents in Texas. Seems like there was some young doctor attending the old man when it happened. He was with him for quite a while, I gather, while Minor was delirious. Anyway, it seems that Minor said a lot of things which apparently upset the young doctor. So the doctor got in touch with our man and gave him the pitch."

"A doctor, even a young one, should have too much sense to take the ravings of a dying man seriously," Colonel Hauser said.

"Probably," Carter said. "But our Texas agent thought it was important enough to pass it along, so I'm giving it to you for what it's worth. Minor kept rambling on about some plan to blow up the Russian Premier."

"Good God, Carter," Colonel Hauser said, "the old goat's been promoting that line ever since Korea. Remember those ads he took in the papers a few years back, suggesting we bomb Russia? Or maybe it was Cuba or China. He's been nuts on the subject for years."

"Yes, I remember. State Department wanted us to clamp down on him at the time. But that wasn't all of it. From bombing he went into some sort of long tirade about the Premier coming here to pay us this visit. Kept yelling that 'We'll get the bastard this time all right. We'll get him this time.' Those were the exact words the doctor reported him using. The doctor seemed to think that in spite of his being out of his mind, he really knew what he was saying."

"Did your man get in to see him?"

"Hell, no. By the time he heard about it, the big shot doctors had taken over, and no one was getting in to see him. I tell you the man is supposed to be dying."

"Well, I wouldn't worry about it too much, Carter," Colonel Hauser said. "Old Minor has always been a publicity hound. Advocated going on strike against the income tax at one time as I recall. Also wasn't he supposed to be tied in with the Sons of Columbia some way or other?"

"He was and is," Carter said. "We have a record on him like a racehorse. Of course, with his money and power, there's never been much we could do to shut him up. But he's been financing a lot of fanatical right-wing groups for years. I'm just hoping that his bunch haven't cooked up something that will create an incident when the Premier arrives."

"I wouldn't worry," Colonel Hauser said. "Rich old eccentrics talk a lot, but they never really do anything. Anyway, the doctor said he was out of his head. Probably just having illusions of grandeur."

"Probably. Just thought I'd tip you off. Since Dallas, I take anything seriously along these lines. One thing we can be sure of this time, at least. Every security measure that can be taken is being taken. It takes one hell of a powerful bullet to penetrate those plastic covers we'll be using."

They talked for several minutes more on general matters and then rang off.

3

Blantz stared at Townsend coldly and spoke in a bitter tone.

"Damn it, I've told you I don't want to be seen coming here. It's dangerous. I'm known. Well known. If the police or FBI should have a tail on me, and it's always possible, this is the last address in America that I should be seen at."

"I'm being seen here all the time," Townsend said. "If I don't care …"

"The situation is different," Blantz replied. "When this is finished, you will be disappearing for a while. You have money, all the money you'll ever need. And if I'm not mistaken, you have much of it salted away in a numbered account in some Swiss bank. You can afford to lay low until it's safe to return. With me it's different. I'm too important a figure just to drop out of sight. I'll be on the scene, and if the finger starts to point to us, as is more than likely, I've got to have a foolproof alibi."

Townsend didn't bother to conceal his sneer. "I believe," he said, "it was you who told me we would be considered heroes."

"We will, once the clamor dies down," Blantz said. "I just want to be sure to be around at the time. Anyway, what is it you wanted to see me about? If it's about the Margulies woman being found, I've already read about it in the papers. Be careful to keep your voice down." He pointed to the closed door of the bedroom. "The less he knows ..."

"He's gone," Townsend said.

"Gone?" Blantz looked up sharply.

"Yes—gone. I sent him away—just before the police came."

"The police!"

"That's right. The police. You should have expected them. I certainly did after I heard the radio report about the finding of the body. So I had Marschalk and Detrie do as fast a cleanup job as they could downstairs. Of course it wasn't possible to get the wall back in, and, in any case, fresh concrete would have drawn attention to itself. We piled up old crates against the hole and pretty well concealed it. We did the best we could with the extra earth on short notice. I short-circuited the lights so most of the basement is in the dark. We couldn't do much, but we did what we could. And then I made Marschalk take Detrie with him when he left. He's promised to keep him out of sight for the next few days."

"But what about the police?"

"A detective. Making routine queries. He knew that I had subleased from the woman. Wanted to know if she had left anything behind which might offer a clue. Of course there was nothing."

"But the other tenants. Suppose one of them told about the trunk she'd left in the basement?"

"Fortunately they were not home when the detective was here. I was in the building alone. And I covered it in advance."

He went on to explain the story he had given the detective.

"You think fast," Blantz said. He couldn't help the note of admiration in his voice. "Do you think they'll be back?"

"It's possible. They may want to talk to one of the girls or the man on the top floor. But I don't believe it will go beyond that. There will be no reason for questioning me again. I only met her twice and then for very brief spells and always with someone else present."

"Except for the last time," Blantz said, obliquely.

Townsend looked at him with a cold eye. "We're in this together, remember?" he said.

"Well what are your plans?"

"We do nothing," Townsend said. "We must stop all work in the basement, keep the door locked, keep up a constant vigil. It will be best if Marschalk and Detrie stay away for the next few days. I have

Marschalk's address in Alexandria, and you can get in touch with him. The other one will be with him. The fat man has a final task to perform here, but it will take him only a short time, and he will do it the day before D-day. I'll be here at all times. We must sit it out and wait. We're all ready at this end—I just hope nothing goes wrong at the other end. I'm still not quite sure how the thing is supposed to work."

Blantz shrugged. "I'm not completely sure I understand it myself. From what Marko has told me, the system is very much like those small button switches you use to control a television set from a distance. You hold the little box in your hand, press a button, and the station changes. Or the sound goes off. Or perhaps the set itself is turned on and off. From across the room, without wires. Only in this case it will be from a distance of several blocks rather than from across the room. And it will not be a television set turned on. It will be a chapter in history."

"A chapter well worth the risk," Townsend said. "Knowing what we'll have accomplished compensates me for the dismal weeks I'm spending in this place."

Blantz was silent for several moments, a thoughtful expression on his face.

"I don't like the idea of Marschalk and Detrie being together," he said at last. "Marschalk is dangerous because he's ambitious, and Detrie is dangerous because he's a fool. Another thing, I don't think it's a good idea for you to be here completely alone. If you should have to go out for something, there will be no one on watch. Someone must be in the apartment at all times, and I think it would be best to bring Marschalk back and let him stay with you. At least he's clever enough to know what to do if someone should come nosing around while you're out—or while you're upstairs with the girl."

"But what of Detrie? We'll need him for the last day."

Blantz nodded. "I'll cope with Detrie," he said. "Keep him occupied so that he stays out of trouble. Yes, it will be best to bring Marschalk back. If trouble should come, he's a good man to have around."

"Trouble?"

"There was trouble when that fool woman returned," Blantz said. "Marschalk came in very handy then."

"Marschalk is a bumbler," Townsend said coldly. "They found the body within less than ten days."

"Indeed they did," Blantz said. "But they haven't found the killer yet. I'm confident they won't." He nodded his head several times. "Yes, I'll see that he returns. He'll be able to relieve you, so you can get out for a decent meal now and then if nothing else. And if there's any difficulty with those two upstairs, or that man on the top floor, well, Marschalk might come in very handy indeed."

"There won't be trouble," Townsend said. "But call Marschalk and be sure you keep Detrie buried until we need him. You'll be at the same number?"

"The same number."

Blantz turned back for a moment as he reached the door. "One thing more," he said. "Just how much control do you have over that girl? How far would she go to protect you if she became suspicious?"

"All the way," Townsend said. "She's a woman in love, or at least she thinks she is, which is the same thing. She'll be loyal. Her only danger is stupidity, and I guard against that by keeping her with me as much as possible."

"And the other girl?"

"So far, she suspects nothing. I'm able to keep an eye on her through the Harrington girl."

"Don't trust either of them too far," Blantz warned, and then quickly left.

4

The thing had been bothering her for some time. A memory in the back of her mind that had been disturbing her ever since she had learned of the murder.

Marty had been with Paul Dabney when Lieutenant Majeska had stopped by to discuss the crime. Each had been badly shocked by the news of the murder, and Marty again felt that odd sense of fear when Paul's detective friend had called to say he wanted to see them. Jan Majeska was hoping one of them might reveal some half-forgotten fragment of information that might have a bearing on the matter.

The three spent a couple of hours together, going over every angle of the case. Marty kept thinking that there was something, some tiny item which she should remember. Which might be of some value. But it failed to come to her and the conference was, for the most part, fruitless.

The trouble was that although both Paul and Marty had known the dead woman, the relationship had been most casual—except for the night Paul found her with the dead bird. They had never met any of her friends and knew nothing of her personal life.

"I can't remember her ever having visitors," Marty had said. "I simply can't understand why anyone would have wanted to …"

"Neither can the police," Majeska said. "That's what makes it so irritating: the apparent complete lack of motive. Yet we know, of course, that there must have been one. This is not a case of an insane killer selecting his victim at random. Not with that previous history of telephone calls and persecutions. There is a motive all right, but we just can't discover it."

It was then that the faint, unborn memory first began to disturb her. Something she'd thought must be important but which persisted in eluding her memory.

And now, as she dropped off the day's mail on the hall table on her way up to her apartment, it hit her.

The key. Mrs. Margulies' outside door key, which she'd left at the house that day. The woman *had* returned to the house on K Street. She had returned on the very day she had disappeared, on the day the police believed she had been slain.

Moments later, inserting her own key into the door of her apartment, she was chilled by the importance of her recollection. According to Majeska, Mrs. Margulies had not been seen from the time she'd left the hotel on that fatal morning. But she *had* come to the house on K Street. Could something have happened to her here?

And what had attracted her back to the house in the first place? She was supposed to have taken a plane to the Coast that afternoon. Would she have wasted valuable time to stop off just to leave a key which she could easily have dropped in any mailbox? It was hardly likely that she'd have stopped by merely to say goodbye. It must have been during the daytime, and she would have known that neither Paul nor the girls would be home. So if she'd come to see anyone, it would have had to have been Jerry Townsend.

But Townsend had said nothing about such a visit.

Marty quickly closed the door and went to the telephone. She must call Paul at once and tell him about it. He'd know what to do.

She reached Paul's secretary a couple of minutes later and was told that Dabney had had to make an unexpected trip to New York. He would be telephoning his office the first thing in the morning. The girl wasn't sure where he was staying in New York.

Marty asked to have Paul call her the moment he called in; she stressed that it was important.

She hung up and then dialed Police Headquarters and asked to be connected with Lieutenant Majeska. The desk sergeant transferred her to Homicide; she was told that the lieutenant was out but, if she would leave her number, he would call her back when he checked in. She left her number and again hung up.

Marty was wondering if perhaps she should have given the information she had to someone else, when she heard the key in the door. She turned as Joan Harrington entered the apartment.

5

When Joan walked into Townsend's apartment, her face was livid, and she was shaking with anger. Jerry turned to her with a forced smile. The girl was becoming impossible. Her nerves had been on edge for days, and it seemed that when she wasn't nagging at him, she was complaining about everyone else.

"Now what, baby?" he said.

"Jerry—Jerry, make me a drink please."

"Sure." He reached for the bottle of Scotch on the table next to the couch. "What happened? Have you and that roommate of yours been …?"

She reached for the glass, gulped, and then spoke, her voice tense with suppressed anger.

"I guess we've finally had it out," she said. "It seems when she got home she went into the bathroom and found one of those things that you use. She told me she was fed up having her place—her place, imagine—used as a house of assignation. She suggested that I pack up and find a place of my own."

Jerry shrugged. "So—go ahead. You can stay down here tonight if you like, and tomorrow …"

"It isn't that simple, Jerry. I'm on that lease and half responsible for the rent. And, anyway, it was my apartment originally, and I took her in to share it. I am not going to have anyone tell me I have to get out."

"In that case, don't," Jerry said. "Why not tell her to take off? In fact, I'll be damned glad to assume her share of the rent, and I'll even go further. You go up and tell her if she will leave—leave right now—I'll pay for a cab to move her, for a hotel for the next few days while she finds a place, and I'll cover any incidental expenses."

Joan shook her head. "She wouldn't do it, Jerry. She feels that it is her place and she wants me to be the one to move."

Jerry sighed. Damned fools, he thought. Here he had only a couple of days or so more to go, and this had to happen.

"Well, what was it all about anyway?" he asked. "Hell, she knew about us ..."

Joan blushed. "That only started it, Jerry," she said. "Then we started talking, and we got on the subject of you and she said things that I just can't forgive her for. She's jealous, Jerry. Jealous of us because we are in love and are happy. She's a vicious, self-righteous little bitch."

"What did she say about me?" Jerry asked.

"Oh, it started about that thing in the bathroom and then I thought I had her calmed down and we were talking about Mrs. Margulies and she was telling me about finding the key and how she knew Mrs. Margulies must have been here the day she disappeared and that you must have known about it and ..."

"What the hell are you talking about?" Townsend said quickly. "What has Mrs. Margulies ...?"

"I'm trying to tell you, Jerry," Joan said. "It seems that Marty found a key to the front door that Mrs. Margulies left on the hall table that day she disappeared. In any case, she suddenly remembered it and she says that you were home all day, and so you must have known she came to the house."

"Has she told the police about this?" Jerry's voice was sharp.

"She said that she had forgotten it until today and that she is waiting for either Paul Dabney or that detective friend of his to call her back and that she is going to ..."

Townsend quickly stood up, interrupting her.

"Wait here," he said harshly. "Stay right here until I get back." He moved fast, opening the door to the bedroom and beckoning to Marschalk.

"But, Jerry ..."

"I said wait! Make yourself another drink—make me one. I'll be right back." He nodded to Marschalk as he opened the hall door. A second later, the door closed behind him, he hesitated and turned to his companion.

"I heard her," Marschalk said. "Now what."

"We've got to shut Marty up before she gets those telephone calls," Townsend said in a low whisper.

Marschalk smiled wryly and without humor.

"Not again," he said, his voice sarcastic. "Don't tell me you are going to repeat ..."

"Don't be an utter damned fool," Townsend said. "We can't do anything to her. Just keep her from seeing anyone or saying anything. Hell, you don't think I want to have another woman disappearing from here at this time, do you? Good God, that's all the police would need to take this place apart. But right now we are going upstairs, and we are going to see that she is kept out of circulation for the next few days. I want you to stay with her, while I come back down here and get Joan cleared away. Then we can make some sort of plan."

"I've been wanting to stay with that babe for some time now," Marschalk said.

Townsend grabbed him by the arm. "Don't get any ideas," he said. "You are not to touch her. Understand? Just keep her quiet. Tie her up and gag her if you have to, but that's all. Until I have a chance to get back."

A moment later, and he rapped sharply on the door of the second-floor apartment.

Townsend was breathing heavily when he returned to his own apartment some five minutes later. His eyes were pinpoints of fury, and he was wiping blood from the long triple scratches on the right side of his face.

Joan looked at him with alarmed eyes.

"I'll kill that little bitch," he muttered. "By God, before this is over I'll ..."

He stopped speaking suddenly and reached for the drink Joan had poured. Making an effort to control himself, he took the half-empty glass from his mouth and slumped on the couch next to her. Reaching over, he pulled her close and kissed her brutally on the mouth.

She moaned and pressed against him.

"Oh, Jerry ..."

Her hands reached out and he leaned quickly back.

"Later," he said. "We have to talk."

She stared at him wide-eyed.

"Did she ...?"

"It's nothing," he said, wiping the scratches again.

"Jerry," she said, "Jerry what's happening? You didn't ...?"

"I didn't do anything," he said. "I told her off and I got Marschalk to stay with her, so I could come down here and talk with you."

"What's going on Jerry?" Joan asked. "What's happening anyway? What is this all about? Why is your friend up there with her?"

She stopped suddenly and stared queerly at him, a thoughtful look in her watery eyes.

"Jerry," she said in an almost soundless voice. "Jerry, this hasn't to do with Mrs. Margulies, has it?"

Her face slowly lost color and her eyes grew large. Her hand went to her mouth.

He reached out, pulled her close and brushed her hand away. His lips met hers and for several moments he just held her until her slender body had relaxed. He spoke then, barely taking his face away from hers.

"It's not what you think," he said. "Nothing like that. You must believe me and have faith in me. Nothing happened to the woman while she was here. She just came and dropped her key and left."

"But why didn't you tell the police?"

"Joan—Joan, just please listen. Good God, you trust me, don't you?"

"Of course I trust you, Jerry," she said.

"Then listen. Just keep quiet and listen to me."

"But, Jerry ..."

He pushed her away and glared at her. "I asked you if you trusted me?"

She nodded, dumbly.

"Completely and without reservation?"

"I love you, Jerry," she whispered.

"Well, I love you. Now be quiet and listen to me." He hesitated for several moments and then, reaching over and taking her hand in his, he began to speak.

"I can't tell you everything," he said. "And you mustn't question me. You must merely listen and believe in me.

"You see," he went on, "I have decided to stay with the group of patriotic Americans who believe that the welfare of our country comes before anything else. I believe that no personal sacrifice is too great, no risk too dangerous, no ..."

She watched him, fascinated, as he continued speaking. She didn't really hear what he was saying or understand what he was getting at. She only knew that the man she loved was deeply earnest.

The fact is, that he told her nothing really. He merely ranted on about patriotism, his devotion to a cause, and the need for secrecy.

After several moments she interrupted him.

"But what has this to do with Marty and with Mrs. Margulies and this house?"

"Everything," he said, "everything. What we are doing—and I can't explain and you will just have to trust me for a few more days—but what we are doing here is of supreme importance. We cannot afford the interference of publicity now. We cannot have police snooping around trying to solve some obscure murder which has nothing to do with us at all. So we can't have that damned girl upstairs setting off alarms which would bring in the authorities. We need a few more days. And so we will just have to hold her for the time being and see that she calls no one."

"And then …"

"I promise you that by Monday afternoon it will be all over. We will release the girl unharmed. And by Monday evening you and I, Joan, will be on a plane for South America. It will all be over and done with."

"You mean …"

"I mean that you and I are going to be married Monday morning. But in the meantime, I need your help. My friend Marschalk is upstairs with the girl now. You are to go up and stay with them. Marty will be held in the back room. You must answer the phone and the door, should anyone come. You must explain that Marty has been called home to wherever she comes from in the Midwest. Now here is the way it will work, here is what you must do. Listen carefully."

CHAPTER NINE

1

A really competent policeman realizes that first-rate detective work consists of ordinary, dull, routine investigative activity as well as the use of keen deduction. Jan Majeska went one step further: he felt that both functions, the legwork and the brainwork, should be handled by the same officer whenever possible.

A man questioning witnesses might often get all of the facts, but still not know quite what to do with them. On the other hand, Majeska believed that it was only in the most unrealistic fiction that a brilliant detective was able to lounge in a dressing gown, sip a glass of champagne, go over the reports of the work of others, and come up with the proper answer.

As a result of his theory, he found himself spending Friday afternoon of June first on the Eastern Shore of Maryland, parked at the side of the road so that he and his small colored companion could watch an endless stream of passing traffic.

The boy had not been hard to find. His name was Calvin Roosevelt Jones; he was ten years old, and extremely bright for his age. It was he who had witnessed the theft of a length of heavy chain from the site of a construction job sometime previously. He had reported the incident to the State Police well before the same chain had been discovered around the body of Carolyn Margulies and identified by the head of the construction firm.

Young Jones had been fishing around dusk in a small creek over which a new bridge was being constructed. He had seen a car drive up, stop, and a man get out. The man had broken into a work shack and come out dragging the heavy length of chain.

The youngster, moved both by a sense of duty and a sense of self-protection—he was frequently in the vicinity fishing—made his report the following morning, after telling his family of the incident.

He was not sure what kind of car it was, but thought it might have been a truck or pickup. He wasn't sure of the color, had not seen the man close enough to say more than that he was tall and broad-shouldered. But when Majeska talked with him, he said that the car seemed sort of familiar and that if he were to see it again or one like it, he would probably be able to identify it.

And so, on this very slender evidence, the lieutenant had packed the youngster into his car, driven out to Route 50 where the traffic was heaviest, and now they were sitting and watching cars. They had been there for two solid hours, and three times the youngster had pointed out vehicles which vaguely reminded him of the one he had seen that evening at dusk.

The first vehicle had been an orange-yellow taxicab. The second had been a small Volkswagen hauling a two-wheeled trailer. And now the third one had again been a car towing a rented trailer. What baffled the detective was the child's remark.

"No, sir, mister," he said. "I'm sure. It wasn't a trailer. I would remember if it'd been, but it wasn't. But every time I see one of them small trailers, it sure reminds me of that car. Not every trailer, but just one now and then."

He couldn't doubt the child's sincerity or his desire to help. But it was confusing.

"Well then, son," he said, "how about that first one? That yellow cab. You said it also reminded you."

"Yes, it did. It certainly made me think of that car. But I still can't say why."

"And you are sure you didn't see the license?"

The boy shook his head. "No, sir, I didn't. It was too dark. Can't even say if it was Maryland."

It was only after the fourth partial identification, some half hour later, that Majeska decided to give up. This time it was a small pickup truck with an orange cab.

Again something about the vehicle had reminded the child of the car, but again he wasn't quite sure. So Majeska decided to call it a day. He drove the youngster to his home and gave him three one-dollar bills for the time he had taken up. The child refused the money, but Majeska forced it on him. He told the boy he'd been a big help and that he was a smart lad—to try and keep thinking about it. Maybe it would come to him.

Driving back to Washington, he tried to dismiss the matter from his mind. It had been a fruitless day, and the Eastern Shore had yielded nothing he hadn't already known. Well, it was just one of those things.

But somehow or other he was unable to dismiss it completely. The child had been so sure, and yet still unable to be consistent in his identifications. Majeska again began to think about it.

Four vehicles. A yellow-orange taxi, two cars hauling trailers, and a pickup truck. Each had reminded him of a single vehicle, and yet each had been different. There was no doubt that the child was honestly trying to be helpful. He could have faked it easily enough had he wanted to. Just identified any sort of conveyance at random. But he had been cautious, tried to be absolutely sure.

There must be some common factor to all four, some way in which each resembled the murder car. And yet the murder car must have been different in some way from each of those four vehicles: otherwise one would have qualified.

Certainly the truck and the taxi were completely different. And why just those two cars drawing trailers of all the dozens of trailers that had passed by? Remembering back, Majeska suddenly tensed.

He nodded quickly. Yes, that was it. Both of those trailers had been rented, U-Drive-It trailers.

But why the taxi? It hit him almost at once. The taxi had been that same orange-yellow color. And then immediately the rest of it fell into place. It hadn't been a trailer, of that the child was positive. But he had partly identified a pickup truck.

Ten minutes later Jan had the Eastern Shore Barracks of the Maryland State Police on the telephone. He learned that there was a local U-Drive-It branch, and the State Police agreed to pick up the youngster and take him there. They would let him see the trailers, the rental trucks, and each type of vehicle handled by the firm. Majeska would call back when he reached Washington.

2

Marko flicked the solid-gold cigarette lighter and, when it failed to work, cursed and tossed the cigarette on the floor of the car. He turned toward Blantz who sat behind the wheel slowly guiding them through the heavy traffic.

"And you have been holding the girl at the house against her will? You must be insane. You should kill her. Your friend didn't hesitate to kill before when it was necessary."

"It isn't a case of killing," Blantz said. "Don't you understand? We simply can't afford to have another missing woman; not from that house at least. Not after the business with the Margulies woman. It would be suicide. We must have her available if someone should come looking for her."

"But if they do?"

"There is the other girl. As long as we don't kill the first one, the other girl will front for us. Will explain to whoever may show up. But should we do away with the Eden girl, the other one would crack up."

"And you are sure of this second girl?"

"She's in love with Townsend," Blantz said. "A woman will do anything for the man she is in love with. Or at least, some women will. This one will."

"She must be a fool then," Marko said. "And what is to happen to the girl afterward? What is to happen to both of the girls? I have met Townsend, and I hardly believe that he will want to be encumbered ..."

"Townsend has his own plans," Blantz said. "It is not my concern, and certainly not yours, as to how he wishes to dispose of the woman. Of either woman. This is too big, too important, to permit any one person, or any dozen persons, to stand in the way. So you need not worry about the girl or her friend. You have no need to worry about anyone except yourself."

"I have everything to worry about. I would like the rest of my money as soon as …"

"As soon as the job is finished," Blantz said. "That's the agreement."

"I shall hold you responsible," Marko said. "You are the one I contracted with, and you are to remember one thing. If I fail to receive payment when it is due, there will be no second chance. You understand?"

"Do you think I'm a fool?" Blantz said. "You'll receive your money as agreed. You were hired because of your reputation, so you may be assured I take that reputation seriously."

Marko nodded and stared at his tiny hands. He spoke in a low, disinterested voice.

"You would do well to eliminate Townsend when it is over," he said. "He is young, a stupid fanatic. Dangerous."

Blantz ignored his remark.

"When will you activate the switch at the house?" he asked. "I have no desire to be there once you've made the final arrangements."

"I shall visit the house on Monday morning. The switch will be activated. But there will be no danger. Not until the moment I receive the phone call and press the button on this small box I hold in my hand."

Blantz looked down for a moment and blanched slightly when he saw the small, square box in the man's tiny hands.

"And that," he asked, "that is all it will take?"

"That is all."

3

She was frightened, more frightened than she had ever been in her life. Fear is supposed to paralyze a person, but Marty Eden was not paralyzed—she had never been more alert in her life. And she knew very well what was happening to her.

She sat crouched at the far corner of the couch, her legs folded under her and her arms crossed over her breasts. Although she tried not to watch him, she couldn't seem to keep her eyes away.

Marschalk was getting drunk, had been drinking steadily for the last three hours. Ever since Joan had left them to go downstairs and be with Townsend. At first he had tried to get her to drink with him, but she'd refused. He'd sulked for a while but then, as he continued to refill the shot glass from the whiskey bottle, he'd changed. He'd become good-natured and tried to draw her out and this had been worse. She understood only too well what he had in the back of his mind. She wondered now if he was drinking to build up his courage.

For a moment or so she had been tempted to take a drink with him in the hope that eventually he would become sentimental and relaxed. But she quickly realized that he would never become sentimental, and the liquor certainly did nothing to relax him.

She wondered whether he'd be more dangerous drunk or sober, but she knew, in either case, that she'd have no control over it.

Her eyes passed over him again and then went on to the window at the side of the room. The curtains were drawn. For a moment she was tempted to make the attempt, to spring up and hurl herself through the glass of the window. Someone would see her; it was still broad daylight. But she abandoned the thought. She knew she would never make it. He was fast and ruthless, and he was on constant guard, despite his drinking. Had been ever since she'd tried screaming.

That had been an hour ago, when she'd thought she'd heard someone outside on the street.

He'd been on his feet and across the room even as the sound left her throat. One hand had grabbed her, closing off the yell. And then he had slapped her, back and forth across the face with his huge open hand. Brutally. She'd finally fallen, and he'd picked her up, half crushing her.

"I'm not going to gag you, and I'm not going to tie you up," he'd said in a cold, emotionless voice. "But try that again and I'll beat you until there isn't an inch of your lily-white body that won't be black and blue."

She stared into his face, trying to control the tears which the pain had brought to her eyes. His own eyes were half closed and he had a strange, half smile on his lips. She suddenly realized that he wanted to beat her, that he would take pleasure in doing it.

"Now go back and sit down and behave yourself," he said.

She had tried to talk to him then, tried to find out why she was being held. How long he was going to keep her there. But he'd refused to tell her anything.

"But when will you let me go?" she begged. "Don't you realize I'll be missed; that people will be looking for me. That my friends ..."

He shrugged his great shoulders.

"Nobody will be looking for you," he said. "As long as your girlfriend is around to explain, nobody will be looking for you."

She'd turned away then and closed her eyes, involuntarily shuddering.

She didn't understand it, didn't know what it was all about. But one thing she did know: she was in terrible danger. It wasn't only him. She knew what he wanted, and she knew it would only be a matter of time before he took her. But there was something else. Something to do with the house itself and with the murder of Carolyn Margulies.

She was convinced they had been involved in the murder, but it went a lot further than that. Something was happening in this house, something evil.

She thought then of Joan, Joan whom she had believed she knew so well. Joan was going along with it, condoning it and covering for them.

She remembered Joan's words.

"Just do what they say and everything will be all right," Joan had said. "I can't explain to you, but it has to be this way. Just do what they say and they won't hurt you. On Monday they will let you go."

She had been too shocked, too confused to say a thing. None of it made any sense at all.

And Joan had lied. Joan was there when the telephone call came from Paul, and she'd lied to Paul and told him that she, Marty, had been called back home to Duluth because her mother was ill. She had lied to other people about her.

And now she was gone, had been gone for a long time. She hadn't taken her things with her, so perhaps she would be back, but there was no way of knowing. And in the meantime she was alone with this great hulking brute who was rapidly becoming drunker and more courageous. That is, if courage was the word to use for what she knew he was preparing to do to her.

Oh, God, if only Paul would come. If anyone would come. But she knew it was useless to hope. She'd been hoping ever since that moment when the two men had crashed into her apartment. It was Sunday afternoon now. Another day. Twenty-four more hours. But then what?

Again she looked over at Marschalk.

Twenty-four hours wouldn't help her. Joan was lying if she said it would. She was sure these men were already involved in one murder. Why would they worry about another? No, twenty-four hours wouldn't help. She'd be lucky to be alive in twenty-four hours.

Marschalk stood up and tossed down the remainder of the liquor in his glass.

"Looks like you and I are going to spend the night alone," he said.

4

Joan Harrington twisted her long, slender, naked body so that she was able to put her arms around him as he lay beside her. "Hold me, Jerry," she said. "Hold me tight. I'm frightened."

"There's nothing to be frightened of," he said, forcing the note of concern and affection. His strong lean hands caressed her, and he kissed her eyes so that she was forced to close them. "You're tired," he said. "It's been a long day. Why don't you sleep?"

She felt his body tense and begin to draw away from her, and she clutched him tighter.

"Make love to me again," she said, breathlessly. "Make love to me."

"You should try and sleep," he repeated.

"I can't sleep, darling," she said. "Oh, God, I do love you so. Please— please hurry and ..."

He sighed and his hands moved and found her small breasts, and he forced his mind to become blank as he went through the movements. He couldn't stand her voice, and so he closed his mouth over hers and she began to moan as her body set up a rhythm. He took his mouth away and she muttered and cried out, and it was then that the shrill sound of the telephone interrupted.

Quickly he moved over and away from her, thankful for the diversion. She tried to draw him back but he had the receiver in his hand. He listened for a moment and then said, "Just a minute."

"I've got to go out for a while," he said. "I want you to stay here until I return."

Joan nodded dully as he replaced the receiver on the bedside phone.

"Jerry," she said, "can't you tell me? Can't you let me understand?"

"You said you love me," he said shortly, pulling away and half turning. "You told me ..."

"Oh, God, I do love you. Can't you tell by now? It's only—only that

I'm frightened. Marty—what's going to happen to her?"

"She'll be all right," Jerry said. "I told you that nothing is going to happen to her. After tomorrow we'll be gone. She won't be hurt and we'll be gone."

"But if you could only tell me ..."

He turned and reached for her.

"This is the only thing I can tell you now," he said, his voice rough and hard. "This!"

5

Sunday newspapers throughout the nation carried not only the full report of the Russian Premier's rather long and tedious speech which he had made before a full session of the United Nations but editorials commenting on that speech. The consensus was that the Communist world, through the mouth of the Premier, was making a definite overture toward peaceful coexistence with the West. The general note was one of optimism and confidence.

No one, of course, was childish enough to assume that an official state visit, a motorcade down Pennsylvania Avenue, a meeting on the White House lawn between the heads of two great governments, and the usual social hubbub which surrounded such events would really solve any basic problems. But there was a general feeling that the entire thing was a step in the right direction.

The Premier himself had declined to issue any statements following his United Nations appearance, apparently not wishing to detract from the dramatic impact of the following day's activities. But every news medium in the nation would be ready on Monday to report in depth on those activities, and the nation more or less breathlessly awaited what the morrow might bring.

6

In a way he half regretted he had ever had the place bugged. They had lied to him, and for once in his life he would have been just as glad not to have known about it.

A hundred times Gordon Franklin Minor had lain on the great bed in the air-conditioned master bedroom of the ranch house and leaned down to turn this or that switch so that he might eavesdrop on employees, friends, or guests as they spoke in what they fancied was the privacy of one or another of the rooms of the rambling structure.

A hundred times he had heard himself discussed, a hundred times he had known who was being honest and who was being dishonest with him. A hundred times he had acted on the information he'd obtained secretly over the microphones.

But this time—well, it would have been better if he hadn't heard.

They had told him that he had a chance, that he was getting better and would live through this one. But they'd lied. It was really strange. He was dying; he was to all intents and purposes already as good as dead.

God, what hypocrites they really were. It had been the specialist from Boston, the very best heart man in the country if not in the world, who had pronounced the sentence. The man who only an hour ago had smiled at him and said he'd be well again.

But that isn't what he'd said when he'd returned to the great library and talked with his associates. Not what Minor had heard over the secret intercom.

"He'll never last out the night. God knows it's a miracle that he's lasted this long. Six times now his heart has stopped; six times he's been pulled through. Right now he's all right. But at his age, in his condition, he simply can't go through another one. And he's bound to have another attack: they have come with increasing frequency."

It was amazing how clear his mind was, amazing that he had the strength to press the button that turned off the receiver from the hidden microphone. Amazing that he was able to press the other button that summoned Tashi, the houseboy.

They had left him alone and called the nurse from his room at his request, and now he understood why they had pampered him to this extent. They knew he was as good as gone, and what he did no longer mattered. But they didn't know the reserves he still had left.

The houseboy nodded when he explained in his feeble, barely audible voice. He put the call in on the private line and made sure he had the right party on the other end before he took the instrument to the bed and held the mouthpiece so that the old man could speak into it.

He didn't waste words.

"You are to go ahead with the contract on Mr. B.," he said. He repeated it twice. "Tomorrow, at exactly twelve-thirty. Not a minute before or a minute later. Keep a tail on him from now on. And be sure. Completely sure."

He waited a moment and then, without another word, nodded, and the houseboy removed the instrument and replaced the receiver.

Five minutes later Minor again spoke with the specialist whom he had summoned from the library. He was very weak now, and it cost him a tremendous effort to make himself understood.

"No point in fooling me anymore," he said. "I'm dying, and I know I'm dying. Only one request. If I die tonight, the news is not to be released until late tomorrow afternoon—Eastern Daylight Time. I must have your absolute promise."

The doctor had no way of knowing that his prediction had been overheard, but something told him that there would no longer be any use in trying to fool the old man.

Quickly he pledged himself to honor this last request. It might be difficult, but a dying man deserves to have his last wish observed.

The old man closed his eyes, and the doctor quietly left, summoning an assistant to return to the room and stay by the bedside until he might be needed.

He knew that it couldn't be long.

CHAPTER TEN

1

For the first time in his life, Detective Lieutenant Jan Majeska was deliberately disobeying an order. It wasn't a specific order aimed directly at him. It was a general police emergency order, broadcast to every member of the force.

He had heard it over the radio as he and Carol were having breakfast late on Monday morning. Every off duty police officer in the District of Columbia was informed that he was to report immediately for assignment to posts along the route that the Russian Premier would be taking in his parade from Union Depot to the White House, at noon or shortly thereafter.

Majeska was not due to report in until noon, so the order did very definitely apply to him. On the other hand, he was working on an important murder case, and in a sense was actually on duty twenty-four hours a day. It was all rather technical.

The thing was that Majeska was really on to something hot. He could feel it in his bones. That sixth sense he had had so often in the past. He couldn't justify it on any logical grounds, but he was convinced that he was on the verge of cracking the Margulies Case.

Late on Sunday night, he had completed his check of the local U-Drive-It agencies and found out that a pickup truck had been rented on the day the woman had disappeared. The same model truck identified by the child on the Eastern Shore.

It hadn't been easy, especially on a weekend when most of the employees were away. But persistency had paid off, and he had finally reached the U-Drive-It manager. He'd met the man at his office in the small hours of the morning, and the record was there.

One pickup truck rented to a Robert Marschalk. An out-of-state address, an out-of-state driver's license. But the name and license had checked out over the teletype.

There was no local address.

The manager remembered certain things. The fact that the truck had been hours overdue when it was returned. The condition of the vehicle when it had been brought in.

The mileage. Enough to travel to the Eastern Shore and back.

From the condition the pickup had been in, it was very possible it may have figured in some minor accident. So Majeska had called the traffic bureau. Of course, on a Sunday night, most of the records in the traffic department were not available. But he had put in his request and he knew that now, early Monday morning, the information would be there. It would take a little more time, but had this mysterious Robert Marschalk received a ticket for some minor infraction, it would he listed.

It could very well be the missing key.

He had asked the FBI for a routine check on Robert Marschalk. He should be getting the answer on that at any moment.

It was one hell of a time to be pulled off the case. Certainly not the time to walk away from it to do patrolman duty along a line of march.

It was while he was reaching the decision not to comply with orders that the phone call came.

Carol answered it, getting up from the table and going into the living room. She was back a moment later.

"Paul Dabney," she said. "He seems upset. I couldn't quite understand what it was all about, but it has something to do with that girl of his. Seems she's missing or something, and he wants to talk to you."

He almost didn't take the call. He didn't want anything, anything at all, to distract him. But then, suddenly remembering that had it not been for Paul, he probably would never even have been aware of the Margulies murder, he had a second thought on the matter. Paul had first introduced him to the woman. Paul …

He dropped his napkin on the table and went to the telephone.

"… and I became worried for some ridiculous reason," Paul Dabney said, "so I returned to Washington early this morning. I got in some time shortly after three, and when I arrived at the house there were no lights on. I went up to my apartment. Guess I was sort of half hoping she might have left me a note. Especially after I got that message in New York about its being important I call her as soon as possible. But there was no note. It bothered me. Well, to make it short, I sat around and smoked a couple of cigarettes and finally I couldn't stand it anymore, so I went down and knocked at their apartment. Took a long time, but finally Joan—that's Joan Harrington, her roommate—came to the door. Opened it on the night chain. Said that Marty had been called home to Duluth."

"And then what?" Majeska asked.

"I went back upstairs. And I started worrying. I'm still worrying."

"Have you tried to reach her in Duluth?"

"I don't have an address, and, when I asked Joan for it, she didn't have it either. I telephoned Marty's office a few minutes ago, and they haven't got it—and she hadn't called in or given them any message that she was going away. I don't know why, but after that message, about its being important to get back to her as soon as I could …"

"Just a minute, Paul," Majeska interrupted him, "just a second."

There was something about Paul's last remark. And then he got it.

"Paul," he said, "Paul, when did you say she called New York and left that message?"

"Why, why it was late Friday. I was out and I didn't get back to the hotel until late at night and didn't pick up the message itself until Saturday. Tried to get her all day Saturday but there was no answer. It wasn't until Sunday morning that I finally was able to reach Joan."

Majeska was silent for several minutes, and at last he spoke.

"It's damned odd, Paul," he said. "She called me also on Friday and failed to reach me. Left a message asking me to get in touch with her as soon as I came in. I didn't get in until Saturday night, and I called but there was no answer, and I guess I just sort of forgot it. Figured if it was important she would call back. Paul, where are you now?"

"I'm at the office. Got in a few minutes ago. But I'm worried. Can't exactly say why, but I think I'll go back to the house and see Joan. Maybe, well, I hate to ask you to go out of your way, but I'd sure consider it a favor, Jan, if you could meet me there."

Majeska hesitated for several seconds. "Paul," he said, "I'd like to, but I was just leaving to see someone about something which I think could be very important. Instead of going back to your apartment, why not meet me and then, as soon as I'm through, we'll go to the house together?"

"Where will you be?"

"I want to see the manager of a U-Drive-It agency on the south side of town. Suppose I give you the address and you meet me there. Say in half an hour?"

Dabney quickly agreed.

2

Marko arrived at the house on K Street at ten-thirty on Monday morning, June fourth. He walked over from the hotel room shortly after he'd had breakfast in a nearby luncheonette. He carried a small suitcase.

Townsend opened the door at his first ring. He was obviously nervous and his face was unusually pale. He let the fat man in wordlessly and, once in the apartment, carefully put a finger to his lips, nodding toward the door that closed off the rest of the apartment.

"Detrie, one of the ones who worked on the tunnel, is inside," he said. "Will you be able to do what you have to do without help?"

Marko nodded.

"How long will it take and then what happens?"

"I'll be in the basement no more than twenty minutes," he said. "When I am through I return to the hotel. According to the newscasts this morning, that procession will leave Union Station at approximately twenty minutes after twelve. I shall have my radio on, and the moment they leave I will put in a phone call and get you people on the wire. Someone must be here, watching out of your front window. At the moment the car is exactly opposite the front of this house, you must tell me. It will happen then."

Townsend nodded.

"I shall be here until ten after twelve," he said. "I will wait until you call. And then I will put Detrie on the phone. Either he, or the other one, Marschalk. One or the other will give you the signal."

"And you?"

Townsend shrugged. "My affair," he said shortly.

"Exactly," Marko said. "But what of Mr. Blantz? Blantz is to be at my hotel at the crucial moment. There is a little matter which must be taken care of at that time."

"Blantz has told me to tell you to expect him. He'll be there."

The fat man grunted. "I'll be getting on with it," he said and turned to the door. "Be absolutely sure that no one goes downstairs. If they should, I will not be responsible for the consequences."

"Be equally sure you make no mistake with that little box of yours until the proper time," Townsend replied sourly. "I have no desire …"

"Handle your end of it and I will handle mine." Marko turned and started downstairs.

Walking to the window, Townsend looked out and saw a police car parked a few doors down the street. The driver was talking with a man who was standing beside a small black coupe. The man nodded and climbed in his car and switched the ignition key.

Townsend realized that the police were clearing all vehicles from the line of march. He looked at his watch and then turned and went into the bedroom.

"Our friend is in the basement," he said. "He will be through in a few minutes. I must go upstairs for a short time. Unless it is Blantz, let no one in and do not answer the bell. You'll be able to see who it is through the window if anyone should knock."

He walked over to the dresser and opened the top drawer and took out a long, rectangular silk scarf.

"I shall only be a short time," he said.

Marschalk answered his knock and Townsend knew at once from the appearance of his eyes and the way that he staggered as he stood by the door that the man was drunk. His eyes quickly went to the couch where the two girls sat.

Joan was at the far end, staring at the floor. She didn't look up as he entered the room. Marty Eden sat hunched in one corner. One of her eyes was purple and black and frozen closed, and the other one stared at him maliciously.

Townsend nodded toward Marty. "Take her into the bedroom," he said to Marschalk. "I want to be with Joan alone."

Marschalk reeled as he stepped across the room. He leaned down, reaching for her arm, but Marty quickly leaped to her feet. "Keep your filthy hands off me," she said.

"Are you all right?" Townsend asked, half closing his eyes as he watched the other man.

"Sure—sure, buster," Marschalk said, slurring his words. "You don' have to worry about me."

"Then just get her into the other room and stay there. And don't cause trouble. I don't want any trouble now."

"If this animal touches me again," Marty began, but Townsend quickly interrupted her. "Oh, shut up and get in that other room or we'll gag you," he said. "And you, Marschalk. Remember what I said. Get in there with her and watch her. That's all. Just see that she keeps quiet. No trouble. You understand?"

"Yeah, sure, I understand."

Marschalk swept the half-empty bottle off the library table as he followed Marty through the doorway.

Townsend slumped on the couch.

"Packed?"

Joan looked over at him, her eyes frightened. "He won't hurt her again, will he, Jerry?"

"No, he won't hurt her, Joan," Townsend said. "I asked if you were packed."

"I'm packed, Jerry."

"Come here."

She moved and half turned so that she was facing him, her body next to his.

"I bought you a present, Joan," he said.

"Oh, Jerry—Jerry. What's happening? I feel—I don't know, darling, but I feel ..."

"I said I bought you a present, Joan. Something I have been wanting you to have for a long time now."

She shook her head slightly, as though not quite understanding. Her eyes were on his and she didn't notice his hand as it reached into his jacket and he took out the scarf.

"Do you like it, Joan?"

Her eyes dropped, and she saw the square of paisley silk in his hands.

"Oh, Jerry," she said. "Jerry, darling, you didn't—you didn't have to get me any ..."

"But, Joan, I wanted to. I wanted to, Joan. Here, let me see how it looks on you. Let me put it around your lovely, slender neck. Let me …"

There was no sound at all. Merely a moment of thrashing, wild activity under his weight as he held her down and his mouth crushed the sound back in her throat in a final kiss.

3

"You know, of course, about the ticket?" the man said, raising his head and looking first at Majeska and then at Paul Dabney.

"The ticket?" Jan Majeska quickly cocked his head as he straightened in his seat and faced the manager of the U-Drive-It branch.

"Why, yes. Got it in the mail this morning. Apparently the police department sent it to the party who had rented the pickup, and, when there was no response, they mailed it on to us as the owners of the vehicle. Just a second and I'll call my secretary. It came in this morning and she brought it to my attention." He turned and pushed a buzzer on his desk.

Two minutes later and the detective was carefully reading the summons.

Robert Marschalk, license Fx 866-554-098, Missouri, driving a motor vehicle with District of Columbia tag E-6652, had been served a summons by Officer Patrick Martens on May eighteenth, on K Street. He was charged with failing to have a red flag on material extending beyond the body of the truck he was driving. He was ordered to appear in court the following Tuesday at ten o'clock.

Majeska turned to the manager of the rental agency.

"Would you mind if I used your telephone?" he asked. "It is rather urgent."

He not only was glad to oblige, he insisted that the detective have the use of his office as long as he needed it. Leaving, he closed the door to give them privacy.

Majeska at once dialed Headquarters and asked to be connected with the precinct station out of which Officer Martens worked. While he waited for his connection to go through, he turned and spoke to Paul Dabney. Briefly he told him what had happened, explaining about the truck and its use in taking the body of Carolyn Margulies to the Eastern Shore where it had been discovered.

"I don't want to worry you, Paul," he said, "but I somehow have the feeling there is a connection between the Margulies case and your missing girl. Both women lived at the address on K Street; both mysteriously disappeared."

Dabney's face went white. "Good God," he said, "you don't believe …"

"I don't know what to believe," Majeska said. "But we know that this car was used to haul away the body of a woman who had lived at the K Street house. This traffic ticket establishes that the truck was near that house on the day the woman was last seen alive. I'm trying to reach the man who gave out that ticket. He may have some bit of knowledge which could be valuable."

He ceased talking suddenly and pressed the receiver to his ear. A moment later he nodded and said, "Fine. If you can reach him on the radio, ask him to call me at this number. It is extremely important."

Hanging up, he again turned to Paul. "Martens is on patrol and will be calling back. In the meantime, I want to telephone the FBI and see what they have been able to dig up on Robert Marschalk."

Five minutes later he again replaced the receiver on the phone. He was visibly excited as he spoke to Dabney.

"They were able to get a check on this Robert Marschalk," he said. "That is if it's the same man. From the address I have on the driver's license, I can't help but think that it is. Their man came from St. Louis and so does ours."

He looked down at the pad on which he had been scribbling notes.

"Marschalk is thirty-two, six feet three, weighs a hundred and ninety-five. Blond with blue eyes. Long police record of petty crimes and a conviction of assault and battery and statutory rape. The reason the FBI has been interested in him is because he is a member of the Sons of Columbia. They think he is one of their strongarm boys."

Dabney looked up sharply.

"Sons of Columbia? That's the outfit that Jerry Townsend, the man who rented Mrs. Margulies' apartment, is tied in with. My God, Jan, it is all beginning to add up."

"It is more than beginning to add up," Majeska said. "A few days ago a bulletin came through the office, warning all police officers to expect possible trouble from the Sons of Columbia when the Russian Premier arrives. Seems some nut or other was overheard talking about a crazy plot to …"

Majeska suddenly stopped speaking and leaped to his feet. "Paul, it's insane, but it is just barely possible." Again he hesitated and looked at his wristwatch. It was five minutes after twelve.

"We're going to the house on K Street," he said. "The Russian will be passing in front of there any minute. Come on, Paul!"

He started for the door and as he did the telephone shrilled and he hesitated. A moment later he grabbed the receiver from the hook.

"Martens?" he asked.

He spoke for several moments, trying to refresh the officer's mind about the traffic ticket he had given some time back.

When he hung up he spoke quickly to Dabney. "He thinks he remembers the incident," he said. "The truck was carrying heavy building lumber. He didn't know what it was for, but he remembers seeing the car parked in front of the K Street house a short time after he gave out the ticket. Let's get moving."

"Wouldn't it be quicker to report to Headquarters?"

Again Majeska checked his watch. "The procession will be leaving Union Station any second now," he said. "I don't know what's going on in that house, but by the time anyone gets there, it could be too late."

He reached for the telephone and a moment later was asking for Police Headquarters. He spoke swiftly and urgently, making his points as carefully as possible.

"Only the commissioner himself," he said. "Important? My God, it's more than important! No, no one else will do." He hesitated a moment and then spoke again, rushing his words. "Good, then connect me through to him at Union Station. Don't waste a moment. It is absolutely vital!"

4

Marschalk was as drunk as he'd ever been. He'd known that he was going to get drunk, known that, sooner or later, he might doze off and fall asleep. And so he had made the girl lie down on the bed, and he had tied her hands behind her and her ankles together. She had fought him as well as she could, but he had forced the gag into her mouth and tied that also.

She lay sprawled on her back, her skirt pulled askew and her bare thighs exposed, her one good eye wide with fear.

He'd hesitated, staring down at her, and then he turned and went into the living room and opened a fresh bottle. He'd have a couple of belts and then … He didn't even notice Joan's body on the couch.

When he returned to the bedroom, he took the switchblade knife out of his pocket and flipped it open. Marty drew back, shuddering, as he moved toward her.

Marschalk cocked one eye and smiled. "Afraid, baby?" he asked. "Don't be. I'm just going to make it more comfortable for both of us."

His hand moved with amazing swiftness, and the knife blade slashed through the twine binding her ankles. He dropped the knife and tore the gag from her mouth.

"We'll keep the wrists tied, honey," he said. "I remember those nails of yours."

She looked up and past him and saw the clock on the dresser. It was exactly thirty-two minutes after twelve.

Watching her face, he saw the direction in which she was looking, and instinctively he turned to see what had attracted her attention. As he did, she leaped to her feet and then, within a split second, she was across the room.

Her body struck the curtain covering the window, and she heard the glass shatter as it broke.

She felt something tearing at her as she hurtled through the frame.

Her head turned as she started down the fire escape, and she saw his silhouette framed in the window.

As her feet touched the ground in the garden behind the house, she stumbled and half fell, and when she started to rise, his body struck her and bore her down.

His breath was a hot flame, and the words struck her like a blow in the face.

"I've waited for this too long," he said. "Too long."

His hands tore at her, and she felt the fabric of her dress give until there was nothing between them. She started to cry out, and it was then that the world seemed to be torn asunder as a million giant firecrackers exploded in her brain and the very earth quivered and shook.

5

Francis Blantz left the hotel at twelve o'clock on Monday morning. He was very careful to see that his watch was correct: he wanted to time things exactly.

When he got into his car and turned it in the direction of the station, he was carrying a briefcase. He was very careful of the briefcase as he drove, keeping it at his side, one hand resting on its lock.

He didn't want to be late, but he didn't want to be too early either. It would never do to give the money to Marko until the thing had actually been accomplished. On the other hand, he didn't want to be in the neighborhood a second longer than was absolutely necessary. The sooner he got away the better.

In a way it was a shame having to turn all that money over to the other man, but after all he really couldn't complain. He had already taken his own cut. Once or twice he had vaguely entertained the idea of refusing to make the final payment, but had quickly abandoned such thoughts.

Cheating a senile old man like Gordon Minor was one thing. Playing around with a character like Marko was something else again. Marko was a professional killer. It wouldn't be healthy to hold out on him.

He would get to the hotel at twelve-thirty. He would probably be in the lobby when it happened, and he was quite sure that he would be able to hear the explosion. He would be upstairs at twelve thirty-two.

He drove very carefully, holding to a steady speed. He was very observant, keeping an eye out for a possible tail or for casual police. He didn't want any trouble, any possible last-minute accident.

But he completely failed to observe the small black sedan that pulled out of the parking space across the street from his hotel when he had left. He didn't notice it on the several occasions when it was directly behind his own car as he progressed through the city streets. Even if he had, it is very doubtful that he would have recognized either of its two passengers: two large, rangy men with an oddly Western look about them; cold-eyed men who looked as though they might have been guards in a Nevada gambling house at some time or other.

At twelve-thirty on the button he found a parking space directly opposite the rather seedy, rundown hotel where he had his appointment. He twisted the key in the ignition, stepped out, and rounded the car to drop a coin in the parking meter. And with the attaché case tightly clutched in his hand, he turned to cross the street.

6

Jerry Townsend waited until twenty-two minutes after twelve to put in the call to Marko. He was white with anger. Marschalk had not come down, and he was sure that the man would be too drunk by now to be of any use. He had himself to think of, and time was running short. He knew that the parade would be leaving Union Station any moment.

His small transistor radio was turned on, and he was listening to a running broadcast from the station. The announcer had just said that, although there had been some slight unexpected delay, the procession was about to start.

And so he called into Detrie and told him to stand by. He had already instructed him as to what he was to do.

"Marschalk is still upstairs," he said, "but you stay here on the phone whether he shows up or not. I count on you completely."

Marko's voice was cold with fury when Townsend reached him, but Jerry didn't try to explain. He merely said that he was turning the receiver over to his companion and to stand by.

Seven minutes later he had packed his single suitcase and was ready. He made one final check to see that Detrie was still on the telephone, and then left the apartment.

He could see through the glass of the front door that the streets were already crowded with sightseers. He would have to hurry: it would take time to get a safe distance from the house.

Again he looked at his watch and now was shocked to see that it read twelve twenty-eight. He must have read it wrong the last time, or the packing had taken longer than he'd expected.

Quickly he threw open the door and started down the steps.

It was only then that he saw the three men starting up the same steps from the sidewalk.

They were not in uniform, but he knew at once they were police.

"Jerry Townsend?"

He hesitated only the briefest of seconds and then, without a word, he dropped his bag and turned and ran back through the front door, locking it after himself. He wasn't halfway down the hallway when the door was smashed open and the three officers rushed into the house.

7

Marko sat in the chair in front of the desk, facing so that he was able to look out of the fourth-story window and observe the street four floors below. He held the receiver of the telephone in one hand, while on the table, within reach of his other hand, was the small lethal box containing the highly intricate electronic switch that would be activated when he pressed the button. Across from the switch box was the chronometer which was guaranteed to keep perfect time or as near perfect time as man had been able to devise an instrument to measure. The chronometer showed exactly twelve-thirty.

Sweat stood out on the fat man's brow, and he cursed under his breath. He reached for the gold cigarette lighter, and as usual it failed to work. He tossed it back on the bed.

They were late—and Blantz was late.

Again he cursed out loud. God, the ways things were screwed up! He regretted ever having become involved in the matter in the first place. A bunch of stupid amateurs and fanatics.

The thing was insane.

And now for two minutes there had been no sound at all on the phone when he had spoken into the instrument.

He wondered if the man Detrie had panicked, and they had all left the place.

And what of Marko's money? The rest of the money he was to receive from Blantz?

His eyes traveled from the clock to the window and he looked down and across the street. That's when he noticed Blantz's car parking at the curb.

He breathed heavily, leaning forward to watch as the foreshortened figure of Francis Blantz stepped from behind the wheel to the street.

He was watching a second later as the sound of the staccato blasts reached his ears, and his eyes widened as he saw Blantz whirl and then sink to the pavement.

The attaché case he was carrying skidded halfway across the street.

Marko watched only long enough to see the small black sedan cut out and swerve around the parked car and race with engine wide open up the street.

He noticed the uniformed patrolman as he ran from the corner toward where the body had fallen.

He leaned back from the window and slowly began to take the telephone receiver, which he still held, away from his ear. It was then that the voice reached him.

"Who is this, please?"

He held the receiver closer and again the voice reached him.

He moved the receiver away from his ear and stared at it. And then he spoke into the mouthpiece.

"Who is this?"

"This is Detective Sergeant Morrissey. Who am I speaking with?"

Without answering, Marko slowly took the receiver from his ear and replaced it on its cradle. He stood up, a dazed expression in his eyes.

Looking over at the chronometer, he saw that the hands pointed to exactly thirty-three minutes after twelve o'clock.

He belched slightly and then his hand reached out and he pushed down sharply on the button of the electronic switch box.

CHAPTER ELEVEN

ITEM:

The following excerpts are from a news story appearing in the early-morning edition of the *Washington Star*, dated Tuesday, June fifth.

"Police officials late last night issued a statement accrediting the noontime tragic explosion on K Street yesterday to a defective gas main. At an early hour this morning the death toll stood at more than fifty-two persons, few of whom have been identified at this time. At least a hundred and fifty more were injured and hospitalized.

"No one yet has established what was the cause of the disaster which, but for a sheer caprice in timing, could well have taken the lives of the Russian Premier as well as his party, who were due to have passed the exact location of the tragedy at the time the explosion took place. It is known that only minutes before the official party was to leave Union Station on its way to the White House, where the President waited to greet the high Soviet official, there was an unaccounted delay.

"Among the few identified victims of the holocaust was a resident of the house on K Street, which was the focal point of the explosion.

The body of Jerry Townsend, 27, believed to be a student, was identified by fingerprints which were on file in the Federal Bureau of Identification. Several other bodies were found in the smoldering remains of the fine old Georgian mansion, which was almost totally destroyed.

"An amazing coincidence of the tragedy was the fact that a Miss Martha Eden, also a resident of the building, was discovered unconscious, but apparently not seriously injured, in the garden behind the shattered structure. The fact that she was still alive may be due to her having been partially protected as a result of the death of a second person. The body of a man, tentatively identified by papers found on his person as Robert Marschalk of St. Louis, Mo., had apparently struck Miss Eden after it had been blown from the building and in falling had covered her so that she was protected from the debris which showered down on both of them.

"Miss Eden, although still unconscious at a late hour last night, is believed to be out of danger. She was identified by Paul Dabney, a resident of the house on K Street, who was not in the building at the time of the disaster, but was less than two blocks away, apparently one of the spectators of the parade as the Russian Premier's party made their way from Union Station to the White House.

"Federal Bureau of Investigation agents, who have been assigned to the case, have been extremely reluctant to ..."

THE END

www.ingramcontent.com/pod-product-compliance
Lightning Source LLC
Chambersburg PA
CBHW050321160726
48002CB00001B/133